The Tale of
Holly How

The Cottage Tales of
Beatrix Potter

Susan Wittig Albert

BERKLEY PRIME CRIME, NEW YORK

THE BERKLEY PUBLISHING GROUP
Published by the Penguin Group
Penguin Group (USA) Inc.
375 Hudson Street, New York, New York 10014, USA
Penguin Group (Canada), 90 Eglinton Avenue East, Suite 700, Toronto, Ontario M4P 2Y3, Canada
(a division of Pearson Penguin Canada Inc.)
Penguin Books Ltd., 80 Strand, London WC2R 0RL, England
Penguin Group Ireland, 25 St. Stephen's Green, Dublin 2, Ireland (a division of Penguin Books Ltd.)
Penguin Group (Australia), 250 Camberwell Road, Camberwell, Victoria 3124, Australia
(a division of Pearson Australia Group Pty. Ltd.)
Penguin Books India Pvt. Ltd., 11 Community Centre, Panchsheel Park, New Delhi—110 017, India
Penguin Group (NZ), Cnr. Airborne and Rosedale Roads, Albany, Auckland 1310, New Zealand
(a division of Pearson New Zealand Ltd.)
Penguin Books (South Africa) (Pty.) Ltd., 24 Sturdee Avenue, Rosebank, Johannesburg 2196,
South Africa

Penguin Books Ltd., Registered Offices: 80 Strand, London WC2R 0RL, England

THE TALE OF HOLLY HOW

A Berkley Prime Crime Book / published by arrangement with the author

PRINTING HISTORY
Berkley Prime Crime hardcover edition / July 2005
Berkley Prime Crime mass-market edition / July 2006

Copyright © 2005 by Susan Wittig Albert.
Cover art and map illustration by Peggy Turchette. Cover design by Lesley Worrell.
Interior text design by Julie Rogers.

ISBN: 0-425-20613-0

BERKLEY® PRIME CRIME
Berkley Prime Crime Books are published by The Berkley Publishing Group,
a division of Penguin Group (USA) Inc., 375 Hudson Street, New York, New York 10014.
The name BERKLEY PRIME CRIME and the BERKLEY PRIME CRIME design
are trademarks belonging to Penguin Group (USA) Inc.

PRINTED IN THE UNITED STATES OF AMERICA

10 9 8 7 6 5 4 3 2 1

Acknowledgments

I am especially grateful to Dr. Linda Lear, Senior Research Scholar in History at the University of Maryland, Baltimore County, and Research Professor of Environmental History at George Washington University, who has generously shared the results of her research into the life of Beatrix Potter. Her forthcoming biography (its working title is *Beatrix Potter: A Life in Nature*) is eagerly awaited.

I am also indebted to a great many people whose biographical research into the life of Beatrix Potter has made it possible for me to write a fiction that is true to the facts of her life. Their names and the titles of their studies are listed in the Resources section at the end of the book.

Author's Note

The Cottage Tales series explores the life of Beatrix Potter, beloved children's illustrator, countrywoman, and conservationist. The books (*The Tale of Holly How* is the second in the series) cover the years between 1905, when Miss Potter purchased Hill Top Farm in the village of Sawrey, and 1913. If you know something about her life, you will no doubt recognize her, her family, and her friends (including her animal companions), for I have tried to represent them all as accurately as I can. And if you have visited the Lake District of England, you may recognize villages, houses, roads, lakes, and fells, for I have chosen many of these lovely and very real places as settings for The Cottage Tales. Other characters and settings are entirely imaginary, although I've bent every effort to make you believe that they're real, too—yes, even the animals who share their thoughts with us. I believe that Miss Potter would have approved.

Susan Wittig Albert
Bertram, TX 2004

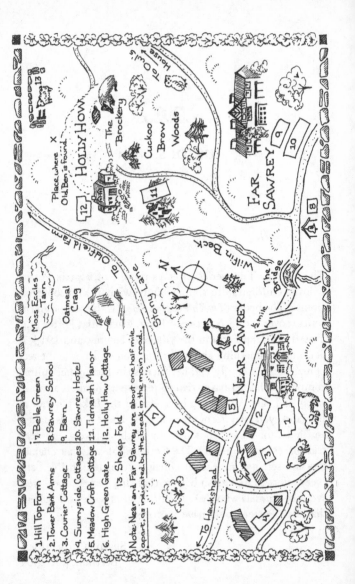

1. Hill Top Farm
2. Tower Bank Arms
3. Courier Cottage
4. Sunnyside Cottages
5. Meadow Croft Cottage
6. High Green Gate
7. Belle Green
8. Sawrey School
9. Barn
10. Sawrey Hotel
11. Tidmarsh Manor
12. Holly How Cottage
13. Sheep Fold

Note: Near and Far Sawrey are about one half mile apart, as indicated by the break in the main road.

❦

Cast of Characters
(* indicates an actual person or creature)

Beatrix Potter*, children's author and illustrator, is the owner of Hill Top Farm, in the Lake District village of Near Sawrey. While the farmhouse is being renovated, Miss Potter stays with the Crooks at Belle Green. She has brought four animal companions to the village with her: *Josey* and *Mopsy Rabbit**, *Tom Thumb Mouse**, and *Tuppenny*, an orange guinea pig.

John and *Becky Jennings* operate Hill Top Farm for Miss Potter. They have three children and a cat named *Felicia Frummety*.

Dimity Woodcock and *Captain Miles Woodcock* live in Tower Bank House, a large house overlooking the road to Hawkshead. Dimity volunteers for parish activities; her brother Miles is Justice of the Peace for Sawrey District and a trustee of Sawrey School. *Elsa Grape* keeps house and cooks for the Woodcocks.

Lady Longford lives at Tidmarsh Manor, a large estate at the edge of Cuckoo Brow Wood. Her twelve-year-old granddaughter, *Caroline,* has recently come to live with her. Also at Tidmarsh Manor are *Maribel Martine,* Lady Longford's secretary and companion; *Mrs. Beever,* the cook-housekeeper; *Mr. Beever,* the gardener and coachman; *Emily,* the upstairs maid; and *Harriet,* the kitchen maid. *Ben Hornby* farmed Holly How Farm, one of the farms belonging to Tidmarsh Manor.

Sarah Barwick has recently opened a bakery in Anvil Cottage.

Frances and *Lester Barrow* own the Tower Bank Arms, the village pub and inn, which is located at the bottom of the hill, below Hill Top Farm. *Ruth Safford* helps Mrs. Barrow with housekeeping and waits tables in the pub.

Mathilda and *George Crook* board guests in their home, Belle Green, at the top of Market Street. George owns and operates the village forge. Also in residence at Belle Green: a Jack Russell terrier named *Rascal* and the senior village cat, *Tabitha Twitchit*.*

Grace Lythecoe is the widow of the former vicar. She lives in Rose Cottage and plays an important role in village affairs.

Lucy Skead is the village postmistress. She and her family live at Low Green Gate Cottage, which is also the village post office.

Margaret Nash is Acting Head Teacher at Sawrey School. She lives in one of the Sunnyside Cottages with her sister, *Annie,* a piano teacher.

Dr. Harrison Gainwell is Lady Longford's choice for the position of Head Teacher at Sawrey School.

Bertha Stubbs and her husband, *Henry,* live in the lefthand cottage in the row of Lakefield Cottages. Bertha cleans Sawrey School; Henry is a ferryman. A gray tabby cat named

Crumpet lives with the Stubbses, but spends most of her time observing and commenting on people's behavior.

Jeremy Crosfield lives with his aunt in Willow Cottage, on Cunsey Beck. Jeremy, twelve, is an artist and naturalist and spends as much time as possible in the woods and fields.

Rose and *Desmond Sutton* live with their six children in Courier Cottage. Dr. Sutton is the veterinary surgeon.

Lydia Dowling is the proprietress of the village shop, located in Meadowcroft Cottage (which will later become famous as the Ginger & Pickles Shop in one of Miss Potter's books). Lydia is assisted by her niece *Gladys*.

Vicar Samuel Sackett is the vicar of St. Peter's Church in Far Sawrey, and serves as a school trustee.

Dr. Butters, the much-loved family doctor, lives in Hawkshead. He serves as a school trustee.

William (Will) Heelis* is a solicitor with an office in Hawkshead and a school trustee. He is a good friend of Captain Woodcock's.

Isaac Chance operates Oldfield Farm, located just to the north of Holly How Farm.

Jack Ogden builds stone walls and digs badgers for farmers in the Lake District.

Professor Galileo Newton Owl, D.Phil., is a tawny owl who lives in Cuckoo Brow Wood. He studies celestial mechanics and the habits of small furry creatures, and makes it his business to know everything that goes on in the neighborhood of Sawrey.

Bosworth Badger XVII lives in Holly How, in The Brockery, the oldest badger sett in the Land between the Lakes.

Bosworth is responsible for *The Brockery Badger History and Genealogy*. A wide assortment of residents and guests lives in The Brockery.

Primrose, Hyacinth, and *Thorn* are three badgers who are kidnapped from their sett at Hill Top Farm.

Tibbie, Queenie, and their lambs are Herdwick sheep living on Holly How, under the care of *Ben Hornby,* of Holly How Farm.

1

Miss Potter Becomes a Farmer

It was high summer in the Lake District. The green meadows and hills were drowsy under the July sun, and there had been so little rain that even the nettles in the lane were limp and parched. The cloudless sky arching over the lakes and fells was the deepest blue, and the wandering breeze was laced with the fresh, sweet scent of wild rose and honeysuckle and the call of the skylark. It was the sort of warm summer day that Beatrix Potter loved, and a great relief after the chilly London spring that made her nose run and her joints ache.

But this morning, Beatrix was not thinking of the lovely weather. She was surveying her pigs.

"Well, now, Miss Potter," said the farmer. "Wha' dustha think? Will they do?"

Beatrix folded her arms and regarded the newly repaired pigsty and the six recently purchased Berkshire hogs, black and white and promisingly plump. "I think," she said after a moment, "that they will do very well. And that they ought to be quite content in their new pigsty." She added dryly, "It isn't pretty, and Mr. Biddle certainly charged us enough, but I daresay it will do, too."

"At least they woan't be runnin' up and down t' Kendal Road, underfoot of t' horses," John Jennings replied in a practical tone. He rubbed his brown beard. "T' auld fence was rotten reet through, top t' bottom and all round. Had to be rebuilt, like it or not."

That was undeniably true. Hill Top Farm, at the edge of the Lake District village of Near Sawrey, had been in the Preston family for half a century before Beatrix purchased it the year before. The buildings had been allowed to run down, the livestock had been sold when Mr. Preston died, and the whole place wore a sad, neglected look that begged to beg for a cleaning and fixing up. In fact, there seemed to be an endless amount of replacing, repairing, rebuilding, and restocking to do—and to pay for. Beatrix was new to farming ("nobbut a reet beginner," the Sawrey villagers liked to say with a sarcastic chuckle), and every day seemed to bring a different and more costly surprise. Beatrix loved her new farm, but the expenses were certainly beginning to add up.

"She's calculating how much those porkers are going to cost before they're bacon," said Tabitha Twitchit, the senior village cat. Tabitha, a calico with an orange-and-white bib, lived at Belle Green, but, like most of the other village cats, went pretty well anywhere she pleased.

"A pretty penny, no doubt," Crumpet commented authoritatively. *"Things always cost more than Big Folks expect."* Crumpet, a sleek, smart-looking gray tabby with a red leather

collar, was an observant cat who made it her business to know everything that happened in Sawrey and considered herself an expert in practical psychology, and the way Big Folk thought and acted.

"Wait until she finds out that pigs never stop eating," Tabitha Twitchet went on with some disdain. *"That'll make her think twice."* Tabitha liked most barnyard animals—horses, cows, chickens, ducks, and even sheep. But she detested pigs, who in her view were greedy, smelly, lazy lay-abouts who deserved their ultimate fate: served up at the holiday table with an apple in their mouths, or made into rashers and tasty Cumberland sausages.

Felicia Frummety daintily licked one ginger-colored paw. *"Mrs. Jennings says that Miss Potter is making a mint of money from those little animal books of hers, so I doubt she'd fuss over the cost of a few pigs."* Felicia lived at Hill Top, where she was supposed to be in charge of rat-and-mouse control. But although she caught one or two just often enough to make people think she was doing her job, the Hill Top rats and mice were mostly left to their own devices.

"How much money Miss Potter makes is no business of Mrs. Jennings—and certainly not yours, Felicia Frummety," Crumpet growled. It was her belief that Felicia (who had been only a ginger cat with no particular claim to distinction before Miss Potter came along and gave her a clever name) had begun to put on airs, as if being the chief cat at Hill Top had some special merit. *"Especially since you don't bother to earn your keep,"* she added with a sniff. Cats who were derelict in their duties were beneath contempt, in her opinion.

"I do too earn my keep!" Felicia retorted, narrowing her eyes. *"I caught a mouse just yesterday. And anyway, what right do you have to criticize me?"*

"She has every right," Tabitha said slyly. *"For one thing, she's much older than you are."*

"*Older!*" Crumpet spat. "*I am not a day older than that hussy!*"

"*Call me names, will you?*" Felicia snarled, unsheathing her claws. "*Why, I'll—*"

"Hod on!" the farmer cried. "Hold that flaysome din!" He threw a dirt clod at the animals, who scampered away to the safety of the stone wall. To Beatrix, he said, "Ben Hornby is sellin' off some of his Herdwick ewes and lambs at Holly How Farm. He keeps good sheep, Ben does, and I've bought two of his ewes and their lambs, to increase t' flock here. Five, all told. Like t' drive up there wi' me tomorrow afternoon to have a look at 'em, a-fore Ben brings 'em down here?"

"Yes, indeed," Beatrix replied promptly. Mr. Hornby was reputed to breed the best Herdwicks in the district. Having Ben Hornby's Herdwicks in her flock would mean a fine crop of lambs next spring.

Hearing the clang of milk pails, she turned to look toward the farmhouse, where Mrs. Jennings was rinsing buckets under the outdoor pump. The seventeenth-century house was built of Lake District stone, in traditional Lake District style, with a slate roof and slate-capped chimneys, eight-over-eight mullioned windows, and a simple porch—a plain, rather austere little house, some might think, but pure in its simplicity and already very dear to Beatrix. When the new extension was finished—a handsome two-story wing that replaced the old lean-to kitchen and added quite a bit of room to the house—the five Jenningses would live there. And she would finally have the farmhouse all to herself.

If it was finished, Beatrix thought glumly. Mr. Biddle, the building contractor who was handling the work, seemed determined to create all sorts of delays and distractions. He liked to pretend that the delays were caused by problems in the drawings she had given him, but Beatrix thought it more likely that he simply didn't like the idea of taking orders from a woman. They had already had several rows, each one worse than the one before. The very worst was yesterday, when he told her that he wanted to tear out the cupboards and the secret, unused staircase—the only way to keep out the rats, he claimed. Beatrix agreed that the rats were a serious problem. But the cupboards and closets and staircase hidden in the wall were among the many things she loved about the old house. Rats or no rats, she was *not* having them torn out! And if Mr. Biddle didn't follow her instructions, she would dismiss him, although it would mean another delay in finishing the house.

But even when the house was finally done, Beatrix knew that she wouldn't be able to live there all year round. Her mother and father expected her to be with them, either at the family home in Bolton Gardens, or on their various holiday excursions, and Beatrix did her best to be a dutiful daughter. Like it or not, she had to spend most of her time in London, where she managed the servants, looked after her mother, and tried to squeeze her own work into whatever time was left over—not a very happy arrangement, but that's how it was, and she did her best to endure it.

It had been on one of their family holidays that Mr. and Mrs. Potter had rented a large house called Lakefield and Beatrix had discovered the twin hamlets of Near and Far Sawrey, nestled between two lakes: Windermere, the largest and deepest lake in England, and Esthwaite Water, which Beatrix thought the prettiest. The names of the two Sawreys always confused casual visitors, for they seemed entirely backward. The hotel, Sawrey School, St. Peter's Church, and the vicarage were located in Far Sawrey, which lay at the top of Ferry Hill, just a mile from Lake Windermere. Near Sawrey, on the other hand, was smaller and less important and farther away, another half-mile further on. But the confusion was cleared up when visitors glanced at a map and realized that "far" and "near" described the distance to the ancient market town of Hawkshead, for centuries the most important settlement in the area. Near Sawrey (*sawrey* was an Anglo-Saxon word for the rushes that flourished along the shore of Esthwaite Water) was only three miles from Hawkshead, whilst Far Sawrey was a half-mile farther away.

Beatrix had immediately felt at home in this little bit of England, which some people called the Land between the Lakes. She loved the fells that thrust skyward beyond blue Esthwaite Water, the velvety green valleys dotted with fluffy white tufts of grazing sheep, the craggy hills strong and unmoving under the dancing clouds, the sparkling becks laughing in the sun. Sawrey was only a day's railway ride from London and less than that from the densely populated Midlands, but the village seemed to Beatrix to be on the other side of the moon. The only way across Lake Windermere was an unreliable steam ferry, whilst the roads over the fells were steep and treacherous. And because Sawrey was isolated, it seemed to Beatrix to be somehow unchanging and unchangeable. This was a welcome thought in the first decade of a new century that had already brought with it more changes than most sensible people welcomed: speeding motorcars, shrill telephones, harsh electric lights, titanic steamships, a new and untried king, and a Liberal government.

From her very first visit, Beatrix had felt comfortable with the quaint, old-fashioned ways of the village, and she was delighted when her parents rented Lakefield for another holiday season. She spent many happy hours wandering along the shore of the lake and sketching in the village. And when she learnt that Hill Top Farm was for sale, she didn't hesitate. She knew she wanted it, and she had the money to buy it: the royalties from her children's books and a small legacy from her aunt. She had paid twice what the farm was worth, the villagers said. She suspected that they were right, for her father's solicitors had arranged the purchase, and she hadn't been permitted to bargain for a lower price.

But the cost hadn't mattered, except as a matter of pride, for Beatrix had the feeling that everything in her life had led up to the moment that Hill Top Farm finally belonged to her, and that buying the farm was the single most important thing she had ever done. From that moment on, she knew, her life would be different.

Beatrix also knew that the farm would not have assumed such an enormous importance if it hadn't been for what happened to Norman. The previous July, just a year ago, Norman Warne, her editor at Frederick Warne and Company, had asked her to marry him. Norman was a kind, gentle man who had encouraged her to keep on drawing and writing her "little books." First, of course, there was *The Tale of Peter Rabbit,* and after that, *The Tailor of Gloucester,* and then several more, very quickly, until they had produced seven books together. She visited his office in Bedford Street frequently, and the two of them exchanged almost daily letters as they worked out the various problems that always seemed to crop up.

But her parents, who had very little enthusiasm for her literary efforts, made sure that Beatrix was always chaperoned on the trips to Bedford Street and refused to allow her to accept even a luncheon invitation from Norman's mother. When she told them that Norman had proposed, they objected, loudly and angrily. Beatrix was a gentleman's daughter, her mother pointed out, and Norman and his family were "in trade" and socially beneath them. Couldn't she see that a Potter could never marry a Warne? Couldn't she see how much she was hurting her mother and flaunting her father's wishes?

But Beatrix knew her own heart. She wrote to Norman to tell him yes and to accept his engagement ring. Even though her parents forbade them to tell anyone other than their immediate families about their engagement and although they could not marry straightaway—not for years, perhaps—Beatrix was determined to make her own happiness. Someday, somehow, she would become the wife of the friend she had grown to love.

But the happiness that she hugged to herself like a sweet, warm hope had quickly turned to a bleak and chilly grief. Norman fell ill with an acute form of leukemia and died a month after their engagement. Beatrix was desolate, whilst her father and mother could scarcely hide their relief that the marriage they dreaded was no longer a threat. Not even the thought of her work could lift Beatrix out of her despair. In fact, drawing and writing now seemed utterly impossible. Norman had not only been her friend and her editor, he had been her best audience, for he seemed to know instinctively what children would like. He had encouraged and guided her at every step along the way. Without him, she was lost. Without him, how could she go on?

But go on she did, and perhaps she was saved by the energy she put into saving Hill Top Farm. To keep the house for herself and yet keep a farmer who could tend the place whilst she was absent, she needed to design an extension and oversee its construction—in spite of Mr. Biddle and all his objections and delays.

And if the old, run-down place were to become a real farm, there had to be farm animals: sheep, cows, pigs, horses, chickens. This was certainly a challenge for a lady who had never thought to become a farmer, but it was a challenge that Beatrix welcomed, for it gave her new things to think about, and a new future to look forward to.

Yes, Beatrix needed Hill Top, and Hill Top needed her. And although her parents complained that her new hobby would distract her from her family duties, even they had to admit that buying a farm was preferable to the awful prospect of a daughter's marrying into trade!

The purchase of Hill Top had been completed in the autumn of the previous year, and Beatrix had come to Sawrey as often as she could get away from her parents. With each trip, she felt more at home in the village, although she wasn't sure she would ever be accepted by the villagers themselves. The men seemed to resent her for buying a farm that might have been bought by a *real* farmer, and the women couldn't understand why an unmarried lady from a wealthy family wanted to live in such a rural place, away from the intrigues and excitements of London. But Beatrix had little time to worry about them, because there was always more to do: overseeing the expansion of the house, rebuilding the dairy and pigsty, redirecting the farm track that went past the door, and acquiring a small herd of cows and the beginnings of a flock of sheep. And pigs.

She turned to look once more at the Berkshires rooting enthusiastically in the mud, and smiled to herself. Yes, the pigs would do, and the Herdwick ewes and lambs from Holly How, if they could be got. Yes. It would *all* do, she thought contentedly. It would do very well.

On the stone wall, Tabitha was the first to speak. *"Ben Hornby's Herdwicks, coming to Hill Top,"* she remarked reflectively. *"Wonder if Tibbie and Queenie will be in the lot."*

"Now, that would be nice," Crumpet said. *"I'm not over-fond of sheep, but Tibbie is certainly pleasant."*

"Sheep," Felicia said in a scornful tone, *"are the stupidest creatures on God's green earth. Not even smart enough to come in out of the rain. And they are always in need of grooming. They have no idea how to take care of themselves."* She licked her right paw and smoothed her whiskers, of which she was very proud.

"They do their jobs, at least," Crumpet retorted smartly, *"which is more than some of us can say."*

Felicia's sharp claws shot out, and Crumpet danced backward, squalling. Tabitha shrieked at the top of her lungs.

"*Stop it,* I say!" the farmer roared. He threw another clod of dirt, and the animals leapt off the wall and scattered into the rockery.

Miss Potter burst into laughter. "What pickles," she said. "I think I shall have to make a book about them."

2

Lady Longford Calls on Miss Woodcock

Dimity Woodcock was in charge of the Sawrey Flower Show again, for the third year in a row. She didn't remember volunteering, but there it was—the committee had simply seemed to take it for granted that she would do it, and (as usual) she hadn't been able to say no.

Now, of course, the second thoughts were beginning to pile up, like ominous storm clouds over the western fells. Dimity was making a list of the judges, and already running into trouble. Mrs. Wharton's judging of the dahlias had caused such an uproar last year that she couldn't be asked back, even though she was already counting on it. If Mr. Threlkild awarded all the rose prizes to Mrs. Belcher again, the other rose fanciers in the village would be absolutely livid. And what to do about—

This gathering storm of second thoughts was broken up

by the sound of wheels on gravel, and Dimity glanced out the library window. A phaeton and matched pair of smart-looking gray horses had just pulled up in front of Tower Bank House, where Dimity lived with her brother, Captain Miles Woodcock. In it were two female passengers.

Dimity's eyes widened in surprise. One of the passengers was Lady Longford, of Tidmarsh Manor, the other her secretary-companion, Miss Martine. Lady Longford was rarely seen in Sawrey these days, and to tell the truth, nobody missed her. She had a razor-sharp tongue, an acid disposition, and a reputation for being mean-spirited and miserly. Since it didn't seem very likely that her ladyship had come on a social call, Dimity concluded that she must have business with Miles. But she would be disappointed, for Dimity's brother had gone to Manchester that morning and would not be back until the next day.

Lucky Miles, Dimity thought ruefully, putting her list into the desk drawer. She cast a quick look in the mirror, smoothed her brown hair, tucked her white blouse into her gray skirt, and went to tell Elsa that they would need a tea tray.

A few moments later, the guests had been shown to the sitting room and Elsa had brought tea and a plate of scones and tea cakes, on the best silver tray.

"I hope you have been well," Dimity said, as she poured tea.

Lady Longford, a tall, strong-looking person with formidable black brows under the brim of a black bonnet, pressed her lips together. "I have not been entirely comfortable, but I fancy I am as well as may be expected for a woman of my age." She frowned. "However, I did not come to discuss my health, Miss Woodcock. I am sorry that your brother is not here, but I trust that you will give him a message from me." She accepted the tea cup that Dimity handed her but rejected Elsa's warm and buttery scones. "I wish you to tell him that it is no longer necessary for the trustees to continue their search. I have located a person to take over Sawrey School."

"To take over the school?" Dimity was so startled that the tea she was pouring for Miss Martine slopped into the saucer. "As head teacher, you mean?"

"Precisely, Miss Woodcock." Lady Longford put up her lorgnette and peered at Dimity. "You do recall, do you not, that the school's head teacher has retired?"

"Well, yes," Dimity said. Of course she recalled it. Miss Crabbe had fallen down stairs and broken her leg, and the villagers had talked of nothing else for months. There had been other difficulties, as well—forgetfulness, shortness of temper, a tendency to make unsupported accusations—although the less said about these problems, the better, Dimity felt. In the end, the residents of Sawrey had agreed that it was not a bad thing that Miss Crabbe had retired from teaching and gone to live in Bournemouth with her two sisters, Pansy and Violet. And most felt that Margaret Nash, who had taught the infants class for the past fifteen years, was doing a simply splendid job as a temporary replacement in the junior classroom. It would be quite satisfactory, the villagers believed and Dimity concurred, if Miss Nash were chosen as the permanent head teacher, and it was widely expected that the four school trustees—of whom Miles was one—would shortly ratify her appointment.

Which was why Dimity was dismayed to hear that Lady Longford (who had a well-earned reputation for getting her way) had someone else in mind for the post. Feeling that she ought to find out as much as possible about Miss Nash's competitor, she said, with a false note of bright interest, "I'd love to hear all about him. The person you have in mind, I mean."

"I daresay," Lady Longford said dryly. "Tell her, Miss Martine."

Miss Martine leaned forward. In her forties, she was thin and meek looking, with scraped-back black hair and sallow skin. She spoke with a strong French accent and was said to be from Paris, although Dimity—who had visited France often as a child—suspected that the accent was counterfeit.

"Dr. Harrison Gainwell," she said primly, "is a graduate of Oxford University, in Theology. Recently, he has been engaged as a teaching missionary in the islands of the South Pacific. He is now looking forward to a quieter, more reflective life. Dear Lady Longford has graciously invited him to be her guest at the Manor until he has found lodging suitable to his position at Sawrey School. Lady Longford will, of course, vouch for his character, reputation, and international experience, all of which are quite impressive."

"No doubt," Dimity murmured, thinking regretfully of Margaret Nash, who was a very fine teacher, admired by everyone, but whose educational experience was of a more local and limited sort. And whilst Lady Longford might not be a favorite of the villagers, she certainly wielded a great deal of influence in Claife Parish. Dimity was enough of a realist to know that the school trustees would have to give special consideration to any candidate her ladyship supported.

Lady Longford put down her cup. "I am certain that Dr. Gainwell will exceed the trustees' highest expectations. Please tell Captain Woodcock that he plans to arrive on Wednesday. Today is Monday, so that will give the captain time to arrange an interview, perhaps Thursday or Friday."

"An interview?" Miss Martine asked, in some surprise.

"I'm sure that the trustees will want to meet him before they agree to appoint him," Lady Longford replied. To Dimity, she said, "Tell your brother that Dr. Gainwell will be glad to put himself at the trustees' disposal."

"Of course," Dimity said with resignation. It really was too bad for Margaret, and for the school. And then, to fill the awkward gap that had opened up in the conversation, she added politely, "I understand that you have another guest. I hope you are enjoying her visit."

"Guest?" Lady Longford frowned.

"Perhaps you don't consider her a guest, then," Dimity replied, wishing she had not brought up the subject. "Your ladyship's granddaughter, Caroline, I mean. I understand that she has been staying at the Manor."

Dimity had got this news from Will Heelis, who was her brother's closest friend and Lady Longford's solicitor. The girl, the only daughter of Lady Longford's estranged son, had been sent from New Zealand on the death of her mother, her father having already died some time before. Lady Longford at first had refused to take the child, but when Will Heelis pointed out that there was no other living relative and Vicar Sackett implored her to do her Christian duty, she had reluctantly allowed herself to be persuaded. The girl had arrived at Easter.

But the situation could not be a happy one, Dimity thought. Tidmarsh Manor was a gloomy, uninviting house, and Lady Longford was very stern. It would be a bleak place for a solitary child who had lost both her mother and her father. Far better if she were allowed to go to Sawrey School with the village children, but that apparently was not to be permitted. There was rumor of a plan to send her to an Anglican convent school in the autumn.

"Ah, yes, Caroline," Miss Martine said, with a sigh that managed to express mingled resignation and exasperation. "One does not mean to criticize, of course," she murmured, casting her glance down. "Although Lady Longford has shown an extraordinary generosity in offering to—"

"I do not shirk my duty," Lady Longford said grimly.

"The girl will be at the Manor until other arrangements have been made for her education. In the meantime, Miss Martine has agreed to serve as her governess."

"I see," Dimity said, feeling a twinge of uneasy sympathy for the child who was Lady Longford's "duty."

"I am merely teaching her literature, music, and French," Miss Martine put in, with a self-deprecating gesture. "Dr. Gainwell has kindly consented to tutor her in maths and natural history. Until she is sent to school, that is. We expect to find an appropriate place for her shortly."

"I see," Dimity said again, and then blurted out, "I was thinking of making a seaside visit next week." Actually, she hadn't been thinking anything of the sort, and it had just that moment occurred to her that the lonely child might like to get away from Tidmarsh Manor. "Only a day or two," she added, "and only if the weather is fine. I should be delighted if you would permit Caroline to—"

"Quite out of the question," Lady Longford said. "You would not find her at all congenial, Miss Woodcock. She is a secretive, sullen child."

"Disobedient, as well," Miss Martine said in a low, regretful voice. She sighed again. "And defiant, one is sorry to say. Her ladyship entered a subscription for her to the *Young Ladies Journal,* but she refuses to read it. One finds such ingratitude inexplicable, doesn't one?"

"One does, I suppose," Dimity murmured.

"Well, then." Lady Longford put down her teacup and rose. "I think this concludes our business. Good afternoon, Miss Woodcock. Your brother may expect a call from Dr. Gainwell."

"I'll tell him," Dimity said limply, and saw them out the door.

3

Caroline Longford Begins a New Journal

The cloudless July morning had turned cloudy by mid-afternoon. Caroline Longford had watched from her third-floor bedroom window as Mr. Beever brought the phaeton round by the front of Tidmarsh Manor and her grandmother and Miss Martine came down the steps, got in, and were driven off, under the shade of their black parasols. Without losing a minute, Caroline turned from the window, pulled the blank account book and pencil out from under her mattress, and flew down the back stairs and out the back-garden door, her long brown braid bouncing down her back. It was a rare thing for both of them—the prison warders, she called them to herself—to be gone from the house, and she didn't want to waste a second of the precious time.

It wasn't as if she didn't have plenty of time to herself, of course. Miss Martine regularly fell asleep by the fire when they were supposed to be having morning lessons, leaving Caroline free to read and draw as she liked. In the afternoon, she was sent out into the garden with Dudley, Lady Longford's spaniel, whilst Miss Martine and her ladyship read and napped. At tea, Caroline was required to pour, for Lady Longford (who was really her grandmother but refused to allow herself to be called Grandmama) seemed to think that pouring tea might somehow transform her into a lady—a frightful fate that Caroline refused to accept, even (or perhaps especially) in her imagination. After tea, she was sent upstairs to read until supper, when Mrs. Beever brought her a supper tray. After supper, she sat in front of the fireplace until it was time to go to bed, writing in her journal, a pretty leather-bound book with her name stamped on it in gold, given to her by her father.

But her writing had come to an unhappy end several days ago, when Miss Martine had found her journal and begun to read it.

"That's mine!" Caroline cried hotly, springing to her feet and trying to snatch the book out of Miss Martine's hands. "It's my private writing. You have no right!"

"I have every right," Miss Martine said, in her fake French accent, holding the little book over her head, out of Caroline's reach. "Lady Longford has given you into my charge, young miss, and I will not permit you to hide anything from me. I intend to see what you are writing about." Her dark eyes were full of a sly, jealous triumph. "Of course, if you prefer, we can take it to her ladyship, so that *she* may read all your shameful secrets and see what an ungrateful girl you really are."

Letting her shoulders slump, Caroline had pretended to give in. But the moment Miss Martine had relaxed her guard and begun to turn the pages, Caroline had snatched the little book and thrust it into the hottest part of the fire, where it burst into bright flames.

"You young heathen!" Miss Martine cried, reaching for the poker to rake the book out of the fire.

But it was too late. The pages charred and curled, sending little flakes of burnt paper flying up the chimney as Miss Martine watched, white with fury. She would never know what Caroline had written: "Miss Martine is no more French than I am, and I am not French at all. And Grandmama Longford is a silly old fool who has been taken in by a mean, cruel woman who only pretends to like her."

It was true. Miss Martine might be meek and submissive to Grandmama's face, but when her back was turned, it was another matter entirely. Caroline had seen the malevolent gleam in her eye, the spiteful twist to her mouth, and was convinced that she had no one's interests at heart but her own, whatever they were.

But whilst Caroline was glad that she had saved her writing from Miss Martine's censorious eyes, she paid dearly for her act, for Miss Martine, in a rage, sentenced her to three days with only milk-and-bread for supper. Caroline hardly missed the food, but she was desolate without her journal.

Writing in it had been her salvation through the somber days after the train on which her father was riding flew off a trestle and plummeted into a New Zealand gorge, killing everyone aboard. It had comforted her through the interminable weeks whilst her mother grew sadder and sicker and finally died, and the even longer, darker months she waited to learn her fate from her father's solicitors. At first, they reported that her grandmother—who had disowned her father when he refused to marry someone she had picked out for him—flatly refused to take her. Another place would have to be found, although they couldn't seem to think where, since there was no other family to give her a home. At last Caroline learnt that her grandmother had agreed to give her a place to stay until a suitable school could be found, so she was put on a ship sailing for England. A rather nice solicitor, Mr. Heelis, met her at the dock in Liverpool and took her to Tidmarsh Manor.

And all during this awful time, Caroline had spilled her feelings onto the pages of her journal, her anger and fear and, yes, even her hope. Her hope that her grandmother might be kind and nice and would like her after all, and that she would not be sent away to school. Her hope that she would have friends in the village, and pets to play with, and—

But what was the use? Her hopes had all been dashed, and her precious journal was a pile of ashes. There was nothing for it but to start all over again, in the blank account book she had stolen from Mrs. Beever's kitchen cupboard this morning. But this time, she vowed, she would not let her private writing fall into Miss Martine's jealous hands— or anyone else's, either. She would keep it where she knew it was safe. And even if it were found, no one but she would be able to read it, because she was going to write it in *code*. What kind of code, she hadn't decided yet. But she would think of something.

So whilst Lady Longford and Miss Martine were drinking tea and telling Dimity Woodcock about Dr. Harrison Gainwell, Caroline was racing along the path that skirted Cuckoo Brow Wood—without Dudley, who was too fat and slow and grumbled a great deal when he was coaxed into going outside the garden. A few minutes later, she was scrambling up the steep, rocky incline of Holly How, (*how* was a Lakeland word for *hill*), to the very top, where shepherds, long ago, had built a tiny stone hut as a shelter against the summer rains and winter snows. A little distance below the hut, in the side of the hill, there was an old, unused entry to a badger sett, mounded about with the dirt that the industrious badgers had dug out of their tunnels and sleeping chambers. The day before, Caroline had hidden an empty biscuit tin just inside the entry, where she intended to keep her journal. Now, she had a new journal; all she had to do was invent the code.

And now, as the July breeze lifted the damp hair from her forehead, Caroline sat down on a sun-warmed stone beside the badger hole and made a list of every letter in the alphabet. Then, beside each letter, she wrote down the symbol or letter she would use to represent it. *M* would stand for *a*, *&* for *b*, *#* for *c*, and so on. It would take a while to learn this new alphabet, but she had a quick mind and an excellent memory. And just in case she forgot, she put the code key into her pocket. She would keep it with her always. Even if someone did discover the book, they couldn't disclose its secrets.

As she worked, Caroline often glanced across the narrow valley of Wilfin Beck, where the little stream glinted in the afternoon sunlight like a shining silver thread. She didn't much like Tidmarsh Manor, which she could see if she leaned forward and looked down and to her left. It was a dark, ugly house, full of selfishness and ill intentions, and she was sometimes awakened in the night by the angry wind slamming the shutters and snarling in the chimney. But she loved the surrounding hills and sheep-dotted fields, whose quiet serenity reminded her of home. The mountains might not be half so high nor the landscape half so wild as in New Zealand, but it was beautiful all the same.

From where she sat, she could also see the slate roof and whitewashed walls of Holly How Cottage, the small Manor farmhouse where Mr. Hornby lived. And she could see Stony Lane, which wound along the shoulder of Oatmeal Crag, on the other side of the beck. She would glimpse the returning phaeton-and-pair in plenty of time to run back to the Manor before her grandmother and Miss Martine reached the front door.

In fact, Caroline saw, there was a vehicle coming along Stony Lane just now, making its way up from the village. But as it came into clearer view, she could see that it wasn't her grandmother's shiny black phaeton, but rather a green-painted cart pulled by a large black horse. Then, behind her, Caroline heard the sound of a foot dislodging a rock. She turned sharply.

"It's only me," Jeremy Crosfield said. "Hope I didn't startle you."

"Not too much," Caroline said, and went back to her work.

Jeremy was just her age, although his serious manner made him seem older. He was the one who had shown her the shepherd's hut and the badger sett on Holly How and places where the best mushrooms grew, and the sweetest bramble berries. Jeremy, whom she had met one afternoon when she went on a reconnoitering expedition outside the garden, seemed to know a great deal about almost everything, which made him a useful person, in Caroline's view. He lived with his aunt Jane in a small cottage near Cunsey Beck and always carried a sketchbook with him so he could draw pictures of animals.

Of course, Grandmama and Miss Martine had no idea about Jeremy, and Caroline knew better than to mention him. If they'd known, they would have forbidden her to see him. They had made clear that the village children were "beneath" her, an idea that Caroline thought was ridiculously old-fashioned and snobbish. At home in New Zealand, she'd been the same as everyone else on the sheep station. These days, Caroline found herself being angry a great deal of the time, and the idea that some people were better than others was just one of the things that made her angry.

Jeremy took a telescope out of the canvas pack on his back. "You can get a better look with this," he said, gesturing at the pony cart on the road.

Caroline put down her journal and peered through the telescope. The horse had a white blaze on its nose and the green cart was driven by a dark-haired man in a gray shirt, with the sleeves rolled up. A yellow dog trotted beside the wheel.

"Mr. Chance, of Oldfield Farm. That's a bit further up the road, past Holly How Farm. The dog's name is Mustard." He grinned. "Mr. Chance calls him that to make people think he bites, but he's not really a bad sort."

With an envious glance at the telescope, Caroline handed it back. "Is this new?"

"Miss Potter gave it to me. The lady who owns Hill Top Farm. I met her when she was drawing frogs for a book. She's famous for her kids' books, my aunt says. *Little* kids," he added, with another grin. "But I wish I could draw frogs as well as she does." He glanced at her journal. "I won't interrupt your writing," he added, taking a pad and pencil out of his pack. "I've come to sketch. But I did want to tell you about the badgers. The ones at the rock quarry not far from where I live."

"What about them?" There were no badgers in New Zealand, but Jeremy had drawn a picture of one for her, when he'd shown her the sett—the badger burrow—on Holly How.

"A badger digger got them a day or so ago," Jeremy said matter-of-factly. "I found the sett, dug up, and the badgers gone. I expect the cubs are dead and the sow—that's the badger mother—will be used for badger-baiting."

"Badger-baiting?" Caroline frowned.

Jeremy's voice had gone hard. "A dog is tossed into a pit or a big box with a badger, and they fight until one of them is dead. People lay wagers on which will win."

Caroline shivered. "It sounds hideously cruel."

"It is," Jeremy said fiercely. "It's against the law, too. But nobody pays attention. After all, it's just badgers, and the farmers don't like them because they get into the grain and the gardens. So everybody turns a blind eye." He sighed. "Sorry. There's nothing to be done. I don't suppose I should have told you."

There seemed to be nothing more to say, so they fell into silence, Caroline writing in her new secret code, Jeremy sketching. After a while, Caroline even forgot that Jeremy was there, and became so absorbed in writing about the unhappy scene that had led to the burning of her journal that the tears began to spill down her cheeks. She was wiping them away with the back of her hand, hoping that Jeremy would not notice and think that she was just being a weepy girl, when she saw the black phaeton appear around the bend in the road. With a sigh, she put her journal into the biscuit tin.

Jeremy looked up from his work with a grin. "Want me to close my eyes so I won't see where you're hiding it?"

Caroline shook her head. "I want you to know where it is," she said. "That way, if anything happens to me, you can come and get it." She gave him a serious look. "Although of course, you won't be able to read it, since you don't know the code. Just burn it."

Jeremy regarded her with a frown. "What do you mean, if anything happens to you?"

"Oh, I don't know," Caroline said. She thought of her father's train falling into the gorge, and her mother's dying, and having to leave the sheep station and come to England to live with a grandmother who didn't like her. She shrugged fatalistically. "You can't tell what's going to happen, that's all. I have to go."

Jeremy shoved his sketchbook and telescope back into his pack. "I'll go with you as far as your garden."

The two of them went away downhill, leaving Holly How deserted and alone once more, to enjoy its wide view of the peaceful Land between the Lakes and the soft touch of the warm afternoon breeze on its rocky flank.

4

Bosworth Badger Is Mystified

But Holly How was not deserted, for a rather substantial stripy fellow had just emerged onto his porch, eager for a bit of fresh summer breeze to blow the cobwebs out of his mind. The porch was the front entrance to The Brockery Inn, one of the most highly regarded hostelries in the Land between the Lakes, and the stripy fellow was Bosworth Badger XVII, The Brockery's proprietor. The name "Brockery," of course, was derived from the Celtic word *broc,* for badger, and throughout the Lake District, badgers (who were thought to be rather disagreeable creatures) were known as "brocks."

Bosworth sat down in the rocking chair on his front porch, blinked several times against the bright sun, and lifted his face to sniff the pleasant, heather-scented breeze. Now, badgers are rather near-sighted, but even Bosworth could not fail to notice the two young persons sitting not far away, beside one of The Brockery's many side entrances, one that had not been used for some time. The girl seemed to be writing something, whilst the boy was apparently drawing pictures.

Bosworth was accustomed to the fell walkers who occasionally climbed Holly How, and to the village boys who played explorer amongst the rocky crags. And he was always on the lookout for the detestable badger diggers who might come to the sett with their dogs and badger tongs and potato sacks, aiming to catch an unwary badger. But whilst Bosworth recognized the young fellow as someone who visited Holly How from time to time, he had not seen the girl before, and he regarded her inquisitively.

She was writing in a book. Bosworth was well acquainted with books, for he himself was an historian of some repute. Upon the death of his father, the Honorable Bosworth Badger XVI, he had assumed responsibility, not only for The Brockery Inn, but also for the official *History of the Badgers of the Land between the Lakes* and its companion project, the *Holly How Badger Genealogy*. The *History* and *Genealogy* were recorded in some two dozen leather-bound volumes in The Brockery's library—quite the nicest room in the sett, Bosworth always felt, with its comfortable fire and leather armchairs and the carved oak table that served as his desk. In fact, he had spent the last hour there, recording the details of a kidnapping at the rock quarry at Hill Top Farm, from which a mother badger and her two young cubs had been recently taken by badger diggers. It was a tragic event and deserved to be recorded for future generations.

Bosworth had never seen a young female person writing, and he was intrigued, especially when he saw that she was crying. He was a soft-hearted fellow who found it difficult to turn away from a creature in distress. Lodgers temporarily down on their luck—like the fox with the injured leg, and the family of rabbits whose burrow had been flooded—were permitted to stay at The Brockery even when they could not pay their bill. And although he recalled the Badger First Rule of Thumb ("Do not on any account approach a human, for they are not trustworthy"), Bosworth began to wonder whether he should go over and inquire if there was something he might do to help.

However, just as he was hoisting his bulk out of the rocking chair, the girl stopped writing, wiped her eyes, and stowed her book in a biscuit tin. She and the boy exchanged a few words, after which she pushed the tin into . . . yes, into The Brockery's side entrance! Then the two of them walked down Holly How together, in the direction of Tidmarsh Manor.

Bosworth frowned. He had no objection to the young person's concealing her writing in his side entry, but he thought he ought to know what sort of writing it was, in case of—well, just in case. So he went round the hill, located the biscuit tin, and took out the book, which bore the legend *Kitchen Accounts* on its black leather cover.

Bosworth smiled. Ah, Kitchen Accounts. As the proprietor of The Brockery, he had to deal with things like this on a daily basis, so Kitchen Accounts were familiar, although he didn't know quite why the girl should have been weeping over them—unless, of course, the Accounts were overdue or in a muddle, which frequently happened at The Brockery, in spite of Bosworth's best efforts. But when he opened the book to the first page, he saw to his great surprise that these accounts were not written in any language that he could read.

"Why, bless my stripes," Bosworth muttered. He turned the page in some puzzlement, for he was a linguist as well as a historian, and knew a great many languages. But Page Two

was much like Page One, written in writing that looked exactly like writing. The sentences (if that's what they were) began with a capital letter and ended with a period, but in between there was only an unreadable jumble of letters, numbers, and symbols:

Sr%jm# kqm sp*nn ergx2.

Frowning, the badger turned the book upside down to see if this might improve matters, but finding that it did not, turned it right-side up and studied it again. At last, in some puzzlement, he returned the book to the biscuit tin and the biscuit tin to its hiding place and sat back on his haunches, thoughtfully scratching his chin with his right hind paw and wondering what he should make of this mystery.

Indeed, it was the second mystery (the third, if one counted the badger kidnapping at the Hill Top quarry) that Bosworth had recently encountered. Very early that morning, just as the sun had peered over Claife Heights to inquire what sort of day it was going to be in the Land between the Lakes, Bosworth had ambled around the hill and down, aiming for the sheep fold above Holly How Farm. The meals at The Brockery were ably prepared by Parsley, a young badger of some culinary talent, but Bosworth liked to go out for breakfast once a week or so. Earthworms were plentiful under the dew-wet grass of the stone-fenced fold, which was chiefly used at sheep-clipping time and when the ewes and lambs were to be sorted and sold.

The farmer, old Ben Hornby, was evidently intending to sell some of his Herdwicks, for the evening before, he had put two ewes and three lambs in the fold. Bosworth (who had quite a wide view from the rocking chair on his front porch) had watched him do this. It was quite natural, then, that the badger should expect to have company for breakfast—not a problem, of course, since badgers and sheep have shared the same fellsides and patches of tasty turf for eons.

Indeed, Bosworth was rather looking forward to hearing the latest gossip from Tibbie, the chief Herdwick ewe, who could always be counted on to know the news. The Herdwicks were given free range upon the fellsides, for they had an unerring sense of direction and a very strong sense of place. They were heafed to their native pasture, it was said, and required neither shepherd nor bell-wether to take them to and from the fell. On their travels, Herdwicks were always encountering other Herdwicks who came from as far away as Dungeon Gyll or Borrowdale or even Seathwaite Tarn, and there was always a great deal of news to trade. In fact, the animals always said that Herdwicks were better than newspapers, and that they could tell you anything from the price of wool in Carlisle to the weather in Ambleside to the number of lambs that had been born that spring. Bosworth was hoping that Tibbie had heard some word of a young badger of his acquaintance who had stayed briefly at The Brockery and then headed west and north, beyond Ambleside.

But he was to be disappointed, for when he reached the fold just after sunrise, he found the gate standing open and the enclosure empty. Tibbie, her twin lambs, and the other ewe and lamb were gone. For a moment, the badger stared around him, wondering whether old Ben Hornby had had second thoughts about selling his sheep, or whether a fellwalker had happened along and opened the gate, or whether Tibbie and the others had, for their own good reasons, decided to lift the hasp on the gate and take themselves off somewhere else.

But badgers abide by the animal axiom that it is an impropriety to inquire into the whereabouts of one's absent friends and companions, for life in wood and field is prone to accident. (This is obliquely expressed in the Seventeenth Badger Rule of Thumb, which says, "Hold a true friend with both paws, but be willing to let him go when the time comes.") And anyway, Bosworth knew that life is made up of things that go as one expects and things that don't, so it is well to be flexible and adapt oneself to the current circumstance. And since what was wanted at this moment was breakfast, Bosworth ignored the fact that the fold was empty and began to poke his nose here and there under the grass. Within the half hour, he had completely satisfied his appetite for earthworms and was on his way back to Holly How.

But the mystery of the missing sheep had bothered the badger all the while he carried out his ordinary responsibilities of the day: discussing The Brockery's dinner menu with Parsley; overseeing the two young rabbit maids, Flotsam and Jetsam, as they swept and dusted and made the lodgers' beds; inventorying the items in the Supplies and Necessities Closet; reading his post, which contained a chatty missive from a distant cousin who lived in the Wild Wood, far to the south; and penning that sad note in the *History,* regarding the kidnapping of the mother badger and two cubs from the Hill Top sett.

And now, to the morning's mystery of the missing Herdwicks, Bosworth could add the equally puzzling mystery of the afternoon: What was the meaning of the unintelligible writing in the girl's Kitchen Accounts? What sort of secret might be concealed in such cryptic sentences as the one that kept teasing Bosworth, as if it were a puzzle to be solved, or some sort of mystic chant:

Sr%jm# kqm ɛp*nn ergx2.

5

Sarah Barwick Makes a Mess

The afternoon had turned overcast and sultry, and Sawrey drowsed in the growing July heat. Clouds of tiny midges—thunderflies, people called them—very small and black, and thought to be a sign of a coming storm, gathered in the air all over the village. In the garden of Tower Bank House, they annoyed Dimity Woodcock no end. She had tucked a sprig of rue behind one ear and a sprig of southernwood behind the other, hoping that the herbs' strong scents would fend them off, but to no avail. And whilst thunderflies didn't bite or sting, they got in one's eyes and one's mouth and were certainly aggravating.

The garden had been without rain for too long, and Dimity was trying to catch up with the gardening chores, which probably seemed as overwhelming to old Fred Phinn (who came twice a week to putter around the borders) as they did to her. The lettuces, past their prime, were ready to bolt; the parched-looking roses and lupines, drooping with heat exhaustion, pleaded for a good sprinkle; and the couch grass, chickweed, and groundsel, always especially insubordinate at this time of year, were clearly plotting a major invasion of the flower borders.

But between the thunderflies getting into her eyes and the disagreeable recollection of Lady Longford's words still ringing in her ears—not to mention the ominous cloud of second thoughts regarding the Flower Show that hung over her head—Dimity could not keep her attention on her tasks. At last, with a sigh of exasperation, she threw down her garden trowel, got to her feet, and brushed the leaves from her skirt. There was no use in trying to work when she was vexed—and she was certainly vexed this afternoon. What she needed was a cup of tea and some good, strong, mind-rattling conversation. And the only place in the village where she could get both together was just on the other side of the stone wall along the edge of the garden, at Anvil Cottage, where Sarah Barwick lived.

Sarah Barwick was a newcomer to Sawrey. In the previous autumn, she had inherited Anvil Cottage upon the death of Miss Agnes Tolliver, an elderly lady who had been greatly respected for her many good works. The villagers were astonished when they learnt that Miss Tolliver had not left the cottage to her nephew, as everyone naturally expected, but to the daughter of a man whom she had loved in her youth and had been forbidden to marry. Most people in Sawrey had an inborn wariness when it came to off-comers like Miss Barwick and Miss Potter, who had purchased Hill Top Farm at about the same time that Anvil Cottage landed so unexpectedly in Sarah's lap. However, the villagers understood that such things, whilst regrettable, were beyond their control, and most had had settled into a cautious acceptance of their two new neighbors.

But if the village thought that Miss Barwick might become another Miss Agnes Tolliver, they were mightily mistaken, for it soon became clear that she was one of those "New Women" who were always pointing out ways that women could take charge of their lives and change things for the better. The most striking evidence of this was her appearance, for Miss Barwick, whilst she occasionally dressed like all the other respectable Sawrey ladies in a dark serge skirt and a white cotton blouse, much preferred trousers. In fact, she had several pairs in different colors—black, brown, blue, and dark green—all fully cut for maximum comfort, and she wore them on every possible occasion. Dimity privately thought that Sarah looked quite smart in her trousers, and even her brother Miles had been heard to comment that it was rather a sensible get-up, if somewhat outlandish. But the rest of the village could express nothing but consternation.

The second thing that had alarmed the village was Miss Barwick's green bicycle. Bicycles had long since ceased to be a novelty, of course. Henry Stubbs bicycled to and from his work at the ferry landing every day, and the boy who carried the newspaper from Hawkshead came on a bicycle, as did several of the men who worked on outlying farms. And there was the Esthwaite Vale Cycling Club, sporting gentlemen who cycled as fast and as far as they could through the moors and fells. Sarah Barwick, however, was the only female in the district who regularly rode a bicycle, and in *trousers*! The village was shocked, and several had forcefully suggested to the vicar that he discuss the matter with Miss Barwick, which he wisely declined to do.

Dimity herself suspected that behind this criticism was the recognition that women who rode bicycles enjoyed an

unusual degree of mobility, and that mobility led to inde-
pendence, and *that*—as all of the men in the village very
well knew—might create all sorts of problems. Why, a wife
who rode a bicycle to Hawkshead in the afternoon might
not arrive home in time to cook her poor husband's supper,
and him bone-weary after a day's hard work. And if she was
gadding about on her bicycle, who would iron his shirts or
scrub the floor? Yes, indeed, in more ways than one, Miss
Barwick was a danger.

As Dimity looked over the wall in the direction of Anvil
Cottage, she saw the sinister green bicycle leaning against
the fence. Concluding that its owner was at home, she went
through the gate between their two gardens and down the
path, and knocked.

"Yoo-hoo, Sarah!" she called. "It's Dimity. I'm in dire
need of some tea and talk. Are you free?"

"Oh, bother," said a very cross voice.

Dimity sighed. "Well, of course, it can wait, if you're
busy. I'll come back later."

Sarah had her own bakery business at Anvil Cottage, and
she was usually busy with something or another—making
scones and Cumberland sausage rolls or baking bread or ex-
perimenting with this or that new recipe. But baking was
the sort of thing one did with one's hands whilst one talked,
and Dimity and her friend had enjoyed a great many con-
versations and pleasant cups of tea whilst Sarah mixed and
kneaded and stirred and stoked the stove and wielded her
rolling pin.

"Oh, BLAST!" the voice roared. This was followed by a
loud clattering noise, as if something had fallen from a height
and rolled across the floor. "No, not *later*," the voice said.
"Now. And of course, you're not a bother, Dim. Or a blast,
either—that's just my tongue talking. But do mind your feet
as you come in. There's treacle and milk all over the floor."

"Treacle!" Dimity exclaimed, standing on the threshold. "And milk?"

"Yes, treacle and milk," Sarah said grimly. "Puddles of it." She was on her hands and knees with a scrub brush and a bucket of soapy water. "And sugar. And flour."

"Sugar and flour," Dimity said in a wondering tone. She looked down at a spreading patch of brown treacle, which was streaked with milk, dotted with several volcanic islands of sugar, and dusted with flour. Sarah's kitchen was never spotless, far from it, but Dimity didn't remember ever seeing such a catastrophe as this. "I don't suppose I should ask what happened," she remarked tentatively.

"It's these damned thunderflies," Sarah replied through her teeth. "*They* did it. What I need is some flypaper strips, but Lydia Dowling says she's sold all they had." She scrambled to her feet and brushed her hair out of her eyes with the back of her hand.

No one could call Sarah Barwick handsome, for she had a horsey face, a freckled nose, and a square, determined jaw—attributes rarely considered beautiful in a woman. But her dark hair was thick and shining and her eyes revealed both intelligence and humor. She was wearing a skirt today, tucked up and showing a trim ankle, and Dimity saw treacle smeared on her cheek, treacle dribbled on her white apron, and white flour dusting her hair.

"And if it's not completely cleaned up," Sarah went on grimly, "the treacle will get into all the cracks, and then there will be ants. And if thunderflies aren't *evil* enough," she added, dropping to her knees again and applying her scrub brush fiercely, "ants are positively diabolical."

"But I don't see how the thunderflies managed to—"

"Oh, you don't, do you?" Sarah looked up with a dark scowl. "Well, I wouldn't have upset the treacle pot if I hadn't been trying to slap the flies out of my eyes. And when I tried to catch the pot before it rolled off the table, the milk jug flew off. And when the milk went, the sugar canister fell over and the lid came off and it spilt. And just now, when you came to the door, I hit the table leg with my elbow and down came the flour bin." She bit her lip and her mouth twisted. "Don't look, Dim. I'm going to cry, and I'm an awful sight when I cry."

"I won't look," Dim said compassionately. "Stay where you are, Sarah, and I'll get another bucket. This is a job for two."

Sarah sighed and rubbed her nose. "It's a job for ten, or—better yet—a team of floor-cleaning fairies. But thanks, Dim. I'm desperate. I'll take all the help I can get."

So for the next half hour, the two women scrubbed and scraped and emptied buckets of dirty water and filled fresh ones, until the milk and treacle and sugar and flour had been washed completely off the floor.

"Well," Sarah said, getting to her feet, "I don't think this floor has been so clean since dear Miss Tolliver was alive. I can bake a very nice loaf of bread, but I daresay I'm not nearly the housekeeper she was." She made a rueful face. "The flour does have a way of getting all over, even when I'm careful."

Tactfully, Dimity said, "I see that the kettle is hot. I'll make us some tea." And five minutes later, the two were sitting down to freshly brewed cups of tea and a plate of Sarah's lemon bars, which were decorated with tiny bits of candied orange peel.

"Cover those lemon bars, Dim," Sarah said, handing her a napkin, "or the thunderflies will track all over them with their nasty little feet. And then tell me what you came to tell me. You sounded as if you were dreadfully upset about something."

"What I came to—" Dimity laughed. "Oh, for pity's sake, Sarah. Your calamity drove mine right out of my head."

"If a little thing like treacle could distract you, your calamity must not have been so calamitous after all." Sarah took out a packet of cigarettes and lit one. Cigarettes, along with the trousers and the bicycle, marked her as a New Woman.

"Yes, it is," Dimity replied, sobering. "It's horrible. It's appalling. For Margaret Nash, at least. And for the children at the school. And on top of all that, there's the Flower Show. Mrs. Wharton can't possibly be permitted to judge the dahlias again, or we shall have a rebellion on our hands. But I don't know how to tell her without—" She was interrupted by a knock at the kitchen door. "Why, Miss Potter!" she exclaimed in surprise, glancing up. "I didn't know you were back in the village! How very nice to see you."

"I thought we agreed," Sarah said sternly, "that we would all use first names. Hullo, Beatrix. If you'll look down, you'll see that you're walking on the cleanest floor that ever was."

"How extraordinary," Beatrix said, bending over for a close examination. "It's cleaner than Mathilda Crook's kitchen floor, which is saying a great deal, considering that she washes it every morning, whether it needs it or not." She straightened, her china-blue eyes twinkling. "I don't suppose I ought to ask how it got to be so clean."

"A great lot of treacle and milk and even more elbow grease," Sarah rejoined cheerfully. "However, all's well that ends well. Dim has a story she's dying to tell us, though. You'll want a cup of tea whilst you listen. And you should try one of my lemon bars, too. You'll like them." She got up and fetched another cup, poured it full, and set it in front of Beatrix. "All right, Dim," she commanded. "Fire away."

With a sigh, Dimity told Beatrix and Sarah about Lady Longford's visit. "It's her intention," she added, "that the trustees interview Dr. Gainwell as soon as possible after he arrives. She insists that he's the best-qualified person for the job. Anyway, he's the one *she* wants," she added, "no matter whether he's qualified or not."

"I don't understand," Sarah said, frowning. She tapped her cigarette ash into her saucer. "Who is this Lady Longfellow, that she can dictate who is going to be the next head teacher?"

"Longford," Dimity corrected.

"Oh, I know her name," Sarah said, waving away several inquisitive thunderflies. "I know where she lives, too, for I've delivered there. Her cook, Mrs. Beever, orders two loaves a week of my best white bread, and wants a ginger cake for this coming Wednesday. Her ladyship professes a great liking for my ginger cake, it seems. She thinks it helps to settle her stomach. I oughtn't speak ill of a customer, I suppose. But who *is* she?"

"She's the wealthiest woman in the district," Dimity replied. "And a truly disagreeable old thing. She mostly keeps to herself these days, and we don't see much of her in the village. But until he died, her husband was involved in everything—judging agricultural shows and being president of the Sawrey Institute and buying a piano for the school and helping out the poorer families with coal during the worst of the winter. He was a bit of a busybody, but his heart was in the right place. He was also a school trustee—which, I suppose, makes her think that she has the right to interfere."

"And who is this Gainwell person?" Beatrix asked, with interest. "What is his chief claim to fame?" She looked at Sarah. "These bars are very good, Sarah. When I go back to London, I'd like to take some with me. My mother would enjoy them, I'm sure. She's very fond of sweets."

"Smashing!" Sarah exclaimed. "P'rhaps you'll spread my

reputation amongst the gentry, and my fortune will be made." She stubbed out her cigarette. "Yes, Dim, what about Gainwell? Pray tell, who is this intrusive chap?"

"He's a graduate of Oxford," Dimity said glumly. "In Theology, Miss Martine said. He's apparently just come back from the South Pacific, where he was a missionary. So you see, he has superb credentials." She gave a discouraged sigh. "While there can't be a better teacher than Margaret, her educational background can't compare to his. Oh, what a *wretched* muddle this is turning out to be!"

"It does seem to me," Beatrix said, licking her fingers, "that the trustees might have acted sooner."

"Right," Sarah said. She twisted her brown hair around her finger, discovered a treacly clump, and made a face. "Here it is July, and school starting before you know it. Not to fault your brother, Dim, but if he and the other trustees had done what they were supposed to do, Margaret would already have the position, and old Lady Longflop would have to find another place for her fair-haired boy."

Dimity came to Miles's defense. "Well, it's not entirely their fault. The trustees have been waiting for a letter of commendation from the previous head teacher, you see. They expected the letter weeks ago, but there have been . . . well, difficulties. I understand that the vicar has communicated with Miss Crabbe—she and her sisters are in Bournemouth— and urged her to write. The trustees are all on Margaret's side, of course," she added. "They couldn't think more highly of her. And the villagers, too."

"Well," Beatrix said, in her usual practical way, "I don't see that there's anything that any of us can do, except you, Dimity. You might remind your brother—discreetly, of course—that the whole village is behind Miss Nash and that if the trustees have so little sense that they hire someone else, there's likely to be an uprising."

"I'll certainly do that," Dimity agreed. "But do you think p'rhaps we should let Margaret know what's going on?"

"I'd say no to that," Sarah replied, with great firmness. "Margaret's a very good sort of person, quite levelheaded, really. But she's nervous enough about this situation already. I mean, there's a substantial difference in salary, as I understand it, and with her sister being sick for the past six months and not able to work—" She sighed. "Well, I certainly know what it's like to wonder where the next little bit is coming from."

"But orders are picking up, aren't they?" Dimity asked hopefully. "I hear such good things about your baking. Even Elsa Grape admits that your muffins are superior to hers."

Sarah had started the bakery business from scratch, based on her experience in working for her father and her uncle in a bakery in Manchester. But she'd had to invest in a new kitchen range and other baking equipment, and although the better-off housewives could afford to buy bread and cakes and sausage rolls instead of baking for themselves, there were many others who couldn't. Dimity wasn't surprised to hear that Sarah was struggling.

"Business will improve, I'm sure of it," Sarah said stoutly.

"It might improve faster," Beatrix replied, "if more people knew about it. You're right on the main road, Sarah. Have you thought of putting your cakes and bread on display in your front window, where travelers can see them and be tempted as they go past? Your sausage rolls, too—nice for a quick bite, or to put in a pocket for later. Pity to go hiding your light under a bushel."

"But I'm usually in the kitchen," Sarah objected. "I won't hear customers knock. And if I'm not in the kitchen, I'm out on my bicycle, delivering."

"Then put a bell on your door, as the shops do," Beatrix

replied. "And ask one of the village girls to mind things whilst you're out and about."

"What good ideas," Dimity said admiringly. "You're quite the businesswoman, Beatrix. But I suppose you have to be, don't you?"

"The little books have taught me to look out for opportunities," Beatrix said with a small smile. "You know, I published *Peter Rabbit* myself, because no one else was willing to take a chance on the thing. And I thought almost from the beginning that there might be a demand for Peter Rabbit toys, so I made one myself out of rabbit fur, with whiskers pulled out of a brush, and a blue coat. I've even patented him. But now people are wanting to make all sorts of things like tea sets and games and wallpaper borders and the like, and I have to think about licenses and royalties. It's rather fun, actually."

Sarah nodded. "Well, I have to admit that the bell is a smart notion, and the window. I'll give them a try—although I'm not sure I can afford to pay someone to mind the place whilst I'm gone." She bit her lip vexatiously. "I'm not complaining, you know—I'm just saying that I understand Margaret's situation. It's not easy to make ends meet when there's sickness in the family. That's why I don't want to tell her about this other candidate. She doesn't need extra worries heaped on."

"If we don't tell her, someone else will," Beatrix replied. "You know how this village is." She made a face. "One can't take one step without a half-dozen people telling one what one *ought* to do. I've been getting all sorts of advice about the improvements at Hill Top."

"I'll just bet you have," Sarah said with an ironic laugh. "Did anyone mention the new road you poked through the wall?"

"Oh, of course," Beatrix said. "People say it's ugly, and they're right. But it's ugly because it's new, and because all the fern has been pulled from the wall, which leaves it very bare. But mostly they ask why the extension is taking so long to finish. Which of course is Mr. Biddle's doing. If he would just get on with the business—" She threw up her hands with an expression of frustration. "What a great bother. All the man wants to do is argue over this and that and almost everything! Yesterday, he was proposing to tear out the cupboards and the little staircase in the wall. He says it is necessary to stop out the rats, when I know perfectly well there are better alternatives."

"Those beautiful oak cupboards beside the fireplace?" Dimity asked, horrified. "Oh, dear. I do hope you didn't allow it!"

"Of course not," Beatrix replied. "We had a frightful row—which isn't likely to be the last, at the rate we're going." She wore a rueful look. "I'm rather afraid I let my temper get the better of me. I think I startled him."

Dimity had to smile at that, for when she had first met Miss Potter, she had formed the impression she was a very meek person—an impression that more recent experience had corrected. If Mr. Biddle was not yet aware that Beatrix's mild manner concealed a quick temper and a tenacious resolve, he soon would be.

"You shall have to put Mr. Biddle into one of your little books," Sarah said decidedly. "He repaired the slates on my roof. Stubborn as the day is long, and hates like anything to do business with a woman. Tell you what, Bea—you can draw him as a donkey."

At that, Beatrix threw back her head and laughed heartily. "Dear Sarah," she said at last. "You *are* good for the soul. Here I was, thinking I was the only woman the wretched man had ever dealt with. Yes, indeed. If I ever do a donkey book, I shall have Mr. Biddle in mind. And now that I've a clearer picture of him, perhaps I shan't lose my temper quite so easily. Donkeys can't help being donkeys, after all."

"Speaking of books," Dimity remarked, "my cousin wrote from London that she saw *Jeremy Fisher* in a bookstore window." Beatrix had been drawing *Jeremy* the previous autumn. "What are you working on now?"

"It's called *The Tale of Tom Kitten*," Beatrix replied. "I got another idea for it this morning, when I was watching the cats pushing and shoving one another on the stone wall at Hill Top." Her smile was crooked. "But I always find it difficult to settle to drawing whilst I'm here. There's so much to do, in addition to all the renovations. Tomorrow afternoon, Mr. Jennings and I are driving up to Holly How Farm to look at some Herdwicks Mr. Hornby has sold us. I must confess to admiring the breed, even though it is quite out of fashion these days."

Sarah laughed, delighted. "Fancy the famous Miss Potter, a shepherd. But I daresay the children who read your books would understand."

Dimity stood. "I'm afraid I must be going. I really must come to terms with Mrs. Wharton and the dahlias."

"You could just cancel the dahlias," Sarah said. "Who would miss them?"

"That wouldn't work at all, I'm afraid," Dimity said. "Everybody enters dahlias. It's Mrs. Wharton who needs canceling." She paused. "So it's been decided that we won't tell Margaret about Lady Longford and Dr. Gainwell?" She wasn't sure that this was the right thing to do, but Sarah was always so *positive* that it was hard to argue against her.

"That's the plan," Sarah said. She shrugged. "Anyway, who knows? Maybe this Gainwell fellow will decide to go back to Borneo or New Guinea or wherever he's been, and then Margaret would have worried for nothing."

"If we don't tell her," Beatrix said quietly, "we shall have to expect that someone else will do it."

Which, of course, is exactly what happened.

6

Miss Nash Hears Some
Unpleasant News

Margaret Nash had always felt some irony in her summer situation.

June and end-of-term never came soon enough. She was delighted to pick up the last pair of wellies, dust the last eraser, and turn the key on the Sawrey School door, imagining the great pleasures waiting for her in the garden and the kitchen and at the seashore, where she and her sister Annie usually spent a fortnight. But her spirits always began to sag about the middle of July, and it wasn't long after that when she began actually looking forward to the end of the summer holiday and the return to school, inspired with a sense of change and renewal and the expectation that this year's crop of students would be even better than the last.

This year, the anticipation that gripped Margaret was even stronger than usual, partly because Annie had been ill

and they had been unable to get away for their usual fortnight's holiday, but mostly because she hoped (if that was the
right word for an emotion that included desire, anxiety,
trepidation, and the fear that she might not quite be up to
the task) that she was to be named the new head teacher at
Sawrey School, where for the last nine years she had taught
the infants class. She was thinking about this as she stood at
the table in the kitchen of the cottage that she and Annie
shared, the middle of the three linked cottages that were, as
a group, called Sunnyside.

"Margaret, what *are* you doing?" asked Annie, rolling up
her sleeves as she came into the kitchen. She had just finished teaching a piano lesson—little Angus Williams—and
Margaret was distinctly grateful. Angus could be counted
on to do his part in the school chorus, but he was nothing
but thumbs, and heavy thumbs at that, when it came to the
piano. No sense of rhythm, either.

"What am I doing? Why, I'm peeling potatoes, of
course." Margaret looked down and broke into helpless
laughter. She had pared a new potato until it wasn't much
bigger than a marble. "I suppose I was thinking," she said
apologetically.

"Don't think with a knife in your hand, dear," Annie remarked, brushing the brown hair out of her eyes and tying
on her plain cotton apron. She chuckled. "It's downright
dangerous."

Margaret glanced at her sister, glad to see a return of her
light, teasing smile. Annie hadn't been dangerously ill,
thank heaven, but she was not robust, and even a slight cold
was enough to provoke a bout of pneumonia. She'd been
sick since April and had to give up her job at the post office
in Far Sawrey—only a half-mile, but much too far for her to
walk, especially during the spring rainy season. Doing without her salary had been difficult, but things were easing up

now that she was able to teach piano again, which brought in enough so that they could pay Dr. Butters for his visits and the medication. And the new position, when it came through, would bring a substantial salary increase. Annie wouldn't have to go back to the post office. And she could take only the serious piano students, which would please her.

With a little shiver, Margaret pushed the thought away. She was not one to tempt fate by counting too heavily on something that had not yet happened, even when it seemed a virtual surety—although now that Miss Crabbe had finally written the letter, it did appear that things were moving forward at last.

Annie opened the oven and took out the iron pot in which they always baked their Monday tatie-pot supper. She took off the lid, allowing a savory cloud of steam to rise, gathered up Margaret's peeled and quartered potatoes, and plunked them into the pot on top of the mutton, black pudding, carrots, and onions.

"Let's give this another forty minutes," she said, replacing the lid and sliding the pot back into the oven. She straightened, smiling. "I won't offer you a penny for your thoughts, because I can guess them. I saw Miss Crabbe's letter to the trustees on your desk."

Margaret scraped the potato parings into the pail that they filled daily for their neighbor's pig, who lived in a small pigsty at the back of the garden. "The letter was a good one, I thought, and it was nice of her to send me a copy. What did you think?"

"I think she could have written sooner," Annie remarked sternly. "And she certainly didn't give you anything more than your due—and that grudgingly, the old witch." She poked up the fire in the kitchen range. The Sunnyside cottages, where the Nash sisters had lived for nearly a decade, were constructed of stone and shaded by large beech trees;

they were always so cool that the fire was welcome, even on a warm July evening.

Margaret had to agree with her sister, although she wouldn't have gone quite so far as "old witch." Miss Crabbe's recommendation that she be promoted to head teacher (sent to the school trustees, with a copy to her) had come very late, and it had not been written with anything like the enthusiasm for which Margaret had hoped. But she knew that the trustees would take into account both Miss Crabbe's reputation for being parsimonious with her praise, and the unhappy circumstances that had shadowed her departure. Miss Crabbe would have come back to teach after her broken leg had mended if Captain Woodcock and Vicar Sackett had not been adamant that it was time for her to retire, and she could not be expected to endorse even Margaret without reservation. Anyway, Captain Woodcock had assured her that Miss Crabbe's letter was just the final formality. The trustees would act on her appointment as soon as they had it in hand.

"So we should be hearing something in the next few days, then," Annie said. She put a spoonful of tea leaves into the blue and white china pot and poured in hot water from the kettle.

"I truly hope so." Margaret sighed.

There shouldn't really be any suspense, since Captain Woodcock had told her that there were no other candidates for the position. But Margaret had learnt not to count her chickens before they were hatched. Time enough to imagine herself as Sawrey head teacher—head teacher! what a wonderful title!—when the trustees actually made the appointment. It was a temptation, though, to think about it. She had very much enjoyed the challenges of teaching the junior class and doing the work of the head teacher, with all of the increased responsibilities. She bit her lip. It would be very hard for her to step aside in favor of someone else, someone who—

Annie put the kettle back on the range with a bang. "Do stop dithering, Maggie," she said decidedly. "You know you have nothing to worry about. Why, the trustees haven't placed a single advertisement. They certainly mean to promote you to head teacher. It's only a matter of—"

"Good evenin'!" shouted a comradely voice at the kitchen door. Margaret turned to see their neighbor, Bertha Stubbs, an ample, untidy woman who lived just around the corner, in one of the Lakefield cottages.

"Are you two home?" Bertha inquired, unnecessarily, since both Margaret and Annie were standing in front of her. "You're not sittin' down to supper reet this verra minute, are you?"

"Oh, bother," Annie muttered, turning to take off her apron.

"Do come in and have a cup of tea, Bertha," Margaret said, suppressing a sigh. Bertha Stubbs was the daily woman at the school, and Margaret saw more of her during the term than she wanted. Bertha was one of those women who did her best work to the accompaniment of loud and long complaints, and her casual spitefulness—sometimes hidden, sometimes not—wasn't always easy to tolerate. But one had to be neighborly.

"Thanks," Bertha said with satisfaction. "B'lieve I will."

Margaret smiled. "We've only just put the potatoes on, so supper won't be ready for—" She caught Annie's glance and amended her sentence. "For ten minutes or so. They cook quickly, you know, when the oven is hot."

Bertha settled her bulk in a chair at the kitchen table and waited whilst Annie poured tea. She put both elbows on the table, dropped three cubes of sugar into her tea, stirred, and drank deeply.

"Thought there was something y' should hear," she said, putting down her cup with a bang. "If y' haven't already, that is. Which y' may have, seein' that it's important."

"Oh, really?" Margaret asked politely. Bertha's news, whatever it was, was always important, even when it was only a bit of common gossip that everyone had already heard. "What's happened?"

"I've just been up to Tower Bank House, havin' a bit of a chat with Elsa." Elsa was Bertha's brother's widow, and one of Bertha's closest friends. Bertha leaned forward, narrowed her eyes, and lowered her voice. "She told me that something big came up this afternoon. Name of Dr. Harrison Gainwell."

Annie, who had little patience with Bertha, was more direct than Margaret. "Don't hint, Bertha," she said in an exasperated tone. "Who is Harrison Gainwell? And if you've only just heard about him, how can you think that we might have?"

"I thought mappen y' got some advance word." Bertha leaned back in her chair with a smug look, obviously feeling the significance of what she was about to say. "He's a grad-u-ate of Oxford University, that's who he is. Lady Longford wants him to be t' new head teacher at Sawrey School."

"The new head teacher—" Margaret gasped.

"How does Elsa know this?" Annie asked, her voice like steel. "Where did she hear it?"

"Why, where else but t' sittin' room at Tower Bank House?" Bertha replied innocently. "Lady Longford and that companion of hers called this afternoon, to tell Miss Woodcock to tell the captain that t' trustees could stop lookin' for a new head teacher, 'cuz she has found him. Elsa heard what they said when she took in t' tea."

"She eavesdropped, you mean," Annie said acidly. Elsa's reputation as a source of important village information was enhanced by her position as cook-housekeeper in the home of the Justice of the Peace. It was generally reckoned that the gossip she gathered had the stamp of authority on it—as it usually did.

"Well, I wouldn't go so far as to say she *eavesdropped*," Bertha said in a judicious tone. "But she did hear what was said. Gainwell's a mission'ry from t' South Pacific." She rolled her eyes. "Elsa says a gentl'man who can civ'lize cannonballers can cert'nly teach Sawrey School."

There was a moment's silence. Finally, Annie broke it. "Cannibals, I think you mean, Bertha. Although I'm not quite sure that I see the connection between civilizing natives and teaching children."

"Well," said Bertha distantly, "that's what Elsa says."

Margaret tried to speak, but found that she had to clear her throat twice before she could manage to get the words out. "I . . . I'm sure Dr. Gainwell will do an admirable job," she said. She found that she could not see through the tears that suddenly welled up in her eyes. Hastily, she pushed back her chair. "If you'll excuse me, I just remembered something I have to do upstairs." She stood and fumbled her way to the door, feeling Bertha's sharp glance like a knife between her shoulder blades.

"It's all right, Maggie," Annie said. "You can do it later." Margaret paused with her hand on the knob, realizing that Annie did not want to give Bertha the satisfaction of knowing that she had delivered a telling blow.

"There's no call to fret, Miss Nash," Bertha remarked, with some sympathy. "It won't come to nothin', cannonballers or not. Everybody's hopin' that t' trustees'll give t' place to you." She pushed her empty cup forward. "Is there more tea in that pot, Annie? Another cup would go down right well."

Annie stood and went to the kitchen range, where she

opened the oven door, took out the iron pot, and lifted the lid. "I think our supper is just about ready, Bertha. If you don't mind, that is."

Bertha sighed heavily. "Well," she said, putting both hands on the table and hoisting herself to her feet, "I s'pose I'd better get home and see to Mr. Stubbs's meal. Steak and kidney pie tonight, is what it is." She cocked her head to one side and added, thoughtfully, "Mission'ry, eh? Wonder if he's got any magic lantern slides, like that gentl'man who give that speech at t' Sawrey Hotel last year. He was a fine talker, he was. And them pictures of brown nekkid baby cannonballers with dirty old crab shells strung around their fat necks. Well, all I've got to say is—"

She was still saying it as Annie closed the door behind her.

"Oh, Annie!" Margaret cried, and burst into tears.

Annie held her sister in her arms. "Don't cry, Maggie," she whispered. "I'm sure the trustees will realize that you're the better choice for the school. They can't possibly mean to hire a man who doesn't know anything about—"

"But he's a graduate of *Oxford*!" Margaret wailed disconsolately. "He's Lady Longford's candidate! And you know that she always gets what she wants, no matter how horrid it is for other people."

This time, Annie couldn't think of anything comforting to say.

7

Word Gets Around

Naturally, the news of Dr. Gainwell's candidacy for the position of head teacher did not remain a secret for very long. Fifteen minutes before Bertha Stubbs was making her unwelcome announcement to Margaret and Annie Nash, Elsa Grape was passing the news along to Grace Lythecoe, the widow of the former vicar, whom she met on the street just outside the door of Rose Cottage. From inside the cottage came the vibrant sound of Caruso, Mrs. Lythecoe's canary, warbling a series of complicated trills up and down the scale. Elsa knew, of course, that Grace Lythecoe, having been the wife of a vicar, was not one to gossip, but she was the first person Elsa encountered, so she was the first to hear Elsa's news.

"I'm sorry that her ladyship has seen fit to intervene in the selection process," Mrs. Lythecoe said gravely. "And

I very much hope, Elsa, that you will keep this information to yourself. The school trustees will have a difficult enough time dealing with the facts of this matter without having to deal with the inevitable gossip, as well. I'm sure you don't want to cause them any more anxiety than necessary, do you?"

"Oh, no, Mrs. Lythecoe," Elsa vowed, her eyes widening. "Of course not, Mrs. Lythecoe."

And then, without hesitation, Elsa hurried to the Tower Bank Arms, the village pub, which sat on a hill on the opposite side of the main road through the village. There, she went looking for her friend Mrs. Barrow, the wife of the pub's proprietor. She found her in the grassy garden behind the Arms, folding freshly dried bed sheets from the clothesline into a wicker laundry basket, and told her story.

Frances Barrow listened with a growing apprehension, and was much distressed by the implications of Elsa's report. She hurried into the pub to inform her husband, who had just brought up a fresh keg of beer from the cellar and was tapping the bung, that Miss Nash would not be the new head teacher, after all. Lady Longford had just overruled the trustees' appointment and awarded the position to her own man, a Dr. Harrison Gainwell, a missionary from Borneo. Mrs. Barrow was highly incensed at her ladyship's intervention in school affairs, since her very own Margaret had just been promoted to the junior class, which her mother had expected would be taught by Miss Nash.

It did not much matter to Mr. Barrow who taught his daughter, as long as the girl learnt her lessons and behaved herself, but he quite naturally believed that this news might be of some interest to the other parents in the village. So that evening, when the men began to gather at the Arms for their nightly half-pints and the monthly dart tournament (which always drew a much larger than usual crowd), he mentioned it to three or four of the early arrivals, who mentioned it to those who came later, and so on. Of course, there was always a great deal of noise in the pub, singing and shouting and clinking of glasses and such, and it wasn't always possible to hear exactly what was being said. But by closing time, most of the dart players in both Near and Far Sawrey—that would be at least half of the men in the twin villages—had heard the facts of the matter, at least in a general way. They knew that a gentleman of outstanding education, character, and amazing courage (they were a little unclear as to whether his name was Gainfellow or Galsworth) had been unanimously appointed by the school trustees to take over Sawrey School, his entire salary being underwritten by Lady Longford out of gratitude for his having rescued the three children of a fellow missionary from the cooking pot of a savage tribe of head hunters.

It was this thrilling tale that the wives of the village learnt from their husbands at breakfast, and which they shared amongst themselves, with further embellishments, as they met one another in the street or the post office or the village shop or across the garden fence. And since the village women cared little about Dr. Gainfellow's adventures in Borneo and a great deal more about the fate of dear Miss Nash, they were soon speculating sympathetically about what would become of her.

Most of the speculators felt that she would stay on as the faithful teacher of the infants class, as she had for the last nine years, whilst others believed that she would suffer such a humiliating loss of face that she could never stay in the village and would most certainly be forced to look for another teaching position. In fact, Bertha Stubbs (who met several of the women in the queue at the post office a little before lunch time) reported having seen Miss Nash in her back garden early that morning, airing several valises and looking terribly upset. It was clear that the two sisters were packing to leave.

Having heard this intriguing bit about the valises, Agnes Llewellyn's daughter Mary wondered out loud to Lydia Dowling's niece Gladys just how quickly the Nash sisters' cottage would be let—if they actually moved house, of course, although perhaps they wouldn't, since Annie had been so ill all spring. Gladys, in her turn, met Hannah Braithwaite, wife of the village constable, and happened to mention that it looked as if the Nash sisters might go to the south of England, with the hope of a new position for Miss Nash and a kinder climate for Annie, who suffered so with her lungs.

Hannah became very excited when she heard this bit of news, because Miss Nash's cottage was larger and nicer than Croftend, where she and the constable and their three children lived, cheek by jowl, as it were, in only two small bedrooms. It had a much larger garden, too, with room for a pig and chickens, which would mean eggs and bacon. Not to hurry things along, of course, and Hannah certainly didn't wish the Nash sisters any ill luck, the good Lord forbid. But she did so hope that once the cottage was empty, she and Constable Braithwaite could obtain it. Who better to have it than the village constable?

Except, as Mathilda Crook pointed out when she heard of Hannah's hopes, the Nash cottage would very likely go to Dr. Gainfellow (or Galsworth—some had heard one name and some the other), who would necessarily be looking for a place to live. And since he was a bachelor (no one knew this for certain, of course, but a missionary to Borneo couldn't possibly have a wife, could he?), he would certainly make a handy fourth at bridge and fill in the gap at the table when Captain and Miss Woodcock entertained.

And speaking of Miss Woodcock, who had thus far

fended off several highly suitable offers of courtship (to the village's great distress), would it not be delightful if she and the new head teacher would strike up a romantic friendship, fall in love, and marry? After all, Miss Woodcock—whose brother might decide at any moment to take a wife who would displace her who would have to find a new home in which to live out her spinsterhood and a lonely old age—was seriously in want of a husband, and a former missionary from Borneo would be a perfect choice.

So it was that by the time the mothers finished their Tuesday baskets of ironing and called in the children for their lunches, Sawrey School not only had a new head teacher, but Miss Nash and her sister had up sticks and gone to the south of England, leaving their cottage to the Braithwaites or to Dr. Worthwell, who was to marry dear Miss Woodcock.

As most people know, in a village, word gets around very fast.

8

An Unfortunate Accident

Beatrix didn't hear a word of this gossip, for she had spent the morning at Hill Top, happily making pencil sketches for *The Tale of Tom Kitten*. She had borrowed a kitten from one of the stone masons, and drew a few pictures of it, although it was a mischievous little creature and not very anxious to sit still. Then she went inside and made some preliminary sketches of the kitchen and bedroom for the interior scenes. She had already written out the tale in a penny exercise book and calculated that she'd need a couple of dozen paintings to illustrate it. She was hoping to finish the project within the next few months, and was already thinking ahead to the next book, which she had decided would be a story about the rats that seemed to be everywhere, and into everything.

Making the indoor sketches was not as pleasant as it might have been. Beatrix very much enjoyed going into the house whenever she got the chance, but Mrs. Jennings—who had never been enthusiastic about staying on at Hill Top Farm after Beatrix took possession—always made her feel uncomfortable, as if she were intruding. And when she did go in, she couldn't help noticing that the place needed a good airing and cleaning, top to bottom, something that was understandably hard for Mrs. Jennings to do, with two small children and a new baby to care for. And then there was Mrs. Jennings's cheap machine-made furniture and religious pictures and bric-a-brac, which made the old rooms look cluttered and shabby.

Beatrix could hardly wait until the new extension was finished and the Jenningses had moved into it, and the main part of the house was her very own. She would furnish the rooms with authentic antiques that would fit the spirit of the old house, and she already was happily looking for the curtains and rugs, the dishes and fireplace implements and pictures that would make Hill Top her home. Her very first home—in spite of the fact that she wouldn't be able to live there the year round, as she desperately longed to do.

So, all things considered, Beatrix was just as glad when Mrs. Jennings didn't ask her to stay to lunch. She went back to Belle Green and ate a sandwich and a bowl of soup. A little while later, Mr. Jennings brought the pony cart—pulled by Winston, a shaggy brown pony with an alert, self-confident air—to collect her for their drive to Holly How Farm, to have a look at the sheep she had bought.

The Crooks' dog Rascal trotted out to the cart with her. A fawn-colored Jack Russell terrier, he lived at Belle Green but counted the village as his home-at-large. And since she boarded at Belle Green when she came to the village, he seemed to have appointed himself as her escort.

"I'd like to go along," said Rascal politely, giving her fingers a lick to show his respect.

"Do you mind if we take the Crooks' dog?" Beatrix asked. "I think he'd like to go with us."

The farmer grinned. "'Spose if I said no, he'd just trot along behind. Jump in, Rascal."

The narrow track of Stony Lane glistened in the afternoon sunlight as they drove along. The thick green hedge was filigreed with the delicate tracery of honeysuckle and blackberry and veiled with feathery plumes of travelers' joy, whilst beyond the hedge, the green bracken climbed the shoulder of the hill. The little road snaked upward and out of the village and draped itself across the slope of Oatmeal Crag, above the emerald green water meadows on either side of Wilfin Beck, dotted with the plump white shapes of grazing sheep. Beyond lay a stubble-field where the men and their massive draft horses had just finished cutting the summer's hay, the haystacks as golden and proud as temples in some exotic land. It had been a dry, hot summer thus far, the best kind of weather for haying, so most of the hay had been cut and stacked. The next regular farm chore, sheepshearing, would begin in another week or so.

With Rascal on the seat beside her, every now and then giving her chin a quick lick, Beatrix looked around with pleasure. She had loved the countryside since her earliest childhood, when her family went to Scotland for their summer-long holiday. Then, nothing was sweeter than a long walk through the meadows and woods, listening to the wind through the fir trees and watching for a glimpse of the fairies that came out at night to dance on the green turf. Now, she loved to walk up Stony Lane to sketch at Moss Eccles Tarn, the small lake behind Oatmeal Crag. And she enjoyed riding through the countryside with Mr. Jennings, for he had farmed in this area for quite some time and was usually willing to share what he knew about the land and the people. When she first met the farmer, he seemed taciturn and withdrawn, but now that they were better acquainted, he was proving a regular gossip, and much friendlier than his wife.

Just now, he pointed with his pony whip at a tall, frowning house that stood well off to their right, on the other side of Wilfin Beck. It was built of gray stone, with a gray slate roof and narrow windows that gleamed like steel in the afternoon light. A fortress, grim and uncompromising, it was half-screened by gloomy fir trees, and behind it rose the dark wildness of Cuckoo Brow Wood.

"Tidmarsh Manor," Mr. Jennings remarked. "Sad place, that."

"*Sad?*" Rascal asked. He shivered and moved closer to Miss Potter on the seat. "*I call it sinister.*"

"Why so?" Beatrix inquired encouragingly.

"*Why sinister? Because Dudley—Lady Longford's spaniel—says there's trouble brewing.*" Rascal looked up at Miss Potter, whose pink cheeks were even pinker with the heat. "*Dudley is fat and rude and nobody much likes him. But he knows what's going on at the Manor.*"

"If tha doan't hush thi noise, Rascal," Mr. Jennings said sternly, "tha can'st get down and walk." To Beatrix he replied, "'Tis sad because Lady Longford's husband died, and her son—t' young Lord Longford—went off to New Zealand and bought a sheep station."

"Really," Beatrix remarked with interest, remembering that Dimity Woodcock had named Lady Longford as the person who had nominated a candidate for the school.

"Oh, aye. Great pity, 'twas." Mr. Jennings pulled his brows together and pursed his lips. "Lady Longford had it in mind that t' lad would marry t' Kittredge daughter and take over t' estate, which by rights he should've done, o'course." He flicked a fly off Winston's shoulder with a light touch of the whip. "But he didn't like t' girl, 'spite of

t' fact that t' lands join, and raised a great protest against
t' marriage. His mother told him to go away and ne'er come
back. So he ran off to New Zealand and married a sheep
farmer's daughter, and then got killed in a t'rrible train crash,
and now there's no one to keep t' fam'ly line goin' or manage
t' Tidmarsh estate." Mr. Jennings concluded his speech with
the satisfied air of a man who has managed to pack a great
many complicated details into one brief narrative.

Beatrix flinched as if she had been touched by Mr. Jennings's whip, for the story was rather too near her own. "Oh,
dear," she murmured, thinking that parents could be extraordinarily cruel when it came to managing their children's lives. It did no good and caused nothing but pain, all
round.

"There's the granddaughter," Rascal pointed out. *"Of course,
she's half a New Zealander, Dudley says, which is the reason the
old lady turns up her nose."*

"There would be somebody to inherit," Mr. Jennings
went on, "if Lady Longford would have her, but she won't.
T' son had a daughter, y' see. Now t' girl's father is dead and
her mother, too. She's stayin' at t' Manor, sin' she has
nowheres else to go. Caroline, she's called."

Caroline. It was the name of Beatrix's favorite cousin,
Caroline Hutton. She cast a glance back over her shoulder at
the house, which stood gaunt and forbidding behind the
firs, with an air of desolate isolation.

"It looks a lonely place for a child," she remarked, feeling
an immediate sympathy for the girl who was exiled there.

Perhaps because she herself had not had playmates in the
usual way, Beatrix was not very comfortable with the village
youngsters who tormented the ducks and chased cats and
stole birds' eggs. She was much more at ease with quieter
children, especially with girls who enjoyed books and art—
girls like herself, when she was younger. Now, she thought

of how she would have felt if she had been shut up in that dark, menacing house, and shivered. If Caroline Longford was timid and impressionable, she might well be terrified, especially when the wind whistled down the chimneys and battered at the windows.

"Lonely? Oh, aye," Mr. Jennings agreed. "Nobody on t' place but a housemaid or two and t' Beevers—Mrs. Beever cooks, Beever keeps t' garden and drives t' phaeton when it's wanted. And there's t' companion to Lady Tidmarsh. Miss Martine. She's giving t' girl her lessons 'til she goes off to school."

"The child needs an animal to keep her company," Beatrix said decidedly.

As children, she and her younger brother Bertram had kept all sorts of animals in their third-floor nursery at Bolton Gardens, frogs and lizards and snakes and mice and even a bat and an obstreperous raven. Over the years, her pets— Punch, her frog; the splendid Belgian rabbit she called Peter Piper; and Mrs. Tiggy-Winkle, a dear little hedgehog who had died quietly just a few months ago—had become even more important to her. They had served as models for the drawings she used in her little books and had gone everywhere with her. On this trip, for instance, she had brought her pet rabbits and mouse, as well as a guinea pig named Tuppenny, about whom she wanted to make a story. In fact, she had already written it out some two years before, calling it *The Tale of Tuppenny*. But she had decided instead to do the Kitten book, set at Hill Top Farm. If Lady Longford's granddaughter would like to borrow her guinea pig—

"*Don't think so,*" Rascal said confidentially, into her ear. "*Dudley says that Miss Martine doesn't approve of—*"

"Doubt she'd be allowed, Miss Potter," Mr. Jennings said.

Beatrix frowned. Not allowed to have animals? That would be a hard thing, and a lonely life, indeed.

"Talkin' of animals," Mr. Jennings said, pointing again, "dust tha' see t' top of Holly How? Up there is a very old badger sett, older'n any others between t' lakes, some say. Doan't know how many badgers live there, but it's home to rabbits, and likely a fox or two. Most of t' setts between t' lakes has been dug, some of 'em dug more'n once. But Lord Longford 'ud nivver let anybody meddle with t' sett on Holly How, and auld Ben has carried on t' way his lordship wanted. So there's badgers there, I expect."

Beatrix looked where the farmer was pointing, at a rocky hill outlined against the sky. She had studied and sketched quite a few wild creatures, but not badgers, who were nocturnal animals and quite shy. "The only badger I've ever seen," she said thoughtfully, "was a very old, very fat badger in a traveling circus. I felt rather sorry for him. They're not much liked by farmers, I understand."

"Some say they eat chicks and eggs in t' hen coop," Mr. Jennings replied, "but them 're mostly careless folk who don't shut up their chickens proper." He paused, frowning. "Somebody dug t' sett down by t' Hill Top rock quarry a few days ago. Badger-baiters, most like. There's some in this village that doan't mind takin' a chance on a fight 'twixt a badger and a dog."

Rascal growled deep in his throat. His father had been tossed into a badger pit once, and although a stalwart warrior, had barely lived to tell the tale. Badgers were known as stout fighters who employed both tooth and claw—and they had long, sharp claws—against their foes. He himself was brave, but he should not like to go up against one.

"But the law prohibits badger-baiting," Beatrix replied with a frown, not sure whether she felt sorrier for the badger or for the dog. "Not to mention that the diggers were trespassing on Hill Top property." And that made the badgers *her* badgers, didn't it? Not really, of course, since one couldn't own a wild animal. But the idea that somebody would steal a peaceable animal out of its home made her angry and indignant.

"Did t' law ever stop anybody who wanted to do a thing?" Mr. Jennings remarked with such scorn that Beatrix felt that her response had been naïve. Perhaps the village constable wasn't interested in enforcing a law that protected animals. And as far as trespassing went, many of the poorer people in the district gathered berries and mushrooms wherever they could be found, and shot hares and rabbits and pheasants for their dinner tables. Who was to draw the line between poaching a rabbit for a meal and digging a badger for entertainment?

They went along a little way in silence, until the road crested the steep shoulder of Oatmeal Crag and began to creep cautiously down into the valley. They crossed Wilfin Beck at a stony ford where small fish flashed like quicksilver in the shallow water, and drove along a well-used cart-track toward a cottage, its whitewashed walls topped by a roof of gray Coniston slates. The front of the house was covered with pink roses, and there was a blue door.

"Holly How Farm," Mr. Jennings said, as they drove down the track. "Hornby'll be waitin' for us. He's glad to sell us those sheep."

"I hope he's not wanting to sell because there's something wrong with them," Beatrix replied.

Mr. Jennings shook his head. "Not a bit of it. Ben Hornby's Herdwicks are t' best between t' lakes, b'yond a doubt. No, t' truth of it is that his knees are allus givin' him trouble these days—and then there was that bad business with t' barn last winter."

"The barn?"

"Aye. Caught fire and burnt to t' ground. Disheartened him some, I expect. Told me he aims to retire and go to live with his daughter up Keswick way, although he's keepin' that dark, so doan't go telling it around." He chuckled dryly. " 'Course, his daughter may not have him. Auld Ben's not t' easiest man in t' world. Gruff and growly, much of t' time."

Rascal gave an ironic chuckle. *"He's like an old bulldog, always snapping and showing his teeth. Not one to suffer fools, gladly or otherwise."*

Mr. Jennings paused, as if he thought he might have said too much. "Auld Ben's nivver a bad man, for all his tempers. And he's fair. Whatever else tha may think of him, he's fair."

"When he quits farming," Beatrix said thoughtfully, "will he put the farm up for sale?" Of course, she reminded herself, Hill Top Farm demanded every penny she could scrape together, and she had recently bought that two-acre pasture across the road. It was silly to be thinking of acquiring any more land. Still—

"T' farm's not his," Mr. Jennings said. " 'Tis a manor farm, let to him by Lord Tidmarsh under tenancy for his lifetime. Lady Longford might sell it when auld Ben quits, though. Now her son's dead, there's nae reason to keep t' estate all in one piece." There was a note of disapproval in his voice, for the farmers and villagers generally felt that the breakup of the large estates invited wealthy outsiders to come in and purchase property, creating instability. "Isaac Chance, at Oldfield Farm, just up t' way a bit, tried to buy it, but her ladyship told him it's Ben's, long as Ben wants it." He shrugged. "Expect Isaac Chance'll put in his bid soon as Ben makes it known he's leavin'."

"I see," Beatrix said, thinking that perhaps she should keep an eye on the situation. She probably had no business with another property—at least until she had managed to get Hill Top under control—but it was something to keep in mind. The cart had stopped in front of the cottage gate, and she climbed down, glancing around with an even greater interest. The farm looked to be in apple-pie order, buildings painted, fences mended, garden weeded and hoed— although behind the cottage and off to the right, she could see the ruins of a burnt barn.

Rascal jumped out of the cart and Mr. Jennings got out and looped the pony's reins around the gatepost. "Auld Ben doan't like to be kept waitin'. I see t' door's standin' wide, so he's expectin' us."

The blue front door opened directly into a kitchen with a large stone fireplace and a ceiling supported by two huge, hand-hewn oak beams. A plate, cup, knife, and fork sat on the table, ready for the next meal, and there was a pot of soup on the back of the kitchen range. It was a queer thing, though, Beatrix noticed, for the fire had gone out some time before. The range was cold.

Just as queerly, Ben Hornby was nowhere in the house. They went around to the back, and then to the barnyard and the garden, Mr. Jennings calling all the while.

"He's prob'ly up at t' fold with our sheep," he said finally. "He promised he'd have 'em penned well a-fore we came, but happen he didn't get round to it 'til now. We'll just walk up Holly How to t' fold."

With Rascal at her heels, Beatrix followed Mr. Jennings along the narrow path. It zig-zagged across the steep green hill behind the ruins of the barn, ending about halfway up at a stone-walled enclosure snuggled against the hill at the foot of a rocky outcrop. But Ben Hornby wasn't at the fold, either—and what's more, the gate was open. There were sheep grazing on the hillside nearby, but the enclosure was empty.

"Perhaps he forgot," Beatrix said, frowning. It was distinctly annoying to think that they had come all the way up here for nothing, especially when there were so many other things she might have done this afternoon. She could have continued the drawing she'd begun that morning, for instance, or gone to the house to see what Mr. Biddle was up to and make sure that he hadn't touched the cupboards.

Mr. Jennings was shaking his head. "Forgot? Not auld Ben. Not likely. Least, not where sheep're concerned. And he's already been paid for two ewes and three lambs, which was what we agreed to."

"Well, then, where is he?" Beatrix pointed at five nearby sheep, who were watching them curiously. "Those must be our sheep."

A shaggy ewe left her lambs and came in their direction, baaing. *"I'm glaaad you're here,"* she cried, raising her right foreleg in a stiff salute. *"Something very queer has haaappened, and needs sorting out. You see—"*

"I b'lieve they're ours," said Mr. Jennings, scratching his beard. "See t' lug marks in their ears? The larger one's Tibbie, if I recall a-reet, and them are her twin lambs, o'er there. And that one's Queenie, and that's her lamb. But I can't think where Ben's got off to."

"Excuse meee," the ewe bleated diffidently. *"If you'd only allow me to tell you—"*

"Don't even try," Rascal said. *"They don't understand, you know."* He gave Tibbie a searching look. They had met at the last sheep-shearing, if his memory served him correctly. He hid a grin, thinking that the last time he had seen her, she had been naked. She was much prettier in her wooly coat, although her fleece was certainly in need of a good wash.

"Baaa." Tibbie sighed gloomily and lowered her head. *"Anyway, there's nothing to be done now. Perhaps if you haaad come—"* Another deep sigh. *"But even then, you couldn't haaave changed anything. It's too late to shut the stable door after the horse has bolted, aaas the Norwegians say."*

"Changed what?" Rascal demanded crossly. Sheep were

always so fatalistic, and Herdwicks were annoyingly proud of their Norwegian ancestry. *"What's going on here, Tibbie? Why aren't you in the fold? Where's old Ben?"*

Tibbie rolled her eyes. *"I suppose you'll just haaave to see for yourself."* She began to climb up the craggy outcropping, with Rascal scrambling at her heels. *"Not that it will do any good, of course."*

Beatrix was watching the animals clambering up the rocks. "Do you suppose Mr. Hornby might have been taken ill?" she said to Mr. Jennings. "Perhaps we should look around."

"Suit thaself," Mr. Jennings said curtly. He was obviously very much put out. "I'd say we go back down to t' farm-house and leave a note on t' door. Happen Ben's been called away somewhere, sudden-like, and meant to be back a-fore we came. His table was laid, and his supper was on t' range."

"But the fire was out," Beatrix called over her shoulder. "It must have been *yesterday's* supper."

She spoke breathlessly, for she was already scrambling up the steep slope after the animals. A few moments later, she had reached the top of the craggy pile of rocks, where a few sparse bushes had managed to root themselves in the stony earth. The ground fell off into a deep gully, a small stream dancing and chattering below. It was not quite a cliff, but almost. Beatrix took one look over the edge and gasped.

"You see?" said the ewe, with a resigned sigh. *"As I saaaid, nothing to be done."*

"How do you know until you go and look?" Rascal snarled, and launched himself down the slope of rock scree in a head-long, precarious slide.

"Mr. Jennings!" Beatrix cried. "Come quickly!" And she followed the little dog down the face of the cliff, arriving barely upright at the bottom.

But by the time Mr. Jennings had joined her at the foot of the steep slope, Beatrix already knew that there was nothing that could be done for the gray-haired, gray-bearded man sprawled, crumpled and unmoving, facedown on the rocks beside the stream.

"I told you so," bleated Tibbie. *"But nobody ever baathers to listen to a sheeeep."*

"Ah, poor fellow," Mr. Jennings breathed, and bent down to turn the man over. There was a deep gash on his forehead and blood on his face and on the sleeve of his gray shirt. "Ben! Ben Hornby! Cans't tha hear me, Ben?"

"I'm afraid he can't hear you," Beatrix said in a practical tone. "He's dead. And he's been dead for quite some time."

Mr. Jennings straightened, took off his hat, and looked down at the old man with a lingering sadness. "Well, Ben," he said at last, "tha wust ever a crusty old fellow, but always fair minded, and that's t' best that can be said for any man, high or low." To Beatrix, he said, "There's nothing more to be done here, Miss Potter. It's a verra unfortunate accident, is what it is. We'd best drive back to t' village, and I'll fetch Captain Woodcock up here. He's t' Justice of t' Peace and—"

"I don't like to leave the poor man all alone," Beatrix interrupted. "You go for the captain, Mr. Jennings. I'll stay with Mr. Hornby."

Mr. Jennings frowned. "But it's none of thi affair, Miss Potter. This is village business, and—"

"And I am a resident of the village, so it is my business. Now, go and get Captain Woodcock, please."

"And the constable," Rascal put in. *"Mr. Jennings needs to fetch the constable, too."*

Beatrix was thinking about the way villagers had responded when poor Miss Tolliver had died the previous autumn. Within a few days, some of them had had her murdered, in spite of Dr. Butters's finding of death by heart failure. It would be no different this time, she supposed. In which case—

"It might be a good idea," she added, "if you would also fetch Constable Braithwaite." A quick investigation would do a great deal to put the gossip to rest, although people like Mrs. Crook and Bertha Stubbs and Elsa Grape *would* talk, no matter what the authorities said.

"I'll do that," Mr. Jennings said, and sighed. "Well, if tha'rt determined to stay, Miss Potter, then tha must. But keep t' dog here. I'll be as quick as I can." And with that, he was gone.

Beatrix sat on a rock, and Rascal lay down at her feet. Clouds shadowed the afternoon sun and a cool northern breeze had sprung up, carrying a hint of rain, and she shivered. Her own brush with death—Norman's death, just eleven months ago—was still fresh in her mind, and seeing Mr. Hornby, so unexpectedly, so *irrevocably* dead, brought the grief back, as sharp and biting as new vinegar. Sudden death was cruel, whether the victim was as young as Norman or as old as Mr. Hornby, and she felt the tears start.

But tears were dangerous, for they threatened to dissolve her determination to put the loss and disappointment of the past behind her, and after a moment, she brushed them away with the back of her hand. One had to get on with life. And life certainly had a way of getting on by itself, no matter who died or who lived on to mourn the passing.

She looked up at the wooly sheep peering over the rocky crag, watching her with what seemed like an intense but benign curiosity. Since she had already bought and paid for the sheep, they should be taken down to their new home at Hill Top Farm. She would ask Mr. Jennings to arrange for that as soon as he returned. It seemed a trivial sort of thought to be thinking in the face of death, but even trivial thoughts had their purpose, she had found. If one made oneself think about the things that one had to do—not with a sort of superficial attention but as if doing the thing really mattered—it did help one to get on.

On the top of the crag, Tibbie gave an inquiring bleat. Rascal answered with a consoling bark, and not far away, a woodpecker drummed a reassuring rat-tat-tat on a hollow tree. Beatrix managed a small smile. Yes, life went forward, in spite of deaths and accidents and appalling things one wished had never happened. She looked down once again at the body that lay at her feet.

And that was when she noticed that old Ben Hornby had died with something clutched tightly in the fingers of his right hand.

9

Bosworth Badger Is Interrupted

Bosworth Badger had spent the afternoon in The Brockery library, immersed in his work on the *Holly How Badger Genealogy*. There, the history of the many branches of the Holly How badger family was set down in great detail in the leather-bound volumes. One could find family trees with the names of parents and offspring, dates of births and deaths, and a great many fascinating stories of various badger accomplishments, travels to distant places, and new settlements. (A very important Badger Rule of Thumb makes it clear that every young male badger is expected to leave his place of birth and establish a new sett of his own, unless the senior male badger of the sett has elected him to receive the Badger Badge of Authority, which entitles him to manage the sett.)

Both the *History of the Badgers* and the *Genealogy* went

back many generations, to the first settlement of badgers at
The Brockery, which occurred around the time that Bonnie
Prince Charlie had ridden from Scotland almost to London
and then had been chased back to Scotland again. On the
first page of this historical record was pictured, in full color,
the famous Badger Coat of Arms, with twin badgers ram-
pant on an azure field, bearing a shield on which was written the family emblem,

De Parbis, grandis acerbus erit

("From small things, there will grow a mighty heap"),
which Bosworth had always taken to refer to his family's
habit of digging out their remarkably extensive burrows
one small bit at a time, and piling the dirt outside the near-
est door.

The *History* and the *Genealogy* had become a matter of
great pride to succeeding badger generations, and maintain-
ing them was one of the most important obligations of the
badger who held the Badger Badge of Authority. Bosworth
had done his best, for he knew it would be of enormous
value in the future, when later generations of badgers would
look back with wonder at the lives of their ancestors. He
was, however, confronting a very substantial difficulty, for
he was the last badger in a long line of well-known Holly
How badgers. He had not been inclined to marry and establish his own sett when he was a youth, for he had been a
reckless and wandering sort of badger, anxious to go as far
afield and enjoy as many adventures as any young badger
possibly could. He had returned to Holly How only when
his father had written that he was dying and ready to pass
on to him the Badger Badge of Authority.

By this time in his life, even if Bosworth had wanted to
look for a wife and begin a family, it was entirely too late.

He was getting on in years and, whilst he was still an active and energetic badger, his muzzle was turning gray and he knew that there would come a time when he would no longer be able to do all he was doing now. Bosworth did not regret his failure to sire offspring, for he was thought of as a *pater familias* by the animals who called The Brockery home and he considered all of them to be his true family. But he did regret it where the *Genealogy* and the *History* were concerned, for it was unthinkable that these should come to an end for lack of an authorized badger to maintain them. However, there it was. He had to face it. When he was gone from Holly How—and that might not be such a far distant event—there would be no one to continue the great work.

With a heavy sigh, Bosworth got up from the desk and went to add another stick of wood to the fire. It might be a very warm July afternoon out-of-doors, but down here, in the endless burrows and tunnels and chambers of the sett, it was always cool enough for a fire. He paused to look up at the portrait of one of his ancestors, who looked down at him with what seemed to be a frown of reproach. Bosworth knew why. He had failed in one of his most important duties: to identify a young male badger worthy of wearing the Badge of Authority and carrying on the great work of the *History* and the *Genealogy*. He sighed again, a guilty sigh. He had not done all he could, and he knew it. He—

His thoughts were interrupted by a light rapping at the library door, and the badger frowned. This was the third time in an hour that Flotsam, or perhaps it was Jetsam (there was no telling those two rabbits apart) had come in with an inconsequential question. One hadn't been able to find the lemon polish, and the other had noticed that the hedgehog hadn't slept in his bed for the last two nights and wondered if he had gone off without signing the register. Really, was it too much to hope for a few hours of uninterrupted privacy so that a badger could carry out his important work?

"Yes?" he growled. "Which of you is it this time? And what the devil do you want?"

But the animal who had knocked on the door was neither Flotsam nor Jetsam, but Parsley, the talented young badger who did all of The Brockery's cooking. She was still wearing her bonnet and shawl, suggesting that she had just come back from above ground. Her paws were shaking and she was visibly upset.

"Excuse me, Mr. Badger, sir," she cried, pulling off her bonnet, "but a terrible thing has happened, and I think you should know about it."

"A terrible thing?" Bosworth asked in alarm, thinking at once of the old tunnel that led to the far side of Holly How, which was in need of shoring up and which had been threatening to collapse. Or perhaps one of his lodgers had suffered an accident, or run afoul of a dog, or—

"Oh, yes, sir," Parsley said, her large bright eyes brimming with tears. "I went out, you see, to get some mushrooms for our dinner tonight." She took a deep breath and seemed to steady herself. "I was thinking of a veal and ham pie, you know, made with puff pastry, which I thought would be very good. There's a recipe in Mrs. Beeton's Cookery Book, a fine recipe, except that it doesn't include mushrooms, and the idea came to me that Mrs. Beeton's pie would be much improved if I added a few mushrooms." She paused, took a lace hanky out of her apron pocket, and blew her nose. "Oysters might be another possibility, or sweetbreads, but I'd be hard put to find any fresh oysters hereabouts, unless I should go down to the Sawrey Hotel and meet the fish man who comes over from Kendal. But one has to order ahead for oysters, which in any event should only be eaten in months which contain the letter R, and July doesn't, of course. And as to sweetbreads, I hardly think—"

"Stop, Parsley!" roared the badger, but in a kindly way, for he knew that it was Parsley's habit to talk all the way *around* a story two or three times before she could manage to open the front door and step into it properly. He softened his tone. *"My dear girl, I have not one iota of interest in the presence or absence of sweetbreads, or what one must do to have oysters, or whether there is an R in July. What is this terrible thing you've come to tell me about? I do hope nothing has happened to any of our friends."*

"Well, not to say a friend, sir, but rather a neighbor." Recalled to her narrative, Parsley began to weep again. *"Oh, sir, it was dreadful, really it was—just too dreadful for words!"* She gulped down one or two sobs, which appeared to stick like dry biscuit in her throat and render her speechless.

Bosworth sighed. With a grizzled forepaw, he patted her gently on the shoulder and said, in a coaxing tone, *"I'm sorry, Parsley, but there's no getting around it. It may be too dreadful for words, but you shall simply have to reach down inside yourself and pull them out. Now, be a reasonable animal and give it a go, please."*

"Thank you, sir. I'll try, sir." Parsley took a deep breath and hung her bonnet over her arm. *"Well, then, I decided on mushrooms, instead of oysters or sweetbreads. I thought a pint of them might do very well, and there are usually some rather fine Chanterelles growing near the stream at the foot of that little rocky bluff not far from the sheep fold on Holly How. So I put on my bonnet and shawl and took a basket and went out to look for them, and instead I found—"* She screwed her eyes shut as recollection overtook her. *"Oh, indeed, sir, it was such an awful sight that I hardly know how to—"* She began to cry again, big, gulping, noisy sobs.

"There, there, dear," Bosworth said, scarcely knowing himself what to say, for a female's tears always made him feel helpless. *"Pull yourself together and finish your story. It's only*

words, you know, just one after the other, skipping and plodding, as it were, all the way to the end."

Thus encouraged, Parsley began to tell her tale, with a great many parenthetical asides and explanatory footnotes, but finally it was all out. She had gone to the gully to find the mushrooms, and had been distracted by a pair of dippers, bickering over a choice water bug that one of them had fished out from under a stone, and then by a chatty red squirrel who wanted her to know that his cousin's nest at the back of Oatmeal Crag had been raided by a pine marten, who (happily) had been frightened off before any of the babies could be hurt—the usual sort of woodland gossip that animals share when they are out and about.

At last, Parsley had got close to the spot where she had seen the Chanterelles growing. But not a stone's throw away, she saw a person sitting on a rock with a dog at her feet. The person was the lady from London who had bought Hill Top Farm the previous autumn—Miss Potter, her name was—and the dog was one of the village dogs, a Jack Russell terrier called Rascal, with whom Parsley had a nodding acquaintance. And beside the lady, on the ground, as still as a stick, lay old Ben Hornby.

Bosworth gaped, taken aback. *"On the ground? He was having a nap?"*

"Oh, no, sir," Parsley said sadly. *"Mr. Hornby was . . . he was dead, sir."*

"Dead!" Bosworth exclaimed, horrified. *"Are you sure?"*

"Oh, yes, sir. He didn't move and didn't move, and Miss Potter was trying not to cry. And then finally she reached down and took something out of his hand. So, sir, I should have to say that he was dead."

For a moment, Bosworth stood still, stunned. And then, unbidden, a recollection of the last time he had seen Ben Hornby sprang into the badger's mind. From his vantage point at the top of Holly How, he had looked down and across the shoulder of the hill and glimpsed Ben at work, penning Tibbie and the other sheep in the fold.

Bosworth frowned. When was that? Evening before last, was it? And then, early yesterday morning, when he'd gone to the sheep fold to indulge himself in a breakfast of earthworms, he had found the gate open, and the sheep gone.

The badger's frown deepened to a scowl. The sheep were gone, and their owner was dead—and not in his bed, either. Something was terribly amiss here.

The first thing that leapt into Bosworth's mind, of course, was the suspicion that the old farmer had been the victim of thieves. Sheep stealing was a rare thing in the Land between the Lakes, but not, sadly, unknown. Why, only the year before, a dozen very fine Blue-faced Leicesters had disappeared without a trace from a meadow on the other side of Esthwaite Water, and nothing had been seen of them since. And about that same time, a farmer's boy, on his way to market in Hawkshead with six of his father's best Herdwick ewes, had been attacked and the sheep stolen. Yes, it had happened before, and it would undoubtedly happen again, humans being the greedy animals they were, always wanting what belonged to other humans.

"Did you notice, Parsley," he asked somberly, *"whether any of Mr. Hornby's Herdwicks were in the neighborhood? Tibbie or Queenie or their lambs?"*

Parsley shook her head, snuffling. *"I didn't stop to look. I was that frightened, you see, sir, that I ran away just as fast as my paws could carry me, and came straight home, without stopping for anything. I know that Mr. Hornby always looked out for us here at The Brockery, and I thought you would surely want to be informed. It seemed the sort of thing you'd want to make a note of. In the History, I mean."*

"Yes, of course," Bosworth said heavily. It was true. Ben

Hornby had always guarded The Brockery from any threat of disturbance, just as old Lord Longford had done when he was alive. Now that Ben was gone, who would look out for them? With a deep sense of foreboding, he added, *"I'm greatly obliged for the report, Parsley. I shall make a note of it straight away."*

The badger went to the shelf, pulled down the last of the leather-bound volumes, and placed it, open, on the desk in front of him. Then, taking his quill pen in his paw, he dipped it into his silver ink pot, and set down the date. Beneath that, in his best and most careful penmanship, he wrote:

Old Ben Hornby found dead today on Holly How.

He paused and looked at Parsley. *"I don't suppose,"* he said, *"that there was any way for you to guess how Mr. Hornby died."*

"Oh, no, sir," Parsley said sadly. *"I just supposed that he tumbled down the cliff and hit his head on a rock. Wouldn't you say, sir? As to how he might have come to tumble, or when, I couldn't say, sir. It might have just happened, or he might have died some time ago."*

Bosworth sighed, and added the phrase *manner of death unknown* to what he had already written. After a moment's thought, he added *time of death undetermined.* Then, having thought again, he dipped his quill in the ink pot once more, and wrote:

Whereabouts of 2 Herdwick ewes and 3 lambs unknown. Sheep thieves suspected.

"Thank you, Parsley," he said, putting down his quill pen and blotting his words with a bit of green blotting paper. *"I know that this has been quite a trial for you. You may go back to your work now, my dear, and we shall all look forward to a nice veal and ham pie with mushrooms for supper."* He closed the *History.*

Parsley took two steps toward the door, and then threw up both paws. *"Oh, Lor', sir!"* she cried. *"There aren't any mushrooms! I ran away and left the basket behind, sir! Oh, how careless of me!"*

"I daresay you had other things on your mind," said the badger comfortingly. *"The basket is a small loss, my dear. And I am sure that we shall enjoy your excellent pie with just as much pleasure as if it were full of mushrooms."*

"It's kind of you to say so, sir." Parsley blew her nose. *"But I still think—"*

"Goodness, it's teatime already," Bosworth said, with a glance at the clock on the mantle shelf. *"Perhaps you would be so good as to send one of the rabbits with a cup of hot tea with lemon and a small plate of something."*

"Oh, yes, sir. I shall, sir." This time, the young badger got as far as the library door. She stopped with her paw on the knob, turned, and said, in a brighter, more cheerful voice, *"But I do have a bit of good news to pass along, sir. I'm sure you heard about my aunt Primrose and her two young badger cubs, who were kidnapped from the sett down by the rock quarry at Hill Top Farm."*

"Yes, I did hear about that, Parsley," Bosworth said sorrowfully. *"It's very regrettable. But I didn't know that the victims were relatives of yours. Does anyone know what's happened to them?"*

Parsley sighed. *"Well, Aunt Primrose is still missing, and the little girl badger—Hyacinth, her name is. The general understanding—according to the magpie who told me all this—is that Jack Ogden took them. He's been seen around the village again, I'm sorry to say."*

At the sound of Jack Ogden's name, the badger shuddered. There were several well-known badger diggers in the Land between the Lakes, but Jack Ogden—also an itinerant waller (a man who built the dry-stone walls that took the places of fences in the district)—was the most notorious, and a serious threat to every badger.

Parsley was going on, with some relief. *"But the boy badger, Thorn, he's been found, I'm very glad to say. Jeremy Crosfield came across him wandering through the meadow down by Cunsey Beck. His leg's chewed and of course he's terribly distressed, but he's not otherwise injured—at least, that's what the magpie said."*

"Jeremy, is it?" said Bosworth in a comforting tone. *"Well, that's all right, then. The other village boys aren't terribly trustworthy, but that one's a sensible youngster, more sensible than some of the grownups. Your little cousin will be well taken care of."*

"We can only hope so, I'm sure, sir," said Parsley. *"Well, then, I'll see to your tea."* And with that, she bustled off.

When she was gone, the badger opened the *History* once again, to the earlier entry he had made regarding the missing badger family. *Thorn found by Jeremy Crosfield,* he wrote. *Primrose and Hyacinth still missing.* And then, frowning darkly, he added, *Jack Ogden suspected.*

10

Captain Woodcock Is Summoned

Captain Miles Woodcock had been Justice of the Peace for Sawrey for several years. The position required him to hear complaints, witness documents, certify deaths, deal with disturbances of the peace, and the like, so he found himself involved in almost every aspect of village life—something he had not intended when he came to the Lake District. Miles had served honorably in Her Majesty's Army in Egypt and the Sudan, where he had earned a bad leg and malaria and begun to think that he might like to live a quieter life in a place that was very green and cool, where the sun did not blister one's skin and the natives harbored no more than a mild resentment toward outsiders. The tiny Lake District village of Sawrey—located well off the beaten track and distant from the alarms and excursions of Empire—seemed as tailored to his exact specifications as his favorite shooting jacket.

And so it had proved, for the most part, especially after his sister Dimity came to live with him and assume the running of their small Tower Bank household: the cook, Elsa Grape; the housemaid, Molly; and old Fred Phinn, who came twice a week to assault the weeds and butcher the grass. Sawrey suited Dim just as well as it did him, and she seemed to get on comfortably with the villagers in ways that he did not. She always knew the latest gossip and could tell him what people were thinking and saying, most of it rather petty and inconsequential, Miles thought.

Just now, however, upon his Tuesday-afternoon return from a two-day trip to Manchester, she had told him something rather more urgent.

"A missionary from the South Pacific?" he exclaimed incredulously, dropping into a sitting-room chair. "With an Oxford degree? Why under the sun would a man like that want to teach in Sawrey? He'd be about as happy here as an elephant in a back garden."

Dimity picked up her knitting. "I fancy he must have the same motive as you, Miles. He wants some peace and quiet. Life in the South Pacific must be almost as difficult as the war in the Sudan."

"I doubt it," Miles replied sulkily. The trustees had already decided that their best course of action was to name Margaret Nash as the new head teacher, a decision in which Miles heartily concurred. In fact, they would have made the announcement the previous week, if they had received the letter they had requested from Miss Crabbe, which had only just arrived. And now there was *this* to deal with.

He picked up the Kendal newspaper and unfolded it to a front-page story about the aftermath of the San Francisco earthquake, which had devastated the city some three months before. He stared at the page, unseeing, for a moment, then rattled the newspaper and demanded, rhetorically, "And just what gives Lady Longford the right to barge in here like a juggernaut, flattening everyone with her schemes and intentions, and tell us who to hire?"

"I'm sure she's only doing what she thinks is best for the school." Dimity's voice was unhappy. "The trouble is, you see, that Dr. Gainwell actually sounds a much better candidate than Margaret. In terms of experience and education, I mean. He would be a real feather in Sawrey's cap, wouldn't he?"

"I suppose." Miles sighed. "Although I don't think there's a better teacher anywhere than Miss Nash. She's taught in the school for nearly a decade and understands the children in a way that an outsider cannot. This fellow might be a feather, but she's . . . well, she's the school's bread and butter."

"Well, if she's so crucial to the school's well-being, you and the trustees should have named her already," Dim said, frowning down at her knitting. "Do you know what the villagers are saying, Miles? That Margaret is so unsettled by the fact that this man is to be appointed head teacher that she has accepted a position in the south of England, which would be better anyway for poor Annie's lungs. And that they've given leave to the Braithwaites to take their cottage, unless, of course, it goes to the new fellow, who will surely want a house, unless Lady Longford has invited him to live at Tidmarsh Manor. Oh, *bother*!" she exclaimed crossly. "Now I've dropped a stitch. No, two, and several rows back."

Miles dropped the newspaper and stared at his sister. "Taken a position in the south of England! Given their cottage to the Braithwaites! That's utter nonsense, Dim, and you know it! That sort of village tittle-tattle isn't worth listening to, let alone repeating."

"Of course it's tittle-tattle," Dimity said, attacking her knitting with a crochet hook. "But that's the villagers for you. They will talk, and most of it's rubbish, but sometimes there's more than a kernel of truth in their gossip. I daresay Margaret won't want to stay if she's passed over for the head-ship—not for very long, anyway, although I doubt that she'd leave us in the lurch this fall." She held up her knitting. "There, all fixed. It wasn't as bad as I thought."

Miles was scowling. "Of course Miss Nash won't leave us in the lurch," he growled. "She's to be our new head teacher, and that's the beginning and end of it."

"I hardly think it's as simple as that, Miles." Dimity put down her knitting and regarded him with a narrow-eyed frown. "You know Lady Longford. She will be appalled if she thinks that you've given the post to a less-qualified woman than the man she's proposed. She may even decide that you've done it just to spite her—and you know what trouble she's capable of causing. In any event, you shall have to in-terview Dr. Gainwell, and as quickly as possible, too. Miss Martine says he's arriving tomorrow."

"Tomorrow!" Miles sighed again. "Well, I suppose I should be glad about that. At least we can get this over with and get on with the school's business." He rubbed his chin. "You don't suppose Miss Nash has heard any of this, do you?"

"Of course she has. Bertha Stubbs made it a point to tell her." Dimity shook her head. "I think you should talk to her, Miles. Reassure her. She must be awfully anxious about all this."

Miles shook his head. "I can't do that, you know, Dim. I'm one of the trustees." He paused. "But you could, you know. If you wouldn't mind." He added plaintively, "You wouldn't, would you? If she's down in the dumps, it might cheer her up to know that none of this has anything to do with the trustees—or with her. It's all Lady Longford's put-up."

Dimity frowned. "Are you sure you want me to do that—before the interview, I mean. What if the other trustees . . ." She let the sentence trail off.

"Oh, blast." Miles sighed. "I suppose you're right. Well, we'll just have to get it over with as soon as possible, then." He raised the newspaper again, feeling that the business about the headship had been settled, at least for now. But his sister hadn't quite said all she had to say.

"Did you know that her ladyship's granddaughter is staying with her?" she asked. "Caroline, her name is."

"Heelis told me," he said. "She's Bruce's daughter, you know. Lady Longford put up a fuss about having her, but Heelis and the vicar finally forced her to agree." He and Bruce—the young Lord Longford—had become friends shortly after his arrival in Sawrey, and they'd stayed in touch after Bruce had gone off to New Zealand, fleeing, Miles knew, from the marriage his mother had arranged for him. "A pity the old lady couldn't bring herself to accept his refusal to marry Kittredge's daughter," he added. "It wasn't a good match—they would have been miserable together. But perhaps, now that the girl is actually here, she'll win her grandmother over. Children have a way of doing that."

"Not in this case, I daresay," Dimity replied. "I offered to take the child for a seaside trip, and was told that she was not companionable. Secretive, sullen, and disobedient, was the way Miss Martine put it." She paused, frowning. "It sounds a perfectly awful situation, Miles. I just wish there was something we could do to help the child."

"Stay out of it, Dim," Miles said firmly. "I know that your intentions are good, but meddling will only make things worse for everyone, including the child. I—"

He was interrupted by a loud rapping at the front door. Miles went to answer it himself, since the rapping had an urgent sound to it. He opened the door to see two men, Constable Braithwaite and John Jennings, the farmer at Hill Top, standing on the doorstep.

"Sorry to interrupt, Captain, but you're needed," Constable

Braithwaite said. He was a short, stocky man with a florid complexion, his hair and eyebrows so blond they were nearly white. "A death," he added, an oblique way of explaining that Miles was being summoned in his official capacity as Justice of the Peace.

"A death?" Surprised, Miles glanced at John Jennings, who was standing uncomfortably by, his hands in his pockets, his cap pushed to the back of his head. "No one in your family, I hope, Jennings."

"Nay," Jennings said gruffly. "T'is auld Ben Hornby, of Holly How Farm. Verra bad accident, Cap'n. Fell off a rock cliff and broke his head. Miss Potter and me, we found him when we went up Holly How to see t' sheep we're buying."

Ben Hornby, Miles thought regretfully. The old man had certainly had his share of troubles this year. First his barn had burnt, then his milk cows had died, and now—

"Miss Potter's up there," the constable put in. "Insisted on stayin' with him."

"No matter what I said to her," added Jennings, with mixed disapprobation and reluctant admiration. "Reet stubborn lady, that one. Knows her mind."

Knows her mind indeed, Miles thought. He already knew that much about Miss Potter, from his dealings with her the previous October, when she had helped to close down a ring of art thieves. He reached for the hat that hung on the peg beside the door.

"Well, we'd best be going, then," he said. "Let's take the motorcar. It's faster."

"Oh, aye, Captain," the constable replied, his round face wreathed in smiles. Braithwaite was always up for a ride in Miles's new teal blue Rolls-Royce, which had caused quite a sensation in the village when Miles brought it home from Kendal the week after Easter. Not an entirely positive sensation, either. Many of the villagers had grumbled that the

Captain's motor was only the first, and that their narrow lanes would soon be jammed with those fast, noisy, *dangerous* vehicles. There wouldn't be any peace or safety left in the world.

Jennings, who had been one of the grumblers, gave a shrugging assent. "Allus a first time, I s'pose."

Miles raised his voice. "Dimity, I've been called away."

"Nothing terribly serious, I hope," his sister said, coming into the hallway. "Hello, Constable, Mr. Jennings." She looked at Miles inquiringly.

"Old Ben Hornby has had an accident," Miles said. "He's dead."

And with his sister's pitying exclamation ringing in his ears, he led the way out to the motorcar, parked in the stable beside his little filly, which he had given to Dimity. It was a shame about Ben, he thought again, sadly. How much bad luck could one man have?

11

Rascal Has a Tale to Tell

"Rascal—riding in a motorcar?" cried Tabitha Twitchit, her amber eyes widening with incredulous surprise. *"You're lying, Crumpet. I don't believe a word of it!"*

The gray tabby licked her right forepaw and smoothed down her ear. *"Believe it or not, however you like, Tabitha,"* she replied with careless disdain. *"What you think doesn't change what I saw."*

It was nearly supper time and the two cats were enjoying the balmy evening on the back steps of Belle Green. The afternoon rain had failed to arrive, the evening sun was just dropping through a wispy veil of peach and lavender clouds above the western fells, and the twilight was filled with the drowsy calls of birds on their way to roost. Belle Green was the large white farmhouse at the top of Market Street where Rascal lived and Miss Potter boarded when she came to the village. Tabitha, a calico with an orange and white bib, now lived there too, Mrs. Crook having offered her a home upon the death of her mistress the previous October. And Crumpet spent a great deal of time at Belle Green, where the mousing was first-rate. Tabitha was far less energetic than she had been in her younger days, and was content to let the mice do as they liked.

"*I'm telling you that I saw him myself, just a few minutes ago,*" Crumpet went on. "*He was sitting in the rear of Captain Woodcock's new Rolls-Royce, behind the Captain and Miss Potter. I don't see how you missed it, Tabitha. The motorcar was making an appalling clatter. It sent every chicken in the village into cackling fits.*"

"Hello, ladies." The two cats turned to see the subject of their conversation come trotting around the side of the house. Rascal's tail was up, his eyes were bright, and he was looking very pleased with himself.

"*Tabitha missed seeing the Captain's motorcar,*" he said, "*because she was having a nap on the top shelf in the pantry. That's where she always goes after tea.*"

"*I was not asleep in the pantry!*" Tabitha exclaimed defensively. "*I was keeping a close eye on a pair of impertinent mice who have been making free with the cheese.*"

"*Is that so?*" Rascal barked sarcastically. "*Well, then, Tabitha old girl, if you've been watching those mice so closely, perhaps you can tell us just how it is that they managed to—*"

"Oh, hush," Crumpet said, feeling that she was losing control of the conversation. "*We've more important things to do than bicker amongst ourselves. I want to hear about your ride in the motorcar, Rascal.*" She stood and stretched, fore and aft, her jealousy overcome by her eagerness to hear the details. "*Did it go awfully fast? Did the tires kick up dust? Was it exhilarating? Was it spine-tingling?*"

"*It wasn't nearly as exhilarating and spine-tingling,*" Rascal said, lifting one paw and studying his toenails with a maddening calm, *"as finding old Ben Hornby dead."*

"Dead!" the astonished cats chorused. *"Ben Hornby?"*

"Dead as a doornail," Rascal said. *"Found him myself, on Holly How, beyond the sheepfold."*

"You found him?" Tabitha cried.

Crumpet frowned, feeling annoyed. Dogs always had more exciting adventures than cats did. They were invited to go to agricultural shows and fairs and foxhunts, not to mention being asked to ride in motorcars. There was something fundamentally unfair about—

"That's right, I found him," Rascal said proudly. *"One of the Herdwicks—Tibbie, it was—showed me where he'd fallen off a cliff, but I was the one who reached the body first. And that took some doing, let me tell you, because he was lying at the foot of an appallingly steep slope. Miss Potter only came later, and after her, Mr. Jennings. Then Captain Woodcock and Constable Braithwaite finally arrived, to begin the official investigation."* He shook his ears and gave a heavy sigh. *"And now, if you two will excuse me, I think I'll go and see if there's any food in my bowl. It's been quite a day, and I'm tired and hungry. Finding bodies is hard work, believe me."*

But Crumpet had planted herself in front of the kitchen door. *"Not so fast, Rascal,"* she said firmly. *"You're not getting a bite to eat until you've told us everything, in great detail."* She scowled. *"And without exaggeration."* Rascal was known to embroider his tales from time to time, to the point where it was sometimes hard to distinguish the facts from the fiction.

Rascal insisted that he was giving them the facts, but his story actually seemed like an invention. He started with the pony cart trip up to old Ben's farm, then told them about the climb to the sheepfold on Holly How and the conversation with Tibbie, and concluded with the finding of old

Ben's twisted body at the foot of the cliff and Miss Potter's discovery of a clay pipe in the dead man's fingers.

"That gave Captain Woodcock and the constable something to puzzle over, you can be sure," he added. *"The question is, where did it come from?"*

"A clay pipe?" Tabitha lifted her head, blinking. *"But why should that be puzzling? Lots of people smoke clay pipes. Maybe Ben was standing at the top of the slope, having a smoke, when he missed his footing and fell."*

"But Ben didn't smoke, you see," Rascal replied. *"At least, that's what Mr. Jennings said. So they're wondering—"*

"So they're wondering if somebody was with him when he fell?" Crumpet broke in. She was beginning to feel the prickle of rising fur across her shoulder blades, a sure sign that something significant was under discussion. *"Was he . . . pushed?"*

"Really, Crumpet." Tabitha wrinkled her nose crossly. *"You always imagine the very worst about every situation. You're never happy unless you've conjured up some mystery or another to poke your nose into."*

"Well, was he?" Crumpet demanded. Old Ben Hornby was known around the village as a difficult man to get on with. He'd alienated a great many people over the years and made enemies of several, some fairly recently. Crumpet herself could name names, if it came to that, and doubtless everyone in the village could, too. It wouldn't be at all surprising if somebody had finally decided to take matters into his own hands. *"Come on, Rascal,"* she said urgently. *"Answer the question. Was he pushed?"*

Rascal sighed. *"I have no idea, Crumpet. The sheep are the only ones who might have seen what actually happened. I intended to talk to them and find out if they could tell me anything. But Miss Potter insisted on staying with old Ben's body, and I felt I had to stay with her. And by the time Mr. Jennings got back with the constable and Captain Woodcock, the sheep were nowhere in sight. You know how those Herdwicks are, always on the move. They probably went over the top of Holly How."*

"And you wanted to ride in the captain's motorcar, so you didn't go looking for them," Crumpet said in an accusing tone.

Rascal frowned. *"I wouldn't put it that way, exactly."*

"Well, I would," Crumpet muttered darkly, although she had to admit to herself that she probably would have done the same thing. There was no doubt about it, the first chance she got, she was going for a ride in that motorcar. For a moment, she forgot all about the matter at hand and began to picture herself whizzing along at the astounding speed of fifteen miles an hour, the horn tooting merrily, the wind ruffling her beautiful gray fur, the chickens fluttering out of her way, everyone in the village enviously watching her progress, just as if she were a Royal.

"Oh, I wish," she began dreamily. *"I wish I could—"*

"And I wish," Tabitha interrupted in a sharp tone, *"that the two of you would stay with the subject, instead of flying off in a dozen different directions. Forget the motorcar. What we need to know is what really happened to Ben Hornby. So how are we going to find out?"*

"I suppose we could go back to Holly How and look for those sheep," Rascal said. *"Tibbie might know something, if we can get her to tell."* He frowned. *"But I don't know what good it will do for us to know. Even if we find out what happened, it's impossible to tell the Big Folk. They can't understand what we say."*

"Be that as it may," Tabitha replied in a lecturish tone, *"it's important to know what happened. It sounds as if there were no witnesses other than the sheep, so let's go up to Holly How and find them. Come on!"* And with that, she jumped off the step and onto the path.

Stubbornly, Rascal shook his head. *"I am not going anywhere until I've had my supper. Finding dead bodies is hungry work, and I haven't had a bite to eat since—"*

"*Well, go and do it, then,*" said Tabitha bossily, tossing her head and switching her tail. "*Crumpet and I will wait right here.*"

Crumpet sighed and rolled her eyes. Really, if you gave Tabitha Twitchit an inch, she would take a mile.

12

Miss Potter Makes Up Her Mind

While Crumpet, Tabitha, and Rascal were having their conversation on the back steps of Belle Green, Beatrix had gone to her room to freshen up for supper. The motorcar ride—her first ever—had been highly interesting, but she had to comb and pin up her hair, which had been blown every which way, and wash the dust from her face. And, of course, her friends were waiting to be fed: Josey and Mopsy Rabbit, Tom Thumb the mouse, and Tuppenny, the guinea pig, all of whom lived in large, comfortable cages on a sunny shelf in her second-floor room.

She filled their dishes with food and water, spoke gently to them as she stroked their soft fur with her finger, and knelt beside their cages as she watched them settle down happily to eat. She still enjoyed having little pets to care for and make stories about, and they were always good company and a relief from her mother and father, who were constantly telling her what to do and how to think and feel. Peter and Mrs. Tiggy and Benjamin Bunny and her other pets had brightened her life and made her smile during some very dark times, and she would always be grateful.

These days, however, the Hill Top Farm barnyard animals—the pigs and cows and sheep and horses—called out for her attention. The sheep on Holly How, for instance. *Her* sheep, the ewes and lambs that had been bought and paid for, who had been grazing on the fellside when she and Mr. Jennings went to look for them, but who had disappeared by the time the constable and Captain Woodcock arrived. Tomorrow morning, she and John Jennings would have to go up to Holly How and see if the Herdwicks could be found and taken down to Hill Top, where they now belonged.

She sighed. Also tomorrow, she had to talk to Mr. Biddle and try to get him to hurry up the work on the house, and most especially to do something to stop out the rats. And then she would have to find Tabitha Twitchit and get a few sketches for the new book, a very simple story about three naughty kittens who lost their clothes to a family of ducks. But simple or not, the drawings required time and attention, when there was Mr. Biddle and the house to worry about, and the missing sheep and—

But downstairs, Mrs. Crook was putting supper on the table and it would soon be time to eat. Beatrix stood up, unpinned her curly brown hair in front of the mirror, and brushed it smooth again, thinking all the while. Her pets had been an enormous comfort to her, and she knew that Lady Longford's granddaughter, who must be lonely in that huge, dark house, would benefit from having a quiet, loving companion. Tuppenny, for instance, who was well-mannered and always very cheerful. On her way to Holly How in the morning, she'd be driving right past the Manor.

If she appeared at the door with Tuppenny and offered to lend the little creature to Caroline for a few days, her lady-ship couldn't really say no, could she?

Beatrix didn't usually do this sort of thing, appearing without invitation on somebody's doorstep and handing in a guinea pig, as if it were fresh laundry or a cod from the fish man's cart. But she knew she had something of a local reputation—"that lady writer from London who publishes ever so many of those sweet little books for children"—and she was willing to trade on it when there was good reason. Lady Longford was reputed to be an irascible old woman who liked nothing better than to have her own way, but surely she couldn't be so mean and petty as to deny her grand-daughter the pleasure of a quiet, clean little animal in a cage—especially if it was offered by a well-known children's writer.

Beatrix slipped the last pin into her hair and turned around. She had made up her mind. "Enjoy your dinner, Tuppenny. Tomorrow, you're going to have an adventure. A young girl needs help, and you are exactly the right sort of creature to help her."

"The right sort of creature?" Tuppenny was not a very brave guinea pig, and he hadn't had much experience of the world. Miss Potter's announcement struck him as more than a little ominous. *"What d'you suppose she means by 'going to have an ad-venture'?"* he whispered worriedly to Josey Rabbit, who was nibbling a fresh green lettuce leaf. *"Who is this girl? What kind of help does she need? Where am I going?"*

Josey, who hated to be bothered with silly questions, es-pecially when she was eating dinner, flicked her ears impa-tiently. *"I couldn't hazard a guess."*

"An adventure, Tuppenny," Mopsy Rabbit said, very seri-ously, *"is something like a quest."*

"What's a quest?" Tuppenny asked, feeling that they might be going in circles.

"An expedition undertaken by a knight to achieve something or other very important, such as slaying dragons, or rescuing damsels in distress."

"Slaying dragons?" Tuppenny repeated, dismayed. *"The kind that breathe fire, you mean? That sounds . . . dangerous."*

"Probably," said Mopsy, in a practical tone. *"Well, if there's danger, you shall simply have to face up to it. Be as brave as possible and do the best that you can in the circumstance. We're in the countryside now, and it's not at all civilized, you know. We have to be prepared for anything."*

"Anything, anything!" twittered Tom Thumb the mouse, who had a nervous disposition and was inclined to fly into hysterics at the slightest provocation. *"Stoats, ferrets, badgers, weasels—all sorts of appalling anythings, and all appallingly fierce!"* He flung his paws and his tail into the air and began to run in circles. *"We're doomed, I tell you, doomed! Oh my whiskers, if only we were back in London, safe, luxurious London, where I could comfort my poor soul with concerts and museums and champagne suppers and balls. Stoats and badgers! Weasels and stoats!"*

"Stoats?" Tuppenny asked, his nose twitching. *"What's a stoat? And what's a badger? Are they creatures I'll have to . . . to fight off?"* His nose twitched harder, his fear almost overcome by the unhallowed imagination of battle, and a vision of himself as a Very Brave Guinea Pig, arrayed against a thronging crowd of badgers and stoats (whatever those were), with a fire-breathing dragon just on the other side of the hill. *"Do you step on a stoat? Should I carry something to swat them with?"* He suddenly brightened. *"I suppose I shall need a sword, shan't I? One can't have a go at a dragon without a proper sword."*

Tom stopped running in circles and stared at Tuppenny. *"Step on a stoat?"* he scoffed. *"I'd like to see you step on a stoat. It would swallow you whole in one bite, it would. And what good do you think a sword would be against a dragon? Why, a dragon would breathe on you and turn you into a tuppenny's worth of toast."*

At that, Josey laughed. But Mopsy scowled at the mouse. *"Tom is just trying to frighten you, Tuppenny. Dragons are entirely imaginary. And there are no stoats or ferrets or weasels anywhere nearby."*

Tuppenny might not be the bravest (or the brightest) guinea pig in the world, but he was by nature an optimistic fellow, and he was determined not to lose heart, no matter how many weasels and badgers might be lying in wait for him. He swallowed his fear, sat up on his haunches, and began to comb his fur with his paws, brightening as he did so, and thinking how orange and sleek and attractive it looked, exactly the right sort of fur for a Very Brave Guinea Pig to wear when he went on a quest.

"Well, well, well," he mused, *"perhaps there will be danger, and wild animals, and even a dragon or two. But never mind. A guinea pig must persevere, especially when there are damsels that require rescue."* He paused, and scratched his ear, and frowned.

"Mopsy," he said, *"what's a damsel?"*

13

"Not an Accident?"

Captain Miles Woodcock did not park his motor car in the Tower Bank stable after he brought Miss Potter back to the village. Instead, he drove on to Hawkshead, where he located Dr. Butters, the physician who served the area. The doctor, a tall, thin man with a gaunt face, reddish hair, and a gingery moustache, listened to his description of the situation, nodded twice, and said, "I'll get my horse. But it may be a while, I'm afraid. I have to look in on Mrs. Rice, who will be delivering in another week."

"I don't suppose there's much hurry," Miles said. "It's not a criminal matter." He pulled his brows together. "Although there is that puzzling bit about the tobacco pipe. He was holding it in his hands when he fell."

Frowning, the doctor picked up his black bag. "Ben? With a tobacco pipe? That's odd. He left off smoking some

while ago, on my advice. I'd be mightily surprised if he took
it up again." He sighed. "Anyway, I'll see you there."

"There" was the large stone shed behind the captain's stable where Constable Braithwaite and Mr. Jennings had
brought Ben Hornby's body. By the time the doctor arrived,
dark had fallen, the bats were flitting out of the stable,
and the nightjar's eerie call (considered an ill omen by super-
stitious villagers) rattled through the meadow. Inside, the
scene was illuminated by several lanterns and a half-dozen
flickering candles. The old man, respectfully covered with
a sheet from Dimity Woodcock's linen cupboard, was
stretched out on a wooden table.

The doctor took off his coat, rolled up his sleeves, and
went over old Ben's body with great care and attention,
humming between his teeth as he worked and making occasional quiet comments, which the constable dutifully wrote
down in his notebook. The captain looked on, Mr. Jennings
having gone home to his supper as soon as the body was
safely delivered.

The examination went on longer than might have been
expected. When it was over, the doctor beckoned to both
Miles and Braithwaite.

"I want both of you to look at this," he said, pointing to
a welt about an inch wide, across the whole of Hornby's
back, just below his shoulder blades. It was outlined on
both sides by a large, dark bruise, the width of a man's arm.
"This bruise is fresh," the doctor said. "From the degree of
lividity, I'd estimate that it was inflicted immediately prior
to death." He paused, then repeated, "*Immediately* prior to
death," glancing at them to make sure they took his point.
"In living tissue, bruises have a way of repairing themselves
quickly. If Ben had been struck—oh, say, two days before he
died, we'd see a different coloration."

Miles let out his breath in a slow whistle. "And what

kind of instrument would inflict such a bruise? A walking stick?"

"P'rhaps," the doctor said. "It's impossible to say. Show me the instrument, and I'll tell you whether it's a candidate for our weapon."

"Weapon!" the constable exclaimed in surprise, breaking his silence for the first time. "You're sayin' that this was *not* an accident?"

"That's what I'm saying," Butters replied grimly. He glanced at Miles. "Did you search the place where he fell?"

"The constable and I went up there," Miles said, "and had a good look around. Of course, if he was struck by a walking stick—"

"It went home with whoever used it," the doctor said, finishing the captain's sentence. "I'm afraid that there are a great many uncertainties here, gentlemen." He began to roll down his sleeves. "But one thing is clear. Faced with this evidence, I cannot certify Hornby's death as accidental. Harry will have to convene an inquest."

"Harry" was Harry Lamb, the King's Coroner for the district. "I agree," Miles said soberly. "I'll get word to him first thing tomorrow." The coroner would summon a jury as soon as possible, and charge it to return one of three verdicts: homicide, suicide, or misadventure—and if the evidence warranted none of these, they would return an open verdict.

The doctor pulled the sheet over Ben Hornby's face. "Damn shame," he said sadly. "Ben Hornby wasn't everybody's friend, p'rhaps, but he was a good man."

Miles nodded. Not everybody's friend.

And somebody's enemy.

14

In Which the Professor Joins the Search

The summer night had grown dark by the time Tabitha, Crumpet, and Rascal went trekking off to Holly How. The moon had not yet risen as they reached Holly How Farm and began their search for the sheep, but the stars were shining like tiny beacons in the heavens. Rascal led the way up the rough track, since he was a dog and got out and about a great deal more than the two village cats. And anyway, he knew the territory and was acquainted with the sheep and felt confident that, under his leadership, they would quickly find Tibbie and Queenie and the lambs.

But their search was futile. Climb as high and call as loudly as they might, up one side of Holly How and down the other, even as far afield as the ominous edge of Cuckoo Brow Wood, where the dark trees rose up in an impenetrable wall of shadows, Tibbie and Queenie and their lambs were nowhere to be found. The moon had flung its silvery veil over the meadows by the time they gave up and started wearily back down the zig-zag path.

"*It's all your fault, Rascal,*" grumbled Crumpet, whose paws hurt from walking over the sharp stones. "*You should have made Tibbie tell you what she knew straightaway.*"

"*Crumpet's right,*" Tabitha put in sourly, pausing to catch her breath. "*If you'd done that, we wouldn't have had to come looking. And we'd know what really happened to old Ben.*"

"*Oh, give it up, will you?*" Rascal replied in a weary tone. "*Even if I'd asked, she mightn't've said anything useful. You know how sheep are, all dithery and doltish. Terrible gossips, and half the time, they don't get their facts straight.*"

"*Better than no facts at all,*" Tabitha retorted stiffly. "*Really, Rascal, you—*"

The rest of her words were drowned out by a great rushing sound in the sky above them, as a menacing shadow with outstretched talons sailed low over their heads.

"*OWL!*" shrieked Tabitha hysterically, and dove for the hedgerow. "*Run for your lives!*"

There was a thud in a nearby oak and the whole tree seemed to shudder as an enormous owl settled himself onto a branch, shook his feathers, and gave out a fierce, interrogative "*Whooo goes there? Stop and declare yourselves immediately!*"

Taken completely by surprise, Rascal had flattened himself against a large rock with his paws over his eyes. Tabitha had gone headfirst under the hedge, so it was left to Crumpet to reply. She screwed up her courage, tried to steady her voice, and said respectfully, "*Good evening, Professor. It's Crumpet, Tabitha, and Rascal, from the village. I trust you are well, sir.*"

The professor—for this was none other than Professor Galileo Newton Owl, D.Phil., a very old, very large tawny owl—was known by every animal in the Land between the Lakes, and by a great many of the Big Folk, as well. He lived in a great hollow beech tree at the top of Cuckoo Brow Wood, where it spreads out over Claife Heights before tumbling down the steep slope to the very edge of Lake Windermere. The professor enjoyed an international reputation for his scholarship in celestial mechanics, with a particular emphasis on navigating by the stars. And this with very good reason, for he spent the hours from midnight to dawn searching the sky with the telescope he had installed at the very top of his beech-tree observatory, and making notes in his celestial logbook.

The professor was also widely respected for his studies in applied natural history, with a special interest in the nocturnal habits of scaled, winged, and furred creatures, and their particular tastes. He carried out this research from dusk to midnight, high above the fields and woods. There was not much in the Land between the Lakes that escaped his observation—or so he thought, at any rate.

"I am perfectly aware of whooo youoo are," the professor said in a tone of great aggravation. *"What I mean too know is why youoo village animals are bumbling about on Holly How at this time of night."* He turned the flat disc of his face from one side to the other, and the light seemed to gleam behind his eyes. *"What is the exact nature of your business?"*

Rascal stood up and wagged his tail, only a little braver now that he knew to whom they were speaking. The professor was a commanding bird with a very low tolerance for impudence and a very great willingness to employ his powerful claws and razor-sharp beak. But he might also be a helpful bird, and it was entirely possible that he could further their search.

"We are looking for five Herdwicks, sir," he said. *"Tibbie and Queenie and three lambs—the sheep that old Ben Hornby sold to Miss Potter. We are hoping that they can clear up the mystery of what happened to him."*

The owl raised his great wings and flapped them twice, ferociously. "What *happened tooo Ben Hornby?*" he screeched. He always became very angry when one question was answered by reference to a previous question. It was an impertinent fallacy that he simply could not tolerate.

Rascal cleared his throat and told the professor the same story he had told to Crumpet and Tabitha earlier, although with a great deal more hesitation and much less confidence, for the owl's fierce, unblinking gaze unsettled him. But at last he came to the end of his tale, took a deep breath, and sat back on his haunches, waiting.

There was a long silence, whilst in the distance another, lesser owl hooted and nearer by, a pair of frogs began to trade insults. Finally, the professor spoke. *"Yooou are telling me that old Ben Hornby is dead?"* he demanded wrathfully, his round, luminous eyes growing even rounder and more luminous. If there was anything more infuriating than impudence, as far as the professor was concerned, it was the discovery that an important event had occurred without his knowledge or consent. *"How did he die? Was it an accident?"*

"That's exactly what we want to know, sir," said Rascal nervously. *"We were hoping the sheep could tell us, since they were grazing nearby, and may have seen what happened. But we looked all over Holly How and couldn't find them, and—"*

"Gooo hooome, all of yoooou," commanded the professor in a tone of weary exasperation. *"Gooo straight home and straight tooo bed, where yoooou belong. I will look for the sheep. And when I find them, yoooou can be sure that they will tell me what they know about Ben Hornby's death."*

And with that, he raised his professorial wings, flapped them heavily, and lifted himself into the night sky above Holly How, where he sailed for several hours, surveying the fellsides and valleys for the five missing Herdwicks. But to his annoyance and puzzlement, he was no more successful in his search than had been the village animals, for no matter how far he flew or how hard he looked, the sheep were nowhere to be found.

At last, the professor solaced himself by pouncing with an unnecessary violence upon a young and unwary vole who had ventured too far from his den under the rocks. He bore the vole home to his beech tree, which could be distinguished from the other beech trees at the top of Cuckoo Brow Wood both by its size and by the fact that it bore a painted notice board beside a low wooden door at the base of the tree, announcing:

G.N. OWL, D. PHIL.
OBSREVER AT LARJE
MIND YR HED!

The door, and the interior stair onto which it opened, were designed for the convenience of those of the professor's guests who could not fly, and he rarely made use of them. Now, he flew straight up to his sitting room, high above the mossy forest floor, where he got out the best white table-cloth and spread it on the table, which he laid with the best china, silver, and crystal. Then he lit a fat beeswax candle, poured a glass of elderberry wine, and sat down to enjoy a hearty midnight supper of fresh vole, along with a tin of sardines and some pickled eggs and cream crackers.

After this entirely satisfactory repast the professor retired to his library and looked up a scientific paper he remembered having read a year or so earlier, "The Deleterious Effect of Voles (*Microtus agrestis*) upon the Vegetation of the Lake District." The paper argued that voles were bad for meadows because they dug up the turf, exposing the grass roots to the air, and that too many voles could completely ruin a meadow in only a few days.

Yes, indeed, the owl thought with satisfaction, replacing the volume on the shelf and preparing to fly up to his observatory for a night's examination of the stars, he had done a very good thing by reducing the vole population, if only by one. Tomorrow night, he would make it two voles, and leave off the sardines.

Upstairs in his observatory, the professor pointed his telescope at Venus, very large and bright, which seemed to hang just out of reach above the lake. And then, by accident, he happened to hit the telescope with his wing and knocked it askew, so that it pointed elsewhere. He looked through it as he bent to straighten it, and blinked in great surprise.

The professor had found the missing sheep.

15

Miss Potter Makes a Delivery

Beatrix had planned to go up to Holly How with Mr. Jennings early the next morning, but when she walked to Hill Top Farm to meet him, she learnt that he wouldn't be going anywhere very soon. The evening before, he had stepped out the door and sprained his ankle badly. He was sitting in a chair with his leg propped on a stool in front of him.

"Looks like we'll have to put off gettin' those sheep," he said ruefully.

"I can at least go and get them and put them into the fold," Beatrix replied. "I'm sure I can gather up the two ewes without any difficulty, and their lambs will follow." She spoke with a great deal more confidence than she felt, but they *were* her sheep, and sooner or later, she was going to have to learn to work with them. Anyway, she had a delivery to make at Tidmarsh Manor, on the road to Holly How.

"Well, I don't s'pose it'll hurt to try," Mr. Jennings said doubtfully. "But who's to hitch up Winston? And who's to drive him?"

"Why, I can do both," Beatrix said, this time with real confidence. She had driven her first pony fifteen years before, and counted herself an excellent driver.

So a little while later, Beatrix was driving past Anvil Cottage, where she saw Sarah Barwick, standing in the street, surveying her front window with satisfaction. Beatrix pulled Winston to a stop. "It looks splendid, Sarah!" she exclaimed.

Truly, the window did look very nice. Sarah had pulled the curtains aside in a kind of drape and set a low table behind the glass. On it were displayed a Dundee cake, a plate of scones, a tray of various tea-cakes, and a vase of flowers.

Sarah grinned triumphantly. "I've already sold three scones to a fell-walker going past, and it's not even nine o'clock yet." She smoothed Winston's mane. "Where are you and your pony off to so early this morning?"

"To Holly How, to look for some sheep I've bought."

"Oh, are you, then?" Sarah asked with interest. "I'm supposed to deliver two loaves of bread and one of my ginger cakes to Mrs. Beever, the cook at Tidmarsh Manor. But there's a big hole in my bicycle tire, and I've no way to patch it quickly."

"I was planning to go to Tidmarsh Manor myself," Beatrix said. "Would you like me to deliver your order?"

"I'd rather you deliver *me*, if you don't mind," Sarah replied. "I've been wanting to talk to Mrs. Beever about that person Lady Longford has in mind for Margaret Nash's job. If you'll take me, I'll be glad to give you a hand with rounding up your sheep."

"Perfect," Beatrix said promptly. "I'd love the company— *and* the help."

"Hold on a shake, then," Sarah said. "I'll get my basket

and my hat and pop across the way and ask Lydia to keep an eye on my door, in case of customers. Who knows? Those scones might all be gone by the time we get back!"

Five minutes later, Beatrix and Sarah were at Belle Green, where Beatrix went upstairs to get her guinea pig. She brought him out in a lidded wicker basket, and was putting him into the cart when Rascal ran around the house.

"I want to go too!" he barked excitedly. Without waiting for an invitation, he jumped into the cart. *"Ready or not, here I am!"*

"What a fine, frisky fellow," Miss Barwick said with a smile.

"He doesn't look like a sheep dog," Miss Potter said, "but perhaps he can help us put them into the fold. What do you think, Rascal?"

"Delighted, if I can," Rascal said promptly. *"The cats and I had a go at finding them last night, though, without any success. We searched high and low and couldn't find them, and finally had to leave it to the professor."* He felt this ought to be said, although he knew that Miss Potter couldn't understand him. He peered at the orange guinea pig through the little window in the basket. *"Where are you off to this morning, pig?"*

"Not the foggiest," the guinea pig replied cheerfully. *"It's a quest, that's all I know. In aid of a damsel in distress, with possibly a dragon or two thrown in for good measure."* He sat up, crossed his forepaws, and sniffed the air, his shoe-button eyes sparkling. *"A lovely day for a ride in a pony cart, isn't it? On such a splendid day, splendid things are bound to happen, wouldn't you say?"*

The logic of this conclusion escaped Rascal, especially with distressed damsels and possibly dragons in the offing. But if the guinea pig wanted to take a cheery approach to life, that was his business.

It was a bright, sunshiny morning, with puffy white

clouds sailing overhead, the hedges filled with birdsong and blooming roses, the fields glowing with the bright yellow of cinquefoil and stonecrop. Winston was frisky, tossing his head and picking up his neat hooves, and they rattled along the narrow lane in fine style. On the way, Miss Potter told Miss Barwick about finding old Ben Hornby, dead, at the foot of the slope. Miss Barwick was much surprised, although she hadn't known Mr. Hornby, and wanted to hear all the details. Listening to the two ladies discuss what had happened, and looking around him at the lovely green hillsides, Rascal thought that there was no lovelier place in all England than this Land between the Lakes, and that it was very sad that old Ben Hornby would not waken to another such fine morning.

In a little while, they approached a large, forbidding house that was shadowed by somber, spreading pines and yews. The guinea pig began to shiver as Miss Potter turned the cart into a lane that was so overhung with trees and vines that it was rather like a dark tunnel.

"I'm afraid there's been some . . . some mistake," he chittered nervously, peering through the little window in the side of his wicker basket. *"Why are we going here? I'm on my way to an adventure."* His shiver became a shudder, and he shook from nose to tail. *"I'm sure that no self-respecting damsel would be found in a place like this."*

"It's Tidmarsh Manor," Rascal explained. *"Where Lady Longford lives. I can't think why Miss Potter would want to take you there, unless she means to give you to Lady Longford."* He paused. *"I must say that her ladyship doesn't strike me as a damsel in distress, although—"*

"Give me away!" the guinea pig squealed, horrified. *"Abandon me in that awful place? Oh, no!"*

"Whoa, Winston," Miss Potter said, stopping the cart on the gravel drive in front of the house. She looped the pony's reins around the cart wheel, climbed down, and took

Tuppenny's wicker basket off the seat. Miss Barwick got down as well.

"I'll go round to the kitchen," she said, picking up a basket of baked goods. "That's where I make my deliveries."

"I'll meet you back here, then," Miss Potter said. To Rascal, she added, "You stay with Winston and watch the cart."

"*I will*," said Rascal, feeling that he had been given an important assignment.

"*Wait!*" Tuppenny shrieked, flinging himself against the side of his basket. "*Hold on a bit, Miss Potter, do! Surely you can't mean to leave me here! I may have made some very foolish boasts last night about fighting stoats and dragons, but I am not at all a Brave Guinea Pig. What's more, I'm supposed to be going on a quest, and rescuing damsels in distress, and all that sort of thing. Oh dear oh dear oh dear!*"

To tell the truth, Beatrix felt every bit as nervous as the poor guinea pig. But when she knew that she was right, she became very stubborn and refused to let herself be deterred, no matter how apprehensive she might feel. This was one of those occasions. Tuppenny's cage in her hand, she marched up to the massive front door, where she knocked.

The door was opened by a white-capped, white-aproned maid. "Deliveries at the back, miss," she said severely. Then her eyes widened and her hand flew to her mouth. "Oh, Miss Potter! So sorry. I didn't realize it was you."

"Hello, Emily," Beatrix said pleasantly. "How nice to see you. And how is your sister? Such a well-behaved child." The maid was Mrs. Crook's niece, and Beatrix had met her and her little sister at tea at Belle Green.

"Oh, she's just lovely, thank you, miss," said Emily, her chubby face wreathed in smiles. "And she adores the Mrs. Tiggy-Winkle book you gave her. Fair readin' it to shreds, she is!" She stepped back, holding the door wide. "Come in, do, and I'll let her ladyship know that you're here."

In a few moments, Emily was back to show Beatrix into what seemed to be the morning room, a large, high-ceilinged room wallpapered in red and green cabbage roses, with a red wool carpet on the floor and red velvet draperies at the windows. The numerous tables were laden with bric-a-brac, potted palms filled the room's four corners, and the arms and backs of the stuffed sofa and chairs were covered with crocheted antimacassars.

"Miss Beatrix Potter," Emily announced, very primly, and left, closing the door behind her.

Beatrix placed Tuppenny's basket on the floor and went toward an old lady in a black silk dress, white lace cap, and black lace fingerless mitts, who was sitting in a large armchair with a fat, slobbery King Charles spaniel at her feet. In the corner behind her sat another lady, also in black, a demure, meek look on her face. Miss Martine, no doubt, Beatrix thought. Her ladyship's companion.

Beatrix was usually quite shy, but she had an unflagging interest in human nature. She was especially fascinated by the many and various expressions on people's faces, for they always seemed to reveal a great deal of what lay hidden beneath. If one were observant, one might almost look *through* the expression as through a window, and see whatever there was to see within. At this moment, Beatrix fancied that she could look through the decorous look on Miss Martine's composed face to something sharp and disquieting, and she shivered involuntarily.

At that moment, she became aware of a man standing at the window. He turned and came forward with alacrity, and she saw that it was Vicar Sackett.

"Why, good morning, Miss Potter," he exclaimed with pleasure. "This is a *very* agreeable surprise, I must say!"

Beatrix was not surprised by the relief she heard in the vicar's voice. He was gentle and scholarly and often rather vague, no match for such difficult parishioners as Lady Longford. To tell the truth, Beatrix was relieved to see him, too, for she fancied that Lady Longford might be more amenable to her request in the presence of the clergy.

Lady Longford's pince nez hung on a gold chain around her neck. She put it on and peered critically at Beatrix's tweed skirt and jacket. Beatrix knew that she did not cut a stylish figure, but her comfort and the durability of her clothing meant a great deal more to her than her ladyship's opinion.

"And who is Miss Potter?" Lady Longford inquired abruptly. The spaniel, hearing the tone of her voice, gave a low, disagreeable growl.

Vicar Sackett hurried to make introductions. When he was finished, Lady Longford said, in an arch, autocratic tone, "So you are the female owner of Hill Top Farm. It seems an unlikely purchase for a person from London. I wonder whatever possessed you to buy it." Without waiting for Beatrix's reply, she went on. "But no matter. I've always been amused by the foolish things that people do with their money. Your books—would they amuse me? I have not been entirely well lately, and I am always glad of amusement."

"I rather doubt that your ladyship would be amused by my children's books," Beatrix said with as much equanimity as she could muster. A sharper reply had come to the tip of her tongue, but the habitual reticence and self-control she practiced with her mother—who also had a habit of making critical remarks—stood her in good stead, and she suppressed it. "I understand that your granddaughter Caroline is staying with you."

There was a silken rustle in Miss Martine's corner, and a slight clearing of the throat. Lady Longford frowned. "The girl is here for the present," she replied, "although she will be going off to school as soon as an appropriate place has been found. Why do you ask?"

"I have brought something to help her pass the time," Beatrix said. "An amiable creature—a quiet little guinea pig—who will be a very pleasant companion for the child." Not giving Lady Longford a chance to voice an objection, she added, in a firm voice, "I have found that small animals are a wonderful comfort to those who have no playmates, particularly young girls who have suffered losses, as I understand Caroline to have done. The guinea pig is only a loan, of course. I shall have to take him back to London with me when I go at the end of the month."

Miss Martine cleared her throat again. "If your ladyship will forgive me for intruding," she said deferentially, "I hardly think it suitable. The child has been both insolent and unruly. One should not reward disobedience."

Beatrix cast another look at Lady Longford's companion. She saw a thin, narrow-shouldered, sharp-faced woman of indeterminate age, her hair snugged back tightly, her eyes glittering like the eyes of a hawk. Beatrix was suddenly overwhelmed with sympathy for Caroline Longford, who had to do her lessons with Miss Martine.

The vicar spoke in a placating tone. "Well, well, I'm sorry to hear that. It is very wrong of Caroline to be disobedient. But what child hasn't, from time to time? And I'm sure that your ladyship appreciates the girl's difficult situation. She is a stranger in a strange place, bereft of all that is familiar and comforting. The loan of Miss Potter's little pet seems to me quite providential, exactly what the poor child needs to help her feel at home. And perhaps it will make her more mindful of her duty." He smiled earnestly at Lady Longford. "A little animal—it is a small thing, after all, wouldn't you agree?"

"Indeed." Lady Longford pressed her thin lips together. "It is such a small thing that I doubt it will have the substantial benefits you suggest."

The vicar's mouth drooped sadly.

"But if Miss Potter is willing to lend the creature, and if the girl will engage to care for it—"

"Of course she will, of course she will," exclaimed the vicar. "And I think—forgive me, please, for being so bold as to venture an opinion—but I believe, I truly do, that this will be a turning point for the child."

Miss Martine gave a delicate cough. "My dear Lady Longford," she said, "I really do not think it appropriate to—"

"Thank you," Beatrix said briskly, determined not to allow any intervention. "I'm glad that it's been settled." She picked up the cage. "If I may, I should like to take the animal to Caroline and tell her what must be done for him."

"Oh, very well." Lady Longford gave a dismissive wave of her hand. "Ask Emily to show you upstairs. Miss Martine will remain here. We are awaiting the momentary arrival of Dr. Harrison Gainwell, who is to be the next head teacher at Sawrey School."

The vicar shifted. "I fear that her ladyship somewhat anticipates," he said with an uneasy gravity. "Dr. Gainwell is indeed a strong candidate, very strong, and would be a credit to any school. However, the trustees feel that our dear Miss Nash—"

"Dr. Gainwell has my unqualified support," Lady Longford interrupted shortly, raising her chin. "And I am sure that he will have yours as well, Vicar." She looked at Beatrix through her pince nez. "You must be anxious to get back to your farming duties, Miss Potter. I won't detain you."

"Thank you so much for your thoughtfulness, Miss Potter," the vicar managed politely. Beatrix heard the note of desperation in his voice and knew that Tuppenny's victory over Miss Martine was a small thing in comparison to the battle royal that was about to be waged over Dr. Harrison

Gainwell. Understanding that the interview was concluded, she picked up the guinea pig's cage and left the room with a feeling of positive relief. She was very glad that *she* was not one of the school's trustees.

16

Caroline Meets Miss Potter

Caroline Longford looked up as Emily opened the door and a strange woman stepped into the room, carrying a wicker basket. She was a plump, rosy-cheeked person with quite remarkable blue eyes, dressed in tweeds and sturdy shoes. She wore an air of imperturbable practicality.

"Who are you?" Caroline asked suspiciously, narrowing her eyes. In the months she had been at Tidmarsh Manor, she had seen her grandmother, Miss Martine, the Beevers, and the two maids—never a visitor. She slid a book over what she had been writing and put down her pen.

"I am Miss Potter," the lady said, in a light, pleasant-sounding voice. "I own Hill Top Farm, down in the village, and I come up from London, when I can, to see how the farm and the animals are getting on."

"Oh," Caroline said, recognizing the name. "You're the

lady who gave the telescope to Jeremy. The one who draws frogs and puts them into books."

"Frogs and rabbits and hedgehogs and mice," Miss Potter said, raising the lid on the wicker basket. "So you know Jeremy, then. I'm glad. He's a sensible young man."

"What's that?" Caroline asked curiously, coming close and looking into the basket. In it was a small creature with very long, silky fur—mostly orange, with bright glints of gold and patches of golden brown—a twinkling nose, and shiny black eyes that looked up at her with great apprehension. He wasn't a mouse or a rat, and he didn't have ears like a rabbit. She had never seen anything like him.

"He's a guinea pig," Miss Potter replied. "Guinea pigs come from South America, you know, and they make wonderful little pets. This one is called Tuppenny. He's quite a fine fellow—at least, that's his personal opinion. And even though he tends to self-conceit, I really must agree." She smiled. "I wonder if you might like to take care of him for a fortnight or so."

The smile seemed to transform Miss Potter's face, and Caroline was aware of a kindness and sympathy in her china-blue eyes, quite unlike anything she had experienced since she came to England. It dissolved her suspicion in a flash, and made her think of the happy security she had known when her mother and father were alive, when she felt safe and cared for. It was almost as if Miss Potter were an old friend of the family, *her* family, *herself,* not her grandmother or Miss Martine.

That Miss Potter should have this comforting effect on her was surprising, but it was so wonderfully welcome and so immediately penetrated her natural reserve that Caroline didn't for a moment question it, or Miss Potter's offer. She thought fleetingly that perhaps she was dreaming, or that Miss Potter was some sort of fairy godmother, like the one who had come to Cinderella. But she was wide awake, so it couldn't be a dream. And Miss Potter and the guinea pig—who was making little snuffling noises—were quite undeniably real. And anyway, Caroline didn't believe in fairies.

"I can keep him? For a whole fortnight?" She reached into the basket and stroked the whisper-soft fur. "What a dear little creature he is," she said, half under her breath, "and what a beautiful color." She paused, remembering Oliver, the orange tabby cat who had lived in the barn at the sheep station, and felt a sudden pain of homesickness so sharp that it made the tears come to her eyes. "Of course. I'd love to take care of him."

And then she withdrew her hand and pinched her lips together, brought back with a jerk to the bleak reality of things. "But it will never work. Miss Martine won't let me. She has no patience for anything, not even poor old Dudley."

"Dudley?" Miss Potter asked.

"Grandmama's spaniel. He's old and disagreeable, although some of that is Miss Martine's fault. She pinches him when Grandmama isn't looking, which makes him very cross and apt to snap. She pinches me, too, when I'm disobedient." Caroline stopped. She never talked on like this to anyone, let alone a stranger. What had come over her?

Miss Potter's blue eyes had darkened at the mention of pinches, but she said only, "I'm glad to say that your grandmother has already given her permission."

Caroline was dumbfounded. "She *has?*"

"Yes, she has, and has given instructions to Miss Martine." Miss Potter added, as if in apology, "Tuppenny is only a loan, however, until I have to go back to London. But if you like him, and would like to have a guinea pig of your own, we'll see if it can be arranged."

Caroline seriously doubted that Miss Martine would permit *that,* but perhaps she shouldn't be so quick to judge, since Miss Potter was apparently capable of miracles. "Thank you," she said. And then, feeling that this wasn't quite enough, added, "You are very kind." She paused. "May I take him out and hold him?"

Miss Potter nodded, and in a moment, Tuppenny was nestled in Caroline's cupped hands, making a soft gurgling sound. "I think Jeremy would like to draw him," she said after a minute. "He draws animals, too, you know. Rabbits and squirrels and mice. Whatever he sees."

"Yes, I know," Miss Potter said. "Jeremy's quite a good artist. Where did you meet him?"

"On Holly How, where I go sometimes when I'm supposed to be walking Dudley in the garden. I'd love to know some of the other children in the village," Caroline went on hesitantly, "but Grandmama doesn't think I ought to. It's because she imagines I'm better than they are, which is a lot of rubbish. She doesn't think much of me, either, though." She could taste the bitterness in her words. "I'm only in the way, especially now that Dr. Gainwell is coming. She'll be glad to have me go off to school."

She stopped. There she went again, talking and talking, and saying nothing of any importance at all. But Miss Potter was looking at her with an expression of interested kindness, and there was that feeling of having known her for a very long time. Caroline felt she could say anything to her, and she would be neither surprised nor critical. She would simply . . . listen.

Miss Potter stood silent for a moment, her head cocked to one side, regarding her seriously. Then she said, very slowly and thoughtfully, "It is a sad thing, Caroline, but mothers and grandmothers do not always know all they ought to know about daughters and granddaughters. It is not something they should be blamed for, exactly—the fault is in the way their own mothers and grandmothers brought them up. But this means that we must find our own way toward being happy and useful, even when it is not the expected way."

Caroline was so astonished at this that she could say nothing at all.

Miss Potter lifted her hand and touched Caroline's cheek. "You must look out for yourself, my dear, and be as brave as you can. If there is any way that I can help, I would be glad to do so. And now," she went on briskly, without waiting for a reply, "let me tell you what you will need to know in order to properly care for this little fellow. He is inordinately fond of freshly cut grass. He delights in apples, too, and carrots, and celery. But bread and butter are not good for him, and no matter how he begs—he is quite an accomplished beggar—do not in any circumstance allow him to have a lump of sugar. And you should ask Mr. Beever if he can find you a large, deep box for him to live in, and put some hay in the bottom of it, and a dish of water, and—"

For the next few minutes, their attention was fixed on Tuppenny. When they had finished, Miss Potter straightened up. "Well, now. I must go. I've brought a friend with me, and we're going to Holly How to look for my sheep."

"You've lost them?" Caroline asked.

"I don't think so," Miss Potter said cheerfully. "See that you take good care of Tuppenny, my dear."

"I will," Caroline said. She pulled herself up quickly. She had been about to fling her arms around Miss Potter and thank her, but she stopped herself in time, and merely held out her hand and said, in a formal way, "Thank you for letting me look after Tuppenny. I will be very good to him."

"I'm sure you will," Miss Potter said with a smile, and left.

As she went down the stairs, Beatrix thought about the girl, and wondered. She was a serious child, with an intelligent, listening look—a self-reliant girl, not the sort to be terrified by the wind rapping at the shutters, or even by Miss Martine, glowering at her from the fireside whilst she did her lessons. Not a pretty girl, if one judged by the standard of accepted prettiness, which was dimpled and snub-nosed, with a pink and white complexion and golden ringlets. This one was brown haired and olive skinned, with a sharp nose, firm brows, and a definite mouth—strong features that would undoubtedly come into their own when she was a woman, but which were considered very much a drawback for children. Like Beatrix's own nose, which had been criticized by no less famous a personage than the great portrait painter, John Millais. He had once told her that her face was spoilt by the length of her nose and upper lip.

And what was that she had glimpsed on the paper that had been only half-covered by the book Caroline had hastily slid over it? It had looked very much like code writing, something that Beatrix understood very well.

For when she was just a little older than Caroline, she had begun keeping a journal, in her own privately invented code, so that nobody else—and most especially her mother—could read it.

Beatrix smiled, remembering.

17

Miss Barwick Has a Conversation

This was the fourth week in a row that Sarah had made a delivery to Tidmarsh Manor, and she was beginning to feel like a regular at the kitchen door. Mrs. Beever was a cheerful and gossipy sort. Sarah always looked forward to having a cup of tea and a bit of a chat with her in the big old barn of a kitchen, which had been built back in the days when the Manor cook prepared meals for dozens of family and servants.

Today, however, Sarah had an ulterior motive for her visit. The more she reflected on what Dimity Woodcock had said about Lady Longford's candidate for Sawrey School, the more she wanted to know the inside story. Both of the Beevers—Mr. Beever worked in the garden and drove her ladyship's phaeton—had been in service at the Manor for over two decades. If Mrs. Beever was willing to talk, she could probably give a behind-the-scenes glimpse into what was going on.

"Well, and there you are, Miss Barwick!" exclaimed the stout Mrs. Beever, her round face brightening as she looked up from two large pheasants she was jointing. "I was about to give you up for lost, and fearin' that I'd have to add another baking to t' day's work, with a guest expected and all." She scowled at a girl who was scraping carrots over a basin at the far end of the kitchen table. "You can get along a little faster with those carrots, Harriet. That knife isn't a feather, y' know. Put some muscle into it, my girl."

"Yes, Mrs. Beever." Harriet heaved a heavy sigh, but Sarah did not notice that the knife scraped with any greater force.

"I would have been here earlier," Sarah explained, "but my bicycle tire went flat, so I drove up with Miss Potter, from Hill Top. She brought something for Lady Longford. For her ladyship's granddaughter, that is," she corrected. She put her basket on the table, removed the red checked napkin that covered it, and took out two loaves of bread and a large ginger cake, wrapped in white paper. "And here you are. The bread you ordered, and Lady Longford's cake, baked fresh this morning." She took out another package. "And a half-dozen muffins, extra, for Mr. Beever's tea. I'm sure they're not as good as your own," she added, "but they might save you some work."

"Well, now," said the cook warmly, "that's very kind of you, I'm sure, Miss Barwick. Her ladyship does appreciate your ginger cake. She has it along with a glass of ginger beer, for her stomach, you know. The poor lady has a world of trouble with that stomach of hers, and it's not gettin' better." She dropped a pheasant leg into a bowl and covered the naked bird with a cloth. "These flies," she said crossly. "There's no end to 'em. I had a packet of flypapers in t' pantry, but I've mislaid it, and now I'm payin' t' price. Mislaid that new kitchen account book, too. It'll be my head next." She went to the range where a kettle boiled. "You'll have tea, won't you?" And then, without pausing for an answer, said, "Miss Potter's the lady who writes and draws, isn't she? And what's she brought for our young miss? One of them animal books of hers?"

"Not a book," Sarah said, pulling out a chair and sitting down at the kitchen table. "A guinea pig."

"A guinea pig!" Harriet's knife stopped altogether, and her eyes grew large. "One o' them lit'le furry creatures what squeaks and runs about? Lor', I'd pay a fortnight's wages for one of them, I would."

"You won't have a fortnight's wages to spend if you don't smarten up with that knife, my girl," Mrs. Beever said darkly, pouring boiling water into a china teapot. To Sarah, she said, "A guinea pig, is it?" She gave a short laugh. "Well, Miss Martine is the one who looks after Miss Caroline. She'll put her foot down on that plan, for sure. Miss Potter will just have to carry her guinea pig back home." She opened a tin and shook several biscuits onto a plate.

"Oh, that would be a great pity!" Sarah exclaimed. She frowned. "Why would Miss Martine refuse to let Caroline have a pet? I had a guinea pig once. It was only a little creature, very gentle and clean. Not nearly the trouble of a dog or a cat or even a rabbit."

"Why?" Mrs. Beever pulled her brows together into a scowl. "Because Martine is a mean, heartless woman and a troublemaker, that's why." She cast a stern glance at Harriet. "Tales are not to be carried outside this kitchen, of course."

"Oh, of course," Sarah murmured. "I won't say a word, I promise."

"Not meanin' you, Miss Barwick." Mrs. Beever poured them each a cup of tea. "It's Harriet here needs remindin'. But she'd be a fool to let Martine catch her carrying tales,

she would. That woman has ears like a hawk. Eyes, too."
Her voice took on a self-pitying note. "And not an ounce of
sympathy in her soul for poor folks who work their fingers
to the bone to make her comfortable, even though she
landed on her feet when she came here, and no mistake."
She lowered her bulk into a chair and eyed the ginger cake.
"Wonder if I shouldn't try a bite or two of that cake before
it's sent up to her ladyship."

"Oh, please, yes, Mrs. Beever," Sarah implored. "Tell me
if it meets with your approval."

"Well, if you think so," Mrs. Beever said. She cut a generous slice of cake and took a large bite out of it, casting her
eyes upward and chewing critically. "I daresay it'll do, Miss
Barwick." She licked her lips and leaned forward, lowering
her voice. "Just between you and me, her ladyship isn't
eatin' hardly anything these days. Scarcely a bite. The trouble's in her stomach, y' see."

"I'm so sorry to hear that," Sarah said fervently. "It's so
terrible that she doesn't have an appetite for food, especially
when she has such a good cook in her kitchen."

Mrs. Beever accepted the compliment with a modestly
down-turned smile. "Yes, very sick. Dr. Butters was here
twice last week, and she always improves after he's been, although he can't seem to find out what's ailin' her. But she
says your cake helps to settle her stomach—it's t' ginger,
I'm sure. My old auntie, who knew all about such things, always used to swear by ginger for t' mulligrubs and colly-
wobbles. Ginger tea, ginger snaps, candied ginger, ginger
cake. And since her ladyship fancied your cake 'specially, I
vowed she should have it, although I'll have to wait until
Martine is lookin' t' other way and take it to her myself."
She became confidential. "Martine said she shouldn't have
it, y'see."

"I'm very glad her ladyship likes it," Sarah said with

genuine feeling. She frowned. "But why doesn't Miss Martine think she should have it?"

Mrs. Beever looked cross. "She says it's because she don't believe in them old folk remedies, like ginger. But if you ask me, it's t' price. Since her ladyship's been ill, it's Martine what manages t' household accounts. She goes over 'em with a fine-tooth comb, lookin' for things to cut out." She pursed her lips. "Mean, she is, t' most penny-pinchin' person I ever did meet, except for when she wants something special just for herself, and then it's naught but the best. That bread of yours, that fine white bread you brought—that's for *her,* y' see. She has it for her breakfast every mornin', four pieces, toasted, with a special marmalade she gets from London and three rashers of bacon and a soft-boiled egg, two minutes and no more."

"My goodness gracious," Sarah said, raising her eyebrows.

Mrs. Beever's voice was mounting in a scornful crescendo. "Brought up to her *room,* she has to have it, on a tray with a white cloth, like she was as good as her ladyship, and not a plain servant like t' rest of us. While Beever and Emily and Harriet and me has *my* bread and *my* marmalade down here in t' servants' hall."

"Which is every bit as good, I'm sure," murmured Sarah. "Probably much better."

"Well, of *course* it is," Mrs. Beever said. Now fully engaged with her subject and growing huffier and more scornful by the minute, she pushed on. "And I had another girl here in t' kitchen, y' know, to do t' washin' up and scrub t' floors and t' like, and Martine sent her off. Not a word of proper notice, neither."

Harriet spoke up unexpectedly. "She give t' push to Ruth last month, too, so now there's only just Emily upstairs, to do all them beds, and t' fires, and t' floors and carpets and dust t' furniture. 'Tis a good thing she's not very bright, or she'd hate it." The knife met the carrot with greater energy.

"What a pity," Sarah said. "How long has Miss Martine been with her ladyship?"

"Too long, if you ask my opinion," Harriet muttered, and gave the carrot such a great whack that it broke in two pieces. "We was all right here before she came. Not to say happy, o'course, but we was all right, and there was 'nough of us to get t' work done proper, which there ain't now, and more to eat, too." She gave a loud sniff.

"Nobody's asking your opinion, Harriet," Mrs. Beever said disapprovingly. "And if you know what's good for you, my girl, you'll keep a civil tongue in your head when you're around that woman. Talk saucy to her and you'll find your-self gettin' t' push just like Ruth, and I'll be havin' to do all your work my own self." To Sarah, she said, "A year Mar-tine's been here. A year this month." She sighed. "Not a good year, neither, sad to say. And now there's this new man comin' . . ."

It was the moment Sarah had been waiting for. "You're speaking of Dr. Gainwell, I suppose."

"Oh, you've heard 'bout him?" Mrs. Beever gave her an inquiring look. "Folks down in the village are talkin', are they?"

"To tell the truth, Mrs. Beever," Sarah replied in a wor-ried tone, "it's all anybody's talking about." She leaned for-ward. "Everyone's worried about Miss Nash, of course. We thought she was to have the position, and everyone knows what a good teacher she is. And now—" She held out her hands. "Well, I was hoping you might have some idea about what's going on, and whether anything could be done."

Mrs. Beever pulled down her mouth. "I feel sorry for Miss Nash, I cert'nly do, and that's a pure fact. When I heard about it, I was near twizzled up inside, as Harriet will tell you. Don't seem fair that this man can step in and pull

Miss Nash's place out from under her. Right's right, after all." She appealed to Harriet. "That's exactly what I said, now, wasn't it, Harriet? Right's right, after all."

"That's what y' said," Harriet agreed. "Them are the very words."

"And all 'cuz Martine thinks he's so important and wonderful." Mrs. Beever threw up her hands. "But I don't know what can be done, and even if I did, I couldn't open my mouth. If Martine heard me meddlin', she'd be down on me in a flash. Why, she'd prob'ly give *me* t' push."

"Miss Martine?" Sarah frowned. "What does she have to do with this? It was her ladyship who recommended Dr. Gainwell to the trustees."

"That's as may be. But her ladyship hasn't never met t' gentleman, I can tell you *that*. Not to speak ill of him, of course," Mrs. Beever added cautiously, "for he's said to have an Oxford eddy-cashun, and he's a missionary and no doubt a godly man. But it does seem to me that her ladyship is going a bit too far, on just Martine's say-so."

"I see," Sarah said thoughtfully. "I wonder—how did it happen that Miss Martine came to Tidmarsh Manor to be Lady Longford's companion? They were acquainted, I suppose. Longtime friends, perhaps?"

"Friends?" Mrs. Beever snorted. "It wasn't that way at all. Mrs. Stewart was before Martine, and a right nice person she was, too, calm in her disposition and patient with her ladyship, who can be trying at times."

"T' say t' least," Harriet put in.

"To say t' least," Mrs. Beever agreed. "Mrs. Stewart had been with her ladyship since before old Lord Longford died, y' see, and we all liked her. But she had to go back to Carlisle to take care of her old mother. Her ladyship advertised through an agency, and Martine was the only one who answered."

"The only one?" Sarah asked, surprised.

"I was mystified at that myself," Mrs. Beever said, "but we're a bit out of the way here, if somebody's looking for grand society. And her ladyship has never been what y' might call generous." She glanced up at the clock on the wall and pushed back her chair. "Gracious me, just look at that time, and me not finished with t' pheasant yet! Harriet, put down that knife and fetch a dozen potatoes out of t' bin. It'll be luncheon a-fore we know it, and t' new gentleman here, and us not ready with t' meal."

Sarah drained her teacup and put it down. "Thank you for the tea," she said. "I hope the ginger cake does Lady Longford some good."

"So do I, Miss Barwick," said Mrs. Beever devoutly, and hoisted herself up. "I truly do. A trial her ladyship may be, and a sore one at times, but we'd all hate to lose her." She frowned. "Harriet, what did I tell you? Go and get those potatoes, girl. Right now!"

18

"Blood!"

As Miss Potter and Miss Barwick drove the pony cart up Stony Lane on their way to Tidmarsh Manor, Sawrey Village was already beginning a busy summer's day. Cottage windows were flung open wide to the softest of breezes on this fine summer's day, quilts were hung to air in the sunshine, dust mops flapped from open doors, hearths were swept, ranges stoked, kitchens tidied. Youngsters were sent to the vegetable gardens to pull onions and cut lettuces for the noonday meal, wives walked down to the butcher shop in Far Sawrey to purchase their midweek knuckle of beef, and husbands bent to their various industries in workshop, barn, and field.

Rose Sutton, the wife of the veterinary surgeon, opened the door to the surgery at the back of Courier Cottage and said good morning to young Jeremy Crosfield, who lived with his aunt near Cunsey Beck. Jeremy occasionally brought in-jured wild creatures to be repaired by Dr. Sutton. Today he was carrying a badger cub, a small, gray animal with a striped head and a short, round snout.

"Oh, poor baby," Rose said, clucking sympathetically, bending over for a close look. As the mother of six young Suttons and a regular assistant in her husband's surgery, she was well acquainted with the needs of infants, human and otherwise. "He wants feeding up, he does. He looks as if he's starving. And one hind leg's been chewed, I see. Where'd you get him, Jeremy?"

"Somebody dug out the badger sett at the Hill Top rock quarry," Jeremy said with a kind of grim ferocity. "The mother and the other cub are gone. I found this little fellow wandering across the meadow. He's almost big enough to survive on his own, but that bad leg needs to be seen to." He stroked the badger's stubby snout. "I thought p'rhaps Doc-tor Sutton could mend him. And tell me how to manage him until he's old enough to manage for himself. I don't have any money to pay," he added matter-of-factly, "but I'd be glad to run errands and clean cages."

"Well, bring him in, then," Rose said cheerfully, "and we'll ask the doctor what's best to be done."

At Belle Green, Mathilda Crook pegged her freshly washed sheets to the clothesline in the yard, with an ear cocked to the usual village sounds: the metallic clang-clang-clang of her husband's hammer in his smithy just down Market Street from their house; the buzzy rasp of Roger Dowling's carpenter's saw in the joinery next to the smithy; and the ir-ritated tone of Hannah Braithwaite's voice as she called one of her children from the door of Croft End.

Hanging the washing was a pleasant task on a warm day

when there was just enough breeze to shake out the wrinkles, and Mathilda Crook dallied, keeping an eye out to see who might be passing up and down Market Street. She had some interesting news, and she was anxious to share it. If a suitable person did not happen along in the next little bit, she might just take off her apron and walk down to the post office, where she was bound to meet someone or other.

But she didn't have to. Next to Belle Green, at High Green Gate, Agnes Llewellyn put her granddaughter into her brand-new wicker pram, covered it with a cheesecloth drape to keep off the flies and thunderflies, and pushed it into the garden so Baby Lily could get some sunshine and fresh air. Lily's mother had gone into Hawkshead to do some shopping, leaving the baby in her mother-in-law's care. Agnes was always delighted to oblige, since Lily was her first grandchild and the object of enormous grandmotherly pride.

Taking a basket, Agnes went to pick some raspberries for a tart for supper, noticing with annoyance that the magpies, those rascally birds, had been at the berries again. She picked all there were (not quite a cup) and went to see whether there were enough strawberries to eke them out. But the magpies had got them, too, the naughty things. She was turning to go back to the house when Mathilda Crook came hurrying to the fence, a damp shirt over her arm and several wooden clothes pegs in her hand.

To Agnes's annoyance, Mathilda didn't say good morning or how are you or even inquire about the baby's cradle cap, which Agnes had been treating with a salve made from elder flowers and calendula. "S'pose you've heard all about poor old Ben Hornby's accident," was what she said, in that irritatingly triumphant voice she used when she had some especially savory bit of news.

Agnes was forced to admit that she hadn't heard anything about Ben Hornby, accident or otherwise.

Mathilda clucked pityingly, whether at Ben's fate or at Agnes's ignorance was not quite clear. "Tumbled down Holly How and broke his head on the rocks," she said in an authoritative tone. "That's what Miss Potter said, last night at supper. She and Jennings found the old man when they went to look at some sheep Miss Potter bought. Likely he'd had a bit too much to drink."

Agnes said she was greatly distressed to hear this, although she ventured the opinion that there might be some in the village and the surrounding countryside who would not be terribly unhappy to learn of old Ben's demise.

"Oh?" Mathilda asked. She made a show of shaking out the damp shirt and running her thumbs across the collar to press out the wrinkles. Her "Now, who would that be, Agnes?" was light and unconcerned, but Agnes could hear the curiosity burning in the question.

She tossed her head. "You mean," she replied, feigning great surprise, "you don't remember what happened last winter? Why, I thought that you, of all people, Mathilda . . ." She let her voice trail off and shook her head as if in disbelief.

Mathilda frowned. "What was it about?"

"About cider," Agnes replied knowingly, drawing it out. "December, it was."

"Cider?" Mathilda asked, puzzled.

With great patience, Agnes said, "Why, the cider that Toby Teathor stole out of old Ben's cider house, of course."

Mathilda was forced to admit that she couldn't remember anything about Toby Teathor's stealing cider, which gave Agnes the opportunity to be pitying in her turn.

"Well, p'rhaps you never heard it. Mr. Llewellyn sold one of our cows to Isaac Chance, at Oldfield Farm, and Isaac was the one who told him. Toby was working for old Ben, and helped himself to a keg of Ben's cider. Ben caught him red-handed and had him up before the magistrate. Expect Toby won't be sorry to hear about the accident."

"Oh, *that*," Mathilda said in an airy tone. "I thought you were talking about something *important*." She gave the shirt a good shake. "Well, I s'pose I'd best get back to my clothes-hanging."

"And I'd best get on with these berries," Agnes said, feeling put out.

She carried the raspberries into the kitchen and put them into a bowl. Then she took off her apron, smartened up her hair, and pushed Baby Lily's pram down Market Street to the village shop.

The shop, which was located in Meadowcroft Cottage and run by Lydia Dowling (the wife of Roger Dowling, the village carpenter), stood at the corner of Market Street and the road that went east to the Windermere ferry and west to the market town of Hawkshead. It occupied two downstairs rooms, and was stocked with the sorts of things that the villagers needed on short notice: bacon and sausages, eggs, tea and coffee and sugar and snuff, tins of treacle and condensed milk, fresh vegetables and fruit from the village gardens and orchards, needles and threads and buttons, candles and boot-laces and hairpins and three-a-penny candies for the children. Lydia and Roger lived over the shop with their niece Gladys.

Agnes parked Baby Lily beside the shop door, adjusted the pram's wicker bonnet to keep out the sun, and went inside, where she found Lydia filling a jar with peppermint candies and Gladys measuring a length of white lace. Agnes bought a tin of tea, a packet of soap powder, and some red buttonhole twist, and then turned to see a small basket of luscious-looking red raspberries, displayed beside a box of dewy fresh lettuce, a pyramid of purple plums, and several heads of cabbage.

"Fresh-picked?" she inquired cautiously, with a covetous look at the tempting raspberries.

"This very mornin', before breakfast," Lydia Dowling assured her. "T' magpies have been that bad, goin' after them even a-fore they're ripe. But I managed to get enough for Mr. Dowling's dinner, and thought as how somebody else might as well have the rest, or t' birds'll get them, too. There's not quite enough there for a tart, but if you had a few to go with them—"

"How much?" Agnes asked.

"Tuppence ha'penny," said Lydia.

Agnes nodded. "That'll be all right, then." As she paid for her purchases, she remarked, "I s'pose you've heard about Ben Hornby's accident. Had a bit too much to drink and fell down Holly How."

" 'Twa'n't no accident," Lydia said firmly. She blew her dark, fly-away hair out of her eyes. "That's accordin' to Hannah Braithwaite, who got it from Constable Braithwaite, who went up to Holly How with Captain Woodcock, after Miss Potter and Mr. Jennings found t' poor auld soul." She paused to take a handkerchief out of her pocket and wipe her forehead. "My, it's warm today. Wonder if it's fixin' to storm."

"It wasn't an accident?" Agnes asked, her eyes widening.

"Oh, you haven't heard?" Gladys asked, with barely suppressed excitement. "Mr. Hornby was yarked hard, 'crost the shoulders. And he was holdin' a tobacco pipe in his hand when he died." Gladys was a plump, full-figured young woman in her twenties, with thick auburn hair that she twisted into ringlets. She had a habit of smiling widely (flirtatiously, her aunt thought), so as to show off her very white teeth.

"Gladys," Lydia said, frowning. "I don't know that you should be tellin' folk what t' constable—"

THE TALE OF HOLLY HOW

"Oh, tush, Lydia," Agnes said, waving her hand impatiently. "What does Mr. Hornby's pipe have to do with it not bein' an accident, Gladys?"

"I'm sure Mrs. Llewellyn woan't tell anybody, Aunt." Gladys leaned across the wooden counter and lowered her voice. "It wa'n't *his* pipe, y' see. Mr. Hornby had bad trouble with his lungs and had to give up 'bacco years ago. And what's more—"

"And what's more," put in Lydia, not to be outdone by her niece, "t' pipe had some letters scratched on t' stem. An H an' an S." She looked at the raspberries. "I doan't have anything to cover these with, Agnes. Can you just set them in t' peramb'lator with t' baby? You can bring t' basket back t' next time you're down this way."

"That'll do," Agnes said. "An H an' an S?"

"That's what Hannah Braithwaite says," Lydia replied. "T' constable saw it himself."

"Has to be t' person t' pipe belongs to, wouldn't y' say?" Gladys put in eagerly. "Which means that it must have been somebody named H-something S-something who pushed Mr. Hornby down Holly How and killed him."

"Pushed him!" Agnes exclaimed with great interest.

"Well, yes," Gladys said. "How else would t' poor auld man have ended up at t' bottom, with a clay pipe in his hand?" She looked solemn. "Seems t' me we've got a suspect, and his name is H. S."

"H. S." Agnes mused. "Well, it's not Toby Teathor, that's for sure. His initials are T. T."

"Toby Teathor?" Gladys asked.

"He stole some cider out of Mr. Hornby's barn last winter, and was had before the magistrate over it," Agnes replied importantly. "Toby's not o'er-fond of the old man, I fancy." She frowned. "But since it's an H and an S we're lookin' for, Henry Stubbs is the first that comes to mind. I can't think why Henry would've done it, though."

"Or what he'd be doin' up Holly How," Lydia said. "Our Henry's not the sort for goin' out of his way, if you know what I mean."

Agnes knew what she meant. Henry, a bow-legged, weak-eyed little man with sandy whiskers, was Bertha Stubbs's husband and a well-known frequenter of the Tower Bank Arms, the local pub. He helped operate the Windermere ferry, except on days following an especially convivial evening at the Arms, when he was, as Bertha delicately put it, "under the weather."

At that moment, Baby Lily put up a cry, and Agnes gathered her purchases and said goodbye to Lydia and Gladys. She put the packages into the pram with the baby, and the basket of fresh raspberries, and, still thinking about the mysterious person with the initials H. S., pushed the pram up Market Street and around the corner and down the side street to the post office. There, she parked Baby Lily's pram in the narrow garden in front and joined the queue, which also included Mrs. Lythecoe, the widow of the former vicar, and Rose Sutton, the wife of the veterinary surgeon. Two of Rose's younger children, a boy and a girl, were playing under the hedge outside.

Rose was buying a stamp and telling Mrs. Lythecoe over her shoulder that some badger diggers had pillaged a sett at the rock quarry on Hill Top farm and only one little cub had survived, and that one badly chewed, and Jeremy Crosfield, who was quite a nice boy, had brought it to Dr. Sutton to be mended.

"Oh, dear," Mrs. Lythecoe said sympathetically, "those wretched badger diggers. The wild things have a hard enough time of it. They ought to be left alone."

"You're cert'nly right," Agnes agreed, joining the conversation. "There'd be less of it, if 'tweren't for the badger-baiting. It's against the law, and Captain Woodcock stops it whenever he can. But too many men come home with their pockets inside-out, and there's nae a penny for milk the next seven days."

"Who's next," called Lucy Skead, the postmistress—quite unnecessarily, Agnes thought, since she could clearly see that Mrs. Lythecoe was waiting in line, and Agnes right behind her. But then, Lucy always liked to exaggerate her importance. Rose moved aside to lick the stamp and put it on her envelope, and Mrs. Lythecoe stepped forward and put a small package on the counter. Lucy peered at the address as she put it on the scale and adjusted the balances.

"Sending something to your sister?" she remarked. "Those gray gloves you was knitting last week?" Lucy was an inveterate snoop and knew every villager's business as well as they knew their own—and sometimes sooner, since every letter passed through her hands before it reached its intended recipient.

Mrs. Lythecoe only smiled, however, and Agnes took advantage of the momentary silence to say, quite casually, "I s'pose you've heard about Ben Hornby being pushed down Holly How?"

"One and six," Lucy said to Mrs. Lythecoe. "You must have put a tin of something in with t' gloves, to make it so heavy. Or a jar of your plum jam, p'rhaps?" Bright eyed, she took a sideways step so that she could see Agnes, whilst Mrs. Lythecoe counted out coins. "Aye, we've heard about it, Mrs. Llewellyn. Scand'lous, it is. Simply appalling."

"Pushed?" Mrs. Lythecoe turned around and gave Agnes a frowning look. Her gray-streaked hair was twisted up under a wide-brimmed straw hat. "Really, Agnes, it's not a good idea to spread rumors before all the facts are known. The inquest won't be held for at least a week, and—"

"Oh, but he *was* pushed, Mrs. Lythecoe!" Lucy broke in eagerly. "That's t' facts. I heard it from Mrs. Jennings herself, and everybody knows that Mr. Jennings was right there when they found that clay pipe in Mr. Hornby's dead fingers, with t' letters H and S on it." She shuddered delicately, as if possessed by the shivery image of swift and violent death. "It's disgraceful, what t' world is coming to these days, wouldn't you say?" Without waiting for a response, she rushed on. "It's them strangers bargin' through t' village, if you ask me. Fell-walkers and cyclists and t' likes, dozens and dozens of them trampin' and ridin' their bicycles along t' lanes, and climbin' t' fences, and never botherin' to close a gate, so that t' livestock get out and go wandering all over t' place. Why, I've heard old Ben Hornby complain more'n once, standin' right on that spot on t' floor where your two feet are planted. And t' latest was just two days ago."

"Complain about what, Lucy?" Rose Sutton asked, presenting her stamped letter to be put into the canvas mail bag. She turned around to look through the door at her children. "Jamie Sutton," she said sternly, "don't you go bothering around that perambulator. Mrs. Llewellyn's little grandbaby is having a nap. You'll get a smack if you wake her."

"Lily's all right, Rose," Agnes said impatiently, wanting to hear what Lucy had to say. "What was it that Ben Hornby was complainin' about, Lucy?"

Obviously enjoying their attention, Lucy dropped the letter into the bag and followed it with Mrs. Lythecoe's package. She straightened a stack of forms and moved the pen and inkwell a fraction of an inch to the right before she answered.

"About them fell-walkers from Manchester leavin' his gates open when they climb to t' top of Holly How," she replied. "It was more than he could bear in silence, he said. In fact, them're his very words. 'More than I can bear in silence,

Mrs. Skead,' he said. Put out, he was, and you couldn't blame him. 'They're going to find themselves in verra serious trouble, mind my words,' was 'xactly what he said." She paused and added darkly, "If you ask me, old Ben saw one of them fell-walkers openin' his gate and took him to task and got himself killed for his pains."

"If you know of a suspect who should be questioned, Lucy," Mrs. Lythecoe said severely, "you'd better tell Constable Braithwaite. Far better that than gossiping to us."

"But we're not gossipin'," Agnes protested. "We're simply discussin' matters."

"And I *have* told t' constable, Mrs. Lythecoe," Lucy chirped. "I told him this mornin', as soon as I heard t' poor old gentleman had been found dead. I thought of it straightaway, y' see."

"Gentleman, was he?" Rose Sutton inquired archly. "Not to speak ill of the dead, of course, but gentlemen pay their debts, whilst Mr. Hornby—" She was interrupted by a shriek from outside, a splintering sound, and a loud wail.

"Mum, oh, Mum!" a child's voice cried. "Jamie's *kilt* the baby!"

And at that, all four women rushed out of the post office, to find the wicker perambulator lying wheels-up in the grass, whilst a small boy in short pants stood by, howling lustily. His hands were red, there were red smears on his face, and his bare legs were red-spattered.

"Blood!" Lucy cried, her hands going to her mouth. "Oh, Lor', the child's covered in *blood*!"

"The baby!" shrieked Agnes, falling to her knees to paw through the wreckage of perambulator and packages and bedding that littered the ground. "Where's Baby Lily?"

"Jamie, I *told* you!" shouted Rose, aiming a swat at the boy's behind. "What have you done with Mrs. Llewelyn's baby, you naughty, naughty boy?"

"I really don't think," Mrs. Lythecoe began firmly, "that it's as serious as—"

"He's kilt her, Mum," the girl said in a tittle-tattle voice. "I told him not to, but he wouldn't stop." She pointed an accusing finger. "She's there, just under the hedge, kilt dead. All over blood, top to toe."

But Baby Lily had not been killed, as they quickly discovered. The instant she was retrieved from under the hedge she began to shriek at the top of her lungs. And it wasn't blood that smeared her face and clothing. She was covered with the juice of the red raspberries into which she had fallen when Jamie tipped the perambulator as he climbed into it to get the berries.

"I'm sorry, Agnes," Rose Sutton said in a repentant tone, as they gathered up the baby, the packages, and the wicker pram, the bonnet of which was obviously smashed beyond any repair. "I don't know how I can make it up to you."

"I'm sorry, too," Agnes replied stiffly. "I don't know what my daughter-in-law will say when she comes back and sees what's become of her new pram that she was so proud of." She sighed. "And now it seems we won't be havin' tart tonight, after all. I've got barely a cup of raspberries at home, and the ones I got from Lydia Dowling are all smashed."

"I'll be glad to give you a jar of bottled rhubarb," Mrs. Lythecoe offered helpfully. "I always think that raspberries and rhubarb make a very nice tart. And I can write out the recipe, if you're not sure how to put them together."

Agnes had to be satisfied with that.

19

Miss Potter Finds a Piece of Evidence

Beatrix met Sarah at the pony cart in front of Tidmarsh Manor.

"I see that you've left your basket," Sarah said as she climbed in, "so you must have managed to leave the guinea pig as well. Mrs. Beever didn't hold out much hope. She was of the opinion that Miss Martine wouldn't allow the child to have a pet of any description."

"She certainly tried," Beatrix said grimly, tucking in her skirt and picking up Winston's reins. "If it hadn't been for the vicar, she might have succeeded. So you've delivered your baked goods?"

"Yes," Sarah said. "And in the process, I learnt quite a bit from Mrs. Beever. I'll tell you as we drive."

"Let's go," Rascal barked authoritatively. *"Winston and I were getting tired of waiting!"*

"We'll be off, then," Beatrix said, looking up at the sky, which was beginning to cloud over. A light breeze was blowing from the west, carrying with it the smell of damp earth and the promise of rain. "It would be good to put the sheep in the fold and get back to the village before there's a shower."

Winston was just pulling the cart onto Stony Lane when they met Lady Longford's phaeton, driven by Mr. Beever and conveying an aristocratic-looking man with gold-rimmed spectacles who held himself very straight. He was elegantly dressed in a ruffled white shirt, black frock coat, gray gloves, and tall hat, which he tipped to Beatrix and Sarah with a slight, supercilious nod, barely acknowledging them.

"Well, la-di-da!" Rascal growled. *"Fine toffee-nose, that."* And he aimed a volley of sharp barks at the gentleman's departing back.

"Dr. Gainwell, I presume," Sarah said dryly, as Beatrix chuckled. "Quite the fine gentleman, isn't he? Doesn't quite fit my picture of a missionary, though. Or a teacher."

"But that's who he must be," Beatrix said, urging Winston forward along the road to Holly How Farm. "Lady Longford said he was expected." She made a rueful face. "He doesn't look like the sort of person who will be very comfortable in Sawrey School. I wonder where Lady Longford met him, and why in the world she thinks a man like that would be a better person for the position than Miss Nash."

"That's just it, Bea," Sarah said. "Her ladyship doesn't know that man at *all*." And as they drove, she told Beatrix what Mrs. Beever had told her about the unhappy circumstances at the Manor, and about Lady Longford suffering serious stomach problems, and about Miss Martine taking over the servants and being a parsimonious manager who seemed intent on saving money by cutting back on staff.

"It sounds a dismal state of affairs," Beatrix said, shaking her head at Sarah's story. "The servants will manage, of course. It's Caroline we should feel sorry for, her grandmother ill and that companion taking over."

"What's she like?" Sarah asked curiously.

"Sturdy, self-reliant. I think she'll do well in spite of everything, although it'll be a pity if she's sent away to school."

Sarah looked surprised. "You wouldn't suggest a governess, would you?"

"Oh, no," Beatrix replied, remembering her own frustrating experiences with governesses. "There's no reason why she couldn't go to school in the village, in my opinion, especially if Miss Nash is the teacher." She sighed. "Although it looks like that might not happen."

A few moments later, they were driving down the lane to Holly How Farm. Beatrix had not expected to meet anyone there, so she was surprised when she drove up in front of Ben Hornby's cottage and saw an old black horse with a white blaze, hitched to a green-painted cart, standing at the gate. A stern-faced, dark-haired man, dressed in canvas breeches, a gray woolen shirt with the sleeves rolled up, and a wool cap, was loading a hay rake and a scythe into the cart, which already contained a potato fork, several wooden buckets, and a stack of baskets. He seemed as surprised to see the two women as they were to see him.

"Good morning," Beatrix said, and got down from the cart. "I'm Miss Potter, from Hill Top Farm, and this is my friend Miss Barwick. And you are—"

"*Isaac Chance,*" Rascal said darkly, springing down onto the ground beside her. "*He's not to be trusted, Miss Potter. He brought a horse to Mr. Crook's smithy for shoeing two months ago, and hasn't paid tuppence toward his bill.*"

"Mornin', ladies." The man tipped his cap. "Isaac Chance. I farm Oldfield, up t' way a bit." He gestured at the cart full of tools. "I heard 'bout Ben Hornby's accident, poor auld soul, and reckoned I'd better get my tools back a-fore his daughter came to clear out his things. Loaned 'em to him after his barn burnt last winter," he added, as if he felt the need for justification.

"*Rubbish,*" Rascal barked sharply.

"*Rubbish, is it?*" snarled a large yellow dog, crawling out from under the wagon and baring his fangs with a growl that made Rascal's hair stand on end. "*Who's that sayin' rubbish, I wants t' know.*"

"*Well, if it isn't old Mustard,*" Rascal said, with an amiable wag of his tail. "*Last time I saw you was when the hounds ran at the Drunken Duck. Thought they'd hauled you off to the bone-heap years back, you old hobthrush.*" Mustard wasn't too bright, in Rascal's opinion, but he was known to be a fierce fighter with a kind of bull-headed courage. He didn't lead a happy life, though. Chance was not a kind master, and Mustard spent a great deal of his time chained to an iron ring in the barn.

Mustard came closer, sniffing. "*Oh, it's you, is it, Rascal? Sorry, I doan't see too well these days. A bit out of your way, aren't ye? What brings you up from t' village?*"

"*Looking for sheep,*" Rascal said, assuming a careless air. "*Two Herdwick ewes and three lambs. You wouldn't happen to know where they are, would you?*"

Mustard gave him an innocent, eyebrows-raised look. "*Me? Why would I know anything about—*"

"Hod on!" Chance aimed a hard kick at Mustard's head. "Stop that yarpin', Mustard, y' fool dog, and get back under that wagon." As Mustard cringed and crept behind the wheel, Chance took off his cap and rubbed his sweaty forehead with his thumb. "Man's got to have tools, or he can't work, y' know—although auld Ben wa'n't one to waste much time workin'." He grinned, showing a broken front tooth. "Not lazy, was Ben. He just had other things he liked to do."

"Indeed," Beatrix said evenly, thinking that, with Ben Hornby dead, there was no one to dispute the man's claim that the tools were his. She frowned. Mr. Jennings had said that Chance had tried to buy Holly How Farm, but had been told that it was Ben Hornby's as long as he wanted it. Perhaps Chance was here now because he was in a hurry to get his hands on some of Ben's other property. On the other hand, perhaps what he said was true. Maybe those *were* his tools.

Ignoring Sarah, Chance leaned nonchalantly against the cart and replaced his cap, his eyes on Beatrix. "I was down to t' village t' other day and stopped by Hill Top for a look 'round. You and Jennings're doin' a fair bit of buildin' there—barn, pigsty, house. Heard in t' pub that you bought t' field on t' other side of t' Kendal road, too." His eyes glinted. "Reet fair lot of money it's all costin', I'll wager."

Without replying to Chance's remark, Beatrix wound Winston's reins around the gatepost, fastening them with extra care. He was steady and reliable, but ponies were ponies, and if there was thunder, she did not want him to pull free and go home without them. She looked at Chance, thinking that there was something about the fellow that she didn't like—perhaps it was the look of discontent around his mouth and the narrowness of his eyes, or the recent whiplash welts on his horse's rump. She felt no inclination to share her personal business with him and was more than a little glad that Sarah Barwick was with her. Not that she was afraid, of course. But still—

"You and Jennings were t' ones who found poor auld Ben, I understand," Chance said in an offhand way. "Wonder how he come to fall off that bit of cliff. Strange thing, wouldn't you say?"

"I'm sure I don't know," Beatrix said, turning to Sarah. "Miss Barwick, are we ready?"

"Whenever you are," Sarah replied, handing Beatrix her hat and squashing her own firmly on her head.

Chance reached into his trouser pocket and pulled out a worn tobacco tin. From a shirt pocket, he produced a small folder of cigarette papers. Taking a loose pinch of tarry black tobacco from the tin, he began to roll a tidy cigarette. He licked the paper, stuck the cigarette in his mouth, and lit it, lifting his leather boot to strike a wooden match against the sole.

"Up there lookin' for your sheep when you found him, was you? Heard you bought some of Ben's Herdwicks." He dropped the match into the dirt and pulled on his cigarette, waiting for Beatrix to answer. When she did not, he added, in an ingratiating tone, "I've some verra fine ewes m'self, y' know, miss. If you can't locate them that Ben sold you, mappen you'll have a look at mine."

"Why, you rogue!" Racal barked, jumping up and down stiff-legged. *"I wouldn't put it past you to—"*

"Watch out who you're callin' a rogue," Mustard growled. *"Want me to come out there and take a nip out of your tail?"*

"Gooseberries," Rascal replied sardonically, knowing full well that Mustard didn't dare come out from under the wagon, for fear of another hard kick from his master's boot.

"Come on, Rascal," Beatrix said. Have a look at his sheep, indeed! By now feeling greatly put out at the man, she looked up at Holly How, rising behind the farmhouse. "Goodbye, Mr. Chance. Shall we, Miss Barwick?"

Chance pushed himself away from the cart, looking alarmed. "You're not goin' up there alone, are you?"

"I am not alone," Beatrix pointed out reasonably. "Miss Barwick is with me."

"And me," Rascal said.

"For what that's worth," Mustard growled. *"You could protect 'em from a mouse or a rabbit, but not much else."*

"Is that right?" Rascal snapped. *"You just stick that ugly snout of yours out here and—"*

"Rascal," said Beatrix sternly. "Stop that and come along."

Chance frowned. "It's lookin' like thunder any minute. And the fell's not a safe place for ladies. Might tumble down and hurt yourself, like auld Ben." He paused. "Where the de'il is Jennings, anyway? Why isn't he with you?"

With a dry humor, Beatrix said, "Mr. Jennings stepped off the porch and sprained his ankle last evening."

Chance gave a harsh laugh. "Well, that settles it. I'll go up there with you ladies and help you look for those sheep."

"No, thank you." Beatrix was polite but firm. "We don't want to take you from your work." She glanced pointedly at the wagon. "You'll want to get your tools home before it rains, I'm sure."

The frown became a scowl. "I still say you shouldn't go up there alone."

"You don't have anything to say about it, Mr. Chance," Beatrix said crisply. "Goodbye." And with that she led the way up the path, Sarah following behind, Rascal dancing at their heels, barely able to contain his glee.

"That was a bit of all right, I'd say, Miss Potter," he barked happily. *"Shan't be bothered by him again, I fancy."*

"I say, Bea," Sarah said in an admiring tone, "you quite surprise me, talking back to that fellow." She shuddered. "Not a very nice man, if you ask me."

"Rather reminded me of a stoat," Beatrix said quietly. "Let's not talk about him, shall we? It's likely to spoil our walk. And let's do keep our eyes open for those sheep."

As they climbed up Holly How, Beatrix noticed that the clouds had thickened and turned gray, a low haze veiled the farther fells, and the western breeze had freshened. Both she and Sarah were strong walkers and they climbed swiftly, with firm, sure strides, taking the same narrow, zig-zagging sheep's path that Beatrix and Mr. Jennings had used the afternoon before.

As they climbed, they seemed to Beatrix to be going farther and farther from all human settlements, into a wilderness that they shared only with the elements and the animals of the moors. There was a wild, free feeling about being up here, with the wind blowing her skirts and lifting her hair. The green slope around them was pocked with rabbit burrows, and occasionally she could see the twinkling of a white tail and the tip of a pink ear. The dry, fine grass whispered under her feet. A cricket chirruped, and high above, beneath the lowering blanket of gray clouds, the sky was traced with the spiraling flight of curlews, and she could hear their plaintive call, *curl-ee, curl-ee.* Beatrix held her head high, savoring the sharp sweetness of the breeze that carried with it the scents of earth and water and growing things, of wild thyme and lichen and moss and heather. The rounded top of Holly How rose above her, with the stone-walled sheep fold off to the left. But the green hillside was disappointingly empty of sheep, and sheep, she reminded herself, were what they had come to find.

"I don't see the sheep anywhere," Sarah said behind her. She was beginning to sound a little breathless. "I suppose that means we'll have to climb to the top, doesn't it? Perhaps they've gone down the other side."

"*I doubt it,*" Rascal remarked. "*I don't think we'll find them.*" It was a known fact that sheep were curious, and of all the breeds of sheep, Herdwicks were amongst the most curious. If they were anywhere on Holly How, they would have already come over to see who was walking across their fell and ask what they wanted.

"There's somewhere else I want to look before we climb

to the top," Beatrix said, over her shoulder. A few moments later, they had reached the stone-fenced fold, and above, on the shoulder of the hill, she could see the place from which Ben Hornby must have fallen. She pointed.

"Over there," she said. "There's a beck at the bottom of that slope. It's steep, but an easy climb for sheep. They might have gone down for water."

"Lead on," Sarah said cheerfully, wiping the sweat off her forehead with her sleeve. "Although I'd like to suggest that when we get there, we might sit down for a moment or two. You're a much better walker than I am, Bea, and to tell the truth, I am jolly tired."

In a few moments, they reached the spot where Beatrix had stood the afternoon before and looked down to the foot of the steep slope. Ben Hornby's body was gone, of course, and Beatrix could see little sign of its ever having been there. There were no sheep, either. The little stream skipped and leapt amongst the rocks, chattering cheerfully to itself and paying no attention to anyone. On the opposite side of the stream there were a few larches and shrub willows, and then the ground sloped upward again.

"That's where we found him," Beatrix said, pointing down. "I thought, of course, that it was an accident, until Constable Braithwaite explained about the tobacco pipe Mr. Hornby was holding in his hand. The constable was sure he didn't smoke, you see," she added. "So it began to seem as if the old man might not have been here alone."

"And this is where he fell from, I suppose," Sarah replied. She sat down on a large rock and looked around curiously. "I imagine the men must have searched this place rather thoroughly, especially if they thought someone else was up here with Mr. Hornby." She paused, frowning down at the ground. "They didn't find anything, I don't suppose? No sign of a struggle or anything like that?"

"If they did, they didn't mention it in my hearing," Beatrix said. "Of course, I wasn't up here with them." She smiled ruefully and seated herself on a rock. "Once I was down there, it was easier to go farther down than to climb back up."

"I believe it," Sarah said, looking down the slope. "I don't see how you ever got down there safely." With a smile, she looked down at her skirt. "An argument for wearing trousers, if you ask me."

For a moment, the two of them were silent, whilst Sarah contemplated the steep slope beneath them and Beatrix studied the area around them, trying to imagine what had happened that might have resulted in a man's death. One man here alone, enjoying a pipe of tobacco, or two men together? A slip of a heel on a rock and an accidental fall? Or an argument that flared out of control and ended with an angry, impulsive shove? Or something else altogether?

But if there was a tale here, there was nothing to tell it. Thick clumps of low bramble bushes grew out of the tumbled rocks, and the stretches of scuffed earth between them were too hard and stony to bear human footprints—or even the hoofprints of the many sheep that had come this way, judging from the tiny tufts of white wool snagged on the sharp thorns. Although Beatrix searched carefully, she could find nothing that suggested what might have happened in this place.

And then Rascal—who had been scouting the area, tracing with his clever nose the many tantalizing tracks and trails that are completely invisible to Big Folk but so immediately evident to dogs—seemed to find something of interest, lying hidden amongst the thicket of briars about twenty feet distant.

He raised his head and began to bark. *"Over here!"* he yipped urgently. *"Miss Potter, Miss Barwick, come here!"*

"What do you suppose that little dog has found?" Sarah asked curiously. "He's certainly excited about it."

"I'll go and see," Beatrix replied, gathering her skirt close around her. "You'd better stay here. Those brambles will tear your clothes." Paying no attention to Sarah's objection, she plunged into the bramble thicket. A moment later, she had returned, somewhat breathless, holding up a pair of long-handled, black metal tongs. "Here it is!" she exclaimed. "This is what Rascal found."

"Yes, but what is it?" Sarah asked, puzzled.

"I have no idea," Beatrix said, turning it over in her hands. "Fireplace tongs? But the points are sharpened, as if they're meant to catch and hold on to something, not just lift it. And they're heavy."

Rascal had followed her out of the briar patch. *"It's a pair of badger tongs, that's what it is!"* he said excitedly, pressing his nose to the tongs. *"They're used to catch badgers. Mr. Crook makes them at his forge."*

"Look at Rascal," Sarah said wonderingly. "He acts as if he knows exactly what this is."

"He probably does," Beatrix said. "I'm always surprised by what animals seem to know—and they always seem to want to tell us, too. It's such a pity we can't understand what they're saying." She paused, looking curiously at the tongs. "These might belong to Ben Hornby, I suppose, but—"

"No, no, NO!" Rascal cried, bouncing up and down. *"Old Ben hated badger-digging with a passion. Old Lord Longford insisted that the sett not be disturbed, and Ben didn't like the idea of people coming around, bothering animals on land that he was responsible for."*

"—But perhaps not," Beatrix went on, raising her voice over Rascal's excited yelping. "At any rate, the constable and Captain Woodcock obviously missed this when they were making their search. Although, to give them credit, they would have had no special reason to search those brambles."

There was a rumble of thunder not far away. She glanced up to see that the sky had grown even darker, and a finger of lightning danced across the fells to the west. "We'd better start back," she said. "I left my umbrella in the pony cart."

"But I thought we were going to the top of Holly How," Sarah objected. "What about the sheep?"

"They've waited this long, they can wait a little longer," Beatrix said practically, and pointed toward the darkening west. "If we don't hurry, we're going to get very wet."

"We'll get wet even if we do hurry," Rascal observed, lifting his nose to the wind. *"That rain is only a mile or two away."*

Rascal's prediction turned out to be true, and with one additional complication. When the three of them reached Holly How Farm, Winston and the pony cart were nowhere to be seen.

"Oh, blast," Sarah groaned. "The pony's gone home without us."

"But I know I tied him securely," Beatrix said. She narrowed her eyes. "You don't suppose Isaac Chance turned him loose, do you?"

"I wouldn't put it past him," Rascal growled. *"He's a thoroughly bad fellow, you can take my word for it."*

"I don't suppose we'll ever know," Sarah said with a sigh. A few raindrops began to spatter down. "How far is it to the village, do you think?"

"Only about three miles," Beatrix said. "Come on."

"Only?" Sarah said, with a laugh. "I just wish that pony had thought to leave the umbrella for us."

As it happened, Winston had not gone far. When they turned off the farm track onto Stony Lane, they saw him waiting for them under a large beech tree and ran toward him with happy exclamations. The rain began in earnest just as Beatrix and Sarah climbed into the cart and Sarah put up the umbrella, which was large enough to cover the both of them.

"I'd give a lot to know whether that awful man let our pony go," she said.

"It's too bad Winston can't tell us," Beatrix said, picking up the reins and clucking to the pony.

"Well, he can tell me," Rascal replied. He ran alongside the pony, who was trotting briskly downhill, as anxious as the others to get home before the hard rain came. "What happened, Winston? Did Isaac Chance turn you loose?"

The pony tossed his head. "You don't think I pulled myself free, do you?" he asked huffily. "I am a well-bred, hardworking pony, and I know my job. When I am told to go, I go. When I'm told to stop, I stop, sunshine, snow, or thunder. But when I'm whipped—"

"So it was Chance, then? He let you loose and whipped you until you ran away?"

"It was Chance," Winston said through his teeth. "A thoroughly unpleasant fellow. And now, if you'll excuse me, I have work to do."

And with that, he picked up his hoofs and stepped even more smartly down the lane.

20

Caroline Overhears a Conversation

Caroline was introduced to Dr. Gainwell at luncheon. When Miss Martine told her that the man had been a missionary in the South Pacific before coming to Sawrey to manage the school, she had been rather interested in meeting him. Her parents had known several missionaries and a few had come to the sheep station to visit—adventuresome men and women, sunburnt, with work-hardened hands and eyes that seemed to see great distances, and interesting stories to tell about places they had been and people they had met, all sorts of people, unchristian heathens and heathenish Christians.

But Dr. Gainwell was not like any of those missionaries. He was a handsome man with a great deal of long, reddish blond hair that he seemed to be constantly flinging out of his eyes, and his hands looked soft, as though he had done no work at all. And if he had any exciting tales about narrow escapes from savage jungle headhunters, or missionaries who had been boiled and eaten by cannibals, he didn't share them at luncheon—although perhaps such stories were too gruesome to be told at table here in England.

In fact, Dr. Gainwell said very little about himself, which made Caroline wonder, since it had been her experience that people who traveled to exotic places usually wanted to rattle on and on until you were sick of hearing them. And although he was all smiles and pleasantries when her grandmother glanced his way, he was something else altogether—something much more watchful and observant—when Grandmama wasn't looking. He spoke to Caroline once or twice, in a soft, slick voice that made her feel uncomfortable. So instead of answering his questions, she pressed her lips together and said nothing.

Miss Martine leaned forward and said, very coldly, "I'm afraid that it is of no use to concern yourself with the child, Dr. Gainwell. She has been sullen and disobedient ever since her arrival in this house. A truly incorrigible young person."

Dr. Gainwell looked down his long nose at Caroline, then back to Miss Martine, and then to Caroline's grandmother. "Oh, no, not incorrigible, Miss Martine," he remonstrated, with a gentle shake of his head. His hair flopped in his eyes and he pushed it back. "No child is truly intractable. The appropriate discipline, firmly and regularly administered, will call forth the desired behavior." The corners of his mouth curled up and he reached out to give Caroline's hand what might have been meant as a reassuring pat. "I do not exaggerate when I say that in my experience with children, I have been quite successful in disciplining even the most unruly."

Caroline pulled her hand back. She did not like the ominous sound of the words "appropriate discipline," and wondered how it might be administered. With a ruler across the knuckles, the way Miss Martine did it?

Lady Longford put down her fork. "Spoken like a true teacher," she said in a brittle voice. "I daresay you shall want to discuss your disciplinary methods with the school trustees, who will be very interested." She patted her pale lips with a napkin and pushed her plate away. "I regret that I am not feeling entirely well today. You will excuse me."

"Oh, dear, oh, dear," Miss Martine said with an immediate concern. She left her chair and went around the table. "Shall I help you to your room?" she asked solicitously. "Would you like me to send for Dr. Butters?"

"That will not be necessary," Lady Longford replied stiffly, reaching for her carved wooden cane and pushing herself up out of her chair with what seemed like a great effort. "You must entertain our guest, Miss Martine, and see that he gets off in good time to meet the trustees. I daresay I shall feel better after a nap."

After her ladyship had gone, Miss Martine turned to Caroline. "You may go to your room as soon as you have finished eating, young miss," she said thinly. "You will not be required again until teatime."

Then, having disposed of Caroline for the afternoon, she smiled at Dr. Gainwell and said, in a much sweeter tone, "Might I suggest the library, sir? We can have our coffee and dessert there. Lord Longford, now deceased, collected a great many books on the natural history of the Lake District, and you might be interested in seeing them."

"Indeed I should, Miss Martine, if you would be kind enough to show them to me." Dr. Gainwell took out his gold watch and looked at it. "However, her ladyship mentioned an interview with the school trustees. I must say, I was not expecting it. It is to be today?"

"The interview is at three, in Far Sawrey, at the hotel.

Beever will drive you." Miss Martine folded her napkin. "I understand that Captain Woodcock will be present, along with Vicar Sackett, Dr. Butters, and Mr. Heelis. Captain Woodcock, the doctor, and the vicar have already been made aware of Lady Longford's interest in your candidacy. Those three can certainly be counted upon to support it. And Mr. Heelis is Lady Longford's solicitor."

"Ah, well, then," Dr. Gainwell said. He glanced at Caroline and added, in a guarded tone, "One feels . . . well, a trifle uncomfortable, as you may appreciate. The position was not advertised. There is no other candidate?"

"A village teacher," Miss Martine said dismissively, "but she has not your credentials, of that you may be sure." She rose with a rustle of silk. "Might I suggest the library, sir?" She raised her voice commandingly, as if she were the mistress of the house. "Emily! Coffee and dessert for Dr. Gainwell and myself in the library!" She looked at Caroline. "To your room, miss," she added.

And with that, the two of them took themselves off down the hallway. Caroline made a face at their departing backs and went upstairs, where she took Tuppenny out of his box. She played with the guinea pig on the floor for a little bit, feeling resentful, then thought of something. Miss Martine had told her to go to her room, and she had obeyed. However, she had not been ordered to *stay* there.

"You'd like some fresh grass, I imagine," she said to Tuppenny. "Let's go out into the garden and you can get some." With her finger, she smoothed the soft orange fur on the top of his head. "If I let you go free in the garden, you'll promise not to run away, won't you?"

Tuppenny gave his nose a twitch. He was still deeply offended that Miss Potter had gone away and left him at Tidmarsh Manor, when he had been led to believe that he would have an adventure, with damsels, and that he would

be able to distinguish himself against the stoats and dragons. He felt totally justified in having a fit of the sulks and
refusing to be comforted, or in running away, or in doing
anything a guinea pig might jolly well choose.

But Tuppenny rather liked the girl, who had a soft voice
and kind manner, and who seemed to be treating him with
an affectionate respect. He didn't suppose it would hurt to
be agreeable, at least for the time being. So he said, with
pretended reluctance, *"I suppose I can promise not to run away.
For the afternoon, at any rate. Which is not to say anything about
tomorrow,"* he added pointedly. *"Tomorrow is another matter.
Tomorrow there may be stoats, and damsels, and perhaps even a
dragon, and then I shall have to—"*

"Good," said the girl, and put him into her apron pocket.

A little while later, Tuppenny found himself up to his ears
in the middle of a delicious patch of fresh green grass where
he nibbled happily, forgetting all about his quest and feeling
that the afternoon was altogether marvelous, in a way that
only a guinea pig at large in a garden could truly appreciate.
The sky had clouded over and the breeze carried the hint of
rain, but occasional fingers of bright sun caressed his silky
fur, and the grass was cool and sweet. The girl sat with a
book in her lap and her back against a low stone wall, watching him to make sure, no doubt, that he would not run away.

But running away was now the furthest thing from Tuppenny's mind, which was instead concentrated on gobbling
down as much of the delicious fresh grass in as short a time
as possible. So for the next quarter hour, the guinea pig
grazed and the girl read in the fitful sunshine, with birds
spiraling into summer song in the sky above them, and
breezes stirring the flowers that bloomed brightly in the
garden all around them, and bees humming seductively
amongst the blossoms, and the sound of subdued voices
mingling with the general blissful hubbub.

The voices, Tuppenny realized after a little while, were drifting out of an open window not far away. A woman's light, high-pitched voice, a man's deeper voice. They were speaking quietly, just above a murmur, which made it necessary to strain one's ears to hear them.

"—should imagine it will be easy enough," said the woman, in a careless tone.

"I certainly hope so," the man said. A tautness had come into his voice. "Although it's not exactly my line, you know. And I hadn't expected an interview. You told me it was a dead cert."

Tuppenny saw the girl glance up alertly from her book and a frown appear between her eyes. She had heard the voices too.

"Well, I must say I expected you to take a somewhat different—" The woman stopped. "No matter. I daresay you will manage it. However, that is not the real problem, you know. The more serious difficulty is—"

The woman went on to explain what this was, but a pair of male meadow pipits alighted on the grass and began to disagree about a particularly attractive nesting site that each of them had promised to his mate. The woman's voice was lost in their clatter.

When the pipits finally settled their argument and flew away, the man was heard to be saying, in a much darker tone, "—expected that you could handle things alone, without any need for—"

"That was before," the woman interrupted sharply.

"Before what?"

"Before *she* came. I tell you, it's all different now."

Tuppenny saw that the girl's eyes had narrowed. She cocked her head, closed her book, and leaned forward, listening intently.

"I'm sure I don't know what you're talking about," the

man said, almost carelessly. "She'll be off to school in a few weeks and then you'll have a free rein to do as you like with the old lady."

"You don't see, do you?" demanded the woman, sounding thoroughly out of patience. "You never could, even when you were a boy, unless it was an inch in front of your nose."

The man was offended. "Well, I certainly don't how the child can threaten the plan. She has no power, no—"

"She threatens it by her very existence," the woman said.

There was a pause. The man sounded startled. "Surely you're not suggesting that we—"

"Sssh!" hissed the woman. "You never know who may be listening." There was a pause, and the sound of rustling silk, and then the window was shut, quite forcibly.

An instant later, the girl had scooped up the astonished Tuppenny and stuffed him into her apron pocket. And then she fled, as if a thousand stoats and weasels and ferrets—and perhaps a dragon or two—were nipping at her heels.

21

The Interview

It was raining lightly when William Heelis led his horse around to the rear of the Sawrey Hotel and turned it over to the stable boy, who put it into a loose box with Dr. Butters's gray mare, next to Captain Woodcock's teal blue Rolls-Royce. Two of the village boys were standing beside the motorcar, staring at it with a half-frightened admiration, whilst their collie dog circled it, growling. Wherever it went, Woodcock's automobile created a stir.

The motorcar was a sign of changing times, Heelis thought to himself with a sigh as he went into the hotel to meet the other school trustees. He would much rather drive a horse, but as a solicitor in Hawkshead, he already knew of several men who were planning to purchase automobiles. This might be a distant corner of England, but like it or not, the future was about to come roaring at top speed down the road and into the most remote village of the Lake District.

The trustees had chosen the Sawrey Hotel as a place to interview Dr. Gainwell because it was directly across the road
from the school building. Afterward, they could take him
for a tour, which would certainly be brief, since there was
precious little to be seen. The thirty pupils were housed in
two wooden-floored, high-ceilinged rooms that had once
served as a chapel, with a lobby for coats and boots and a
separate anteroom where the two teachers had their tea. As
Heelis went up the main stairs of the hotel, he wondered
again why a man of Gainwell's experience and educational
standing would be interested in such an out of the way place.
But perhaps it was only his connection with Lady Longford
that had brought him here, and he was not truly interested
in becoming head teacher at Sawrey School.

At least, this was what Will Heelis hoped, for it was his
opinion—his *settled* opinion—that Margaret Nash ought to
have the position. And after the gossip he had heard at the
Tower Bank Arms a little while ago, he thought that the
sooner the place was offered, the better, for all concerned.
He rapped on the door of the large sitting room at the top of
the stairs—often used for meetings of various clubs and
groups—and went in.

Dr. Butters and Miles Woodcock were already there. The
doctor was standing with his back to the window that
looked out onto the main road, a cup of tea in one hand, the
other hand in the pocket of his tweed suit. Captain Miles
Woodcock, Justice of the Peace for Sawrey district, was sitting in a cretonne-covered armchair, both feet stretched out
in front of him, his fingers tented under his chin. He got to
his feet and came forward as Will entered the room.

"Hullo, Heelis," he said. "Glad you could be here this
afternoon."

"I'm not sure I'm glad," Will said frankly, shaking

Woodcock's hand. He smiled in greeting at the doctor, who was one of the most respected men in the district, the one people turned to in time of trouble. "Good to see you, Butters." He hesitated, then came out with his opinion straightforwardly, as was his usual manner. "To tell God's honest truth, gentlemen, I'm ready to name Margaret Nash and let her get on with the job. And the devil take this Gainwell fellow."

"The devil might not have him." Woodcock nodded at a tea tray on the table next to the window. "Help yourself to tea, Will. I had it sent up, feeling that we might need it." As Will poured a cup and stirred in sugar, the captain added, "As we all know, Gainwell is Lady Longford's candidate. If we turn him down and appoint our Miss Nash, we'll never hear the last of it—nor will Miss Nash, unfortunately. Her ladyship is capable of stirring up all sorts of trouble."

"It won't be the first time Lady Longford has posed a problem," the doctor remarked, turning from the window.

"Right," Will agreed. "That business about refusing to accept responsibility for her granddaughter, as a recent instance. *Tyrannical* is the word that comes to mind."

"Ah, yes. You were involved in that," said the captain, resuming his chair.

"As her solicitor, it was my job to remind her of her familial duty," Will said. "What good old Lord Longford would have wanted, etcetera etcetera. The vicar, as her spiritual adviser, put in a strong word from the moral angle, and between the two of us, we brought her around to our point of view." Will sat down across from the captain, putting his cup on the small table beside him. "I'm not sure we did the girl a good turn, though. She must be lonely, and no doubt she's bullied by her grandmother's companion. I've seen that type before. Meek as you please to the mistress, and a tyrant to the rest of the household."

"And to make matters worse," the doctor said, "the old lady's ill. I've been asked to stop in several times in the last three weeks." He pushed out his lips, frowning. "It's puzzling, I must say. She's better, then she's worse. Some sort of enteric infection, it seems. Responds to treatment for a few days, then flares up again. Her present physical condition is not likely to sweeten her disposition, I fear."

"All the worse for us," the captain said wryly. He paused for a moment and then said, almost reluctantly, "Changing the subject, Will, I suppose you've heard about Ben Hornby."

Will took out his pipe. "Another prickly character. What's old Hornby done now?"

"Then you haven't heard." The captain was somber. "He's come to grief, I'm afraid. His body was found at the foot of a rock outcrop on Holly How yesterday afternoon, by our intrepid Miss Potter."

"Good God!" Will exclaimed in stunned surprise. "Old Hornby, dead? I'm sorry to hear that, I really am. How'd it happen? And what the devil was Miss Potter doing up at Holly How?" Although why he should be surprised, he didn't know. The lady seemed to enjoy tramping about the countryside and turning up in unexpected places. Only a few days before, he'd encountered her when he went up to the little lake behind Oatmeal Crag to do a spot of fishing. She was there, sketching mushrooms or something of the sort, and they'd had a pleasant conversation.

"She'd gone with Jennings to fetch some sheep she'd bought," the captain replied. "She's restocking that farm of hers, you know. As to how Hornby came to fall, that's not entirely clear." He glanced at the doctor. "The coroner has agreed to an inquest. Butters thinks there might have been foul play."

"Foul play!" Will exclaimed.

"He was whacked across the shoulders with a stick or

something of the sort," the doctor said. "The corpse is sporting a substantial bruise."

"That's a sad business," Will said. He tamped tobacco into his pipe and lit it. "Mind you, Hornby was a difficult chap. I've certainly had my share of disagreements with him over the years. But he was a steady fellow," he added, pulling on his pipe, "and always went by the rules—much to the irritation of some."

Having been a solicitor for nearly a decade, Will had had the opportunity to disagree with a great many people. The trick, of course, was to remain on friendly terms with as many as possible, even with those who were arrayed on the opposite side of a particularly thorny legal issue. Will made it a practice to be amiable and even-handed with all, no matter which side they were on, and over the years, the habit had usually paid off in goodwill.

" 'The irritation of some,' " the captain mused thoughtfully. "I say, Heelis, I find that remark intriguing. Who do you think might have had it in for the old fellow?"

"That's hard to say," Will replied. "There was that business with Toby Teathor last winter. Remember? Ben had him up before the magistrate for stealing cider."

"That's true," said the doctor. "Ben had a fierce row or two with fell-walkers, as well. They left his gates open. And then, of course, there's Isaac Chance. Now that Ben's gone, there's nothing standing between him and Holly How Farm. Lady Longford will be glad to let him have it."

"I've always believed that Chance had something to do with that barn burning," the captain said, "but there was no evidence on which he could be charged. And the cows—no proof there, either." He reached into the pocket of his jacket. "However, in this case, we have this."

He held out a clay pipe, of the sort that country people in England had smoked for centuries. In the last half-century, as briar pipes became more readily available and people took to smoking cheaper cigarettes, clay pipes had begun to be seen as old-fashioned and countrified. Now, they were chiefly smoked by older people, both men and women.

Will took the pipe and turned it in his fingers. "So Hornby was smoking whilst he tramped around on Holly How. I don't see what that proves."

"He didn't smoke," the doctor said. He put down his teacup and ran his hand through his graying hair. "That's the thing, you see, Will. He gave up smoking some years ago, on my advice. And when Ben Hornby made up his mind to do a thing, you know, he did it. Stubborn as the day is long."

"Ah," Will said again. He frowned. "I don't suppose there was anything overtly odd about his death. Any sign of a struggle, I mean, at the point where he fell."

Miles shook his head. "I had a look around and didn't see anything. I certainly would like to talk with the owner of that pipe. You've noticed the initials on it, I suppose. H. S."

"Yes. Highly revealing, one might think, if one happened to be a Scotland Yard detective." Will grinned. "H. S., you know, stands for Hiram Swift."

"I didn't know," the captain said, adding eagerly, "Hiram Swift, eh? You're sure of that? Never heard of the man. Is he from this area?"

Will chuckled. "Not a person, worse luck for you, Miles. Hiram Swift is the name of a pottery not far from Ambleside."

"There you are, Woodcock," the doctor broke in with a dry laugh. "That's your answer."

"Hiram Swift has been making brick and tile—and to-bacco pipes—for a half century or better," Will went on. "The clay pipes are mostly smoked by country people, I should think. Some claim they're superior, although I can't say, being a briar man myself." He put the pipe to his nose and sniffed. "You might come closer to tracking the owner of this one if you focused on the tobacco, though."

The captain whistled. "A regular Sherlock Holmes, aren't you? What's so distinctive about that tobacco?"

"You don't recognize it?" Will asked, in mock surprise. "Why, I'm astonished. It's Brown Twist, you know, manufactured by Samuel Gawith, right across the lake, in Kendal. Brown Number Four, if my nose doesn't fool me, cherry flavored." He sniffed again, deeply. "Yes, cherry, without a doubt. I'm partial to rum," he added, handing the pipe back.

"Well, I'd say that narrows down the field a goodish bit," the captain replied with an ironic chuckle. "I'm looking for a country man who favors Hiram Swift clay pipes and Brown Number Four, with a cherry—"

He was interrupted by a light rap on the door. It opened, and Samuel Sackett came in. "Ah, Vicar," all three men said together, and stood.

"Oh, don't get up, don't get up," said the vicar hurriedly, taking off his hat and hanging it on the rack beside the door. He was a tall, stoop-shouldered man with thinning gray hair and a gentle, scholarly demeanor. "Ah, tea," he said, brightening. "Jolly thoughtful of you, Captain. No, no, I'll help myself—please don't bother."

"Any sign of our candidate along the way?" the captain inquired.

"As a matter of fact," the vicar replied, taking his cup to a chair and sitting down with a sigh, "I glimpsed Lady Longford's phaeton driving down the road just as I came into the hotel. Dr. Gainwell should be with us shortly." He shook his head, blinking rapidly. "A difficult business, this, I'm afraid. I spoke to her ladyship this morning, as you suggested, Captain. I fear that I accomplished very little, however, other than possibly antagonizing her. She appears quite determined that her man be offered the position."

"Unfortunate," the captain said.

"Indeed. And even more unfortunately, Miss Nash seems to have been informed that the offer has already been made and accepted." The vicar heaved a heavy sigh. "It is said in the village that she and her sister are preparing to leave for the south of England. The Braithwaites are said to be hoping to take their cottage."

"Leaving for the south of England!" Will exclaimed.

"I have never seen such a village for gossip," the captain said, looking grim. "I doubt very much that Miss Nash would contemplate taking another position without saying anything to us. But I should very much regret it if she and her sister felt any discomfort on our account." He went to the window and lifted the curtain. "Well, there's our candidate." He paused and added, with wry admiration, "My word, just look at the cut of that coat, will you? Saville Row, without a doubt. What an elegant chap he is!"

Will went to the window and looked over Woodcock's shoulder. The man climbing out of the phaeton looked to be in his late thirties, thin and fair-haired and very well dressed.

The vicar joined them. "And credentials as impeccable as the cut of his coat," he said gloomily. "I have the letters with me, should you care to review them. One is from the director of the London Missionary Society, attesting to Dr. Gainwell's outstanding achievements as a missionary. The other is from Dr. Palmer, a man of great reputation in the field of native peoples' education. Both are laudatory." He took a sheaf of papers out of his coat pocket and regarded them with distaste. "Exceptionally so, I'm afraid."

"I think we will look at the letters afterward," the captain said, in a resigned tone.

The interview took a little under thirty minutes, and was

followed by a tour of the schoolhouse and yard. Then Dr. Gainwell thanked them, bowed a polite farewell, climbed back into Lady Longford's waiting phaeton, and was driven in the direction of Tidmarsh Manor. The four trustees adjourned to the upstairs sitting room, where Captain Woodcock opened a bottle of sherry and poured a glass for each. The vicar produced Dr. Gainwell's credentials and letters and passed them around for the others to read. The captain put forward the letter that the former head teacher, Miss Crabbe, had written on Miss Nash's behalf. There were several moments of silence as the trustees digested these.

The captain laid aside Dr. Gainwell's papers and looked up. "Well," he said, glancing around, "what do you say?"

"He's certainly an impressive fellow," the vicar said unhappily. "Presents himself very well—although I must confess that I'm not entirely happy with his views on discipline. Rather more of a spare-the-rod-spoil-the-child man than I think absolutely necessary, for our Sawrey children, at least."

"Perhaps it's because of his missionary work," the doctor said with a dry cough. "Must have been a difficult challenge, teaching natives in those far-flung places. One might find oneself more eager to use the rod in such a situation. And the letters certainly provide an extraordinary endorsement." He turned to Will. "What do you say, Heelis?"

"Odd that he didn't talk more about his travels and experiences," Will replied thoughtfully. The vicar was right: Lady Longford's candidate had made a positive presentation, although Will was puzzled by some of his omissions. He seemed to have little to say about his years at Oxford, for instance, even when given the opportunity to do so. However, as far as Will was concerned, the matter still stood exactly as it had before the interview began, so there wasn't any use in debating the finer points of Gainwell's performance.

"I heard nothing to change my mind," he said flatly.

"Margaret Nash has taught in this school for nearly a decade, and is praised by everyone as a superior teacher. I move that we ask her to accept the position of head teacher forthwith."

"I shall second that," said the vicar promptly, in a tone of great relief. "Miss Nash always has the interests of her students at heart, and disciplines with love, as well as firmness."

"And I agree," the doctor said. "Gainwell might do very well, but Miss Nash will do better."

"Well, then, I'll make it unanimous," the captain said, and lifted his sherry glass. "Gentlemen, to Miss Nash."

"Miss Nash, indeed," said the vicar happily, and they drank. When they set their glasses down again, however, he said in a more apprehensive voice, "Now that it is decided, I suppose we must settle on who is to tell her ladyship—and Miss Nash, of course—of our decision. The sooner, the better, too." He coughed delicately. "If I may, I will remind us that I approached Lady Longford this morning on the matter, and was soundly set down. I should very much prefer it if someone else would undertake the task of telling her."

The doctor lifted both hands. "Not I, gentlemen. Her ladyship is my patient. I must deal with her on a professional basis."

The captain reached into his pocket. "Well, then," he said with a grin at Will, "it appears to be between you and me, Heelis." He took out a coin.

"But she's my client," Will protested. "I have to work with her professionally, too."

The captain ignored him. "Heads or tails, Will?"

"Heads," Will said with a sigh. The captain tossed and held out the coin for Vicar Sackett's examination.

"Tails," the vicar announced, with a sympathetic look at Will. "I'm afraid you've lost, Mr. Heelis."

Will scowled. "The devil," he said. "Begging your pardon, Vicar," he added.

The vicar sighed. "I don't quarrel with your description, my boy." He paused. "It will give you an opportunity to see the girl, though. She was doing lessons this morning, and I missed her. Ask to see her, and tell me how she is."

Will nodded. He was also curious about the welfare of Lady Longford's granddaughter, Caroline, not only because his firm had handled the situation, but because he had been a friend of Caroline's father, Bruce. Will had gone to meet Caroline when she got off the ship at Liverpool and brought her to Tidmarsh Manor. She had been a quiet, serious youngster, not frightened, as some would have been, but watchful and observant. It would be good to see how she'd fared in the three months since she'd arrived.

The vicar took his hat off the rack. "Well, then, if we've finished our business, I must be on my way."

"I'd like to suggest that Will first convey our offer to Miss Nash this afternoon," the captain said, as the four of them started down the stairs. "I don't for a minute think there's any truth to the rumor about her leaving. But it would be just as well to have her 'yes' firmly in hand before we say 'no' to Dr. Gainwell."

"An excellent suggestion," exclaimed the vicar. He bade them goodbye, the doctor went to fetch his gig, and after a few moments, Will and the captain went out to the stable together. As they left the hotel, a seedy-looking old man in a dark shirt, brown corduroy trousers, and dirty canvas jerkin shuffled out of the bar. He caught up to them as they stood beside the captain's motorcar, talking.

"Beggin' your pardon, Cap'n Woodcock," he said in a low, gritty voice. "I got something I think you'd be interested in hearin'."

"Hullo, Charlie," said the captain with a grin. "Haven't seen you around for a while."

"Been out of pocket," said Charlie evasively, tipping back his cap with his thumb.

"In jail, eh? Somebody caught you borrowing a chicken, maybe?"

"Mappen." Charlie glanced over his shoulder as if he did not want to be overheard. Seeing nothing but a boy carrying a bucket of water, he turned to frown suspiciously at Will. "Who's this?"

"A friend," the captain said. "He's all right. What do you have that might interest me?"

Charlie leaned close, and Will could smell the fruity rankness of onions, ale, and tobacco on his breath. "I 'member how you feel 'bout badger-baiting, Cap'n. Thought you might like to know there's a session planned for tomorrow night, since it's known to be a night you reg'lar go to Kendal." He winked. "Thought there might be a lit'le something in it for me, if I was to tell you where and when."

At the mention of badger-baiting, Will saw the captain's jaw tighten, and was not surprised. On the surface, the twin Sawreys looked to be cozy hamlets where disagreeable things rarely happened and there was nothing more ominous in the offing than an evening of darts and drinking at the local pub. Near and Far Sawrey had their dark side, however, as both the solicitor and the Justice of the Peace well knew. After darkness fell, men often gathered in sheds and barns, where unsavory activities took place. Cock-fighting, for instance, and setting dogs on rats, and badger-baiting—all accompanied by a goodly amount of ale-drinking, and frequent fisticuffs, and more cash wagered on the outcome than the participants could afford to lose.

Captain Woodcock, as Justice of the Peace, had done what he could to stop these practices. It wasn't just a matter of cruelty to animals, of course, although there was certainly that. Animal baiting of any kind had been against the law for seventy years, but stamping it out completely was difficult, for there was not much in the way of entertainment in the villages, and some of the men considered the baitings their just reward for a hard week's work. The major problem, as the captain saw it, was the betting that went on at these events. Every farthing wagered and lost was a farthing that would not go to buy milk or shoes for a child, or bread for a family's supper. Will shared the captain's concern. Wives and children had it hard enough without seeing the family's meager livelihood gambled away, whilst the frustrations of loss in the cock-pit often led to brutal violence at home.

The captain regarded the man. "I daresay there could be something in it for you, old fellow," he said quietly. "Where's it to be?"

Charlie shifted his plug of tobacco from one cheek to the other and a crafty look came over his face. "How much?"

"Tomorrow night, is it?" the captain inquired casually, pulling on his motoring gloves. "Well, then, I suggest that we meet at my house and you take me to this place. That's when you'll get your reward."

Charlie put on a crestfallen look. "Don't trust me, then?"

The captain shrugged and reached for his goggles, lying on the motorcar's seat. "You know me for a careful man, Charlie. A half-hour after dark, shall we say? Come round to my side entrance. I'll be waiting for you."

"I'll think on't," Charlie said. He turned, stuck his hands in his pockets, and sauntered off, whistling carelessly.

When he was gone, Will turned to his friend. "Sounds like it might be an exciting evening," he said. "You can count me in on the action."

The captain grinned. "I thought you'd be interested.

Shall we invite the constable, as well? A little more muscle probably won't go amiss—although we won't mention the plan to Charlie. Might frighten him off." He bent over and inserted the crank into the front of the engine. "Stand well back," he cautioned, and gave the crank a hard turn. The engine whirred, grumbled, and stopped. He turned the crank hard again, and this time the motorcar, noisily, sprang to life. Beside it, Will's horse gave a shrill neigh and shied away, and Will went to grab the bridle.

"Thanks again, Will," the captain shouted over the noise. "Give my regards to Miss Nash. And good luck with Lady Longford." He pulled down his goggles, seated his cap firmly on his head, and drove out of the stable. A moment later, Will got onto his horse and rode off.

Neither of the two men noticed the slight figure of the boy, who had put down his bucket and was standing in the corner of the stable, listening intently.

22

Mr. Heelis Delivers the News

Margaret Nash was upstairs, taking blouses and skirts out of the closet and folding them carefully into her leather valise. There had been a rain shower earlier in the afternoon, and the air was hot and sultry. Margaret's hair was plastered to her forehead, her skirt had dust on it, and she felt sticky all over. But it would soon be teatime, and she wanted to get the largest part of the packing done this afternoon, so she and Annie could leave early the next morning.

Her sister appeared at the bedroom door, a look of consternation on her thin face. "Maggie," she said uneasily. "Mr. Heelis is here. I've put him in the parlor."

"Oh, dear," Margaret said, her stomach turning suddenly queasy. She looked down at herself. "I shall have to change and—" She ran to the mirror and picked up a comb. "And my hair, oh dear! And tea. Oh, yes, of course, Annie, go put the kettle on for—"

"He said he hadn't time to stop for tea, Maggie. I think he's in a bit of a hurry. P'rhaps you'd better just go down." Annie gave her a long look, and Margaret read in her sister's eyes the sick misgiving she herself felt. "Would you like me to come with you?" Annie asked, and laughed a little. "Whatever happens, I can at least hold your hand."

Margaret straightened and pulled in her breath. There was no point in flying into hysterics. The world wouldn't end just because a highly qualified man who had the support of the wealthiest woman in the district had been appointed over her. She was an experienced teacher, and if need be, she would look for another position. She wouldn't find a school she loved as much as Sawrey School, and she and Annie would never in all their lives have another cottage that suited them as perfectly as this one. But life would go on—it always did.

"No, thank you, dear," she said, and managed a bleak smile. "I would rather face this on my own. But I shouldn't be sorry to have a cup of tea after he's gone. You can hold my hand then. I'm sure I'll need it."

Annie, usually so self-composed, burst into tears and fled in the direction of the kitchen. Margaret went toward the parlor, rolling down her sleeves and brushing cobwebs from her skirt. Mr. Heelis—a good-looking man, well built, with thick brown hair and a mild expression—was seated on the sofa, his long legs uncomfortably crossed, his hat on his knees. He scrambled to his feet when he saw her.

"Good afternoon, Mr. Heelis," Margaret said, with as much calm as she could muster. She smoothed her hair with her hand. "I've been packing, and I'm afraid that I'm not entirely presentable."

"Packing?" Mr. Heelis asked nervously. "You're not going away, I hope."

The annual holiday had been the subject of much discussion between the sisters. Because of the expenses of Annie's illness, they had planned to spend the summer in Sawrey. But after Bertha Stubbs had brought the news about Dr. Gainwell, they had decided to take a few days at the seaside. If nothing else, it would give them both some variety in their routine and a respite from the unending village gossip.

"Yes, we are," Margaret said. She hesitated, not wanting to share all this with Mr. Heelis, who would certainly not be interested in these private details. "My sister reports that you've already said no to tea, but—"

"That's right," Mr. Heelis said, hat in hand. Margaret's heart sank when she saw his anxious expression. She knew him to be a kind man, and it would pain him to give her bad news. He swallowed. "I'm sorry to be abrupt, but I have another errand this afternoon. I've come on behalf of the trustees to—"

"Please," Margaret said, taking the chair beside the sofa. "Won't you sit down?" Her knees felt shaky, and this was not a conversation she wanted to have standing up.

"Thank you." Mr. Heelis sat back down, replacing his hat on his knees. "I've come, Miss Nash, to tell you that the trustees—"

There was a sudden crash, and a loud shriek.

"Annie?" Margaret cried, starting to her feet in a panic. "Annie? Are you all right?" The only answer was a low moan, and Margaret ran out of the parlor and straight to the kitchen, Mr. Heelis following close behind her.

"Oh, Annie," Margaret cried, standing aghast at the door. It was apparent in an instant that her sister had dropped the hot kettle, spilling boiling water across the table and splashing it onto the floor. "Are you hurt?"

"N . . . no," Annie managed. "Not much, anyway. Only my . . . my arm." She held out her left arm. There was a large patch of red skin and the scalded flesh was already beginning to blister.

"Cold water," said Mr. Heelis authoritatively, "and bicarbonate of soda, in a paste." He jammed his hat onto his head. "I saw Dr. Butters's horse in front of the Arms as I came along. I'm sure he's still there—I'll go and fetch him."

"Oh, would you, please?" Margaret asked gratefully, and Mr. Heelis disappeared through the kitchen door. "Put your arm in the sink, Annie, dear. I'll pour some cold water over it. Where's the bicarbonate?"

"What did he say, Maggie?" Annie looked up at her, her eyes blurry with tears. "About the job, I mean."

"He didn't," Margaret said. "He was just starting to give me the bad news when—"

The door was flung open.

"Miss Nash," Mr. Heelis said urgently, "what I came to tell you was that the trustees very much want you to be our next head teacher. I hope you and your sister are not packing to leave Sawrey, and that you're not planning to give up your cottage. Now, I'm off to fetch the doctor. You can give me your answer when I return."

And the door slammed shut again.

Margaret stared after him, dazed. "Did you . . . did you hear what I just heard, Annie?"

"I think so," Annie said, her eyes large and glowing. "Oh, Maggie, this is wonderful! Too wonderful for words!"

And burn or no, she flung her arms around her sister with a glad cry.

At Tidmarsh Manor, Lady Longford was taking tea in the library, with the windows closed and the red brocade draperies pulled against the afternoon heat. She sat stiffly in the gloom, feeling very unwell and even crosser than usual.

Dudley, her ancient spaniel, lay on the floor beside a potted palm, no doubt feeling as out of sorts as she did. The dog, who was named for her late husband, always seemed to wear an accusing look, exactly as Lord Longford had done in his later years. Miss Martine, silent and dour-visaged, presided over the tea table. Dr. Gainwell had not come down yet. Neither had Caroline, and Lady Longford wondered where she was.

Emily opened the door and announced, in her girlish voice, "Mr. Heelis to see you, your ladyship."

"Ah, Mr. Heelis," Lady Longford said, replacing her teacup in its saucer. The firm of Heelis and Heelis had been the Longfords' solicitors for three decades, and whilst she still preferred the formality of the old Mr. Heelis, the young Mr. Heelis (his nephew) was an acceptable substitute. "You have come to convey the trustees' approval of Dr. Gainwell's new position, I suppose," she added.

"Lemon or sugar?" inquired Miss Martine in a whisper, her hand poised over a filled cup.

"I don't believe I'll have tea, thank you," Mr. Heelis replied. "Hello, Dudley," he said, bending over to pet the old spaniel. He sat down next to Lady Longford. "I hope that your ladyship is well."

"Not very," she said, with a peevish cough, "as you can no doubt see." She picked up her cup, felt her hand tremble, and put it down again. "But you did not come to inquire about my health, I daresay."

Mr. Heelis cast an inquiring glance around the room. "The vicar particularly wanted me to ask after Miss Caroline. Will she be down shortly?"

"I assume so," Lady Longford replied, with a slight smile. She was not surprised that Mr. Heelis should ask to see her granddaughter, for he and the vicar were responsible for the girl's coming to Tidmarsh Manor—and, to tell the truth, Lady Longford now found herself grateful for their persistence. Miss Martine was busily searching for a suitable school for Caroline, but the longer Lady Longford observed the girl, the more she began to think that perhaps she should keep her at the Manor, at least for a year or two. Caroline was a great deal like her father, after all, and something had begun to stir in her heart toward—

"The girl is not here." Miss Martine cleared her throat. "I am sorry to report that she is not to be found."

"Not to be—" Lady Longford stopped, not sure that she had heard correctly.

"Not to be found?" Mr. Heelis echoed, looking from one of them to the other. "I don't understand."

"As I said," Miss Martine returned, in her meek, docile voice, "Caroline is not to be found. She was told to go to her room after lunch, and she obviously disobeyed." She pursed her lips and looked penitently at Lady Longford. "Please forgive me for not telling your ladyship immediately. But you were . . . indisposed, and every effort is being made to find her. The house has already been thoroughly searched, and Beever and Dr. Gainwell have gone to look for her in the woods beyond the garden."

Lady Longford pulled in her breath. "I should have been told," she said sharply. "It was wrong of you to keep this from me."

"I could only do what I felt was right," Miss Martine said sadly. "I know how deeply you are troubled by Caroline's willful disobedience, and—"

"Disobedience?" Mr. Heelis asked sharply. "That is not a word I would use to describe the girl, Miss Martine. I was with her for several days when she first arrived at Liverpool, you know. I would call her inquisitive, yes. And intelligent and resourceful. But hardly disobedient."

"I trust that your ladyship will not trouble yourself,"

Miss Martine went on calmly, as if Mr. Heelis had not spoken. "The girl has no doubt just wandered off, and will shortly be found."

Not worry! Lady Longford thought with alarm of the bleak, windy fell, and the wild wood that rose up behind Tidmarsh Manor and spilt over the top of Claife Heights and all the way down to Lake Windermere. She herself had been lost in that wood once, when she had first come to live at Tidmarsh Manor. She had counted herself lucky when she found her way back.

"But the fells are dangerous!" Mr. Heelis protested. "And it's easy to lose one's way in the woods. What's more, it's been raining this afternoon. Is Caroline in the habit of going outside the garden?"

"She is in the habit," Miss Martine said thinly, "of disobeying. I beg you, Mr. Heelis, please do not concern yourself."

Lady Longford, now feeling much worse than before, shifted uncomfortably in her chair. "I'm sure that the girl will be found and brought in before you leave," she said, trying to make the best of things. "Now, tell me what you and the other trustees thought of Dr. Gainwell."

As an experienced solicitor, Will Heelis was quite capable of tact and diplomacy, and under usual circumstances, would no doubt have given his reply the most careful consideration. At the moment, however, he was preoccupied, as if he were thinking of the girl. He scarcely seemed to be paying attention when he said, in an offhand tone, "Oh, that business. The trustees have settled the matter. They have offered the position to Miss Nash, and she has accepted."

"To . . . Miss Nash?" Lady Longford asked incredulously.

"You must be joking!" Miss Martine cried, jumping to her feet and knocking over the pitcher of milk. Dudley hoisted himself up and hurried over to lick the puddle on the carpet.

Mr. Heelis looked up, startled. "Forgive me," he said. "I was thinking of Caroline, or I should not have answered so carelessly." He took a deep breath. "The trustees were of course impressed by Dr. Gainwell's outstanding educational preparation and experience. He is quite a . . . quite a re-markable man. After extensive debate, however, we concluded that Miss Nash is much more suited to this rural school. She has learnt to work within the school's limited resources, she knows the children's abilities, and—"

"But *I* am the one who proposed him!" Lady Longford cried, clenching her fists in angry frustration. How *dare* those stupid, stubborn trustees go against her wishes! She gathered together all her strength and spoke in a low, steely voice. "After all Lord Longford and I have done for this village, it is inconceivable that the trustees should—"

"I quite understand your ladyship's feelings," Mr. Heelis interrupted firmly, getting to his feet. "However, the decision has been made, and in the end, I rather think Dr. Gainwell will be glad. He surely has other, more challenging opportunities than our little village school. When I see him, I shall offer the trustees' best wishes and their heartfelt gratitude for his—"

"Oh, rubbish," Lady Longford said wearily. She waved her hand. "I don't want to hear any more of this, Heelis. You can tell the trustees that I am angry and disappointed. They needn't look to me for any more support." On his way back to the potted palm, Dudley glanced accusingly at her, as if to remind her that she had not been as supportive as she might.

"I will convey your feelings," Mr. Heelis said gravely. "I know the trustees will be distressed to hear that they have disappointed you."

"But, Lady Longford!" Miss Martine protested, half in

tears. "Surely you aren't going to give in so easily. Surely you—"

"I don't want to hear anything from you, either, Maribel," Lady Longford snapped. "I am tired of being pushed around. I'm going to bed. Send Emily to help me. And go down to the kitchen and tell Mrs. Beever that I want a cup of ginger tea and another slice of that ginger cake. And if she has any candied ginger, she can send that up, too. Right now!"

As Miss Martine rushed from the room, Mr. Heelis stood. "I am sorry to have been the bearer of bad news," he said. "The trustees would not have disappointed you except for a very good reason." As he looked down at her, Lady Longford saw the concern written on his honest face. "If you will forgive me," he went on quietly, "I can see that your ladyship is not well. When I left the village, Dr. Butters was there. Shall I send him up to see you?"

"No," Lady Longford said, and then, as Emily came into the room to help her out of her chair, she changed her mind. "Oh, very well, Heelis. Send him up." To herself, she muttered, "Wherever on earth can the child have gone?"

Mr. Heelis went to the door. "I shall be returning," he said, "as quickly as I can, with a team of searchers."

"Yes, searchers, Heelis, by all means," Lady Longford said. "Emily, mind my shoulder, you wretched girl!"

23

Miss Potter Presents a Clue

Miles Woodcock was at the typewriter in his study, finishing a report on the action the trustees had taken that afternoon and thinking with some puzzlement about the interview with Dr. Gainwell. He had not wanted to make a point of it with the other trustees, since it was clear that there was no contest between Miss Nash and Lady Longford's candidate, but he had felt that the interview left some major questions unanswered. Dr. Gainwell had, for instance, been surprisingly vague about his studies at Oxford and unclear about the circumstances of his missionary work. What's more, he hadn't seemed prepared to deal with questions about the school curriculum or his philosophy of education, although he did have certain views on discipline. In fact, one would almost have thought—

But it did not matter. The man was not their choice, and

THE TALE OF HOLLY HOW 191

they had interviewed him only as a courtesy. In the report, it was sufficient to say that the trustees had considered two candidates and selected Miss Nash, whose work was well known to all. He rolled the paper out of the typewriter, signed the report, and blotted his signature. There. That was done, and Miss Nash could get on with her planning for the year.

He heard a light tap at the door, and his sister put her head through. "Miles, my dear, forgive me for interrupting you, but Miss Potter is here. She says she has something she needs to show you, and urgently."

Miles stood. "Not an interruption," he said. "I'm all finished." He smiled. "Hello, Miss Potter. Come in, do. Dimity, why don't you bring us a cup of—"

"No tea for me, thank you, Miss Woodcock," Miss Potter said. Dimity, with a tactful nod, left the room, closing the door behind her.

Miles had originally shared the view that many of the male villagers held of Miss Potter: that a city woman had no business taking on a working farm, especially one that needed so much attention and improvement. But he had changed his mind last October, when she had helped to recover the Constable painting stolen from Anvil Cottage, and through the months after that, as he witnessed the steady, no-nonsense determination with which she dealt with challenges at Hill Top, and with people like Bernard Biddle, the building contractor who was notorious for causing trouble on his jobs. Beatrix Potter, Miles had decided, was a rare and unusual woman, and he was glad that she had come to Sawrey.

As he went to greet her, Miles noticed that Miss Potter's round cheeks were even pinker than usual, and under her straw hat, her brown hair was in disarray. Her clothing showed signs of being recently wet, and she was carrying something that looked like a pair of long-handled metal tongs.

"Thank you for allowing me to barge in," she said, in her light, high voice. "I won't take up much of your time. But I do think it's important, you see. It's about the death of Mr. Hornby."

"Of course," Miles said gravely. He gestured to a chair. "Sit down, please, Miss Potter. What's that you have in your hand?"

Instead of sitting, she put the tongs down on the desk.

"Miss Barwick and I went to Holly How to look for the sheep I've bought from Mr. Hornby. After a brief encounter with Isaac Chance—"

"Ah. You've met the man, then. What do you think?"

Miss Potter pressed her lips together. "I think," she said decidedly, "that I should not be at all surprised to find my sheep at Oldfield Farm. Of course, I have no proof, only a suspicion. But I intend to have a look."

"I hope you won't go unaccompanied," Miles said, in a warning tone. "I suspect that Chance put a match to the Holly How barn last winter. And he might have been responsible for what looked like an accidental poisoning of Hornby's milk cows. But there was never enough evidence to charge him." He looked squarely at Miss Potter. "Do say you won't go to Oldfield alone."

Instead of replying, Miss Potter pointed to the items on the table. "Miss Barwick and I climbed up the hill to the spot from which Mr. Hornby fell. The Crooks' terrier was with us, and he nosed out the tongs lying amongst the brambles about thirty paces away. It looked as if someone had slung them there. I must confess that I'm at a loss about these tongs. They look rather like fireplace tongs, but—"

"But they're not," Miles said distastefully. "Look at those sharp points. They're badger tongs."

"*Badger* tongs?"

"Designed to catch and hold badgers."

"Oh," Miss Potter said, adding, in a matter-of-fact tone, "By badger diggers, I suppose."

Miles raised both eyebrows. "You know about that?"

"I know that the badger sett at the rock quarry on Hill Top property was recently destroyed," she said grimly. "Now that you've told me what these tongs are used for, I wonder if their owner might have been planning to dig the sett at Holly How. Mr. Jennings says that Lord Longford wouldn't allow the sett to be meddled with, and Mr. Hornby continued to follow his wishes." She frowned. "I wonder— do you think perhaps Mr. Hornby might have confronted a badger digger on Holly How, and there was some kind of altercation? Perhaps Mr. Hornby grabbed the tongs and flung them away, and then fell, or was pushed, over the edge."

Miles stared at her, thinking of the welt across old Ben Hornby's shoulders—a welt that might have been raised by a pair of badger tongs. "By Jove, Miss Potter," he said at last, "you might be right."

"I imagine I am," Miss Potter said. She looked down at the tongs. "Is there any way of knowing whose these are?"

"There might be a tool mark," Miles said, picking them up and reaching for the magnifying glass that lay on his desk. "Many countrymen mark all their tools. If somebody makes off with a hammer or a rake, it's easy to prove who owns it."

Miss Potter sniffed. "I shouldn't think a badger digger would want to advertise his ownership."

"It's against the law to bait badgers," Miles replied, "but it's not against the law to capture them. Where badgers are concerned, I'm afraid that Lord Longford was an exception, rather than the rule. Generally speaking, farmers don't like the animals, because they think they destroy crops and gardens. So they're trapped and dug and generally harassed. And there it is!" he exclaimed triumphantly, having found what he was looking for. He put the tongs on the desk and handed Miss Potter the magnifying lens. "Look at the joint where the handles are bolted together."

Miss Potter bent over, studying the tongs. "It looks like the letters J and O."

"Indeed," Miles said, setting his jaw. "And I think I know who—"

The door opened once more and Miles glanced up. A tall figure was framed in the doorway, his bowler hat under his arm. "I hope I'm not interrupting anything," Will Heelis said. "Miss Woodcock told me to come on in."

"Hullo, Heelis," Miles said. "Have a look at Miss Potter's clue. She discovered this pair of badger tongs on Holly How, lying in the briars not twenty paces—"

"Thirty," said Miss Potter. "How do you do, Mr. Heelis?"

"Very well, thank you, Miss Potter." Heelis smiled. "It's good to see you again. How are you getting on with Mr. Biddle?"

"Not at all well," Miss Potter said, with a hint of a smile. "If things don't improve soon, I fear I shall have to take drastic action."

"Not thirty paces away from the cliff-top where Hornby fell," Miles went on, in a louder voice. He held out the magnifying glass to Heelis. "The tool-mark is there," he said, pointing. "The letters J and O."

Heelis took the magnifying glass and bent over the tongs. "My word," he muttered, after a moment. "So it is." He straightened, frowning. "Found on the cliff-top, you say? So you're thinking that—"

"—That the owner of these tongs knows how Ben Hornby died," Miles said. "What do you say?"

"It sounds likely," Heelis said slowly. "Quite likely, I must say. And it doesn't take much to guess at the identity of their owner. Miss Potter, you are to be complimented on your find. You may have solved our mystery." He cleared his throat, looking first to Miss Potter and then to Miles. "I have other news, however. And not good news, I'm afraid."

Miles frowned. "You're not about to tell me that Miss Nash rejected the trustees' offer, I hope."

"No, no, nothing like that. She's quite pleased. And I delivered our rejection to Lady Longford."

"So the trustees have decided in favor of Miss Nash, then?" Miss Potter put in eagerly.

"Yes, we did," Miles replied. To Heelis, he said, "How did her ladyship take the announcement?"

"She's angry, of course. And rather seriously ill, I think." Heelis frowned. "But that's not the point. The point is that the girl is gone. Caroline, I mean. Lady Longford's granddaughter."

"Gone?" echoed Miss Potter, her blue eyes opening wide. "Gone . . . *where*?"

"Nobody seems to know." Heelis threw up his hands. "I'm told that they've searched the Manor, and that Beever is out now, searching the woods. But Lady Longford is too ill to take much notice, and Miss Martine doesn't seem greatly concerned. And to tell God's honest truth," he added, in a burst of feeling, "I don't trust that woman to have Caroline's best interests at heart."

"I agree with you, Mr. Heelis," Miss Potter said gravely. "I spoke with Caroline this morning. She said that Miss Martine pinches."

"She . . . pinches?" Miles asked, at a loss.

Miss Potter's lips tightened. "It is a method that governesses use to discipline headstrong young women. I know of it from my own experience, for I was exceptionally headstrong, as a girl." She looked anxiously from Miles to Heelis. "But we mustn't stand here talking, when Caroline may be lost!"

"Yes," Heelis said, turning to Miles. "Remember that little boy who wandered away from the Sawrey Hotel? I think we had better assemble the men and dogs, without delay."

Miles put down the tongs. He remembered that lost child very well. They had called out every man in the district to help search, and had found nothing. Somewhere, up there . . . he shuddered. "I agree," he said soberly. "The wood is a wild place. I shouldn't like to spend the night up there, myself."

"To make matters worse, there's another storm coming," Heelis put in. "Thunderheads are piling up in the west. We'll have rain by sunset—a hard rain, from the look of it."

"Oh, dear," Miss Potter said. And then, with determination, "Caroline *must* be found! As quickly as possible!"

"We'll go over to the Arms and ask Mr. Barrow to ring the bell," Miles said.

"Right," Heelis agreed, already heading for the door. "That'll bring everyone out in a hurry."

Mr. Barrow had two children of his own, and the idea that the young Miss Longford might be lost somewhere in Cuckoo Brow Wood was enough to galvanize him into action. He pulled a hand bell out from under the bar, ran out on the steps, and began to ring it as hard as he could. Within the next few minutes, the villagers spilt out of their houses and gathered in front of the Arms to find out what had happened. Hearing the news and realizing the urgency of the situation, the men rushed home to collect rain gear and lanterns, whilst the wives (since the men would miss their suppers) hurried to make meat-and-cheese sandwiches and brew jugs of hot tea to be taken along. Thirty minutes later, about three dozen men were on their way out of the village by horse and cart and on foot, heading in the direction of Cuckoo Brow Wood.

Will Heelis had been wrong about the rain, however. The storm did not wait until sunset—or, rather, the hour at which the sun usually set, for dark clouds had completely covered the sky, and the evening was as black as the blackest night. A fierce eddy of wind swept up dust and sticks and dried leaves and sent them whirling through the air, and there was a rushing sound in the great beech trees as the coming storm whipped their branches. A jagged streak of fire split the dark sky over Esthwaite Water.

And just as the men started up Stony Lane, the heavens opened and the rain came down with a crash and a roar.

24

Bosworth Is Interrupted

One of the unique features of The Brockery, Bosworth Badger had always thought, was the hostelry's many fine doors. There was of course the grand main entrance, where the formal coming and going and greeting of guests took place, with its handsome umbrella stand just inside the door, and on the outside, a fine iron bell-pull and thick cocoa-fiber doormat and an engraved brass plate, announcing:

The Brockery

There were, in addition, a half-dozen informal side entrances, each one conveniently located at the end of a meandering corridor and, on the outside, cleverly camouflaged by heather and rocks. These were used by the occupants on a daily basis, to avoid tracking dirt and leaves into the front hall. There, one found pairs of galoshes lined up in a row, and caps and coats hung from pegs. And at the kitchen entry, there was a special shelf with a bucket and basin and towel for washing up, in case one came in muddy from the garden, and a place to put parcels.

And, finally, there were the many unmarked emergency exits that opened onto the rocky rear of Holly How, which was overrun by tangled briars. These were almost never used as entries, but they were convenient for any of The Brockery's boarders who felt the need to make a hasty exit without attracting attention. (The Badger Fourth Rule of Thumb requires that badgers take no notice of friends and colleagues who find they must depart without begging leave.) Emergency exits were also available for use in the unfortunate circumstance that all of the occupants of the sett had to be quickly evacuated—under attack by badger diggers, for instance. Luckily, this had not happened on Holly How, which had been for quite a long time under the protection of the Longford family, but one always had to be prepared.

This evening, after finishing his supper, Bosworth was ambling about the back hallways of The Brockery. Wearing his oldest dressing gown and a pair of down-at-the-heel slippers, with a candlestick in one paw, a notebook in the other, and a pencil behind his ear, the badger was intent on completing the annual Survey of Renovation Requirements. He had been intending to complete this important bit of regular business for some time. He had, in fact, got a start on it at least twice this week, and once the week before, but it was a boring task and a very dirty one, and somehow it never seemed quite pressing enough to demand his attention.

The Survey required him to inspect the entire sett, which meant going from room to room, through hallways and corridors and passages and galleries and arcades and chambers, some vaulted and very grand, others low-ceilinged and cellarlike, with nothing much to recommend them. Many of these rooms had not been occupied since Bosworth's grandfather's time, and, truth be told, were dreadfully shabby and in need of a good turning out. The dry dust on the floors rose up in clouds and settled on the badger's dressing gown and got into his mouth and nose, sending him into a fury of sneezes. It was not a job for which he could summon much enthusiasm, and he was easily distracted from it.

And at just this moment, having jotted the note that Room 37 required both whitewashing *and* a new carpet, he was distracted once again—this time, by the sound of someone scritching and scratching and stumbling in a hasty way down the sloping corridor outside the chamber, from the direction of the out-of-doors. Feeling rather cross, he went to the door and put out his head to see who it was. This particular corridor had not been in use for quite a while, so it was very dusty, *very*. And here was someone, or something, scrambling in from the outside and stirring up dust—such a thick cloud of dust, in fact, that whoever was doing it could not even be seen.

"*Who,*" Bosworth spoke sternly to the cloud, "*are you?*"

"*Please, sir,*" the cloud said, in a high, piping voice. "*I'm Tuppenny, sir.*"

Bosworth stared. The creature that had emerged out of the settling dust was a . . . well, to tell the truth, Bosworth didn't know what it was. He had met all sorts of animals in his life—stoats and weasels and ferrets and foxes and rats and mice and voles and squirrels and otters—but he had never seen a creature like this, as fat as butter and round as a ball, with long orange fur that was completely disheveled and coated with dust, and black eyes and a twinkling nose and almost no ears at all. And no tail. Not a sign of a tail. The poor creature must have left it somewhere, although of course, a badger could not comment on this without violating the Badger Thirteenth Rule of Thumb: One must not inquire about missing ears or tails, because the world is full of traps and snares and animals are prone to be accidentally involved with them.

"*Tuppenny, eh?*" he said at last, in the sort of pitying tone that one might use to a creature who lacked a tail. "*That's a* who. What *are you?*"

"Please, sir," said Tuppenny, shook himself violently, and sneezed twice. "*I'm a guinea pig.*"

"*Go on,*" scoffed the badger, with a disbelieving laugh. "*Pigs don't have fur, especially orange fur. And they have snouts and very nice curly tails. I've seen all sorts of pig breeds, spotted and speckled and plain and fancy, and you are most definitely not a pig!*"

"*But I am a pig, sir,*" snuffled Tuppenny. Tears welled up in his eyes and trickled down his dusty cheeks. "*My ancestors came from South America, you see. At least, that's what I've been told.*"

"*Oh,*" Bosworth said, now genuinely sorry that he had offended the little chap, who couldn't help being whatever sort of ridiculous, tailless creature he was. "*Well, I'm sure that accounts for it, then,*" he went on, in a kindly, comforting tone. "*Pigs in South America are undoubtedly different from pigs in the north of England.*"

"*P'rhaps,*" said Tuppenny. "*If you'll excuse me for asking, sir, who are you? What are you?*"

"*I?*" asked the badger in some surprise, for he rather fancied that his sort were unmistakable. "*Why, I am a badger. Bosworth Badger XVII, at your service.*"

"*A badger?*" Tuppenny's black eyes grew enormous. "*But . . . but I thought badgers were fierce and unfriendly, like stoats and weasels.*"

"*Badgers can be fierce when fierce is called for. We are unfriendly when threatened, although for the most part, we are quite hospitable."* Bosworth smiled, to show that he was feeling neither fierce nor unfriendly at the moment. *"P'rhaps you're called Tuppenny because you're somewhat less than a guinea, eh?"* Then, fearing that this last remark was might have given offense, Bosworth hurried on. *"Have you come to stay for a few days, then?"*

"I'm not sure, sir," said Tuppenny dubiously, wiping his nose on his paw. *"Actually, I didn't intend to go anywhere at all, but the girl put me in a basket with a hole in the bottom and I squeezed out and went for a stroll. And then after a time I wasn't sure where I was, because all the rocks and brambles all looked alike, you see. And then it began to rain rather hard, and I thought I had better get in out of the wet, so I poked my head into a hole behind a rock, and the next thing I knew, I was tumbling down a very steep slope and when I had got to the bottom I found I couldn't climb up it again, no matter how hard I tried, and I was so frightened you just can't think, sir! So I just came along your hallway, which seems to be in need of a good sweeping out, although I daresay that's not your fault, of course, even though you are a badger. And now I'm here and—"*

"Rain?" whispered Bosworth urgently. *"Did you say it was raining?"*

The moment he had heard the word, his nose had begun to twitch, and he could smell that best and most compelling of all smells, the smell that a badger loves better than any other: the rich, sweet scent of rain-drenched earth and rain-washed air, of wet heather and damp fern and dripping bracken. The magical fragrance penetrated the dark and dusty and very dry hallways of The Brockery and called out to the badger in a sweetly seductive whisper, a slippery, sinuous, sibilant whisper: the enticing murmur of *"Earthwormsss! Earthwormsss!"*

Bosworth inhaled deeply. The whisper was a summons

that reached down into his very soul, tugging at him irresistibly, so that he found himself dropping his notebook and pencil and shedding his dressing gown and kicking off his slippers and muttering to himself, *"Yes, yes, quite right, to be sure."* He took several urgent steps in the direction from which Tuppenny had come, then recollected his responsibilities as a host and turned.

"Well," he said hurriedly, *"now that you are here, Tuppenny, you really ought to stay. Here, take my candlestick and go down that way a bit—slowly, mind you, so that you don't stir up too much dust. Turn right at the first corner, and left at the second corridor, and you will find yourself outside the kitchen."*

"Kitchen?" Tuppenny brightened. *"I wonder if there might be a bit of something to eat. I haven't had anything since lunch, you know. I'm supposed to eat grass, but if there's a bit of sticky bun—"*

"I'm quite sure there is," Bosworth replied. *"Just put in your head and ask Parsley—she'll be delighted to oblige you. And then you can look up one of the rabbits, Flotsam or Jetsam, whichever is handy, and ask her to show you a place to sleep. We've plenty of room, you know, and guests are always welcome here."*

But all the while Bosworth was talking, he was smelling it. He lifted his head and sniffed again. Yes, there it was, that delicious, that delectable odor, the odor of damp earth and fresh green leaves and—

"But please, sir," asked Tuppenny plaintively, *"where is 'here'?"*

"Here? Why, this is The Brockery, of course," Bosworth said, tossing it back over his shoulder, for now he had forgotten all about being a host and was scampering up the corridor in the direction of the opening through which Tuppenny had tumbled. As he ran, the smell of rain-wet moss and damp bracken grew stronger and stronger, pulling him forward with the voluptuous promise of soft earth and earthworms. At last, he reached the steep slope that led up to the opening.

Being a much larger and heavier and more experienced animal—unlike the smaller, quite ridiculous pig—he was able to scramble right up the slope with no difficulty at all and thrust his nose out into the dark, rain-soaked night. And then with one quick shove of his powerful back legs, he was all the way out, into the blustery, blowing darkness and the wet foliage, onto the sweet, rich earth, which felt soft and moist and yielding under his paws.

"Whuff," said Bosworth, expelling all his breath in one great huff and refilling his lungs with fresh, cool air. *"Wheee!"* he whooped, tucking his tail under his chin and turning a complete somersault. *"Oh, I say,"* he cried, landing on four feet and dancing a delighted jig, *"This is simply . . . simply . . . simply smashing!"*

And so, in a giddy delirium of delight, the badger ran through the shadowy briars and brambles, poking his nose into first this and then that bewitching bit of green moss and brown leaf mold, snapping up earthworms and swallowing them whole, or as nearly so as possible, to avoid getting grit in his teeth. Ten earthworms, twenty, thirty—he lost all track, because he was gobbling them down as fast as he could catch them, which was fast indeed, since the earthworms also loved the rain and had come to the surface of the earth as eagerly as he had scrambled out of his hole.

Engrossed in the pleasure of eating as many earthworms as possible, Bosworth had made a complete circle around a pile of rocks as big as a house, before he realized that it was indeed a house—the old shepherd's hut on the back side of Holly How, used only occasionally now, and mostly by fell-walkers. He paused, sat up on his haunches, and lifted his head. There were voices coming from inside the hut, a boy's voice and a girl's voice, and the furtive gleam of a candle. After a minute, Bosworth realized that this was the same pair he had seen a few days earlier, and that the girl was the one who had left the strange writing in one of The Brockery's side entrances. They were having what sounded to the badger like a Very Serious Discussion.

"It was wrong of you to run away, you know," the boy said, in a mildly rebuking tone. "They're all out looking for you. All the men in the village, and the dogs. They think you're lost. And they're afraid you're in danger."

"I *am* in danger, so you can just stop lecturing me."

The boy cleared his throat in a disbelieving sort of way.

"But not of getting hurt in the woods," the girl went on. She sounded angry, and determined, and not at all rebuked. "And you would have run away, too, if you'd heard people saying things like that about you."

"People?"

"Miss Martine and Dr. Gainwell."

"What did they say, then?" The boy sounded as if he was humoring her.

The girl took a deep breath. "I *told* you, Jeremy. I was sitting in the garden outside the library. The window was open and Miss Martine and Dr. Gainwell were in the library. They were talking about *me*."

"Did they mention you by name?"

"No, they just called me 'the girl,' but I'm the only girl at Tidmarsh Manor, aren't I? Anyway, Miss Martine said that I threatened their plan, and Dr. Gainwell said he didn't know what she was talking about, because I'd be going away to school in a few weeks, and then she'd have free rein."

"Free rein?" The boy was puzzled. "Free rein to do what?"

"To carry out their plan, whatever it is," the girl said impatiently. "It has something to do with 'the old lady,' who has got to be Grandmama. Anyway, Dr. Gainwell said he didn't see how I could threaten the plan, because I didn't have any power. And she said he'd never been able to see anything, even when he was a boy, unless it was an inch in front of his nose."

"But I thought Miss Martine and this man had just met," the boy objected.

"That's what they want people to think," the girl said, "but it's obviously not true. They must've known one another for a long time. And I don't think he's a missionary, either. His hands are wrong."

"But if he says you can't threaten their plan, whatever it is, then what do you have to be afraid of? Really, Caroline, I don't understand—"

"But I *do* threaten their plan!" the girl wailed. "I don't understand it either, but she said I threatened it, by my very existence! And he said that she surely couldn't be suggesting that they—" She stopped.

"They what?"

"I don't know," the girl said wearily. "She got up and closed the window, and that's when I ran away. It . . . it sounded as if he thought she wanted to be rid of me."

"Well, they *are* going to be rid of you," the boy said reasonably, "when you go away to school."

"No, not that way. Get rid of me forever, I mean. Make . . . something happen to me. That's why I hid up here. I was in the woods and I heard him calling my name and knew he was looking for me. I ran up here to get away from him."

The boy gave a skeptical chuckle. "Now, really, Caroline, don't you think that you're—"

"I am *not* exaggerating, Jeremy Crosfield!" the girl cried. "I'm not imagining things, either. And if that's what you really, truly think, you can just go away and leave me alone. I can take care of myself, you know. I've been doing it for a long time. I don't need you to look after me."

There was a silence, and then the boy said, quite firmly, "I am not going away, Caroline. I don't understand half of what you're saying, but whatever this is, we're in it together. We've just got to figure out what to do, that's all. You can't stay here—it's too wet and there's nothing to eat. You can't come home with me, because my Aunt Jane is sick, and I don't want to bother her with an explanation, which I couldn't make very well, anyway. What's more, there's nothing to be gained by hiding. All of this—whatever it is—has to be brought out into the open, sooner or later. And the sooner the better, if you ask my opinion. Missionary or not, Dr. Gainwell, is supposed to be the next head teacher. At least, that's what everybody in the village says. So what are we going to do?"

In the dark, rainy silence, Bosworth heard a man's voice calling, faint and far away, and a vole rattled the brambles. At last, the girl said, very low, "I think we ought to talk to Miss Potter."

"Miss Potter?" the boy asked. "How do you—oh, that's right. She came to see you this morning."

"Yes, and brought me her guinea pig. I liked her, straight away. She seems to be able to . . . well, see *through* things, somehow. And through people. I think she already understands about Miss Martine. She'll know what to do. But I don't know where to find her."

"She's staying at Belle Green," the boy said. "She's probably there now, getting ready to go to bed." There was a scraping sound, as if he were standing up. "If you want to talk to her, I'll take you there. But we'll have to go a round-about way, over Oatmeal Crag and down the hill behind Belle Green. Otherwise, we might run into one of the search parties, and they'd take you back to the Manor."

The girl thought about this for a minute. "All right," she said. "We'll go. Just a minute, whilst I get Tuppeny. He's in that old basket over there." Another scraping sound, and then a half-stifled shriek. "Jeremy, he's gone!"

"What? Who?"

"Tuppenny! The guinea pig Miss Potter gave me to look after. I found that basket when I first got to the hut, and I put him into it, and now he's not here! See? There's a hole in the bottom, and he's got out. He's lost! However will I find him? And whatever will I tell Miss Potter? I promised her I should take good care of him."

The badger shook his head. *"Tuppenny? No, he's not lost. He couldn't be better. He's at The Brockery, having a nice bit of late supper."* But he said this to himself, in a low, badger voice, since he knew that humans could not understand him.

"Well, we're not going to find him in the dark, that's for certain," Jeremy said. "I'll come back up here tomorrow and look for him. We'd better get going now, though. If we wait much longer, Miss Potter will have gone to bed."

25

Miss Potter Entertains Guests

Miss Potter had not, in fact, gone to bed. She was in her bedroom, dressed in her old blue dressing gown. She had taken her hair down and was sitting beside the fire, writing in her journal, something she had not had time to do during the past few days.

Beatrix began her journal when she was fourteen. Because she was a very private person and didn't want her mother or her brother or her governess to read what she wrote, she had invented her own secret code, a kind of cipher shorthand—the same sort of cipher (although of course not the very *same*) that Caroline Longford had been using. And because she was sure that no one would ever read what she wrote, she could say exactly what she pleased about everything and everybody.

Tonight, there was a great deal to record. She wrote about

finding Ben Hornby's body, and lending Tuppenny to Caroline, over the objections of the unpleasant Miss Martine. She wrote about meeting Isaac Chance ("an altogether weasely sort of person" she noted), and finding the tongs on Holly How, and learning from Captain Woodcock that they were badger tongs. She also wrote that Miss Nash had been appointed to the position at Sawrey School after all, and—most importantly, as far as she was concerned—that Caroline had gone missing. As she wrote, she heard voices in the street outside the house and knew that at least some of the searchers were straggling back into the village. But there had been no celebratory shouting, and Mr. Barrow had not rung the bell from the Arms, as he promised he would do when the girl was found.

Beatrix frowned. When Mr. Heelis had first told them about Caroline, she had been both surprised and perplexed, for the girl had not struck her as the sort who would wander into the woods or the fells and carelessly lose her way—although, of course, accidents could happen to anyone. Still, now that she'd had time to think about it, she suspected that something else was going on here. If Caroline had not wandered off, she must have run away. Why? And where had she gone?

Beatrix turned down the wick on the paraffin lamp and went to stand at the window, looking out at the rain-wet landscape. The storm had blown off to the east, but streaks of lightning occasionally flickered from cloud to cloud and thunder grumbled along the fells. She pushed the casement window open and let the cool, wet air flow over her body.

As she stood there, watching the lightning and listening to the thunder, Beatrix was very glad not to be in London, where the air was so foul with smoke and soot that she couldn't draw a deep, full, easy breath. In London, she'd be bone-weary and ready for bed almost before it was time to light the lamps, whilst here, she was scarcely tired at all, although she had been busy and active all day, walking and climbing and driving—and dealing with Mr. Biddle.

She smiled into the darkness. Every time she came to Sawrey, she felt better, and clearer, and stronger. She only wished that she never had to go home to London. No, she corrected herself. London was her parents' home, her old home. Her new home, her *heart's* home, was here.

Behind her, she heard the quiet, comfortable sounds of her animals—the two rabbits and Tom the mouse, turning and sighing and snuggling in their beds—and remembered Tuppenny. Perhaps it hadn't been a good idea to leave him at Tidmarsh Manor. Perhaps Miss Martine had made trouble about him, and that was why Caroline had left. It might be a good idea to go up to Lady Longford's in the morning and retrieve Tuppenny, just in case he was the cause of the trouble. It might—

Shadows moved in the garden below. A bush rustled, and an urgent voice called, very low, "Miss Potter! Miss Potter!"

Beatrix looked down, focused, then looked again. Two slight figures were half-concealed in the shrubbery, peering up at her. One was Jeremy Crosfield. And the other was a girl. Caroline Longford! Caroline was safe!

Beatrix leaned out the window. "Hello out there!" she cried, just above a whisper. The Crooks slept on the other side of the house, and had gone to bed long ago, but it didn't do to take chances. "What do you want? Can I help?"

"We hope so," Jeremy said. "Please, Miss Potter, may we come up and talk? We promise to be very quiet."

"I'll let you in," Beatrix said, pulling on her slippers. Taking the lamp, she hurried down the back stairs, slid the bolt on the door, and opened it. "Do come in," she said, drawing them inside. "Why, you're wet through, both of you! And shivering! You must be very cold."

"Not very," Jeremy said stoutly, although Caroline's teeth were chattering and her skirt was clinging wetly to her legs.

"Up the stairs with you," Beatrix said, very firm. "I'll just put the kettle on."

When the kettle was heating on the kitchen range, Beatrix flew back upstairs, sent Jeremy into the empty room next door to dry himself off as well as he could, and found Caroline a towel and a dry nightdress and shawl. Then she hurried back to the kitchen to fix a tray. Ten minutes later, the three of them were sitting on the rug in front of the fire, with cups of hot tea and thick slices of bread and cheese.

"I must apologize for not having anything more to offer," Beatrix said, handing around the last of the cheese. She smiled. "I don't usually entertain guests here, you see."

"But this is splendid," Caroline said, "ever so much better than the hut." She smiled at Jeremy, who was wearing a woolen blanket draped over his bare shoulders, whilst his damp shirt steamed in front of the fire. "We didn't have any bread and cheese and tea there." She stretched out her bare toes to the flames. "And no fire, either," she added gratefully.

"Well, then," Beatrix said, "if you're feeling warmer and more like yourselves, are you ready to tell your story?" And then, as she listened with growing surprise and dismay, Caroline related what she had heard in the garden outside the library that afternoon.

"—And so I stuffed Tuppenny into my pocket and ran away as fast as I could," the girl concluded. "I walked in the woods for a time because I couldn't think where to go. And then I heard Dr. Gainwell calling my name, and I didn't want . . ." She gave Beatrix a furtive glance. "I didn't want him to find me. I remembered the old shepherd's hut on Holly How, and I knew he wouldn't think to look for me there." She sighed and wiggled her toes. "I didn't plan to stay away. I thought I would go back before teatime, you see. But the longer I thought, the more I didn't want to go back. And then finally—"

"And then I heard that Caroline was lost, and that the men in the village were going out to look for her," Jeremy said, taking up the story. "And I thought of all the places she might go—the big hollow beech in Cuckoo Brow Wood, and the dell under the rocks, and the old shepherd's hut. I went looking and found her in the hut, and she told me what she'd heard." His grin was crooked. "I didn't believe it, you know, not at first. And I expect that you don't, either, Miss Potter."

"Let me see if I have it right, Caroline," Beatrix said. "You overheard Miss Martine and Dr. Gainwell talking about some sort of plan, which can't be carried out because of you. Do you have any idea what kind of plan it might be?"

Caroline shook her head. "It has something to do with Grandmama, that's all I know. And I'm a problem because I'm her granddaughter, and my going away to school isn't going to solve it. The problem, I mean."

Beatrix studied the girl gravely, not liking what she heard. It sounded not only mysterious, but ominous, as if there were some sort of conspiracy afoot. "And you thought," she asked, "that the two of them had known each other for a very long time?"

Caroline nodded vigorously. "Dr. Gainwell already knew about the plan, whatever it was. And I'm sure Miss Martine wouldn't talk the way she did to somebody she'd only just met."

Beatrix picked up the teapot. "Which suggests," she said, "that Dr. Gainwell might not be the person he's pretending to be." She paused. "I'm sorry there's no more bread and cheese, but there's more tea in the pot. Who wants some?"

"I do," Jeremy said, holding out his cup.

"I'll have more, too," Caroline said. "And two sugars."

Cradling her cup to warm her hands, she added, "I wondered the same thing, you know. Missionaries used to visit my parents, and they always told us all about their adventures. But Dr. Gainwell doesn't seem to have any stories to tell. And his hands are soft. Missionaries have to work with their hands."

"If he's pretending to be a missionary," Jeremy said thoughtfully, "he might be pretending about other things, too. Like being a teacher." He slid a glance at Beatrix. "You know, don't you, Miss Potter, that he's to be the next head teacher at Sawrey School?"

"Actually, he's not," Beatrix said, putting down the teapot. "The trustees have appointed Miss Nash to the post. Mr. Heelis told me this afternoon."

"Oh, that's smashing!" Jeremy exclaimed happily. "So we can stop worrying about *that,* at least. And Miss Nash can stop worrying too."

"But we still have to worry about the plan, whatever it is," Caroline put in. "We have to do something—only I can't quite think what." She gave Beatrix an anxious look. "You don't think I'm making this up, do you, Miss Potter?"

"No, I don't," Beatrix replied. She didn't want to say it out loud, but she had her own suspicions about Miss Martine. An outwardly meek and docile person whose eyes glittered like the eyes of a hawk and who would pinch a child or a dog was not to be trusted, in her view.

Suspicions were one thing, however, and practical action quite another. But what to do? "I think," she said slowly, "that we ought to look into things a little more carefully."

"Look into what things?" Jeremy asked.

"Well," Beatrix said, "if Dr. Gainwell isn't who he says he is, who is he? But whilst we're thinking about the things that need looking into, there are things that need to be done. Jeremy, on your way home, I should like you to stop at the pub and tell Mr. Barrow to ring the bell, so that people will know that Caroline is safe. And please ask him to send someone to Tidmarsh Manor to let them know, too. Tell him—" She paused. "No, it would be better if I write a note to Lady Longford, I expect. You can give it to Mr. Barrow to be delivered."

"What will you say?" Caroline asked, frowning.

"That you are safe with me, although you are wet and tired and that I've put you to bed. That I will bring you home at her ladyship's earliest convenience."

"It will never be convenient," Caroline burst out bitterly. "Not for Grandmama, and not for Miss Martine and Dr. Gainwell! I don't want to go back." She looked around the room, at the comfortable furniture, the flickering firelight, the drowsy animals. "I'd really rather stay here with you. Please?"

Beatrix smiled and put her arm around the girl's shoulders. "Well, you're here right now, and I'll do all I can to help sort things out. Tomorrow, early in the morning, I suggest that we go to see Mr. Heelis and Captain Woodcock. I want you to tell them what you've told me."

Caroline brightened. "I know Mr. Heelis—he met my ship in Liverpool and brought me here, and he's Grandmama's solicitor. He's a very nice man. But who is Captain Woodcock?"

"He's the Justice of the Peace for Sawrey district, and he knows your grandmother. He'll have some ideas, I'm sure. Now, I'll write that note." Beatrix got to her feet. "But wait—I've forgot to ask about Tuppenny, Caroline. Will someone make sure that he has food and water?"

Caroline and Jeremy exchanged silent glances. Finally, Caroline spoke. "I'm so sorry, Miss Potter," she said guiltily, "but I'm afraid I've . . . I've lost him."

"Lost Tuppenny!" Beatrix exclaimed, dismayed. "But how? Where?"

"There was an old basket in the hut," Caroline said, near tears. "I thought it would be a safe place for him to take a nap—roomier and more comfortable than my pocket. But when I went to get him, he wasn't there. He got out through a hole, you see. He was . . . gone."

"I'll go up to Holly How first thing in the morning and look for him," Jeremy said. "I'm sure I'll find him," he added comfortingly to Caroline. "He's probably still in the hut somewhere."

Beatrix was not so sure. Tuppenny's ancestors might have flourished in the wild jungles of South America, but he himself was not an outdoor animal. He had lived all of his short life in a cage or his wicker traveling basket, and had no experience of the outside world. But he was an extremely curious little animal, and the minute he got out of that basket, he had likely run as far and as fast as he could, delirious with freedom and the opportunity to explore. By this time, he would surely have regretted his escape. No doubt he was wandering across the open fell, wet and lost, easy prey for owls or foxes or stoats.

She pressed her lips together, not wanting to make Caroline feel even worse than she already did. "Jeremy's right, I'm sure," she said, in the most soothing voice she could manage. "Tuppenny will be found in the morning. And then he'll have a tale to tell, won't he?"

Beatrix couldn't know the half of it.

26

Ruth's Revelation

It was late when Will Heelis came down from Cuckoo Brow Wood and learned that Caroline Longford had been found, and that she was staying the night with Miss Potter at Belle Green. He wondered how the girl had found her way to Miss Potter, and why. But mostly he was glad and relieved, for the longer their search had gone on, the more anxious he had felt, picturing Caroline lying sprawled at the bottom of a cliff, like Ben Hornby, or wandering, wet and terrified, through the darkest depths of Cuckoo Brow Wood.

Exhausted and dripping, Will decided to stay the night in Sawrey rather than drive back to Hawkshead, where he lodged with his two spinster cousins, Cousin Fanana and Cousin Emily Jane, at Sandground. They retired early, and his late comings and goings always disturbed them. He took a room at the Arms, jotted a note to Miss Potter to thank her for sheltering Caroline, and gave it to Mr. Barrow for delivery first thing in the morning. Then he surrendered his damp outer clothing to Mrs. Barrow to be dried in front of the fire, borrowed a pair of Mr. Barrow's pajamas, and fell into bed, where he dropped into a restless and fitful sleep.

Early the next morning, he was awakened by a light rapping at the door. "Come in," he called groggily.

"Good morning, sir," said a light voice, and he opened one eye to see a hand putting a tray with a cup of tea and two slices of buttered toast on his bedside table. He opened the other eye and saw a familiar face framed by curly dark hair under a maid's cap.

"Ruth?" he asked, surprised. "Ruth Safford, is that you?"

"It's me, sir," said the young woman cheerfully, going over to draw the draperies so that light streamed into the room. "Sorry to be so early, sir, but Mrs. Barrow thought you'd want to be called. She's brushed your suit, sir, and I've brought it up for you. Your boots and stockings, too."

"But I thought you were in service at Tidmarsh Manor," Will said, sitting up and knuckling the sleep out of his eyes. He was acquainted with Ruth, having a few years before successfully represented her brother John in a case involving a runaway horse and wagon. He had spoken to her several times at the Manor, when he had gone to visit with Lady Longford.

The young woman pouted. "Indeed I was, sir, until Miss Martine gave me the push."

"She did?" Will asked. "Why? And how do you come to be working here at the Arms?" He reached for his tea, frowning. He hadn't understood that it was Miss Martine's responsibility to manage the servants.

"As to why, sir, you'd have to ask Miss Martine," Ruth said crisply. "As to my coming here, Mr. Barrow is my father's cousin, y' see. He thought Mrs. Barrow could do with a bit of help to make up the rooms and serve at table, and I was glad to oblige." She went to the door. "Mrs. Barrow says to say that ye've a lady waiting to see you, and that breakfast is hot downstairs."

"A lady?" Will asked, now even more surprised.

"Miss Potter, sir. And she has Miss Caroline with her." She turned, her hand on the knob. "How would you like your eggs, sir?"

"Scrambled, please," Will said. Miss Potter? he wondered. At this early hour?

"Thank you, sir," Ruth said, and was gone.

Ten minutes later, washed and combed and dressed in his now-dry suit, Will went into the dining room. It was empty except for Miss Potter and Caroline, who were seated at the round table in front of the window that overlooked the Kendal road.

"Good morning, Mr. Heelis," Miss Potter said. "I hope we didn't wake you."

"Of course not," Will lied heartily. "Good morning to you. And to you, Miss Longford. I am glad to see you looking none the worse for your adventure" He smiled as he pulled out the chair and sat down. "I do hope you weren't too awfully lost."

"I wasn't lost at all," Caroline retorted with a hard-edged look that reproached him for his patronizing tone, and flicked one braid over her shoulder. "I was in the shepherd's hut at the top of Holly How."

"Oh, really?" Will asked in surprise. "I must confess, it's not a place I thought to look." He wasn't pleased to hear that she had taken refuge there, since Ben Hornby had fallen to his death not far away. "Ah, thank you, Ruth," he added, as the young woman set a plate in front of him, laden with scrambled eggs, bacon, sausage, kippers, and sliced fried tomato. "Won't you have some breakfast?" he asked his guests.

"Thank you, Mr. Heelis," Miss Potter said politely. "We ate at Belle Green. But a cup of tea would be nice."

"I'll just brew another pot, then," Ruth said. "Won't be a minute."

As Ruth went back to the kitchen, Miss Potter leaned forward and lowered her voice. "I shouldn't have troubled you so early this morning, Mr. Heelis, except that Caroline has something I think you need to hear. I hope you won't mind if she tells her story whilst you eat your breakfast."

"Not at all," Will said, tucking comfortably into his eggs and bacon. But as Caroline talked, he lost that sense of pleasant, relaxed self-indulgence that accompanies a highly satisfactory breakfast. And by the time she had finished her story, he was scowling darkly.

"Are you *sure* that's what you heard?" he demanded.

Caroline regarded him. "I know it doesn't sound . . ." She hesitated, and then her mouth took on a determined set, and in her features, Will could read something of her grandmother's stubborn look. "But that's what I heard. Miss Martine and Dr. Gainwell have some sort of plan, and whilst I don't know what it is, I know it has something to do with Grandmama, and that they think I'm in their way. That's why I didn't answer when I heard him calling my name— out there in the woods, I mean." Her eyes narrowed. "I *am* telling the truth, Mr. Heelis."

"I believe you." Will smiled gently. "Solicitors have to listen to all kinds of people, you know. Some are truthful, and some aren't." He cupped his hand behind his ear and leaned forward. "We develop an ear for honesty, you see. It helps us do our job. And I think you're telling the truth."

"But we don't know enough of the details," Miss Potter said, frowning. "And I can't think how we might find out more."

"We might ask Mrs. Beever," Will suggested. "She's been at the Manor for some years, and—"

"Mrs. Beever doesn't know anything," a voice put in, somewhat scornfully. "She stays in the kitchen. Emily works upstairs, but she curries favor with Miss Martine, and anyway, she's not very bright, which is why she's still at the Manor. You won't get anything out of her."

"Why, hello, Ruth!" Caroline exclaimed, her eyes widening. "So this is where you've come to work!"

"Hello, miss," said Ruth, putting the teapot on the table. "I'm sorry, Mr. Heelis," she added, in a repentant tone. "I couldn't help overhearing what the young miss said. I don't know the gentleman she's talking about, since he's just come, but I have to say that I think she's right about Miss Martine. That person is up to no good, in my opinion. Always so meek and mild to her ladyship's face, but behind her back, it's all brow-beating and bullying."

"I think Mrs. Beever would agree," Miss Potter said with a little smile. To Will, she added quietly, "She told Miss Barwick so when she—Miss Barwick—delivered a ginger cake for her ladyship." At Will's mystified look, she added, "Ginger helps to settle the stomach, you know. Lady Longford has been suffering with stomach trouble."

"That's right," Ruth said. "Anyway, when her ladyship got sick, Miss Martine took over the running of the household, the menus and the supplies and settling accounts and all of that. And giving medicine to her ladyship, and changing out the servants—" She sniffed. "A legacy hunter, is what I call that one. Angling after some little bit in her ladyship's will."

Miss Potter gave her a sharp look. "Medicine? Was this something that the doctor left for her ladyship?"

"The doctor?" Ruth gave her a doubtful look. "I don't

think so. It was something Miss Martine had. A narrow strip of brown paper, y' see. It's soaked in water, and then the water is used to make tea."

"Did you ask her about it?" Will inquired.

"No," Ruth said, with a little shrug. "I just assumed that's what it was. I didn't much like the idea of her making up medicine for her ladyship, though. No more than I liked her other tricks. Didn't seem right to me."

Nor to me, Will thought. He said nothing, but as he glanced up, he caught Miss Potter's eye and had the uncomfortable impression that it didn't seem right to her, either.

He smiled. "I think," he said to Ruth, "that I should like another sausage and rasher of bacon, please."

"Oh, yes, sir," Ruth said. "I'll get it right now. And perhaps for the young miss, too." She turned, then paused. "I hope you don't think I spoke out of turn," she said apprehensively, "or that I said too much. I shouldn't like for Miss Martine to hear that I—"

"No, of course not, Ruth," Will replied briskly. "You've been very helpful. And Miss Martine will learn nothing from us." When she had gone, he leaned forward. "Well, Miss Potter," he said in a low voice, "does this suggest anything to you?"

Miss Potter hesitated. When she spoke, she said just two words—words that might have been incomprehensible to a great many people, but which Will Heelis understood perfectly.

"Mrs. Maybrick," she said.

27

A Breakfast-Table Conference

"All's well that ends well, I suppose," said Captain Miles Woodcock, folding his napkin and pushing his chair back from the breakfast table. "Although it certainly was a trying evening for all of us. Every able-bodied man in the village was out there, beating those woods."

"It's left us with a puzzle, too," his sister said. She put down her coffee cup, frowning. "Why Caroline Longford should come down to the village and go to Miss Potter—instead of going home, I mean. It doesn't seem that she was lost at all, which makes me wonder if perhaps there might have been some trouble at the Manor."

"Trouble?" Miles asked. "What sort of—"

The door opened and his sister's frown dissolved into a wide smile. "Why, good morning, Dr. Butters!" she said cheerily. "How nice to see you so early this morning. What can I get you? Eggs and bacon?"

"Ah, Butters," Miles said warmly. "Dim, ask Elsa for another plate."

"I'll just have coffee, Dimity," said the doctor, holding up his hand. "And a private word with Captain Woodcock, if you wouldn't mind, my dear."

"Not in the least," Dim said warmly, pouring a cup of coffee. "I've a rather unpleasant task this morning, which I have been putting off. But now I really must face up to it, I'm afraid." She turned down her mouth. "The flower show is just a fortnight away, you see, and if Mrs. Wharton is allowed to judge the dahlias again, the whole village will rise up in revolt. Yesterday, the committee asked Mr. Calvin to do it, and he has agreed. I've been commissioned to break the news to poor Mrs. Wharton, although for the life of me, I can't think of a kind way in which to do it."

"You may stop fretting, Dimity," said the doctor, seating himself at the table. "I happened to see Mrs. Wharton on the ferry yesterday. She was on her way to the station at Windermere, to catch the train for London. Her daughter Margaret is expecting twins, and she's planning to be gone for at least a month, perhaps longer. She seemed rather frantic. I daresay that flower shows and dahlias have flown right out of her head."

"Oh, what a blessing!" Dimity exclaimed. "Now I can get on to Mr. Charles and the garden vegetables." She stood. "I'll leave you to your discussion, gentlemen."

"Fine woman, your sister," said the doctor thoughtfully, when Dimity had left the room. "If I weren't married already, she'd be the first I'd ask."

"You wouldn't get her away from me without a struggle," Miles said with a grin. "Although I suppose that's a prospect I should welcome—for Dim's sake. I'm sure she'd prefer a husband and family of her own to life with a dry-as-sticks brother. And since you're not available, I've my eye on Heelis. Haven't said anything to him, though," he added hastily, "so don't you go meddling. He's very shy around the ladies, and will want the right kind of encouragement."

"Heelis, eh? One of the finest men I know. Make Dimity an excellent husband." The doctor's eyes glinted. "And I never meddle in other people's love affairs. I never meddle at all, of course, unless it's something urgent—as it is now. I came to talk to you about Lady Longford."

"The girl's been found, you know," Miles said. "Late last night. It appears that she presented herself beneath Miss Potter's window and asked asylum, as it were. In fact, I saw the two of them—Miss Potter and the girl—a short while ago, going into the Arms. To talk to Heelis, I assume. It was rather late when he got back to the village, so he stayed at the pub."

"I knew that she'd been found," Butters said, "although I didn't quite get the circumstances. Asylum, eh? It's that Martine woman, I suppose." He sipped his coffee and put the cup down. "I was at the Manor last evening, you know. I was called up there to see to her ladyship."

"That stomach ailment again?"

Butters nodded. "It's got me scratching my head, Woodcock. The problem responds to treatment, and she's almost her old self. Flares up again, and she's at death's door. One would almost think—"

The door opened and Heelis came in. "Ah, glad to see that I've caught the two of you together," he said. To Miles, he added, "I'm here so often that you'll think I want to move in."

"Any time," Miles said. "I daresay our accommodations are more pleasant than those at the Arms, and Dimity certainly enjoys your company. Coffee?" At Will's "Yes, thank you," he poured, remarking with a grin, "I trust that you enjoyed your early-morning conversation with Miss Potter."

Heelis took the cup with a wry chuckle. "There's nothing like a village for news, is there?"

"Nothing like," Butters agreed with a malicious twinkle. "Next thing you know, they'll have you and Miss Potter married." Heelis reddened, Miles glowered, and the doctor went on, hastily, "You saw the girl, too, Woodcock says. She's all right, is she? No harm inflicted by her wanderings in the wilderness?"

"She didn't wander," Heelis said. "She spent the evening in the shepherd's hut on Holly How, in the company of young Jeremy Crosfield, and then both of them came down to see Miss Potter. Caroline left the Manor rather precipitously, it appears. She overheard something that troubled her."

Miles frowned. "And what was that?" He and the doctor listened intently as Heelis told them what Caroline had heard outside the library window at the Manor. At the end of it, Miles whistled incredulously. "And you credit this wild tale?"

"Well, it does explain one or two puzzling things, it seems to me," Heelis said. "As I recall, none of us were very impressed by Dr. Gainwell's performance in the interview. He left too many holes, too many loose ends. He left me wondering, for instance, just where he'd served as a missionary. And what his subjects were at Oxford."

"He did seem uncomfortable," Miles said, "although I chalked it up to lack of preparation. I got the idea that he thought the appointment was rather a sure thing, and that he hadn't expected to be quizzed." He frowned. "But this plan Caroline mentions—what do you think it is?"

Heelis looked from one of them to the other. "For that, I'll have to tell you something I learnt from Ruth Safford, a former maid at Tidmarsh Manor."

"Former?" Butters asked. "She's no longer working there?"

"Right," Heelis replied. "Miss Martine discharged her. She's at the Arms now. Served me my breakfast."

Butters gave him a sharp look. "Miss Martine has taken to managing the servants, then?"

"So it would appear," Heelis replied. "There's more, though, Butters—in your line, too, I should think. It seems that she's taken to making medicine." And he told them what Ruth Safford had reported.

"So *that's* it!" the doctor exclaimed, pushing his chair back. He jumped up and began to pace, clasping his hands behind his back. "Narrow strips of brown paper, indeed. By Jove, Heelis, I had my suspicions. But I never—" He stopped, shaking his head, and his voice grew harsh. "I tell you, I have been entirely too naive. I should have guessed."

Miles stared from one of them to the other. "I haven't the foggiest idea what you're talking about, you know. Would one of you care to oblige me with a clue?"

Heelis looked up, his eyes steady, his mouth hard. "Does the name Florence Maybrick mean anything to you?"

Miles put down his pipe, his jaw dropping. "You're joking."

"I'm afraid not," Heelis said in a regretful tone. "Actually, it was Miss Potter who brought up the name. But the minute she said it, I could see the whole thing. Can't you?"

Miles stared at him, incredulous. Yes, he could see it, and he was stunned.

Some years before, in Liverpool, a woman named Florence Maybrick had been convicted for the murder of her husband. The servants had seen her soaking flypaper strips in a basin of water, thereby obtaining the arsenic that she then fatally administered to her victim. The case had become sadly infamous, and anyone who read a newspaper during the time of the trial could not fail to know every detail of the case.

"Heelis is right, I'm afraid," Butters gritted, between his teeth. "All the signs and symptoms are there, Woodcock. Headaches, coldness of the limbs, gastrointestinal difficulties. I've been a blind fool. I didn't make the connection."

"Why should you?" Heelis asked evenly. "Don't reproach yourself, my dear Butters. Intentional poisoning isn't a usual occurrence in your practice, I shouldn't think."

"No, and thank the good Lord for that!" the doctor exclaimed. "My patients have enough troubles."

"So you think Miss Martine is attempting to *poison* her ladyship?" Miles asked, staring at the both of them.

"Arsenic poisoning is certainly consistent with the symptoms," said the doctor darkly.

"And her motive?"

"Ruth Safford claims that she's a legacy hunter," Heelis said, in a grave voice, "and I think it's entirely possible. A wealthy old woman with no immediate family—at least, no family in evidence. Miss Martine probably knew that Lady Longford had disowned her son, and that he had died in New Zealand. She might not even have known about his daughter until the girl appeared on the scene." He shook his head. "In fact, Miss Martine told me some time ago that Lady Longford intended to speak to me about making a new will. Nothing's been done yet, but I suspect that she was laying the groundwork."

"We must act, then!" Miles exclaimed, pushing back his chair. "Her ladyship is in grave danger!"

Heelis shook his head. "I don't think so. At least, not in imminent danger. The old will is still in place, you see. Everything goes to charity. Although I suppose it's possible to make a fatal mistake." He glanced inquiringly at the doctor.

"It's possible," Butters said. "Arsenic poisoning is not an exact science. However, if Miss Martine is indeed a legacy hunter, she must first get rid of—" He pressed his lips together.

"Exactly," Heelis said. "It is likely, then, wouldn't you say, that her granddaughter is in even greater danger?"

Miles stared at him. "By Jove," he whispered. "Yes, I see it. Yes, of course. Miss Martine believed that Lady Longford had no descendents, and when the girl arrived on the scene, she upset the apple-cart entirely."

Heelis smiled grimly. "One can scarcely blame Caroline for taking to her heels, can one?"

"Well, then," Miles said, "the first thing to do is to apprehend Miss Martine, and—"

"I doubt it's that simple," Heelis said. "On what charge? And with what evidence?"

Miles stared at him. "Why, man, attempted murder, of course! On the testimony of that servant you talked to this morning. Miss . . . whoever she is. And then we'll go and look for the flypaper and—"

"But Ruth Safford cannot swear that the poison was administered to her ladyship," Heelis pointed out. "Arsenic-water has other purposes."

"Heelis is right," Butters said heavily. "Mrs. Maybrick argued that she intended to use it for cosmetic purposes. Simple possession proves nothing, I'm afraid."

"But then what?" Miles asked, throwing up his hands. "We can't just stand by and let murder be done!"

"Right, old chap," Heelis agreed, with a glint in his eye. "So let me tell you the plan that Miss Potter proposed to me, and to which I have agreed. Caroline has been detailed to work in Miss Barwick's bakery here in the village for a day or two, where she can no doubt make herself useful whilst she is being kept safely out of the way. And Miss Potter is going to

Tidmarsh Manor to conduct a brief inquiry." At Miles's astonished look, he added, rather sheepishly, "She insists that it is entirely safe, of course, or I should not have allowed her to go." He took out his watch and looked at it. "She's probably on her way by now."

" '*Allowed her to go,*' " Miles muttered ironically, shaking his head. "I doubt if anyone in the world could keep that woman from doing anything she pleases."

28

Miss Potter Conducts an Inquiry

Beatrix was indeed, as Mr. Heelis had said, on her way to Tidmarsh Manor. She had gone first to Hill Top, commandeered Winston and harnessed him to the cart, and was within sight of the old house. It seemed more melancholy than grim to her, now that she knew more about what was going on inside. It was interesting, she thought, the way one's perception of a place—or a person—changed when one knew something more. Just now, she couldn't feel anything but pity toward Lady Longford.

She tied Winston to the post and went up to the front door and knocked. When Emily admitted her, she spoke a few words to her, and was then shown into the morning room, where Miss Martine was engaged in writing a letter.

"I was so sorry to hear about her ladyship's indisposition,"

Beatrix said in her most earnest tone. "I do hope she is feeling better this morning."

"Somewhat." Miss Martine's frown discouraged other queries. "You've brought Caroline back, have you? Has she been sent upstairs?"

Beatrix made a slight gesture. "Since her ladyship seemed so very ill last night, Mr. Heelis suggested that it might be better if Caroline did not return immediately. Youngsters can be so annoying at times, and I know from what you have said that she is not as obedient as one might wish. Mr. Heelis has arranged for her to be looked after in the village." She smiled gently. "I felt that your nerves might be under a strain, too, Miss Martine. Perhaps it would be best if I retrieved the little creature I left yesterday. With Caroline gone, it's really not fair to ask you to care for him."

"Well," said Miss Martine huffily, "it's good that *someone* is considering my nerves, which have been quite badly frayed in this ordeal—her ladyship deathly ill and that doctor totally unable to find a remedy, and then the girl disappearing." She sighed the sigh of a woman who is terribly put upon. "Yes, indeed, take the wretched animal away with you. If you can find him, that is. Emily says he was not in his box this morning."

"I'll ask Emily to help me look for him," Beatrix said, although she knew very well that poor little Tuppenny was lost on Holly How, and that there was no chance of finding him at the Manor. But reclaiming the guinea pig was not the purpose of her visit, in spite of what she had just told Miss Martine. She had come to have an uninterrupted talk with Emily, and when she went upstairs to the school room, she did just that.

"I'm so sorry about the little fellow, Miss Potter," Emily said, twisting her hands together, a despairing look on her round, rosy face. "As you can see, the creature's box is empty. I can't think how he might have got out of his box, or where he's gone off to."

"I'm sure he'll be found under a bed or behind a curtain," Beatrix said in a comforting tone. "When he's discovered, just pop him into his box and take him down to the kitchen, and I'll come and get him."

"Oh, I will, miss," Emily promised, her blue eyes very serious. "As soon as I find him."

"Thank you," said Beatrix, and turned as if to leave. Then she turned back, shutting the door as she did so. "Oh, Emily, I nearly forgot. I wanted to pass along a remark I've heard. About your work, I mean."

"A remark, Miss Potter?" Emily's hand went to her mouth and her eyes widened with distress. "Oh dear! What have I done? I hope I haven't—"

"You haven't done anything, my dear," Beatrix said with a reassuring smile. "I wanted to let you know that her ladyship commented to the doctor yesterday that she just couldn't get along without you." It wasn't true, at least to Beatrix's knowledge, but if Lady Longford could stop thinking about herself long enough to think about Emily, she might say something of the sort.

"That's very kind of her ladyship," replied Emily, with evident relief. "I worry, you know, especially since Miss Martine let Ruth go. But I think she likes me more than she liked Ruth," she added. "Miss Martine, I mean. It's not always easy to please her, but I try to help her all I can—and her ladyship too, of course."

"I'm sure you do," Beatrix said gravely. "You must be an enormous help, especially now that her ladyship is ill. I imagine you do all kinds of things for Lady Longford. Changing her bed linen, caring for her clothes, making sure that she has her medicine—"

Emily, who had been nodding all the while that Beatrix

spoke, suddenly opened her eyes wide. "Oh, I'm not to meddle with medicines. Miss Martine does all the nursing and handles the medicines and such like."

"Oh, of course," Beatrix said. "She makes up her ladyship's medicines, does she?"

"Sometimes," Emily said. "Dr. Butters prescribes things, of course. And Miss Martine wrote away to a friend who's a doctor, and he sent a remedy that Dr. Butters didn't have."

"How very thoughtful of her," Beatrix murmured. "She made up the medicine, then, did she?"

Emily nodded brightly. "It comes in a strip, you know, rather like a flypaper, only of course it's not. It's to be soaked in warm water, in a basin. I wouldn't have known about this, but I happened on her making it a few days ago, you see, and she told me all about it." She smiled confidentially. "I don't like to brag, but Miss Martine tells me things. She says I have promise—as a lady's maid, I mean. She thinks I should go to London, and she's promised to help me find a good place." She tilted her head, her eyes darkening a little. "Of course, I would be sorry to leave Sawrey. But Miss Martine has ever so many friends, and all of them are quite wealthy and live in very fine houses, and they are always wanting ever so many maids, especially good ones. And she says that once I am in London, I will have such fine dresses as you can't think. Silk dresses, and ribbons and lace and—"

"Why, of course," Beatrix said. "I'm sure you will do quite well in London, Emily, although your sister will certainly miss you." She paused. "And after you saw Miss Martine mix the medicine, did you see her administer it to her ladyship?"

Emily nodded earnestly. "In her tea. That's what Miss Martine's doctor told her to do, you see. Use the water to make her tea. It might take a little time to cure the infection,

and she might have to give her ladyship several more doses.
But she's bound to be better soon, the doctor says."

"I'm sure," Beatrix said. "I can see why her ladyship thinks
so highly of you, Emily. You are a very great help to her, indeed." She smiled and opened the door "You don't need to see
me downstairs, my dear. Stay and get on with your work."

And Emily would soon be an even greater help to Lady
Longford, Beatrix thought, for she was the perfect witness,
so innocent of any imagination of wrongdoing that she did
not hesitate to report truthfully what she had seen. And
that made her a danger to Miss Martine. As she went down
the stairs, Beatrix thought that she wouldn't be at all surprised to learn that the letter Miss Martine had been engaged in writing was an effort to find Emily a place in
London, in order to get her out of the house.

But Miss Martine was doing much more than that. As
Beatrix reached the second-floor stair landing, she looked
down and saw Dr. Gainwell, dressed for traveling, set down
his valise and step into the morning room, closing the door
behind him.

Now, Beatrix was not the kind of person who intention-
ally eavesdrops, but even she had to concede that there were
times when one was compelled to set aside one's scruples.
She hesitated for only the briefest moment, then went down
the stairs and stood close to the morning-room door, which
Dr. Gainwell had neglected to close completely.

Inside the morning room, Miss Martine looked up from the
letter she was writing to Mrs. Morant, owner of the Acme
Employment Agency, to see her brother enter the room.

"I've come to tell you goodbye, Mabel." His mouth
tightened. "My bags are packed, and I've asked Beever to

bring the phaeton round." He paused and added emphatically, "Mabel."

"Packed!" Miss Martine exclaimed, feeling suddenly frightened. "You're not leaving me here alone, Kenneth! You mustn't! You *can't*!"

"Why not?" Kenneth said testily. "There's no reason for me to stay. The position that you promised me went to someone else—and it's clear that I wouldn't have been any good in the job, anyway, in spite of your saying I would. And now that I've met the girl, I can tell you that I won't have anything to do with harming her. If she's in the way of your getting the old lady's money, you'll just have to deal with her yourself, Mabel. This whole thing was your idea, anyway."

"It may have been my idea," Miss Martine said pettishly, "but you were glad enough to get the jewelry I sent you, and to sell it and buy yourself those fine clothes. And now—"

"I did that because you promised there wouldn't be any difficulty. You said you were making arrangements for a new will, and when the old lady was dead, we'd sell this place and go abroad." Kenneth gave her a bitter glance. "According to you, it was all going to be so easy."

"It *was*—until the girl came. And then you promised to help me get rid of—"

He shook his head violently. "I never said I'd do that. Killing's not my line of work, no more than school teaching is."

"But if she's still alive to inherit—"

"Oh, leave off, Mabel," Kenneth said disgustedly. "And leave off that dreadful fake accent. I'm not going to help with this scheme of yours, and that's flat." He grinned crookedly. "Don't bother to see me off, my dear. I'll write to you when I get to London."

"I beg you, Kenneth," Miss Martine said desperately. "I

need your help. I can't do this without you. I—" And she began to cry.

Out in the hallway, Beatrix felt she had heard all that she needed to hear, and she didn't want to be caught. She went quickly to the front door and, trying to look as if she wasn't in a hurry, went down the walk and past Mr. Beever, who was waiting behind Lady Longford's pair of smart grays. Untying Winston, she climbed into the cart and picked up her pony whip.

"Winston," she said, low and determined, "we *must* beat those grays down to the village. If you have it in you to go like the wind, now is the time." She flicked her whip lightly on his firm brown rump.

"*Go like the wind?*" Winston's head snapped up. "*Beat those grays?*" He lifted one hoof. "*Well, now, I call that a fine challenge. Hold on to your hat, Miss Potter! Here we go!*" And with that, they were off like a shot.

Beatrix, not quite understanding Winston's warning, failed to hold on to her straw hat. It sailed off her head and into the meadow long before they reached the village and pulled to a stop in front of Captain Woodcock's house—well in advance of Lady Longford's grays.

29

Bosworth Proposes a Plan

Breakfast was one of the very best times of day at The Brockery, it seemed to Bosworth. The breakfast table was always crowded with a great many animals, some permanent boarders, some temporary lodgers, others staying just for the night on their way somewhere else. They were all at their best in the morning, rested and full of exuberant energy and interesting plans for the day ahead—always a wonderful day, because animals rarely worry or imagine the worst of what is to come, as people do. They were generally planning a picnic, or a foraging expedition, or the pleasant completion of chores, or just loafing on a quiet riverbank, listening to the whispering water and whistling birds and watching butterflies whirl through the transparent air.

Breakfast this morning was a particularly lively affair, in part because the table was full. Bosworth sat in his usual place at the head, whilst Parsley sat at the foot, passing the marmalade and toast and boiled eggs and rashers of bacon and pouring additional cups of tea. On the bench to Bosworth's left sat Flotsam the rabbit, and next to her sat her sister, Jetsam, both wearing white aprons and maids' caps. Then a small hedgehog named Thistle who had wandered away from her family and now helped Parsley in the kitchen, scraping vegetables and doing the washing up. Then Parsley, and to Parsley's left, Ramsey Rat, his gray whiskers thick with egg. To Ramsey's left sat an elderly ferret, too blind to see which side of his toast was up, so that he was constantly having to lick butter from his paws. And on the bench next to the ferret, at Bosworth's right, sat Tuppenny the guinea pig, who was happily telling everyone that he was a visitor down from London on the train, and that he lived with Miss Potter, who was a famous artist and made books for children, and that she planned to make a book about him someday, and then he would be famous, too.

"*G'wan,*" said Ramsey Rat scornfully, helping himself to his second soft-boiled egg. "*What's an insignificant scrap of a thing like you ever done that's important enough to make a book about?*"

Tuppenny's face fell, and Bosworth patted his paw. "*Don't pay him any mind, Tuppenny. Every animal has a story, and you will have one, too—some day. You just have to be a little patient. Stories don't grow on trees, you know.*"

Bosworth might have gone on in this reassuring vein, except that he was interrupted by the loud clang of a bell. Someone was tugging at the bell-pull at The Brockery's front door, an authoritative tug, from the sound of it, as if the fellow outside knew exactly what he had come for and meant to have it. There was a second pull, equally authoritative, and Bosworth put down his fork.

"*Go and let whoever it is in, Flotsam,*" he said to the rabbit on his left. *"It's been wet outside, so tell him to leave his galoshes in the hall."*

A few moments later, Flotsam returned, in the company of quite an unexpected visitor. *"Professor Galileo Newton Owl to see you, sir,"* she squeaked. *"And here is your newspaper. It was lying on the doormat."* She wrinkled her nose as she handed it over. *"It's a bit dampish, I'm afraid, sir."*

"Why, Owl, old chap!" exclaimed the Badger, pushing back his chair and getting to his feet. *"Goodness gracious, what a delightful surprise this is! We hardly ever see you down here, you know."*

It was quite true. The owl regularly and generously entertained his friends and colleagues in his beech-tree home, and had even installed a ladder for the convenience of those animals who were not naturally tree-climbers and could not fly up to his lofty tree house, which had (or so it seemed to Bosworth) the giddy habit of swaying in the wind. But when it came to returning social calls to those who lived underground, Owl usually extended his regrets. He was known to feel that there was something . . . well, a bit cramped and closed-in underground, where if he so much as lifted a wing without thinking, he was bound to brush a friend's book off his table or a picture from a wall. The professor much preferred the open reaches of sky, where he could stretch his wings to the buoyant winds and soar high and wide above the fields and vast fells.

However, Bosworth did not push the matter, for he was well aware that the Sixth Rule of Thumb forbade a courteous badger from criticizing other animals' choices as far as living and dining arrangements were concerned—to each his own, as it were, no questions asked. So he motioned to Tuppenny to slide down the bench and begged a clean plate and cup from Parsley. In a moment, Owl was settled before a comfortably large helping of eggs and bacon and toast and a cup of steaming tea. Flotsam and Jetsam went off with their feather dusters; Parsley and Thistle disappeared in the direction of the larder, to confer about the day's meals; and the rat and ferret excused themselves to go to their rooms and get on with their morning naps, the first activity in their plan for the day. This left only Bosworth, Owl, and Tuppenny at the table.

"Well, Owl, what brings you out at such an early hour?" asked the badger, refilling his teacup and sitting back comfortably in his chair.

"Late," corrected the professor, with a yawn that almost split his beak. "It is a very late hour for me, and I must be getting home tooo bed. However, I felt the need tooo consult with yoooou on an urgent bit of business, Badger. It concerns an event that's scheduled tooo take place tooonight, in the field behind the Sawrey Hotel. An appalling event, I'm sorry tooo say." He suddenly became aware of Tuppenny, and scowled. "The story isn't fit for young ears," he said sternly. "Whooo are yoooou?"

Tuppenny twitched his nose nervously. "I'm Tuppenny, please, sir," he twittered. "I'm a guinea pig."

"Not a pig," said the owl firmly, spooning marmalade onto his piece of toast. "Yoooou are definitely not a pig. Pigs dooo not have fur, and yoooou dooo not have a pigtail."

"I've been all through that with him, Owl," said Bosworth, "and it's no use. He insists that he's a pig, and no amount of talking will change his opinion." To Tuppenny, he said in a kindly voice, "Tuppenny, my boy, I expect that Parsley might have a chore or two for you, if you wouldn't mind giving her a hand. Off with you, now, that's a good fellow."

When Tuppenny had jumped off the bench and scampered away, Bosworth said, "Well, then, Owl, what's so troublesome that it can't be said in the presence of small fry?"

The professor turned his head from side to side, to see if anyone else might be listening. *"There's tooo be a badger-baiting,"* he said, with great gravity. *"Tooonight."*

Bosworth set down his teacup with a clatter. There had been few badger-baitings in the Land between the Lakes in recent years, for the Justice of the Peace for Sawrey district had mostly managed to shut them down. He was not entirely surprised by Owl's news, however.

"It's the raid on the sett at the Hill Top quarry," he said soberly. *"Parsley told me that her aunt Primrose—she was living in the Hill Top sett—was kidnapped, along with both of her young cubs. Jeremy Crosfield found one of the cubs, but the other is still missing. Primrose hasn't been seen, either."* He cleared his throat. *"Jack Ogden is the name Parsley heard, in connection with the crime. It seems that the fellow is back in the village."*

The professor looked exceedingly grave. *"I thought as much,"* he said. *"Ogden is a scoundrel of the very wooorst sort, a rascally, criminal fellow. But what's tooo be done, I don't know."*

"Well, something has to be done," said Bosworth, in his practical way. He was very fond of Owl, who was quite a dear fellow indeed, and admirable on several scores. But whilst the professor was respected by all for his intelligence and erudition, he was not known to be a creature of decisive action—except, perhaps, where his meals were concerned. He was quick enough when it came to that.

"Something, indeed," agreed Owl, blinking. *"Further research is called for, I believe, especially in the area of the lax enforcement of existing laws against animal cruelty. I should be very pleased tooo glance through my books and papers and—"*

"I will think of a plan," Bosworth interrupted firmly, *"and then we can discuss it."*

"As yooou wish," said the professor, applying himself, with enthusiasm, to his egg.

While Owl enjoyed his breakfast, Badger unfolded his

dampish newspaper and retired behind it, not to read, but to think. There was silence in the room until the professor was quite done with his meal.

At last the owl sighed deeply and brushed the crumbs from his feathery front. *"I should be glad tooo participate, of course, if yooou will tell me what I'm tooo dooo."* He frowned at the badger. *"I hope, old chap, that yooou will not be tempted tooo take unilateral action. There are likely tooo be a great many men in the group, and some of them will nooo doubt have firearms. I should not like tooo run any unwarranted risks."*

"It depends," the badger replied, *"upon your definition of 'unwarranted.' But I can assure you that I do not intend to go it alone, for that is far too dangerous. Now, listen, Owl. Here is what I propose. Tell me what you think."*

And for the next little bit, the owl listened as Bosworth talked, nodding his head in a benign and owlish fashion, until at last a massive snore confirmed what the badger was beginning to suspect: that the professor had drifted off to sleep. The badger awakened him with a sharp poke, made him listen for five more minutes to an abbreviated version of the plan, and then sent him on his way back to his beech tree. Bosworth knew from long experience that it was no use trying to deal with Owl when it was time for his morning nap.

30

"Whatever Shall I Wear?"

Winston proved as good as his word. He did fly like the wind, so swiftly that Miss Potter arrived at Captain Woodcock's house just as the captain and Mr. Heelis—their jackets off and their shirt sleeves rolled up—were completing the repair of a punctured tire on the captain's Rolls-Royce, and some ten minutes before the Tidmarsh Manor phaeton appeared in the village. This was ample time for Miss Potter to relate what she had learnt from Emily about Miss Martine's administration of a certain "medicine" to Lady Longford, and what she had overheard of the conversation between Miss Martine and Dr. Gainwell, who—it now appeared—were sister and brother.

"Miss Potter," said the captain, rolling down his sleeves and fastening his cuffs, "you astonish me. How you managed to gather all these facts in only a few minutes—"

"Nonsense," Miss Potter replied tartly. "The only astonishing thing is that this foolish pair managed to convince themselves that they could get away with such an outrageous scheme." She pointed up the street. "Dr. Gainwell—although that is not his real name—is coming now, on his way to the ferry. You can question him for yourself."

"We shall," Heelis said, shrugging into his jacket. "Miss Potter, we are deeply in your debt."

"Nonsense," Miss Potter said again, but this time she smiled.

The inquiry did not go on for very long. The two men stopped the phaeton, escorted Dr. Gainwell into Captain Woodcock's library, and subjected him to a series of questions. They already knew the answers to most of these, thanks to Miss Potter. And when Mr. Kenneth Wentworth (his real name) understood that he faced prosecution as an accessory to attempted murder, he became suddenly rather cooperative.

Over the course of the next half-hour, then, it emerged that his sister, Miss Mabel Wentworth (calling herself Maribel Martine), had been sent by a London agency to fill the advertised position as Lady Longford's companion and secretary. When Miss Martine arrived at the Manor and saw the situation—an old woman with a great deal of money and no family to inherit—she began to ingratiate herself with her ladyship. Over the course of the next few months, she devised a scheme whereby she would become Lady Longford's chief legatee upon her ladyship's death—which wouldn't be far off, if Miss Martine had her way. When she discovered that her ladyship had an orphaned granddaughter, she did all she could to discourage Lady Longford from giving her a home. Failing in her efforts, she had contacted her brother and begged him to come to the Manor and help her deal with the problem. She planned to have him appointed as head teacher, which would give him a reason to be in Sawrey—and to stay at the Manor—over an extended period of time. Carrying out his sister's instructions, Wentworth had appropriated the identity of a certain Dr. Gainwell, who had recently been assigned to the South Pacific by the London Missionary Society, where Wentworth worked as a clerk.

"But it was never my intention to harm the girl, you know," Wentworth insisted. "I've done nothing wrong except to impersonate a missionary." He grinned crookedly. "And that, surely, is not a hanging offense."

"You received the stolen jewelry that your sister sent you," Woodcock pointed out. He cast an accusing glance at the man's Saville Row frock coat. "You sold it and you spent the money on clothes. That warrants a charge of grand larceny."

"And you knew of your sister's plan to poison Lady Longford," Heelis added, "which makes you a co-conspirator. Your best chance for leniency, Wentworth, is to testify against your sister and throw yourself on the mercy of the Crown."

Wentworth dropped his head into his hands with a groan.

"As Justice of the Peace for Sawrey district, I am issuing a warrant for your arrest, Kenneth Wentworth," Captain Woodcock said in a formal tone. "The constable will convey you to Hawkshead, where you will be arraigned before the magistrates on the charges of receiving stolen property and conspiracy to commit murder. Meantime, we will apprehend your sister and—"

"Then you'd better hurry," Wentworth said glumly. "Unless I miss my guess, she's planning to leave just as soon as Beever gets back with the phaeton."

Miss Martine was indeed planning to leave, directly after luncheon. She had already packed her bags and quietly set them in the hallway closet, not wanting to call any special attention to her departure. It would be awkward, of course, to answer Lady Longford's questions. In a day or two, after the fuss had died down, she would write and say that her sister or her cousin was deathly ill, and that she had been suddenly called away, and might her outstanding wages be sent, please, to the address at the bottom of the letter.

But in the meantime, Emily was announcing callers. Miss Martine was startled to look up and see Captain Woodcock and Mr. Heelis, standing in the doorway behind Emily. Her surprise turned to stunned dismay when the captain, with a stern expression, told her that he had just sent her brother off to the magistrates' office in Hawkshead, and went on to tell her why. She stared at him for a moment, wondering how on earth he had got the information. Briefly, she considered fainting dead away on the velvet sofa, but rejected that dramatic idea, feeling that it was somehow unbefitting a woman of her strength of character. Anyway, it would only prolong the inevitable. She might as well get it over with.

So she remained upright and heard herself telling the truth in a calm, steady voice that hardly seemed her own, making as much of her brother's involvement as she dared and even going so far as to attribute the idea of poisoning the old lady to him.

"*He* was the one who remembered seeing the stories about Florence Maybrick in the newspapers," she said, applying her white handkerchief to her eyes. "I told him it was a cruel, heartless scheme, but he insisted." She delicately suppressed a sob. "You have no idea how obstinate my brother can be when he wants something. And he wanted Lady Longford's fortune. I was powerless—utterly powerless—to resist him."

When she had said all that could be said, Emily was

called in. The foolish girl, weeping stormily, was compelled to repeat what she had already told Miss Potter—about the "medicine," whilst the captain wrote everything down and asked Emily to sign it. Then Emily pointed the captain and Mr. Heelis to the wastepaper basket where Miss Martine had discarded what remained of the flypapers she had stolen from Mrs. Beever's pantry, not imagining that anyone would understand their significance.

"Thank you for your honesty, Emily," the captain said, folding the girl's statement and putting it into his pocket. "Lady Longford has cause to be grateful, as well."

Emily threw a sidelong glance at Miss Martine. "Does this mean that I won't be going to London to be a maid in a fine house?" she asked in a tearful whisper.

"What do you think, you foolish girl?" Miss Martine snapped. She lifted her chin. "How could I recommend you for a responsible position after the way you have betrayed me?"

"And you can thank your lucky stars for that, Emily," Mr. Heelis said firmly, as Captain Woodcock took Miss Martine by the arm and began to lead her away. "You would not be happy in London, with all the smoke and dirt and noise. And Miss Martine certainly had no intention of getting you a good position. She only wanted to get you out of here, so you wouldn't be able to tell what you saw."

"What is this commotion?" demanded Lady Longford icily, coming down the hall toward them, dressed in her dressing gown and leaning on her stick. "Mr. Heelis, what is the meaning of this? Emily, why are you sniveling so disgracefully? And why does Captain Woodcock have his hand on Miss Martine's arm? Does he think she is going to fly away?" She pounded her stick on the floor. "Miss Martine, I demand to know why these gentlemen have invaded my home!"

"If you will permit me, ma'am," Heelis replied, stepping forward, "I will tell you the full story. It is not a pretty one, I am afraid. But bear with me whilst I—"

Still talking quietly, he accompanied Lady Longford in the direction of her sitting room, leaving Captain Woodcock to take official custody of Miss Martine and the poisonous flypapers, and to tell Emily that her presence would be required before the magistrates, where she would be obliged to repeat under oath what she had seen.

"Before the magistrates?" Emily whispered, her eyes widening. "Oh, my gracious! Oh, my stars! Under *oath*?" She gulped. "Whatever shall I wear?"

"You are a stupid fool, Emily," said Miss Martine, in the cruelest tone she could summon.

31

Miss Potter Feels *Muscular*

It had been a very long day, Will Heelis thought, as he finished his pub dinner at the Tower Bank Arms. A fine dinner,
in fact—nothing at all wrong with the steak and kidney pie
that Ruth Safford had served him, or the blackberry cobbler
and coffee that had finished off the meal. He leaned back in
his chair, took out his pipe, and began to think about all the
things that had happened that day, from the early-morning
breakfast with Miss Potter and Caroline, to the arrest of the
Wentworth sister and brother, now installed in the Hawkshead jail, awaiting arraignment. It had been a long day, a
day full of surprises, and it wasn't over yet.

Ten minutes later, Will had paid for his dinner and was
standing on the front steps of the Arms, when he looked up
to see Miss Potter coming down the hill, on her way from
Hill Top Farm. There was mud on her skirt and dust on her

jacket, and she was swinging her hat in one hand as she walked, whistling under her breath.

Will tipped his bowler hat courteously. "Good evening, Miss Potter."

"Oh!" she exclaimed, and her hand went to her mouth. "I didn't see you, Mr. Heelis."

"I'm sorry to have startled you." He went toward her, noticing how pretty she was when she was flustered. "I wonder if you've heard what happened today?"

"No, I haven't. I've been occupied with Hill Top affairs since I left you this morning." She put on her hat. "I am sorry to tell you that Mr. Biddle and I have come to a parting of the ways. I am tired of being terrorized and bullied by a man in my employ. I have paid him for his work and discharged him."

"Sorry to tell me! Why, I'm delighted, Miss Potter. Good for you!" Will had known Bernard Biddle for at least ten years, and he was aware that the man had harassed and intimidated almost everyone who hired him. No one would hire him if he weren't the only building contractor between Windermere and Hawkshead. "I trust that you are feeling comfortable about what you have done," he added.

"If you want to know the truth, Mr. Heelis, I am feeling *muscular*," Miss Potter replied smartly. "It is surely wicked, and I suppose that some would say I have behaved badly. But it gives one strength to say exactly what one thinks to another, particularly when that other is a man who expects one to curl up and cry."

Will couldn't help chuckling. "Really, Miss Potter, you are an amazing person."

Her cheeks were pink, but she was smiling as she looked up at him. "What I need to do is find another contractor—someone who does not feel that taking orders from a woman reduces him to something a little lower than the earthworms.

There is a man in Kendal, I understand. I intend to go and talk to him tomorrow." She paused. "Now, tell me, please, Mr. Heelis. What happened today?"

Will told her, in every detail, and had the pleasure of seeing her very blue eyes widen as the story went along. He concluded with: "And that, I believe, is the end of *that* ominous scheme. The Wentworths are in custody, and Lady Longford has accepted the situation—with understandable bitterness, of course, at having been so thoroughly duped and so dangerously victimized. She believes, Miss Potter, that you saved her life."

Now the blue eyes were very wide, and the color very high. "I?" she exclaimed. "But I did nothing—except a bit of eavesdropping."

"Now, now, Miss Potter," he chided. "Accept the credit, for it is certainly due. Underneath that crusty exterior, Lady Longford has a good heart. I have high hopes that she will come to accept her granddaughter, over time." He paused. "I have not yet taken Caroline back to the Manor—she seems to be enjoying herself in Miss Barwick's bakery—but I plan to do so tomorrow."

"I am glad to hear that," Miss Potter said decidedly. "If there is any way I can help, be sure to call on me." A shadow crossed her face. "And if you happen to hear that my orange guinea pig has been found, I should be very grateful if you would let me know. I don't hold out much hope, for he was last seen on Holly How, a dangerous place for a very little creature. He's probably already made a mouthful for an owl or a fox."

Will put his hat back on his head. "I shall indeed be on the lookout for him," he said gravely, and added, feeling suddenly shy, "I am on my way to the Woodcocks' for the evening. The captain and I are going out later—we have an engagement in Far Sawrey—but in the interim, we will probably play cards and chat. Miss Woodcock will be there, of course. I wonder . . . would you care to join us?"

Miss Potter looked down at her hands, then away. She seemed to consider the invitation for a moment, but shook her head. "Thank you, no," she said. "Mrs. Crook is expecting me to supper. Besides, I'm not much of a card player."

From the look he saw in her eyes before she glanced away, Will had the idea that there was more to it than that. But there was no point in pursuing the matter, so he swallowed his disappointment and gave her a smile and a nod.

The two of them walked together as far as the path to the Woodcocks' house, where they said goodnight. He stood and watched her as she walked up the street, bareheaded, her stride firm and energetic. Felt muscular for having given old Biddle the boot, did she? Really, a most remarkable woman.

32

We Few, We Band of Brothers

At midsummer, in the Lake District, darkness does not fall until well after ten o'clock, so Will Heelis and Miles Woodcock, with Miss Woodcock, played three-handed bridge and discussed the events of the day.

At ten o'clock, as previously arranged, Constable Braithwaite appeared. Miss Woodcock excused herself, and the three men held a quiet but intense consultation. Having received his instructions, the constable left, and fifteen minutes later, there was a tap at the side entry and Charlie appeared, looking just as seedy as he had the day before, and with the same rank odor of ale, garlic, and onions hanging about him like a malodorous cloud.

They exchanged a few words, and then Will and the captain followed Charlie through the back gate and around the shrubbery. As they reached the narrow footpath that led through the meadows to Far Sawrey, some half-mile away, the constable fell in behind at some considerable distance, keeping the trio just in sight. They walked single file, without saying a word and with no lantern. The moon had risen, casting just enough light for them to see where they were going, and they had no wish to call attention to themselves.

The captain's small group was not the only little band moving furtively through the darkness toward Far Sawrey. Dozens of men from the twin hamlets and the outlying farms and cottages had been looking forward to the night's entertainment, and they were on their way to the event in comradly groups of twos and threes. Lanterns danced like drunken fireflies through the silent dark and bottles of home-brewed beer and ale clinked pleasantly in pockets, as shadowy shapes met and came together and separated, at last converging on the stable at the rear of the Sawrey Hotel.

For the most part, the little bands kept voices low and talk to a minimum. The men knew very well that what they were doing was illegal and that the local Justice of the Peace had done everything he could to suppress such revelries. They also knew, however, that this was a special occasion, deliberately planned for a night when both Captain Woodcock and Constable Braithwaite would be miles away in Kendal, attending a meeting of the Law Enforcement Officers Guild.

There would be no interference from the authorities to mar the merriment.

From a farther distance and a different direction, another, rather more diverse band was making its way toward the stable behind the hotel. In response to the summons passed by word of mouth through field and fellside, a large number of animals had gathered on Holly How, just outside the front door of The Brockery. They listened attentively as Bosworth Badger, standing on a heap of stones, told them why they had been called together, where they were going, and what they aimed to do.

" *'Pon my word,*" drawled a fat, aristocratic-looking vole, curling his tail around his forepaws. *"Sounds a rawther dang'rous thing to do."*

"Of course it's dangerous," snarled a fox, who, under other circumstances, would have made a quick meal of the vole. However, animals are capable of setting certain instincts aside when the good of the community is at stake—and the urgent need to defend the community was certainly reflected in the curious coalition of predator and prey that gathered in the darkness on Holly How that night. An observer might have counted a half-dozen lazy, lay-about voles; a dozen brown field rats from the Holly How rat patrol; a trio of twittering red squirrels with flashing eyes and nervous tails; a pair of foxes; several hedgehogs; an orange guinea pig; three moles; the badger (of course); a very shy pine marten, who kept invisibly to the shadows; a noisy and undisciplined rabble of stoats and weasels wielding large clubs; and Fritz the Ferret, who had come all the way up from the stone bridge on Kendal Road to join the expedition. The owl was there, too, of course, perched on a small tree that sagged under his professorial substance.

As might be expected, the members of this peculiar coalition were not entirely comfortable with one another. The smaller animals tended to huddle together, out of the way of the larger, and the largest tended put out their elbows and take up more than their fair share of the space. Feelings were frayed and nerves were taut and there was a great deal of pushing and shoving and snapping and muttered warnings of *"Mind how you go,"* and *"Have a care of my tail, if you please, sir!"* and *"Hold it just there, not an inch more!"*

The badger raised his stick for silence. *"It is dangerous,"* he agreed gravely. *"Any time we must go amongst men, we are in danger—and some of us may feel endangered by others in this very group. But it is time to put our fears aside. We cannot sit on our tails with our paws folded and let criminals kidnap and make a cruel show of murder. If we allow this shameful event to take place tonight, the shame is on us, my friends, forever and ever! We will not be fit to bear the honored name of ANIMAL!"*

"Hear, hear!" cried the small orange guinea pig, and then hastily shut up, feeling himself at a disadvantage as to size and strength, and thinking that he should leave the cheering to those who were larger and had more experience of this sort of thing.

"Ah," said the vole thoughtfully. He smoothed his sleek gray fur, examined one paw, and said, *"I'm afraid you must excuse me, gentlemen. I have just remembered something pressing that I must do at home."*

The vole's departure became an exodus when he was followed by every single one of the other voles (all of whom had remembered equally urgent matters to which they had to attend), two or three of the older rabbits, a squirrel affecting a sprained ankle, and a mole who claimed to be suffering from a very painful toothache.

Bosworth, reminding himself of the Fourth Rule of Thumb concerning departures without leave, turned his head and took no notice. The professor, however, did not feel obliged to observe badger etiquette, and gave several mocking hoots as the cowards skulked away. Following his lead, the other animals joined in, jeering and shouting taunts after the departing animals, delivering such remarks as *"See if we ever do anything good for you lot,"* and *"Don't come crying to us when you get into trouble and need a hand."*

When the last one had gone, the badger called for silence again. *"Professor Galileo Newton Owl has a few words he would like to share with you,"* he said.

There was a round of polite applause, a respectful *"Let's hear it from the professor!"* and two or three raucous comments from the weasels and stoats, who usually stayed on the rabble-rousing fringe.

"Thank you," said the professor, and lifted his wings. *"Friends, Romans,* countrymen," he cried, *"lend me your ears."* This caused some dark muttering amongst the ranks, and several of the animals were heard to object that they were neither Romans nor countrymen and what did this have to do with anything?

But all fell still as the professor began to recite, with his best Shakespearean intonation, admirable fervor, and a few regrettable revisions, King Henry's famous speech before Agincourt:

> *This night shall e'er be called the Night of Holly How:*
> *He that outlives this fight, and comes safe home,*
> *Will stand a tip-toe when this night is named,*
> *And rouse him at the name of Holly How.*
> *He that shall live this night, and see old age,*
> *Will yearly on this vigil feast his neighbors,*
> *And say, Tooonight is the Night of Holly How:*
> *Then will he strip his sleeve and show his scars,*
> *And say, These wounds I had on the Night of Holly How.*
> *This story shall all gooood animals teach their sons;*
> *Nooo winter's night beside the fire shall e'er gooo by,*
> *From this day tooo the ending of the world,*
> *Without our story told, and we in it remembered:*
> *We few, we happy few, we band of brothers;*
> *For he tonight that sheds his blooood, whatever kind*
> *Of animal he be, shall be my brother!*

By the time the professor was half the way through this stirring speech, a great many hankies had come out of waist-coat pockets and were being applied to wet eyes. And when he had completely finished, he took a deep breath and cried, *"Whooo is with us? Raise your voices, lads!"*

At that, all the animals gave such a mighty shout—a chorus of squeaks, squeals, growls, barks, yips, and snorts—that their clamor might have been heard as far away as Sawrey, if any of the villagers had been listening. They shook paws and thumped each other's backs, and congratu-lated each other on their great bravery, and danced and sang and chanted war cries and generally worked themselves into a fever pitch, the way people do when they're preparing to go to war, until at last Badger raised his stick and shouted, *"Well, then, boys! Let's be off!"*

So at last this motley crew proceeded down the hill in a southward direction, through briar and bramble and over tumbled rocks and across burbling becks and under the omi-nous shadow of Cuckoo Brow Wood. Bosworth Badger led them, followed by the rat patrol, keeping cadence. The pine marten brought up the rear, and the troops were accompa-nied by Professor Galileo Newton Owl, who flew above their heads shouting such encouraging messages as *"Goood show!"* and *"Give it a gooo, boys!"* and *"We few, we band of brothers!"*

Despite the professor's exhortations, it was all Tuppenny could do to keep up the pace, for his legs were shorter by a good bit than the legs of any of the other animals, and he found himself sliding and stumbling and falling over the rocks and tumbling into whatever puddles happened to be in his way. By the time the band of brothers had reached the wooded hill to the north of the hotel yard, poor Tuppenny was scraped and scratched, one ear was badly nicked, one paw was cut to the bone, and his orange fur was wet, matted, snarled with burrs, and disgracefully bedraggled.

But although he was very small, Tuppenny had a very large heart, and he—like the other animals—was appalled at what was to take place that night. So he doubled and redoubled his efforts, manfully doing his very best to keep up. And at long last the company arrived on the dark hill above the stable, stopped to catch their breaths, and peered through the open doors of the building some ten yards away.

33

❧

The Badger-Baiting

And what they saw was, in truth, appalling, a sight no animal should ever have to look upon. A circular area some eight feet in diameter had been inscribed on the dirt floor of the stable, and a temporary wooden fence, about three feet high, erected around the perimeter. Lanterns were hung on poles around this pit, flooding the circle with a garish light and casting flickering shadows on the stable walls.

The pit was surrounded by a throng of laughing, jeering, jostling men, some of them standing on wooden benches they had dragged into the stable for a better view. By their dress, most of the men seemed to be farmers and villagers, but a few—judging from their shiny hats and gentlemen's frock coats and ties—were travelers staying at the Sawrey Hotel. A pair of waiters had come out of the bar and circulated through the crowd with loud cries of "What'll ye have

t' drink, gentl'men? Orders, if ye please! Orders!" Other
men called for wagers and took money, and still others carried small dogs, or jerked them along by ropes tied around
their necks, or shouldered rusty wire cages filled with dark,
heaving masses of rats. For whilst the badger-baiting was to
be the piéce de rèsistance of the evening's entertainment, it
was preceded by several rat-and-dog matches.

While Tuppenny looked on with horror, scarcely able to
believe his eyes, a cage full of rats was tipped into the pit
and a ferocious-looking bull terrier poised over the fence in
his owner's arms. At Tuppenny's side, the commander of the
rat patrol sucked in his breath and put out a restraining paw
to keep one of his troopers from leaping forward.

"*Hold hard*," the commander muttered in a gritty voice.
"*Our turn will come.*"

"*But they'll be killed!*" the trooper cried despairingly.

"*We'll have our revenge,*" the commander said. "*Hold hard,
I say!*"

The man in charge took out a large stopwatch. "What's t'
name of thi dog?" he inquired.

"Butcher," said the dog's owner, who was obviously having trouble holding the animal. "He's a fierce 'un, Jack Ogden. He'll make short work o' this lot."

"Chuck 'im over t' fence, then," said Jack Ogden. "We'll
see how fierce t' beast is." He clicked the stopwatch. "Go!"

To a loud cheer from the spectators in the stable, over the
fence went Butcher. In an instant the frantic rats were racing
around the circumference of the pit, or trying to push through
the gaps between the boards. But Butcher was indeed fierce
and knew his work, and in exactly one minute, fourteen rats
were lying bleeding and kicking in the dirt. Tuppenny could
hear the horrified gasps of the rat patrol, and it was all the
commander could do to restrain his troops.

Down in the stable, the dead rats were picked up by their tails and flung into a basket, and pots of ale and glasses of wine were handed round. There was a brief and noisy intermission whilst Butcher's health was drunk, the winning bets were paid, and wagers laid on the main bout, which was next.

But other things had been going on in the shadowy corners of the stable, unseen either by the band of brothers on the hill or by the spectators whose attention was fixed on the ugly business in the pit. Will Heelis, Miles Woodcock, and the constable had taken up their positions, and stood quietly, waiting for the next event.

Will had his eyes on Jack Ogden, a heavyset, bearded man in a brown shirt buttoned up to the neck, a clay pipe stuck between his teeth. Ogden's massive shoulders and square, hard hands testified to his work as a wall-builder who traveled around the Lake District, constructing the dry stone walls that marked the field boundaries. It was known that he was an expert waller, and he was always in great demand. It was also known that he dug badgers as a sideline, and farmers summoned him when they wanted to be rid of badgers on their property. But there was something else of interest about Jack Ogden, for in the press of people, Will had deliberately got close enough to the man to get a good whiff of the tobacco he was smoking. It was cherry-flavored, without a doubt. And his clay pipe had been made (unless Will missed his guess) by Hiram Swift.

"Gentlemen, attention, please!" cried Jack Ogden loudly. "Tha's all come t' see tonight's chief attraction, and it's near time for t' show to begin! What we have here is a fine, fat badger sow, just dug out of 'er sett. It was close by to t' village, and she was no doubt raidin' all thi wives' gardens. And to make t' match e'en fiercer, we'll throw in 'er cub. And for t' dog—" He held up his hands for silence. "And for t' dog, we have Black Mack, t' terror of t' Lake District!"

"Black Mack!" A cheer went up. "Black Mack!"

Will pressed his lips together, as a cage was brought and two badgers, one large and one quite small, were dumped out of the cage and into the pit. The larger badger, fangs bared and the fur standing up in a ridge along its back, crouched defensively in front of the cub, which squealed and cowered in fright against the wall. Somebody shouted, "Here's Black Mack!" and a large black dog, snapping and snarling on a heavy chain, was produced out of the crowd.

"Go for 't, Black Mack!" a man cried, and Jack Ogden bent over to pick up the dog and toss it into the pit.

This was the moment Miles Woodcock was waiting for. He signaled to Constable Braithwaite, who stepped out of the darkness and blew a shrill blast on his police whistle. All sound ceased, and the captain and the constable went forward into the sudden silence.

"Tha's under arrest, Jack Ogden!" Constable Braithwaite said roughly. "Tha's been warned a-fore 'bout this bus'ness. Tha knows 'tis a crim'nal offense to bait badgers."

"Aw, hell," Ogden said disgustedly.

With that, pandemonium broke loose. The sudden and unwelcome appearance of the constable and the Justice of the Peace panicked the spectators, waiters, and bookies. They turned and broke for the stable doors, pushing and shoving to get out, abandoning their dogs and rat cages and flattening the walls of the pit in their flight. But to this mad disorder was added another, for an extraordinary stampede of animals suddenly charged out of the darkness and through the double doors at the rear of the stable, snapping and yapping and yipping and yelping at the heels of the fleeing crowd with an unearthly, ear-piercing cacophony. To an amazed Will Heelis, it was as if some sort of fantastic zoo wagon had stopped just outside and discharged its passengers, a seemingly infinite horde of brown field rats, squirrels, foxes, moles, stoats, weasels, a badger, and—

He blinked. And an orange guinea pig, which stood on its hind legs, blinking and bobbing its head in confusion, bewildered by the shouting, swirling chaos of men and animals. Without thought, Will bent over and scooped up the little creature and dropped it into the pocket of his jacket.

This madness went on for only a minute or two, and when it was over, the stable was completely empty of spectators—and of animals, too. The two badgers had vanished from the wreckage of the pit, and even the caged rats had somehow managed to escape. As far as Will could see, the only creature left was an enormous tawny owl, perched high in the shadowy rafters, regarding the scene below with a steady, unblinking gaze.

Jack Ogden glared at Captain Woodcock. "Well, now tha's done it," he growled, folding his arms with a surly look. "We was only havin' a bit o' fun, nae harm to nobody. Tha's t' only justice of t' peace in t' whole Lake District that gives a damn 'bout badger-baitin'. And there's nae point in chargin' me, neither. T' magistrate will only let me off with a warnin', same as he's done a-fore."

"Not this time," the captain said gravely. He held something out. "I believe these are yours, are they not?"

"Hey!" Jack Ogden took the tongs he was handed. "Oh, aye. These're my badger tongs. See there?" He pointed with a thick finger. "That's my mark. J.O. Jack Ogden." He grinned, showing a broken tooth. "'Tis nae crime t' dig badgers, tha knows, Captain."

"Yes, I know," the captain said quietly. "These tongs, however, were found on Holly How, at the place where Ben Hornby fell to his death, and they fit the welt that marks Ben's shoulders." He paused. "And what's more, Ben was holding a tobacco pipe, Jack. A Hiram Swift clay pipe." He glanced at Will, who nodded firmly. "That pipe had your tobacco in it. Brown Twist, Number Four, cherry-flavored." He leaned forward and pulled a half-full tobacco sack out of the pocket of Ogden's brown shirt. He held it up, displaying the Gawith label. "An uncommon tobacco, Jack. There aren't many who prefer cherry."

"Hey!" Jack Ogden's mouth opened wide in alarm. "I didn't have nothing to do with that business! You can't tangle me in—"

"We shall see whether I can or not," the captain said. "The handcuffs, Constable Braithwaite. Our friend Mr. Ogden is going to spend the night in the Hawkshead jail. When he is arraigned in the morning, perhaps he will have reflected on the advantages of telling the truth."

Will stood watching as the constable handcuffed the protesting man, took him by the collar, and dragged him out of the stable.

"Well," said the captain, dusting his hands with satisfaction, "that's that. A good night's work, eh, Will?"

"A good night's work," echoed Will. He looked around, frowning. "I don't understand those animals."

"What animals?"

"Why, didn't you see them, Miles? Foxes, weasels, rats— a whole army. Charged right in here and—"

The captain shook his head. "Didn't notice, I'm afraid. My attention was focused on Ogden." He grinned widely. "Did you see his face when I held up those tongs, Will? He had no idea what was coming next. Took him completely by surprise, we did."

Will shook his head, perplexed. "You didn't see the animals?" he repeated incredulously. "They were underfoot, everywhere, yipping and squealing. And if I'm not mistaken, they emptied the rat cages and made off with that pair of badgers."

"Emptied the rat cages?" The captain gave a hearty chuckle. "Made off with the badgers? You're seeing things, Will Heelis!"

"Is that right?" Will asked grimly. He reached into his coat pocket. "What's this, then?" And he pulled out a wet and bedraggled orange guinea pig.

"Doesn't look like a fox or a weasel to me," said the captain, with a quick glance. "More like a fuzzy orange rat, except that he's missing his tail. Anyway, I doubt he's big enough to make off with a couple of badgers." He clapped his friend on the shoulder. "Come on, old chap, I'll buy you a drink."

When the two men had left the stable, another shadow began to stir and in a moment a boy climbed down the wooden ladder out of the loft, a gray cotton sack slung over one shoulder. He stood in the stable doorway, looking out onto the moonlit hill, first one way and then the other, obviously puzzled. At that moment, on his perch high in the rafters, the owl raised his wings, flapped them twice, and sailed into the starry sky, heading north.

The boy looked up at the owl, smiled, and then began to follow.

34

Celebrations

At the Woodcocks' house the next morning, Dimity smiled across the breakfast table at her brother, who was in an extraordinarily good mood.

"I take it," she said, picking up the coffee pot, "that you were able to close down the badger-baiting without any bloodshed."

Miles shook his head. "Not a drop of blood, unless you count Butcher's victims—a couple of dozen dead rats. Butcher," he added, taking the cup his sister handed him, "is a dog."

"A *mean* dog." Elsa Grape came into the room with a plate of freshly fried bacon. "A monster. Rather kill a rat than eat. Kills cats, too."

"I don't want to hear about it, Elsa," Dimity said with a shudder. "What about the badger, Miles? Is she safe?"

"Oh, she got away," Miles said carelessly. "She and her cub. No idea what happened to her. Heelis told me an odd story about invading animals carrying her off, but I was too busy to notice." He grinned. "I was frying a more important fish. We nabbed Jack Ogden, Dim."

"For badger-baiting?" Dimity asked eagerly.

"Won't do you any good to nab 'im for badger-baiting," Elsa observed. "They always let him off. If you'll forgive me sayin' so, Captain," she added in a dark tone, "nobody cares 'bout badger-baiting t' way you do."

The captain looked smug. "I don't think Ogden will get off this time. The evidence we've collected—the clay pipe and those badger tongs—suggests that he was involved in Ben Hornby's death. I'll have to consult with the magistrate before a charge is preferred, although from the welt on the dead man's back, it looks as if he was solidly whacked with those tongs. Of course, there're no witnesses. The case is entirely circumstantial." He frowned at Elsa. "Now, don't go spreading this around the village."

"Of course not, Cap'n Woodcock," Elsa said, looking down her nose with an air of offended dignity. "What do you take me for, a gossip?" She flounced out of the room.

"I shouldn't have said anything in her hearing," Miles said. "She'll never be able to keep it to herself."

"I'll speak to her," Dimity assured him. She lifted her glass of orange juice. "Congratulations on a good night's work, Miles. It sounds as if that man deserves to have some time behind bars." She frowned. "But I should very much like to hear about the invasion that Mr. Heelis mentioned. I must say, it sounds rather curious."

"Sounds rather fantastic to me," her brother said. "Pass the marmalade, would you, Dim?"

* * *

The night before had not ended until several celebratory glasses of ale had been drunk, so Will Heelis had gone to bed once again at the Tower Bank Arms. The excitement of the badger-baiting and the arrest of Jack Ogden now past, he had slept soundly, awaking to the morning sunshine spilling through the window and across his coverlet in a blaze of July glory.

There was something else on his coverlet, though, besides a splash of sunshine. It was the small orange guinea pig he had found in the stable. When he reached his room the night before, Will had dropped the guinea pig into his empty chamber pot and put on the lid, but apparently the guinea pig had pushed the lid aside and climbed out.

"Good morning," Will said, clasping his hands behind his head and staring at the creature. It looked somewhat better this morning, having washed and groomed itself, but there were still snarls and tangles in its fur. "You could do with a good combing."

"*I'm sure I could, sir,*" Tuppenny said humbly. "*You see, I have had a most amazing adventure. I joined a band of brothers—a badger and rats and stoats and weasels and rabbits—who marched all the way from Holly How to rescue a damsel—*"

"Well, I could do with a comb myself," Will said. "And a shave, and a cup of tea, and some bacon and eggs." He threw back the covers, dislodging the creature, and got out of bed. "And then I suppose I had better take you up to Belle Green and see if you belong to Miss Potter." He frowned. "Although how you and those other animals got to the stable behind the Sawrey Hotel is beyond me. It's too bad you can't talk, young fellow. I would dearly like to hear your story."

"*But I can talk!*" protested Tuppenny. "*The problem is you, sir! Won't you at least try to—*"

But Will was whistling cheerily as he went about his

toilet, untroubled by Tuppenny's indignant squeaks. Washed, shaved, and dressed, he popped the guinea pig into his pocket and went downstairs. There, he enjoyed a full breakfast, after which he put on his hat and strode up Market Street to Belle Green, where he knocked at the door and asked to see Miss Potter.

A few moments later, she joined him in the parlor, dressed for travel in her jacket and hat. "Good morning, Mr. Heelis," she said, in some surprise. "You're out and about early this morning. I'm glad you caught me—I was just on my way to Kendal to talk to the man who I hope will replace Mr. Biddle."

"Miss Potter," Will said, "I think I might have found something that belongs to you." He reached into his coat pocket. "Close your eyes and hold out your hands."

With a puzzled look, she did as she was told. And then, the guinea pig squirming in her cupped palms, she opened her eyes wide with a little cry of pleasure.

"Tuppenny! Oh, Mr. Heelis, you've found him! Thank you, thank you!" She frowned down at the little creature. "Oh, you naughty guinea pig, just look at you! Your fur is full of burs and tangles. Where *have* you been? And what in the world have you been up to?"

"Oh, I've been ever so many places, Miss Potter!" Tuppenny cried excitedly. *"And I've had ever so many exciting adventures! I joined a band of brothers who raided a stable and chased out all the men and rescued a damsel in distress and—"*

"I'd like to know that too," Will said thoughtfully. "I found him under the most unusual circumstances." And he told her about the events of the evening before: the badger-baiting, the horde of wild animals invading the stable, and the arrest of Jack Ogden. "Once again, we are in your debt, I'm afraid," he concluded wryly. "If you hadn't found those badger tongs with Ogden's tool mark on them, there might not have been enough evidence to identify the man."

"There may not be enough evidence to convict him still," Miss Potter said. "Unless an eyewitness is found, or he breaks down and tells what happened." She gave him a sideways glance. "Do you think there's any chance of that?"

"There might be," Will said. "He's in a bad corner."

"But I'm even more curious about last night's animal . . . invasion, I think you called it. Tuppenny was with them?"

"Of course I was with them!" Tuppenny cried, jumping up and down in Miss Potter's hands. *"It was just smashing, and all the animals were amazingly brave! They—"*

"It was all very strange," Will said. "Captain Woodcock, for instance, says he didn't see a thing. But he was occupied with Ogden, and there was a great deal of confusion—people running about and shouting, all trying to get out of the stable. And it was rather dark, of course. It was only by chance that I happened to look down and see this little fellow." He smiled. "Is he a model for the book you're working on?"

"No," Miss Potter said, looking flustered. "The book is about three naughty kittens who lose their clothes and cause their mother a great deal of grief." She blushed and looked away. "It's not exactly a sophisticated cast of characters, or a very complex plot. My books are for rather young children, you see. They prefer reading about little animals who get into mischief—nothing very thrilling, I'm afraid."

"I'm quite sure the children would prefer," Tuppenny put in earnestly, *"to read about me, Miss Potter. Talk about thrills! You could tell them all about The Brockery, where the badger lives—really an amazing place, that goes on forever and ever underground. And the band of brothers, and rescuing a damsel in distress. It would make a ripping good story!"*

"I know about your children's books," Will replied, wondering why she sounded so apologetic. Surely she realized how much her work was admired by others. "Some of my young cousins are great enthusiasts of yours—fans, as the Americans say," he went on. "They would be terribly envious if they learnt that I had actually seen a few of your original drawings. Would you show them to me sometime?" When she hesitated, looking almost as if she thought he was making fun of her, he added, "As a reward for returning your guinea pig."

"Of course." She looked up at him, her blue eyes very bright. "I know that Tuppenny is just a guinea pig," she said in a low voice, "but all my animals are very special to me. And I'm sure that Caroline will be very grateful that he is safe—she felt terrible about losing him. Thank you for finding and returning him, Mr. Heelis." She dropped a kiss on the orange head.

"It's cause for celebration, believe me."

There was cause for celebration at The Brockery that morning, too. An extra leaf had been put into the dining table, two benches added, and additional plates and cups and knives and forks laid. As Badger looked down the table on both sides, he was gratified to see that several members of the rat patrol had stayed over, that there were now three hedgehogs rather than just one, and that two moles were seated on either side of Parsley, telling her all about the grand adventure of the previous night as they helped themselves to double portions of sausage.

But most gratifying of all, Bosworth could look down the crowded table and see that instead of there being only two badgers in The Brockery—himself and young Parsley— there were now *four*. For the night before, in that awful, wonderful, soul-stirring raid on the badger-pit in the stable behind the Sawrey Hotel, they had been able to rescue *both* kidnap victims—Primrose Badger and her girl cub, Hyacinth—who had been destined for an unspeakably cruel death.

But there was more.

When the band of exhausted animals had finally returned to The Brockery, Primrose and Parsley put little Hyacinth to bed with a spoonful of treacle and honey and a hot-water bottle for her feet. The others—a pair of foxes, the moles and rats, and a few stoats and weasels—opened a jug of elderflower wine and shared it amongst themselves, dropping wearily into chairs in front of the parlor fire under the benign gaze of Badger's gilt-framed ancestors, whilst the firelight winked on polished brasses and the flames crackled and popped in a most satisfactory way.

As midnight came on, they relived once more the thrilling excitement of the Great Raid (as it was already called), telling one another how the constable's shrill whistle had sounded like a bugle signaling their attack, and how they had charged down the hill and into the stable, disregarding all danger; and how splendidly and with what stunning courage they had fought; and how smartly they had snapped at the ankles of the frightened, fleeing men and the tails of cowardly dogs—yes! even the atrocious Butcher; and how adroitly they had opened the imprisoned rats' cages and released them; and how forcefully they had flattened the fence around the badger-pit so that Primrose and her cub could go free.

They had just opened the second jug and were recalling the long march back to Holly How—the painful climb up the hill, the menacing shadows along Cuckoo Brow Wood, the bottomless chasm over which they had crossed on a shaky fallen tree, the raging floodwaters of the beck they had forded—when The Brockery's front door bell gave three hollow clangs. Flotsam and Jetsam had already been sent to bed, so Bosworth, feeling peevish and out of sorts at being summoned from the congenial company at his fireside, put on his slippers, took a candle, and went to answer the bell.

He shot the bolt and opened the door a crack. *"It is rather late,"* he said crossly into the darkness, *"and it has been a very trying evening. I hope that whatever your business, it is important."*

"Oh, it is, sir!" cried a young voice eagerly. *"It's me, sir. Thorn, sir. I'm looking for my mother and my sister, Hyacinth. I believe they're here. Let me in, sir, please!"*

Bosworth opened the door and saw, to his great astonishment, a badger boy cub standing on his doorstep.

"Thorn?" he cried, in quite a different voice. *"Why, you've been given up for lost, my boy! Come in, come in, oh, come in, do! Your mother will be so very delighted to see you."*

"Delighted" was hardly the word for it. There were cries of joy, and tears of relief, and little whimperings of happiness, and huggings and kissings and strokings, and all the other animals had looked on with astonishment, saying what a joyful reunion it was and how gratified they were to see the little family together again and what a satisfying conclusion it made to a most satisfactory evening.

All this was followed, of course, by the requisite explanations. Whilst a third jug of elderflower wine was opened for the grownups, young Thorn's jacket and boots were removed and he was set to toast before the fire with a glass of warm milk and a dish of Parsley's rice pudding spiced with cinnamon and nutmeg. Thus fortified, he told his tale.

He had managed to escape the brutal badger digger who had destroyed his home at the Hill Top quarry and cruelly kidnapped his mother and sister, but his leg had been badly injured in the attempt. He had been found by Jeremy

Crosfield—"*Admirable young chap,*" muttered Bosworth, "*most admirable*"—who had taken him to the veterinarian for treatment, and then back to the cottage he shared with his aunt, for rest and recovery.

But earlier that evening, Jeremy had put Thorn into a sack and taken him to the stable behind the Sawrey Hotel, where they hid themselves in the loft. It seemed that Jeremy, who occasionally worked as a stable boy, had some sort of plan to disrupt the badger-baiting and rescue Thorn's mother and sister. He didn't get a chance to carry it out, though, for the constable had intervened, blowing his whistle and throwing everyone in the stable into utter confusion. Then the animals had rushed in, adding to the chaos, whilst Thorn and Jeremy watched from the loft, cheering them on. When the raid was over and the men had left the stable, Jeremy had put Thorn back in the sack and climbed down out of the loft.

From that point, Thorn couldn't provide any information, because (of course) he was shut up in the sack on Jeremy's shoulder. But he was aware that the boy was climbing up hills and walking for what seemed a very long way. At last they had stopped, Jeremy opened the sack, and told Thorn that it was safe to come out. And then he had found himself on The Brockery's doorstep and—

"*And now you are safe,*" said his mother. "*We are all three together again, and Mr. Badger has offered us a home. What a great blessing.*" She burst into tears.

Bosworth, who was never quite sure how to comfort a crying female, cleared his throat. "*I think,*" he said gruffly, "*that it is time we all went to bed.*"

And now he could look up and down the breakfast table and see not only the friends who had joined him in the Great Raid, and the victims they had rescued from an unspeakable fate, but four badgers—five, counting himself—and one of them a boy badger, who, when he grew up, might be just the badger to assume responsibility for the *History* and the *Genealogy*.

35

Bo Peep's Sheep

Miss Potter's mission to Kendal was highly successful. It was late afternoon before she returned, satisfied that she had at last found a contractor with whom she could comfortably work, and who might succeed where Mr. Biddle had failed, to stop out the pesky rats. In her room at Belle Green, she changed out of her traveling clothes, checked to make sure that Tuppenny was settling in, and went down to the kitchen for a quick cup of tea with Mrs. Crook. Then, putting on her hat and taking a walking stick, she whistled for Rascal.

Rascal was delighted when Miss Potter asked him to escort her, but he was even more pleased when she began carrying on a conversation with him as they walked up Stony Lane. He had noticed that she seemed to talk to all of her animals in that way—as if they were Big Folk. It was a pleasant habit, and one that made him like her even more than he already did.

"It's been an eventful week," she remarked as they tramped up the hill. "But everything seems to have turned out well in the end. Lady Longford is no longer in danger from that horrible Miss Martine, and Caroline is safely back at the Manor. Jack Ogden will to have to face justice, the badger-baiting was broken up, and Mr. Heelis found Tuppenny—quite remarkable, when one thinks about it. And I've hired a new contractor to replace Mr. Biddle, so perhaps the work at Hill Top Farm will be finished soon, after all." She paused. "As far as I can see, there's only one big problem left."

"The sheep," Rascal barked.

Miss Potter smiled down at him. "I feel like Bo Peep, you know. 'Little Bo Peep has lost her sheep, and can't tell where to find them.' P'rhaps I shall put that nursery rhyme in a book some day." Her smile faded. "Although I can't think that these sheep will simply come home, wagging their tails behind them."

"Why not?" Rascal asked. *"They're heafed to Holly How. That's where they live—at least as far as they know. If they can get loose from wherever they are, they'll go straight home to Holly How. Maybe we should go have another look—"*

"We are going to Oldfield Farm, Rascal. I suspect that the sheep are there, and that Mr. Chance hopes I will buy them from him." Miss Potter thumped her walking stick emphatically. "But if they're mine, I'll recognize them. They have lug marks—both ears are shear-halved."

Rascal knew all about lug marks, of course: slits, notches, or shapes cut into a sheep's ear to establish its owner's identity. An ear that was "shear-halved" had a large scallop cut out of the tip. And farmers like Ben Hornby, who managed land that was owned by the lord of the local manor, were

entitled to mark *both* ears, not just one. Sheep thieves sometimes removed the lug marks by cutting off the ears of
stolen sheep. No knowledgeable farmer would buy a sheep
with no ears, of course, for it was clear evidence of theft. But
Miss Potter was new to farming, and Mr. Chance might
think that he could put one over on her. Rascal wondered
grimly if the Holly How sheep had already had their ears
cut off.

The afternoon sun was dropping toward the west, the air
was warm and sweet, and birds sang in the hedge. Rascal
and Miss Potter walked past Tidmarsh Manor, and then
past the lane that led to Holly How Farm. They had gone
perhaps a quarter-mile farther when they saw, coming toward them, five Herdwick sheep—two ewes and three
lambs—in the company of a large yellow dog, limping
along behind them.

"*Tibbie!*" Rascal yipped. "*Queenie! Where are you going?*"

"*Home, of course,*" sighed Tibbie. "*Where do you think?*"

"*And I'm leavin' Oldfield Farm,*" Mustard growled. "*I've
had all I can take of Isaac Chance's boot, and bein' chained in t'
barn with nothin' t' eat. Even an auld dog like me can learn a new
trick or twa.*"

"How'd the sheep get loose?" Rascal asked.

Mustard shook his head. "*You're not goin' to b'lieve this, but
it was an owl.*"

"An owl!" Rascal exclaimed, thinking immediately of the
professor.

"*I said you wouldn't b'lieve it. He flew down and knocked t'
hasp off t' barn door so's I could get out. Flew to t' sheep pen and
did t' same trick. Broad daylight, and bold as brass, he was.*" He
shook his head again in disbelief. "*Reet maffled me, for sure.
Ne'er saw such a thing in all me life.*"

"Well, for heaven's sake," Miss Potter said, examining
the sheep's ears. "If it isn't *my* Herdwicks, two ewes and

three lambs!" She bent over and stroked Mustard's head. "Thank you for returning them to me, Mustard. You've saved me a long walk, and worry, and a nasty confrontation with Mr. Chance." She straightened up. "I'll take them down to Hill Top Farm. You can go home now."

"*I doan't have nae hoame nae more,*" Mustard said mournfully. "*I'll just tag along with you, if you doan't mind, Missus.*"

"*Taaake us down to Hill Top?*" Tibbie's bleat was disconsolate. "*But we're going to Holly How. Thaaat's where we live!*"

"*Not any more you don't,*" Rascal replied. "*Your new home is with Miss Potter. Old Ben Hornby is gone, you know.*"

Tibbie nodded sadly. "*We saaaw what Jack Ogden did. He didn't mean to kill Mr. Hornby, though. They got into a fight on the edge of the cliff, and there was an aaacident.*" She shuddered from the tip of her nose to the tip of her tail. "*It was appaaalling.*"

"*Too bad you can't testify at Ogden's hearing,*" Rascal said. "*The Big Folk would get on much better in this world if they could hear what we have to say.*" He paused, and the other animals nodded thoughtfully. It was something they had all wished from time to time. The world would be a more harmonious place if all of God's creatures could talk to one another.

"*But now you have a new mistress and a fine new place to live,*" Rascal went on cheerfully. "*You'll like it—really, you will. Lots of green grass, and a hill to climb, and Wilfin Beck running through the meadow for fresh water, and cows and horses for company.*" He added, thinking this would please Tibbie, "*And since you're nearer the village, there will be more chance for news and gossip. And who knows—perhaps Miss Potter will put you into one of her little books.*"

"I don't know about books," said Tibbie, brightening somewhat, "*but news is always nice.*" She sighed. "*Well, if we haaave to heaf to a new place, we'd best get on with the business. It's not easy, you know. Come along, laaambs.*" And with a resigned shake of her wooly head, she set off down the lane with her twin lambs. After a moment, and one last, longing glance up at Holly How, Queenie and her lamb hurried to catch up.

Miss Potter, holding her walking stick like a shepherd's crook, followed the sheep. And in spite of her efforts to make Mustard go back to Oldfield Farm, he tagged along at her heels, with Rascal.

"So you're looking for a new home, then?" Rascal asked, feeling some sympathy for the old yellow dog. Mustard was a country fellow and a bit rough around the edges, but manners weren't everything. He had a good heart.

"A new home," Mustard said, *"and a new job. Some of us has to work for a livin'."* He paused. *"Doan't know any farmers in need of a dog, do you? Experienced herder, handy with sheep and cows. Good watchdog, too—sharp teeth, strong claws, sleeps with both eyes open. Doan't eat more 'n his due, neither."* He glanced at Miss Potter, striding sturdily two paces ahead. *"T' lady farmer, f' instance. She have a dog at Hill Top?"*

"I don't believe she does," Rascal replied.

"She does now," Mustard said, and plodded onward.

36

Life Goes On

After the police raid on the badger-baiting in the Sawrey Hotel stable, life in the twin hamlets of Near and Far Sawrey quickly returned to normal. The Flower Show was well attended and highly praised, although there was a great deal of grumbling about Mr. Calvin's judging of the dahlias. The Esthwaite Vale Cycling Club organized a meet, and the cyclists bought every scone and sausage roll and tea cake that Sarah Barwick had on display in her bakery window. In fact, the bakery's business improved so much that Sarah (who was now called "Sarah Scones" by the villagers) was able to hire Elsa Grape's brother's daughter to help with the sweeping and washing up and mind the shop when Sarah was making deliveries.

Hard on the heels of July's hay-making came August's sheep-clipping, and the farmers were busy with their late summer work. Old he might be, but Mustard settled into his new job at Hill Top Farm as if he had always been employed there, and Isaac Chance (who heard at the pub that Miss Potter had recovered her missing sheep) never even came looking for him.

And then, three weeks after Ben Hornby's death, Isaac Chance himself was dead, kicked in the head by his black horse, Blaze. Some in the village said it was purely an accident, others asserted that Chance had cruelly mistreated the horse and he'd only got what was coming to him. Captain Woodcock said privately to his sister Dimity that he was sorry that he'd never been able to gather enough evidence to charge Chance with burning the Holly How barn and poisoning the Holly How cows, but things had a way of working out for the best, didn't they? Miss Potter, feeling the need for another horse to help out at Hill Top Farm, purchased Blaze and treated his whip welts and his sore hoofs. Once the old horse was feeling more like himself, he seemed eager to get to work.

Tibbie and Queenie and their lambs took up residence in the Hill Top meadow, finding a great deal to like in the sweet green grass and pleasant waters of Wilfin Beck. If they thought back to their former heaf at Holly How, it was only with the vague nostalgia that is often felt for an earlier home, whether that home was entirely happy or not. For her part, Queenie shuddered whenever she thought about being captured and imprisoned in the pen at Oldfield Farm. And Tibbie never wanted to think back on the appalling accident in which Mr. Hornby had been killed. So both were glad enough to get on with their new life at Hill Top.

After the Great Raid, the wild creatures lived on Holly How in contentment and harmony, and the residents of The Brockery were untroubled by further alarms and excursions. Primrose brought a much welcomed new look to the old sett.

Seeing that there was a great deal to be done in the long neg-lected chambers, she undertook their general cleanup and re-decoration, arranging for sweeping out and for whitewashing parties, overseeing the laying of new carpets, and with Hy-acinth's help, sewing bedcovers and draperies. Bosworth Bad-ger XVII, who spent a portion of every day instructing Thorn in the details of the *History* and *Genealogy*, couldn't have been happier with the way things were going. Thorn showed such promise that Bosworth knew he would not hesitate—at the proper time, of course—to hand over to him the Badger Badge of Authority, together with full responsi-bility for The Brockery's management. Bosworth himself had begun to anticipate the day that he would have nothing else to do but sit on his front porch and smoke, or visit Pro-fessor Owl's astronomical observatory, or go looking for earth-worms in the rain on Holly How.

Caroline Longford was also getting on with her new life. Lady Longford, once she was no longer influenced by Miss Martine and was fully recovered from her temporary indis-position, found that she enjoyed being a grandmother, and that it was unexpectedly pleasant to have an active, ener-getic young girl living at Tidmarsh Manor. Of course, there were arguments, and Caroline had to learn to accommodate her grandmother's wishes, but she was delighted when Lady Longford allowed her to have a pair of guinea pigs as pets. She was even happier when it was decided that she should attend the village school, where Miss Nash—to the satisfac-tion of the entire village—had taken her place as the new head teacher. Caroline and Jeremy became even closer friends when Lady Longford allowed Jeremy's aunt to move into the old farmhouse at Holly How, which was much larger and more convenient than the small, damp cottage at Cunsey Beck.

Others did not have so much to look forward to. Jack

Ogden, who had played a part in the accident on Holly How, pled guilty to assault and battery against Ben Hornby, and was sent to prison for a term of ten years. To no one's surprise, he was not charged with badger-baiting.

The Wentworths, brother and sister, were bound over to the autumn assizes in Carlisle on charges of grand larceny and conspiracy to commit murder. Emily had made a new green dress for the trial. However, she would have to share the limelight with Mrs. Beever, who had been told that she would be required to testify to the theft of a packet of flypapers from her kitchen cupboard. Things looked dark for the pair, and it was generally expected that they would be found guilty and receive lengthy prison terms.

As far as Miss Potter was concerned, the coming autumn brought many good things. She had, of course, to get through the difficult time at the end of August—the anniversary of Norman Warne's death. The sharp grief was still there, and the sense that she had lost her only chance to marry the man she loved. But the pain was blunted somewhat by the passage of time and the continued challenges of Hill Top Farm. In September, the plumber put the pipes at the wrong end of the kitchen, but the problem was put right easily enough after she pointed it out. The joiner and plasterer finished the interior of the new addition, and the good weather held long enough to get the roof-ridge put on. It was also dry enough to get the garden dug, and she bought some new bushes at the nursery at Windermere and planted lavender and violets and sweet William. Mr. Jennings purchased fourteen more Herdwick ewes, bringing her flock to sixteen, so there would be a fine crop of lambs in the spring. Miss Potter, with Caroline and Jeremy, helped him cut bracken in the moor and haul it down in the pony cart to use as bedding in the barn.

The news from Miss Potter's publisher continued to be

good. *The Tale of Mr. Jeremy Fisher,* published in July, went into a second printing in September. And after a great deal of putting off, Miss Potter at last finished the drawings for *The Tale of Tom Kitten.* The next book, she had decided, would be about the rude and unruly rats who had invaded the Hill Top attic.

The story would involve a kitten who was put into a pudding, and dog (greatly resembling Rascal) who rescued him.

She would call it *The Roly-Poly Pudding.*

Historical Note

Helen Beatrix Potter was born on July 28, 1866, into a wealthy, upper-middle class London family, and lived with her parents at 2 Bolton Gardens, South Kensington, London. Her life was a quiet but interesting one, filled with reading, visiting art exhibitions, drawing and painting, and traveling on holiday to Scotland or to the Lake District, where she enjoyed the freedom to ramble through the countryside. Beatrix was a delicate child, often ill, and had no childhood friends. She did not go to school (like other girls of her class, she was educated at home by governesses), but she and her brother Bertram, younger by five years, were avid naturalists, assembling their own miniature zoo in their third-floor nursery, where they studied the anatomy of specimens they collected. She was especially interested in fossils and fungi, and by the time she had reached her early twenties, she had compiled a substantial collection of botanical illustrations, a hobby in which she was encouraged by her father.

But Beatrix sketched her pets, too—rabbits, mice, frogs,

bats, lizards, birds. Her drawings of her beloved Belgian rabbit, Peter, led to *The Tale of Peter Rabbit*, which she sent in 1893 as a letter to the son of her favorite governess. Eight years later, Beatrix paid to have *The Tale of Peter Rabbit* privately printed. The little book came to the notice of Frederick Warne and Company, and they published it in October, 1902. An immediate success, *Peter* was followed by *Squirrel Nutkin* (1903), *The Tailor of Gloucester* (1903), *Benjamin Bunny* (1904), *Two Bad Mice* (1904), *Mrs. Tiggy-Winkle* (1905), *The Pie and the Patty-Pan* (1905), *Mr. Jeremy Fisher* (July, 1906), and others, through 1913. Each book was a bestseller, and she soon became one of the most popular children's authors in the Empire.

Beatrix's literary and financial success did not change her life in any remarkable way—until 1905, that is. In July of that momentous year, just days before her thirty-ninth birthday, she received an offer of marriage from her editor, Norman Warne, who had become her closest friend. She accepted his offer in defiance of her parents, who opposed the marriage on the grounds that the Warne family was "in trade." The engagement was disastrously short, however, for Norman fell ill and died of acute leukemia only a month after they exchanged rings.

Her fiancé dead, her hopes destroyed, her life devastated, Beatrix resolved on a new direction. In September, 1905, she agreed to purchase a small farm in the Lakeland hamlet of Near Sawrey, where she and her parents had gone on holiday. It would have seemed a strange idea to her parents, and especially unwelcome to her mother, who expected Beatrix to remain at Bolton Gardens to manage the servants and look after her when she was ill. But the Potters' objections to their daughter's farm must have been tempered by their relief that the marriage "into trade" no longer threatened. The purchase was completed that autumn, and Beatrix began the challenging work of renovating the old farmhouse and restocking the farm's thirty-one acres.

Much of what we know about Beatrix's growing passion for Hill Top Farm comes from her letters. Writing to Norman's sister Millie in April, 1906, she describes the house: "There is one wall 4 ft thick with a staircase inside it, I never saw such a place for hide & seek, & funny cupboards & closets." In July of that year (the same month in which our story takes place), she tells Millie that she has found a swarm of bees and caught them:

> (it isn't quite so valiant as it sounds!) they were lying on the grass near the quarry, we think they had been out all night, & blown out of a tree; they were very numbed, but are all right now & a fine swarm . . . I have bought a box-hive . . . . I borrowed a straw "skep" to catch them in, & put it down over them.

And in August, she proudly reports that she has sold some stone from the small quarry on her property for the repair of Ees bridge, at the foot of Esthwaite Water. "I don't think I shall make much profit . . . but I shall like to see my stone in the bridge." In September, she is cutting and raking bracken for the animals' winter bedding. By October, she is applying "liquid manure" to her apple trees ("a most interesting performance with a long scoop") and planting herbs and flowers given to her by the villagers. The construction work was nearly finished, and on October 12, she tells Millie that she has lit the very first fire in her new library. "It was a great excitement. I laid the fire & lit it myself & it went straight up directly & gives a great heat." The lighting of the library fire must have been a profoundly symbolic and satisfying moment for her. Truly, the life of the farm had become the center of her own life.

For the next seven years, Beatrix's life became more and more complicated, as she juggled her obligations to her parents, to her art, and to Hill Top. She continued to produce her "little books," but the farm and its real animals—its sheep, cows, pigs, and horses—assumed a greater importance with each passing month. While she wrote and drew at least one book a year through 1913, her heart was more and more fixed on Hill Top, on the other Lake District properties she began to acquire, and on the countryside of the Land between the Lakes.

Hill Top Farm, Sawrey, and the Lake District offered Beatrix Potter a new life, full of new hopes and new dreams. By 1913, it had offered her a new love. And thereby hangs yet another tale. . . .

Susan Wittig Albert

Resources

There are a great many excellent resources for a study of Beatrix Potter's life and work and the Lake District of England at the turn of the century. Here are a few of those that I have found most useful in the research for this book and the series as a whole. Additional resource material is available on my Web site, *www.mysterypartners.com*.

Clark, Michael. *Badgers.* London: Whittet Books, 1994.

Denyer, Susan. *At Home with Beatrix Potter.* New York: Harry N. Abrams, Inc., 2000.

Hervy, Canon G.A.K. and J.A.G. Barnes. *Natural History of the Lake District.* London: Frederick Warne, 1970.

Jay, Eileen, Mary Noble, and Anne Stevenson Hobbs. *A Victorian Naturalist: Beatrix Potter's Drawings from the Armitt Collection.* London: Frederick Warne, 1992.

Lane, Margaret. *The Tale of Beatrix Potter,* revised edition. London: Frederick Warne, 1968.

Linder, Leslie. *A History of the Writings of Beatrix Potter.* London: Frederick Warne, 1971.

Potter, Beatrix. *The Journal of Beatrix Potter, 1881–1897.* Transcribed by Leslie Linder. London: Frederick Warne, New Edition, 1966.

Potter, Beatrix. *Beatrix Potter's Letters.* Selected and edited by Judy Taylor. London: Frederick Warne, 1989.

Potter, Beatrix. *Beatrix Potter: A Holiday Diary.* Transcribed and edited, with a forward and a history of the Warne family, by Judy Taylor. London: The Beatrix Potter Society, 1996.

Rollinson, William. *The Cumbrian Dictionary of Dialect, Tradition and Folklore.* West Yorkshire, UK: Smith Settle Ltd., 1997.

Rollinson, William. *Life and Tradition in the Lake District.* Dalesman Books, 1981.

Taylor, Judy. *Beatrix Potter: Artist, Storyteller and Countrywoman,* revised edition. London: Frederick Warne, 1996.

Taylor, Judy, Joyce, Whalley, et al. *Beatrix Potter, 1866–1943: The Artist and Her World.* London: Penguin Group, 1987.

Recipes from the
Land between the Lakes

Sarah Barwick's Lemon Bars

1 14-ounce can sweetened condensed milk
grated zest of 1 lemon
½ cup lemon juice
⅔ cup butter
1 cup dark brown sugar, packed
1½ cups flour
1 teaspoon baking powder
1 cup old-fashioned oats
candied orange peel for garnish

Preheat oven to 350°. Grease a 9"×13" pan. Pour condensed milk into medium-sized bowl; stir in lemon zest and juice. Set aside. In a large bowl, cream butter and brown sugar until light and fluffy. Add flour and baking powder in two additions, beating very well. Mix in the oats. Spread about two-thirds of this mixture evenly over the bottom of the pan, making a smooth, firm layer. Pour milk-lemon mixture over bottom layer. Spread remaining oat mixture evenly over lemon layer. (This is easier if you "dot" it in place, then smooth.). Bake for 30–35 minutes, until lightly browned. Cool in pan; refrigerate for one hour. Cut into 16 squares. Decorate each square with a bit of candied orange peel. Refrigerate.

Mrs. Lythecoe's Recipe for Rhubarb and Raspberry Tart

Pastry for one 10" pie shell
2 cups rhubarb (may be canned, fresh, or frozen), cut into ¼" pieces
1 cup raspberries (fresh or frozen)
¾ cup granulated sugar
4 eggs
½ cup whipping cream
½ teaspoon vanilla

Preheat oven to 400°. Place pastry in a 10" tart or pie pan. Distribute rhubarb evenly in bottom of pie pan and sprinkle with raspberries. In a mixing bowl, whisk sugar and eggs; add cream and vanilla and blend together. Pour egg-cream mixture over fruit and bake in preheated oven for 20–25 minutes, or until tart is firm in center.

Mrs. Beeton's Veal and Ham Pie, Recipe No. 898

Published in 1861, Mrs. Beeton's Book of Household Management was the cookery book that every middle-class Victorian bride asked for when she set up housekeeping. This recipe (which was prepared by Parsley Badger) appears on page 427 in the facsimile edition of the book.

    2 pounds veal cutlets
    2 tablespoons minced fresh savory herbs (parsley, thyme,
       marjoram, sage)
    strip of lemon peel finely minced
    yolks of 2 hard-boiled eggs
    ½ pound ham
    puff crust
    ½ pint of water
    nearly ½ pint of good strong gravy
    yolk of one egg, beaten
    ¼ teaspoon nutmeg
    2 blades of pounded mace
    pepper and salt to taste
    2 cups sliced fresh mushrooms

MODE: Cut the veal into nice square pieces, and put a layer of them at the bottom of a pie-dish; sprinkle over these a portion of the herbs, spices, seasoning, lemon peel, and the yolks of the eggs cut in slices. Cut the ham very thin, and put a layer of this in. Proceed in this manner until the dish is full, so arranging it that the ham comes at the top. Lay a puff-paste on the edge of the dish, and pour in about ¼ pint of water. Cover with crust, ornament it with leaves, brush it over with the yolk of an egg, and bake in a well-heated oven for 1 to 1½ hours, or longer, should the pie be very large. When it is taken out of the oven, pour in at the top, through a funnel, nearly ½ pint of strong gravy. This should be made sufficiently good that, when cold, it may cut in a firm jelly. This pie may be very much enriched by adding a few mushrooms, oysters, or sweetbreads; but it will be found very good without any of the last-named additions.

TIME: 1½ hour, or longer, should the pie be very large

AVERAGE COST: 3 shillings

SUFFICIENT for 5 or 6 persons

SEASONABLE: from March to October

Cumberland Sausage Rolls

1 pound pork

1 egg

3–4 tablespoons dry bread crumbs

1 teaspoon dry sage

½ teaspoon dry thyme

½ teaspoon dry savory

½ teaspoon pepper

½ teaspoon salt

1 tablespoon olive oil

pastry for two pie shells

Preheat oven to 400°. Mix pork, egg, bread crumbs, herbs, salt and pepper. Divide the mixture into 32 pieces and roll into cigar-shaped sausages about 4" long. (Hint: divide the mixture into 4 parts, then divide each part into four. Roll out 16 sausages and cut each into two.) Heat oil in a skillet and fry the sausages until they are browned nicely. Cool. Roll out half the pastry to about ⅛" thickness, and cut in 16 wedges. Place a sausage at the wide end of one of the wedges. Roll up and place point side down on a cookie sheet. When 16 rolls have been completed, roll out the second pastry round and prepare 16 more rolls. Refrigerate the unbaked rolls until you are ready to bake. Bake for 15 minutes, until pastry is golden brown. Serve immediately.

Lady Longford's Favorite Ginger Cake

2½ cups flour
4 teaspoons baking powder
4 teaspoons ground ginger
1½ teaspoons ground cinnamon
½ teaspoon salt
1 cup butter
1¼ cups brown sugar, packed
4 eggs
¼ cup grated fresh ginger root
grated zest of half a lemon
1 teaspoon vanilla
1 cup milk
2 tablespoons confectioners' sugar for dusting

Preheat oven to 350°. Grease and flour a 9" Bundt pan. Sift together the flour, baking powder, ground ginger, cinnamon and salt. Set aside. In a large bowl, cream together the butter and brown sugar until light and fluffy. Beat in the eggs one at a time, then stir in the grated ginger root, lemon zest, and vanilla. Beat in the flour mixture alternately with the milk, mixing just until incorporated. Pour batter into prepared pan. Bake in preheated oven for 45 to 50 minutes, or until a toothpick inserted into the center of the cake comes out clean. Cool in pan for 10 minutes, then invert onto a serving plate. Dust lightly with confectioners' sugar before serving.

Glossary

I have not included as much dialect as I would like in these novels, because dialect forms are difficult to read. One Cumbrian dialect speaker remarks: "It takes a bit of getting used to on paper; it looks very awkward, as if it had forgot to take off its walking boots and clomped onto the nice clean page too rudely." It's difficult to get it "right," too, and there's always disagreement among native speakers as to whether the nonnative writer has represented the sound of this or that word accurately.

The speech of Cumbria (which includes the former counties of Cumberland and Westmorland and parts of Lancashire and Yorkshire) reveals many Celtic, Anglian, and Norse-Irish influences, some of which are demonstrated in this glossary. In the *Cottage Tales,* I have tried to represent just enough of the sounds of Cumbrian speech and include enough of its vocabulary to give an idea of this important and distinctive regional dialect. Some of the words in this list are not dialect forms, strictly speaking, but are uncommon enough that a definition may be helpful. My main source is William Rollinson's *The Cumbrian Dictionary of Dialect, Tradition, and Folklore.*

auld old

beck a small stream (Old Norse *bekkr*)

bell-wether the leading sheep of a flock, who wears a bell around the neck

dustha fo you? *What dustha think?*

fell a mountain or a high hill (Icelandic, Danish, Swedish *fjell*)

flaysome din fearsome noise (*flairt,* to frighten)

happen perhaps (see *mappen*) *Happen she's missed the ferry.*

heafed herdwick sheep instinctively recognize their native pastures, or heafs; that is, they are heafed to their home meadows.

hobthrush a hobgoblin or spirit that can do useful work but is just as likely to make mischief

hod on! stop (Old English, *healdan,* wait, hold)

joiner carpenter

loose box a separate stall for a horse, where the animal is free to move about

lug mark the word is derived from the old Norwegian word *lög,* which means "law." When a farmer cuts a lug mark in his sheep's ear, he is making his lawful owner's mark on the animal.

maffle confused. *Reet maffled me.* It confused me greatly.

mappen perhaps (see *happen*) *Mappen he's lost his dog.*

nae no (said emphatically)

Nobbut a reet 'ginner nothing but a proper beginner.

Pater familias latin for "father of the family," and used by the Romans to designate the eldest or ranking male in the household

pickle a mischievous child or animal. Beatrix Potter dedicated her book *The Tale of Tom Kitten* to "All Pickles— Especially to Those That Get Upon My Garden Wall"

reet right, properly

Sett the system of underground burrows and chambers where a badger colony lives

Tatie Pot A favorite Lake District dish made of mutton, potatoes, carrots, onions, and black pudding (a traditional sausage made of pig's blood, beef suet, oatmeal, and onions). For a recipe, see *The Tale of Hill Top Farm.*

twa two

verra very

wellies waterproof boots, named after the Duke of Wellington

yark to hit with a heavy cudgel